THE INQUISITOR

WATERFYRE RISING 4

NADIA HAN

PROSE & CONCEPTS

Author's Note

Dear Readers,

When you read *The Inquisitor*, you'll see me mention the book, *Finding Your HeART*. It's not a fictional book created for this romantic suspense, but it's an actual journal with prompts and heart-opening activities that I worked on while writing *The Inquisitor*. In some way, I was the inquisitor—searching—for my place in this world. Like many people out there, I was on a quest to find my mark, and creating this journal helped me understand that I didn't need to look outside of myself for validation or any kind of approval.

Writing and creating the art for this journal was my healing journey—an excavation of my heart and soul. Life can get messy, cluttering the heart. No one is immune to this. The journal helped me complete *The Inquisitor* and helped me remember why I write, who I'm writing for, and what brings me joy.

I write for those who believe in happily ever after. I write for those carving out their mark in this complex world. I write for those who are brave enough to be authentic to themselves and to others *despite* what their environment may demand. I write for dreamers, visionaries, and rebels who are too stubborn to give up on their dreams.

In short, I write for you, and I write for me.

So, thank you for reading my stories.

Wishing you a heart-opening journey, wherever that may take you,

Nadia

**For those with the "fyre" to see
"I'm perfect" in "imperfect."**

.

.

.

*"Everything that is made beautiful and fair and lovely is made
for the eye of one who sees."*

– Rumi

COPYRIGHT

The Inquisitor

Copyright © 2023 by Nadia Han

Cover Art Copyright: Nadia Han

Editor: Anna Nesbitt

Copy Editor: Lindsay York at LY Publishing

Proofreaders: Melissa Tarrington

Prose & Concepts LLC

210 Park Avenue, Suite #280

Worcester, MA 01609

www.proseandconcepts.com

Library of Congress Cataloging-in-Publication Data

Library of Congress Control Number: 2023947435

First edition Ebook ISBN: 978-1-952820-48-9

First edition Paperback ISBN: 978-1-952820-46-5

Special edition Paperback ISBN: 978-1-952820-47-2

PROLOGUE

Forrest

I stared at the *pão de queijo* that Grandma Morena made for me and my cousin, Yolanda, and wanted to puke. The delicious cheese rolls should have made me feel cozy. It was my favorite breakfast, made of sweet potatoes and flour—grandma's secret recipe she never shared with anyone except my mom. Mom used to make them for me before she died in a car accident.

I'd never refused to eat them until today. After that murder my friends and I witnessed yesterday . . .

The fear that something horrible could happen to me, my grandma, and Yolanda sat like icy blocks in my gut. Grandma and Yolanda were my only family. I couldn't let anything happen to them. Sleep was out of the question last night. I was dead tired, but wide awake. I'd probably crash around noon.

"Why aren't you eating?" Grandma Morena placed a hand

over my forehead. "You sick?" she asked with an accent that had gotten better over time.

"I'm fine. Just not hungry." I swatted her hand away.

Arching a suspicious eyebrow, Yolanda gulped her orange juice and placed the glass back down. "He got dumped by a girl." She kicked my leg under the table.

"Shut up." I kicked her back. She had a way of causing trouble at the most annoying times.

Grandma Morena whirled around with two hands on her hips, glaring at me. "What did I say to you? No relationships while you're in high school." She waved a finger at me. "Focus on your schoolwork, boy. Girls will come later."

Yolanda smirked, and I gave her the evil eye. *I'll get you back.*

Though there was a hot girl in my science class, I wasn't in any relationship. Yolanda didn't know it, but she just helped me out. Letting my grandma believe I had a girl problem was easier than having to tell her the truth—which I couldn't anyway. I didn't have to admit or deny anything. It wasn't my fault if she believed Yolanda's lie. I just had to maneuver around that obstacle carefully.

My brain was too worried about those men coming after me and my family.

How were my friends coping with this shit? Yesterday at Remington's house, Grayson, Royce, and Arrow were all shaken. Who wouldn't be after seeing someone die? Watching it on TV was different from real life. My body went into a zone I had no control over. It was as though I were playing a video game and some unknown force yanked me into a portal consumed with panic and fear.

But today seemed worse. It was as if my body had more time to let the frightening image sink into my mind. The reality of the murder appeared more vivid. The sound of the gunshot had ripped through the air, sending chills down my skin. I had wished everything were just a dream, and that when I woke up this morning, my life would return to normal. But this was no dream. This wasn't a video game that I could replay to get a better ending.

"Yolanda's always making up crap, *Vó*. Don't listen to her," I said, satisfied that I'd just given the truth, which masked the lie hanging in the air. Rising, I shoved the untouched pancake into a sandwich bag, saving it for later. "I'll have this for lunch, *Vó*."

Grandma tilted her head, eyeing me with suspicion, probably weighing whom to believe.

"Yolanda is the one with a boyfriend," I said, trying to swing Grandma's attention elsewhere.

"He's my study partner for our science project!" Yolanda's quick denial shoved her to the forefront.

"My rules apply to you too, girl." Grandma pointed at her. "School first. Feed your brain. It's important. The other stuff will come later." She whirled and started on the dishes.

After the dangerous escape from Brazil, Grandma had made sure I understood the value of freedom and education, which weren't offered to everyone in the world.

Yolanda got up from the kitchen table and handed an empty plate to Grandma. "Forrest flirts too much with the cheerleaders. They call him the hot nerd." Then she rambled off various scenarios I didn't even remember.

The house phone rang, and my body jerked. Who would call this early in the morning? I stared at the phone for a while.

"Can someone get that? My hands are wet." Grandma looked over her shoulder.

"I'll get it." My heart pounded as I got up from the table,

walked over to the desk by the wall with recipe books, and picked it up. "Hello?"

Silence greeted me, followed by static noises. I slammed the phone back down in its cradle.

"Who was it?" Grandma asked.

"Just static." I squeezed my hand into a fist so no one could see it tremble.

"Goodness. When will the utility company fix the damn landlines in this neighborhood? This has been going on for a week now. They'd better give us a refund on the bill this month."

That knowledge gave me some relief. Last night, I was wary of every little sound in the house. I was afraid those men had discovered where I lived. Even my neighbor's car engine startled me.

"I'm heading out." I jerked a chin toward Yolanda, whose face was red, probably still fuming at me. "Calm down." I tapped her shoulder gently before slinging my backpack over my shoulder. "You're getting your wisdom teeth pulled today."

She snarled at me.

"I'll make you some soup for dinner," Grandma said. "Have a good day at school. Be good."

"Always," I said, trying my best to sound normal.

"Yeah, right," Yolanda mumbled with annoyance. She wouldn't be defiant if I weren't telling the truth. I didn't know if she was dating her science partner, but she started this battle, and she had to learn how to deal with the consequences.

"See ya." I waved at them and left the house.

I headed to a different destination than my high school, which was only a few blocks away. School wasn't on my agenda for today. I needed to be somewhere quiet and made my way to a park with a public garden. It wouldn't be busy during the school day. Though I had excellent grades, I'd played hooky enough times that my grandma would ground me for life if she ever found out. No one knew I went to this garden. Even I didn't know why. It just gave me a sense of peace. It reminded me of my parents, who were expert gardeners.

Wearing my T-shirt and jeans, I plopped down on the grass next to the garden bed. A bumble bee buzzed by and hovered on a dandelion near my thigh. A sunny June day usually made me happy, but anxiety had clouded any joy.

How could I get rid of this? When would this fear and tension go away? Would those men come after me and my friends? Could I trust the man with the slash on his face? Why did he let us go? For all I knew, he could be lying and secretly following me and my friends.

Stop freaking yourself out.

If he wanted me and my friends dead, he would've killed us yesterday. It would have been easier than this.

Needing something to distract me, I stared at the vegetables growing in the garden. Grandma had once brought me here with her friends. They helped make this communal garden flourish. Anyone could come and get herbs, tomatoes, cucumbers, lettuce, and other vegetables.

I'd learned a lot about herbs from my grandmother. I didn't share this with anyone at my school. They'd make fun of me for enjoying something so "girly." My video game buddies knew. They didn't care about shit like this. We were all focused on video games—our escape from reality.

I took out the herb encyclopedia Grandma had given me for Christmas two years ago. It listed all the plants and their medicinal properties. Something about the plants calmed me. The way they just existed—minding their own business while the world went on—fascinated me.

Flipping through the pages, I hoped to find a plant that could cure anxiety. But I had a feeling my illness would take more than some plant. The lack of sleep was taking a toll, and my eyes drooped even though the sun was blazing down on the ground.

A car pulled up to the curb beside the fence and startled me. Vines and bushes made it difficult for people to see into this section. They often came to plant more vegetables using the quiet dead-end road because it had a walkway that linked it to the large parking lot.

I didn't want anyone seeing me here. Not that it mattered. I wasn't trespassing on private property.

A man's voice cut through the silence. "I've wired the money to your account. Don't mention this meeting to anyone —unless you want to die."

The statement sent my skin tingling. *Shit.* I didn't need to witness another crime. The whole reason I was hiding in a garden was to be alone—away from anymore crimes.

I froze as footsteps approached the fence. *Please don't come any closer.* My breathing slowed, fearing they could somehow hear me.

The dense vines created a thick fence between me and the men. Somehow, I plucked up the courage to shift my body to an area that allowed me a view of them between the sparse openings of the vines and bushes. Even if they peeked in, I'd be hidden from them. Though I couldn't see their faces, I noted the crisp black pants and shiny shoes. The red shoes glared at me. I'd never seen anything like them. They looked expensive, bold, powerful . . .

Dangerous.

Red Shoes handed over something to Black Shoes. "These will make your bank accounts fat and happy, Councilor. It will ensure your reelection."

"A reelection would secure our business in the long run."

The men laughed and chatted about political things that

bored the hell out of me. When they left, the way the red shoes hit the ground, like metal to cement, created an eerie feeling in me.

The horrendous red shoes were now etched into my mind like a dormant virus trying to infect me.

CHAPTER ONE

KIERA

Bad luck was like a pesky pimple throbbing on my face. I was aware of its uncomfortable presence and just wanted to be rid of it, but it refused to go away. So when the airline representative named Katie—an anxious girl with blonde hair and hesitant eyes—apologized for misplacing my luggage, I wasn't surprised.

What else can go wrong in my life right now? It was as though there was a gang of little devils flying around my space, teasing and testing me.

I made my displeasure known politely. It wasn't Katie's fault. She was doing her job by notifying me of the unfortunate situation. I couldn't shoot the messenger. I'd worked in customer service during college, so I understood her fear of being yelled at for something she didn't do or had no control over. Hell, even when I became a professional photographer, celebrities with their noses sky-high mistreated me as though I were their servant.

I didn't come from money. Other factors colored my world and gave me a different perspective. That was one reason I turned to photography. I wanted to capture a moment in time. It told a story. I'd always wondered about the hidden story sitting beside the visible photo—the unseen narrative. That invisible story had always called to me.

When I take pictures of fashion models, people see the gorgeous body and clothing that provokes a certain emotion. But what they don't see is the chaos before or after, or the model's personality. The real person behind the layers of makeup, the many angles and poses it took before the last picture. Most of all, no one ever wonders about the person taking the photo.

People loved my work, which was why I never had a problem landing jobs. I enjoyed freelancing because it gave me the freedom to set my rates and to choose my clients. I collaborated with a lot of beautiful people. Some had characters to match the beauty, others made me want to vomit.

Despite being surrounded by beauty and glamor, I hadn't met anyone who saw the real me. Or anyone who wanted to discover the Kiera behind the camera lens. It hadn't bothered me so much before. But now, something had changed.

That one night had changed me, and I wanted to forget it. Why couldn't I?

Enough of the self-pity, Kiera. You have more important things to worry about than a man. A man who probably forgot about you already. A man who's avoided you for too long. A man with a roster of women waiting for him.

Shoving the irritation away, I dragged my one suitcase, carry-on, and purse out of the airport toward an Uber car. The missing luggage was on a different flight, due to arrive tomorrow. I could live with that. It wasn't the end of the world.

I couldn't let stress weigh me down during this trip. I needed clarity to do my job well.

The Uber driver placed my luggage and carry-on in the

trunk while I slid into the back seat of his white Honda Civic. I could've scheduled a livery car to pick me up, but that would've taken longer for confirmation. The Uber was fine, and I'd just expense it later. The driver hopped into his seat, whistling a cheerful tune.

"I'm Juan Torres. Welcome to Austin, Texas. Where to, miss?" He had olive skin, dark hair speckled with silver on the sides, and a goatee with a little braid that ended with a bead.

I rattled off the name of my destination, leaned back, closed my eyes, and sighed. It had been a hectic week, trying to organize my mom's grocery delivery, her medical bills, and other paperwork that needed my attention before I took off to this job.

"Long flight?" Juan asked.

I opened my eyes, and my gaze landed on a pretty girl inside a laminated picture dangling from his rearview mirror along with an air freshener.

"Long week," I confessed. "I'm Kiera, by the way."

"I hear ya. You here for vacation or visiting family?" As he pulled the car away, his body moved with the reggae music blasting in the car. "Want me to turn down the volume?"

He seemed at ease with himself, like there was nothing in the world that bothered him. Perhaps the job required him to be friendly and comfortable with strangers.

"Nah, I'm good. Reggae's cool. Work brought me to Texas, but I'm hoping to steal a few days to explore. Shhh." I placed a finger over my lips. "Don't tell anyone."

He laughed. "Your secret's safe with me. Barton Creek is a nice area by the lake. I want to buy a condo there for my girls." He tapped the picture, sending it swinging back and forth. "The scenic view is breathtaking."

I hadn't been to this area of Texas, and it was another reason I took the job.

"You have two daughters?" I asked.

"One daughter. She just graduated high school and is going to the University of Texas in the fall. The other girl is my wife." He glanced back at me and smiled. "They're the loves of my life."

From the rearview mirror, his eyes gleamed with joy and pride. My chest tightened, wishing I had a father who cherished me and my mom the same way. I didn't know my father. He'd never been in my life, and he didn't care about my mom. Bitterness stung my tongue every time I thought about him. *Be a proton, always positive.* My friend Michelle had made a T-shirt with that phrase on it for her lover. It was true, though.

"You gotta keep the dream alive by *thinking* positive," I told him as I recalled Michelle showing me, Audri, and Natalie her creation. The girls and I had created T-shirts to support an auction.

Laughing, he slapped a playful hand against the steering wheel. "I'm gonna borrow that for my Catherine. It'll get a chuckle out of her. She's been ill. Liver problems. Laughter is good for the heart." His cheerful voice turned serious. "She's cut back on work. My poor baby feels guilty for being sick. Can you believe her?" He shook his head. "I didn't mind taking on a second job. I just want her to get well. Ubering isn't so bad."

"Sorry to hear about your wife." I understood the anxiety over worrying about a loved one's health. Concern for my mom flashed constantly in my mind, especially with her recent diagnosis. "What do you do when you're not driving?"

"Maintenance for a seniors housing complex. Today is my day off."

Nodding, I said, "You're doing a great job, Juan. You make it seem easy."

"Thanks."

For the next few moments, we stopped chatting and let

the reggae music fill the car. I glanced out the window and my heart leaped at the sight of the man driving by in a black SUV. No—that couldn't be him. What would he be doing in Texas?

Stop thinking about him and you'll stop seeing him everywhere.

Releasing a sigh, I concentrated on the passing homes and businesses. Juan might have appeared like a cheerful man, but he carried a dark weight that I knew all too well.

Perhaps talking to a stranger was his therapy. I dug into my purse for the fancy package of travel-sized bottles of lotion, soap, and essential oils. I'd gotten them from a high-end beauty brand I'd worked with recently.

"Here. Give these to your wife. These are limited edition. You'll be her favorite guy." I dropped the package onto the front passenger seat.

He looked over at the package and inhaled the rose scent. "She's going to love these. Thank you. You didn't have to do that."

"You're—"

The car screeched to a sudden stop, and my body jerked. A man wearing a blue tank top and a black cap banged on the driver's side door angrily. My heart pounded with fear as another man squirted something on the windshield and began wiping the surface with a cloth.

"You owe me ten dollars for cleaning the windshield. For twenty, we'll clean the back too."

My mouth dropped open at the unabashed ploy to get cash. I could hear the crooks through the shut window.

Juan's jaw tensed, but he remained cool and collected. He opened his wallet and rolled down the window just enough for his fingers to slip a ten-dollar bill to the guy with the cap. Grinning, the two men retreated to the sidewalk and disappeared, probably waiting for another car to trap. Juan continued down the street as though nothing had occurred.

Appalled and angry, I asked, "What was that all about? Why did you give him money?"

He let out a heavy breath. "If I don't give them the money, they'll block the car, scratch it up, or slash my tires. They get violent." He shook his head. "The city hasn't been able to resolve this issue. The police are having a tough time stopping these guys. They get rid of some for a while. Then you turn around, and they're back. I think our lives are worth more than ten bucks."

I couldn't believe the tactics being used by people these days. People did stupid things online for views and such, so this shouldn't have surprised me. There were homeless people everywhere, even in Providence. I'd given money when asked nicely, but I'd experienced nothing like this brazen entrapment. These criminals knew people would rather pay them than risk having to deal with other consequences. Why didn't these idiots spend the energy they put into defrauding people toward something useful, like getting a steady income?

Wasn't that a billion-dollar question?

Maybe they're desperate, Kiera.

My mom's medical bills flashed in my head, and I could see how desperation forced a person to do unthinkable things.

I'd keep this odd incident in mind when I had to use the rental car supplied by FitFlex during my stay here. What would I have done if I had been driving alone and encountered these guys? I wouldn't have known to pay them, and that could have cost me my life.

Juan turned down a street lined with trees and luxurious homes. They had lovely landscaping and fancy fencing. These homes were set farther apart than the houses near the Austin Airport. I preferred the space. I loved city life, but I didn't want to hear my neighbor's conversation and certainly didn't want him or her to hear mine. One day I'd get a place of my own with a yard and all. But for now, I was happy with my quaint condo that gave me parking during the snow season and where I didn't have to worry about home maintenance.

"I'm surprised those losers are creeping into the nicer neighborhoods. They won't be there for long. The wealthy have a louder voice."

I tried to shake off the odd sensation that became more prominent after the incident. Maybe I'd touched something with a negative vibe. My friends and I had gone to a mystical fair in college where we had psychic readings with tarot cards and all. The lady had used sage to clear my energy. She said it was too cluttered.

I felt cluttered now. Maybe it was time for me to find someone to help me shake this bad luck. I didn't always believe in this kind of woo-woo stuff, but I had an open mind. There were certain things that couldn't be explained logically.

The car drove up to the Sabian Creek Campground, a well-maintained property secluded by woods facing a beautiful lake. The main lodge had three levels with large windows. Several cabins spread all around the complex, allowing for a private oasis.

"It's more beautiful in person," I sighed.

Sunlight sprinkled the lake like a layer of sparkling diamonds. A light breeze blew by, and the waves of diamonds winked as men fished in boats and people walked along the shore. I understood why FitFlex wanted the photo shoot here. The atmosphere would help sell their activewear perfectly.

"I'd love to live in a house by the water one of these days. That's one of Catherine's dreams," Juan said as he pulled into a parking spot by the main office.

"You will. Remember what I said?"

"Yes, ma'am." Smiling, he tapped his temple. "Keep it positive."

After hauling my luggage out of the trunk, Juan saluted me.

"Been a pleasure, Kiera. Enjoy your stay. Sorry you had to experience that unfortunate incident."

"Don't worry about it." I swatted the air. "Thank you for the interesting ride."

I offered him a large tip that also covered the money he'd given those criminals. He'd brought me to my destination safely, and I appreciated that. He had a sick wife at home and was dealing with his problems in a positive way. I had a sick mom, so I knew what he was going through. Though I was now more cognizant of my finances, I couldn't help but be generous with someone who deserved it.

Glancing at the gorgeous, scenic view, I prayed it would bring me the peace and luck I desperately needed.

CHAPTER TWO

FORREST

Sitting in my black SUV in the parking lot of Full Circle Apothecary, I tried to expunge the negative energy that still lingered around me by inhaling for more energy and exhaling the stuff I didn't need. I didn't want to go into my grandma's shop carrying all this darkness. My family must be protected from the evils of the world.

I'd just gotten back from watching my enemy, Afonso Moura, die in a marsh filled with alligators. The location and the method of his death were my decisions. It only made sense that I got to decide how one of the men responsible for my father's death would suffer. I'd been searching for him, along with the gang's anonymous leader, for years. So I'd adjusted my schedule as soon as I heard Afonso had been captured.

Money could buy many things, including information and the right people who were excellent at maneuvering in the darkness. I had other commitments that required my presence in Texas later this week, but the phone call expedited my early arrival.

Watching Afonso suffer while the gators tore him apart

should have eased my dismay, but it didn't. It only intensified the vengeful knots inside me. They only seemed to have multiplied in the past few months. Perhaps finding the leader of the Anacondas would eliminate the growing dread.

I took out my phone and crossed off Afonso Moura's name from my list. Below that was Bento Melo, who had died six months ago. I'd injected a non-traceable drug that slowly broke down his bodily systems before he was fed to the Amazon's anacondas.

These men had changed my life, and they would pay for it.

Two down, and one to go. The leader of the group would endure the worst of my torture. He had to experience the pain he'd bestowed on my father, my mother, my grandmother, and me. I had a creative mind, and it made me feel better to envision the multiple ways he'd suffer.

I'll find you, fucker.

Taking a deep breath, I exhaled, shaking off all the negativity from earlier today. I got out of the SUV and headed to the apothecary's entrance. I yanked the door open and stepped inside. The whiff of sage, frankincense, palo santo, and other herbs slapped my senses awake. I'd gotten used to Grandma Morena's abundant herb collection. Still, whatever she was doing today was too aromatic for my liking.

The shop had been renovated a few weeks ago—and I footed the bill. At first my grandma had refused the gift, but I insisted, using my power of persuasion. After a few weeks of charming her on the phone, she gave in. It was the least I could do. Grandma Morena had raised me, and that was worth more than any amount of money. Growing up, money had been scarce, but it had taught me the value of a dollar. The feeling of scarcity drove me to want more. Lack had a way of making me feel inadequate. It was like a mental disease, and its cure was success, which I now possessed.

Full Circle Apothecary was a store inside a building that my grandma owned. She had used up her retirement fund to purchase the property. She lived on the top floor of her business, making it convenient for her to go to work. It was in a business section close to downtown Austin, Texas, which had excellent foot traffic. This apothecary was her life. People came to her for help with ailments that western medicine couldn't cure. There was wisdom in the way ancient people had healed themselves.

I walked over to a table full of pre-made gift boxes and admired the packaging. The apothecary wasn't just a store. It also held small herbology classes in the backroom for those who wanted to learn the basics. When a thunderstorm knocked down a tree and a light post, hitting the side of the building and causing major damage, I decided it was time for an update. The old building needed new electrical wires and pipes—all of which would have taken a chunk out of her savings. I didn't want her to touch her retirement money, which I'd replenished. I didn't even want her to work. She'd worked hard enough.

A strong body creates a strong mind.

Her words had a special place in my heart. I became a better doctor because she'd showed me to look at medicine from various angles, some of which couldn't be proven by science. She believed the body needed to flow with the energy of the Earth.

Energy is constantly in motion. It's teaching us a lesson. We have to listen to it.

Laughter stirred in the next room where dry herbs were stored in compartments built into a wall. Two customers chatted with Cara Hoang, the loyal sales associate and herbalist. She was Vietnamese-American and taught my grandmother her traditional remedies.

Not wanting to interrupt Cara, I ambled around, admiring

the new meadow green walls with sandy trims. The interior designer Grandma had hired did a wonderful job bringing her vision to life. The rustic display tables, bookcases, and sales counter were all made of wood, giving the atmosphere an earthy and homey feel. This was a place of healing, and yet it made me feel different from my medical clinic and hospital exam rooms. This holistic sanctuary grounded me in a way I couldn't explain. It was like a walk in the woods versus a walk in a sterilized hospital hallway with fluorescent lights and stark white walls.

Exiting the herb room, Cara looked at me, beamed, and held up a finger, signifying she'd be right with me. She turned to the two customers, who each held a brown shopping bag with the store's logo. "Thank you for visiting. See you in a couple of weeks."

After they left, she threw her arms around me. "So good to see you! When did you get here?"

I patted her back. "Happy to see you too. I just arrived a few minutes ago. You doing well?" That wasn't a complete lie. Though I arrived last night, I'd just gotten to the shop minutes ago.

My mother would have been Cara's age if she were still alive. Cara had worked with my grandma since the store first opened seven years ago. She was married to an auto mechanic and had no children. With her short black hair and gentle brown eyes, she had a warm smile that could make a bad day turn good instantly.

"What are you doing here?" Pulling back, she stared at me the way a mother would suspect a child was up to something no good. "You've gotten thinner. Something happen in Providence? What's up with the dark circles under your eyes? Are you eating and sleeping enough?"

I smiled at the slew of questions I didn't want to answer.

Guilt gnawed at me for not visiting as often as I should. I had a medical facility to attend to, along with side projects that occupied a lot of my time. So my visits were rare.

"I missed you and Grandma." I squeezed her shoulder. "That's why I'm here."

"What about me, you oaf?" Yolanda emerged from the back room with a tray of fancy containers that probably held ointment or balm. Three customers entered the shop, and Cara broke away to assist them.

Yolanda placed the tray on the counter and walked into my open arms. Her rose perfume overcame the strong sage. Moving back, she looked up at me and tugged at my hair, making a disapproving expression. "What's up with the long hair?"

She'd lightened her brown hair with highlights that framed her pretty face. She wore a blue dress that matched her sandals. Pride spread through me. My cousin was a good catch, and I was proud of the woman she'd become. She worked as an administrative assistant at some law firm, but helped at the apothecary whenever she had time off. Yolanda and Grandma Morena were my only family.

I tugged at her hair. "Yours is different too. You don't hear me complaining. I like it. Makes you look younger."

Pink dusted her cheeks, but then her eyes narrowed on me. "You calling me old? I'm only three years younger than you. Last I heard, twenty-nine is the new twenty." She studied me from various angles, shaking her head. "Nope, I like you better with short hair. This look makes you seem like a man with no direction. Want me to trim it?"

A man with no direction? Where did she get that from? My hair wasn't even chin length. It grew past my ears, and that was probably as long as I'd let it get, but I wasn't going to divulge this detail to Yolanda, who for some reason disliked my new style.

"No." I swatted her hand away from my hair. "Change is a good thing."

She stepped back and crossed her arms, studying me. "Even your clothes are different. What is this button-down shirt? A Robert Graham! I got you one years ago, and you didn't wear it," she pouted. I didn't remember her giving me any shirt. "And this slim khaki pant makes you look like some European model. What happened to your jeans and polo shirts, preppy boy?"

"They're in my closet. People get bored. They acclimate. You're an herbalist. You should know that energies change all the time—like a woman's mood." I winked at her, but she didn't appreciate it. My experience with the female patients revealed that women's moods varied like a child's crayon box—they came in all shapes, sizes, and colors. "I'm just trying something different."

"Something new, huh?" Yolanda's eyebrows came together. "Why?"

"Why not?" I retorted.

I didn't understand why people were fascinated with my hair and fashion preferences. They should embrace this new look that differed from my usual clean-cut appearance. What was the big deal, anyway? Grayson had called me out on it, and now my cousin too.

Not wanting to continue the ridiculous conversation, I headed to the back office, where my grandmother spent her time sorting herbs. There was nothing wrong with change. People often forgot that change was necessary. Stagnation created diseases. Blood needed to circulate, and energy required constant motion to maintain good health. Yolanda should have known this as well. Maybe she did, but chose not to acknowledge it. Some people had selective hearing and vision.

If there were one important thing that I'd learned as an immunologist, it was the fact that the human body's best remedy was to keep moving. It can heal itself by mimicking nature. This was my personal observation based on years of studying western and holistic medicine. Plants grew because of the change in weather. Some days they required the sun to thrive, while other days, they preferred the rain. This constant change allowed for growth.

The human body was no different. The prescription for my emotional rut was change—hence my longer hair.

Yolanda had unknowingly poked at my vulnerable spot without knowing. She was seeing the exterior part of me, not the true reason. Growing my hair was an experiment, just like the change in clothing preference. No big deal.

Liar. It's more than that.

I slowed my steps as I warred with myself.

So what? Yes, the long hair and trendy clothes thing had a story behind them, but I wasn't in the mood to explain it to anyone.

Maybe I should get a trim and be done with it. I'd return to my usual self and no one would question me about anything.

But that's surrendering.

I didn't surrender. Defeat was not an option. Period. I'd gotten where I was today from working my ass off and maneuvering the dangerous world filled with ruthless, powerful men. Money yielded power, and power made men believe that anything was possible.

The threat looming over me and my friends grew larger each day. Remington, Royce, Grayson, Arrow, and I were discreetly working toward destroying The Trogyn, a powerful crime organization with an extensive global reach. Besides watching my enemy suffer, The Trogyn was the reason I had planned a trip to Texas. My friends and I had discovered an elusive club in Austin, and my colleague had connections to a gathering that could be linked to them. I couldn't let this opportunity slip by without investigating.

My boys and I were taking careful steps to ensure our loved ones were safe. Still, there was a quiet whisper that made me fear that someday this crime organization would attack me and my loved ones unexpectedly.

Who knew that one incident from our teen years could change the course of our lives forever? The past had a power to imprison us more than we realized. I wanted those shackles removed.

As I walked toward the back room, Grandma made her way toward the front and stopped in her steps when she saw me. She blinked, tightened her grip on the basket of dried flowers, and pressed her lips into a thin line.

"What powerful current blew you in here?" Grandma asked, surveying me. She had a lovely accent and learned English at the same school that had taught me in Brazil. "You've lost weight. Working too much and ignoring your health? Money isn't going to prolong your life, boy. When will you learn?" She shook her head. "I thought you forgot about your family."

"Never."

She sneered at my remark, making me wince. Grandma Morena wore her gray hair in a bun with a crystal accessory. She had sharp green eyes that seemed to know everything, and a face etched with wisdom and strength. Her olive skin was a shade darker than mine, which contrasted nicely with the off-white top and full skirt. A pouch of crystals dangled from her belt.

"That's hard to believe when I hardly see you anymore," she said.

Grandma was a petite woman, standing four feet ten inches

tall. Without her, I'd probably be an orphan living a different life.

Guilt stabbed me as I recalled our previous conversations about me being a workaholic. She didn't need to know about the extracurricular activity outside of my medical occupation. Vengeance had reigned supreme for a long time, and staying away from her kept the darkness at bay.

"We talk on the phone."

"Not the same," she huffed, and the bag of crystals shifted on her belt. "That's an excuse for lazy business executives who care more about money than family."

Ouch.

I kept my mouth shut. A man knew when he was going to lose a battle, no matter what excuse he could offer. Feeling resigned, my gaze landed on the crystals. She'd given me a pouch, believing they could ward off evil spirits and such. I prayed she wouldn't ask me about it, because I had no idea where I'd placed it.

Though I loved holistic medicine, crystals and tarot cards weren't for me. Science still ran in my blood. Despite that, I wanted to change the world's perspective on alternative medicine. It didn't get the attention it deserved. But it would one day. I'd make sure of it. It was the future of healing. I'd invested a lot of time and money in this field.

A man with an open mind allowed innovative ideas to manifest. Just because I understood the world of allergies and infectious diseases didn't mean my ambitions ended there.

Ambition was a force of nature. It had helped me survive when the world appeared dark and dire. It had given me strength to obtain the things I wanted. Ambition made me a billionaire.

Grandma Morena flicked an inquisitive look at me. "Why are you growing your hair long?"

Here we go again. This topic was getting boring.

I raked a hand through my hair. "I skipped my barber shop appointment to hop on the first flight to see my favorite grandmother. Isn't that what you wanted?" I grabbed the basket from her hands and draped an arm around her small shoulders, praying she'd change the subject.

She jabbed a strong finger into my ribs. "You don't think I can spot a lie? Don't forget who raised you."

"I've been busy and haven't had time to get a trim. It's the least of my worries."

Those were all truths. I had been busy, and a haircut wasn't a priority compared to the other issues swimming in my head. If she knew I was using this physical change as an experiment, she'd probably understand. But that conversation would encourage more questions.

I didn't have time for that.

"Things okay at the clinic?" she asked, concern weighing on her face.

"It's growing fast. There are three new doctors on rotation now."

"Good." She nodded slowly. "Your parents would've been proud of what you've accomplished." Her tone had softened, and I knew she'd already forgiven me.

My father had died because three vile men entered our home without cause and shot him. My dad was an innocent man, but they didn't want to hear it. He died from an infection he'd acquired from the awful wound. My family didn't have money back then for treatment. Like most areas in the world, Brazil had its political issues where the common people ended up suffering the most. My mom passed away in a car accident when we immigrated to the States.

Their loss changed me, pushing me to become a doctor. It

made me feel better knowing that I had the power to help if my loved ones were hurt.

I squeezed Grandma's shoulder, appreciating her more than she knew. When her shop was in Providence, it had been easy to visit her. But the winter worsened her arthritis, so she moved to a warmer climate and found her niche in a like-minded community of mystics.

Grandma Morena looked up at me. "How long are you staying this time?"

"Three weeks. I've got a few seminars to attend, colleagues to meet up with, and business to review at the Holistic Farm."

"Dinner next Saturday." It wasn't a question, but a firm statement that also served as a command from a woman who had my respect. "After that, I'll think about forgiving you for abandoning me."

Her words cut straight to the quick, and a dark memory flashed in my mind.

Mommy holds my hand, guiding me through the forest behind our house. We follow Grandma Morena as she leads us to a path covered with tall plants. I can't see our village anymore. The only sounds I hear are our feet stomping on twigs. I'm breathing hard because I'm tired. There are so many bugs here. A bug almost flies in my mouth, but I swat it away. Yuck.

I glance at my mom. She looks stressed and scared. I know she's sad because I'm sad too. Mom and Grandma buried my dad in the backyard last night. They thought I was asleep, but I watched them through the window. I couldn't sleep because I miss my dad.

I hate those three men who killed my dad, especially the man with the red birthmark who shot him. They're evil. They killed my neighbors too. I don't understand why this is happening.

The evil men with big guns always come to our town, yelling and pushing people. They pushed my mom's friend, and she fell and hit her head against a pole. Grandma had to help her stop the bleeding with herbs. I wish the police would arrest these mean people, but they don't care. Maybe they're scared too.

I'm only six years old. I'm too small to help.

"Everyone, okay?" Grandma turns around to check on us.

Mom nods and whispers, "We have to hurry, baby boy."

I trip and fall to the ground. "Oww."

Mom crouches to help me up. "Are you okay?"

"Yes."

She pats my cheek. "We have to be quiet. They'll catch us if they hear us."

Understanding, I nod.

"I can hear the river. There's a boat waiting for us." Grandma looks happy. "We're going to a safe place."

"Where are we going, Vó?" I ask, hopeful to not to see those bad people again.

"America."

My grandma, mom, and I were sponsored by my grandmother's friend to enter the United States of America when I was six years old. When I was nine, my mom died, leaving me with Grandma Morena. She raised me and gave me a loving home, shielding me from the cruelty of the world. But I knew how dark it was. I felt the darkness grow inside me the moment those men shot my father. Though America was safer than the villages of Brazil, it carried its own corruption.

Freedom looked and felt different when you'd experienced the alternative.

In order to overcome the darkness, I stepped into it and familiarized myself with its unstable terrain. This was something I wouldn't share with Grandma. She'd be disappointed in me.

I could never abandon Grandma Morena. Doing so would abandon my history—experiences that had formed me into a successful billionaire. Life was one contradiction with many faces. Being open to possibilities had allowed me to see those faces and push them aside to focus on a cutting-edge medication that could change the world soon.

Placing the tray of herb tubes on the marble counter, I met Grandma's eyes. A subtle green that was a shade different from mine.

"I wouldn't trade anything for your cooking," I said.

That was the truth. She made the best traditional Brazilian dishes that were incomparable to any restaurant I knew. *I'm so grateful for this woman.*

"*Sou muito grata por você, Vó.*" I kissed her forehead. Our family spoke Portuguese, and I tried my best to not forget my native language.

Grandma loved it when I spoke to her that way.

With a happy gleam in her eyes, she placed a hand on my cheek. "You've gotten thinner. You working too much? Not eating healthy like I told you to? Is that girl not taking care of you?"

My eyebrows furrowed, unsure of who she was referring to. Yolanda glanced over, looking just as intrigued as Cara, who was ringing up a customer.

"What girl?" I hadn't dated anyone since . . . that night.

"The red-haired girl who didn't even say hi to me when I stopped by the hospital to visit you. You know, the one with the giant melons."

I wasn't sure how to react to my grandma's reference to breasts.

She waved a dismissive hand. "Who dresses like that to work anyway? Those things were practically trying to escape the tight knit top. Maybe she gets patients by giving them heart attacks. They were probably fake like the ones on the celebrities."

Laughter bubbled inside me at my grandma's opinion of Julie Allen, my ex-girlfriend. My relationship with Julie had been nothing serious. It was short-lived and mostly sex-driven. Yes, she had gorgeous melons, which were real, though I wasn't going to inform my grandma about that fact. I was a man who appreciated beauty. But physical attraction faded over time if nothing else was present.

Julie was a hot cardiologist, and she had moved on just as I had. Last I heard, she was dating a surgeon from Mass General Hospital.

My perspective on relationships changed when I encountered a woman who didn't have giant melons, but was more captivating. I craved her like a starved animal. I dreamed about Kiera often. Dreams were the only places where things worked out beautifully between us. Our one-night stand didn't end too well. It had happened spontaneously . . . and regrettably. I didn't regret anything, but she did.

Kiera had darted out of my bed before I even woke. What did that do to a man's ego? *Fuck.* I should stop wondering. It irritated me not knowing what I'd done wrong. I thought we had a fabulous evening. Apparently I pissed her off enough for her to dash off.

I didn't want to think about it anymore. I wasn't her type, and she wasn't mine either. Perfection meant high-maintenance, and I had no time for demanding women.

Yet you can't get rid of her.

She was a virus that had infected me, paralyzing my cognitive thinking. It had been six months, and I still struggled to remove her from my thoughts.

My eyes met my grandma's keen stare.

"That ended a while ago. I'm too busy to date," I informed her.

"Too much isn't good for you either." She jabbed a finger at my chest, then went to add something into a small cauldron sitting in the corner by the incense display.

Yolanda grinned at Grandma's statement.

"Still seeing that guy who lavishes you with jewelry?" I asked Yolanda, gesturing to her new diamond earrings and bracelet.

"Yes, I am." She opened a box and took out handmade soaps, sniffing and sorting them. "Like you, he works a lot."

I'd never met the guy. "When do I get to meet this guy? Has Grandma met him?"

Yolanda nodded. "Well, she spoke to him on the phone. He's busy."

That meant Grandma didn't approve of him. Because if she had, she'd already have invited him to her house for a home-cooked meal. She hadn't mentioned anything about him to me.

A woman with vicious eyes stormed over to my grandmother and slapped a bag onto the table, rattling the tray of herb tubes.

CHAPTER THREE

KIERA

With my luggage and carry-on bag, I made a mental note to take some time for a hike around the camp. I entered the main office, and the air conditioner welcomed me with open arms. Late June in Texas offered humidity, which probably showed in my frizzy ponytail.

A middle-aged woman with a chin-length bob greeted me with a cheerful smile that suited the sunflowers on her blue dress. "You have reservations, darling?"

I returned the friendly gesture with a nod. "Kiera Ford."

She pressed the keys on her keyboard and glanced at the computer screen. "Ahh, there you are. You're with the fashion brand." Leaning onto the marble counter, she grinned. "I already met the hunky coordinator. Your cabin is number sixty-nine. It's just around the corner to the right. The main lodge didn't have any rooms left. But if you ask me, the private cabins are way better." She dropped the keys into my palm. "Enjoy your time here, honey. If you need anything, y'all just holler. I'm Nora."

"Thanks." Holding onto the key, I headed to my cabin.

I had thought the coordinator was Stephanie Patterson. She'd been my contact person with FitFlex for the past couple of months during my negotiation for this job. My schedule had been packed, but they'd offered a deal I couldn't resist. And because of my sudden financial needs, I had declined another offer to work with FitFlex. Besides, the other offer would've taken me to New Zealand. Though I loved to travel, my mom needed me close by. Texas wasn't near Providence, but at least I was in the country, so that made things easier for emergency purposes.

FitFlex was a growing company with celebrities promoting the brand. According to the photo shoot agenda, there would be one female and two male models. I'd worked with all of them before, so this shoot should be smooth sailing. I didn't need the extra drama that often came from supermodels who didn't like my style or were too demanding. Perhaps I could finish the photo edits early and spend a few days exploring, just to clear my head.

When I spotted my cabin, I stopped in my steps and absorbed the scene. "Color me happy." My body instantly relaxed at the splendid view.

The triangle-shaped cabin sat by itself with a private view of the lake. It was made of wood and stones. Interesting designs were etched onto the wooden beams supporting the porch. Trees, floral bushes, and the stone walkway gave it a pleasing curb appeal. Tiny purple flowers dotted the grass and moss. Serenity embraced me like satin over skin. I was a city girl at heart, but I didn't mind this tranquil escape. We all needed an escape now and then to balance out the chaotic energy of city life.

I dragged my luggage onto the stone walkway that led up to the porch with pretty potted flowers. A swing hung on the side, and I planned to enjoy it later.

Lifting my luggage up the two steps onto the porch, I studied the wooden sign nailed to the wall beside the door. Someone had etched in "haha" under the cabin number sixty-nine. *Great.* I prayed the interior of the cabin wasn't also decorated with sexual innuendos. I hadn't been intimate with a man for a while, and right now that was the last thing on my mind. Work and worry had sent my libido down the drain.

"Excuse m-me," a male voice called out.

I turned to face a young man wearing a black tank top and cargo shorts. He had curly brown hair, a narrow face, and dark eyes that scrutinized my body, making me feel uncomfortable. He had scars on his forearm, and his right hand trembled.

"Hi. I'm Kiera," I said, trying to be friendly.

The man stepped onto the porch with his worn sneakers and gave me a nod. "I'm Hank P-Peterson. I live over th-there." He pointed to a cabin that was twice the size of my cabin. I couldn't see the entire cabin, as it was tucked back behind several trees. I wouldn't have noticed it if he hadn't pointed it out.

Note to self: check out the campground. Make note of your surroundings.

Growing up with a single parent, my mom had drilled into me how important it was to be aware of my surroundings. I didn't have a father or a brother to protect me, so I'd had to learn how to protect myself.

"It's nice to meet you, Hank."

"How long are y-you staying h-here?" he asked, glancing around the cabin and looking nervous.

"Whenever the job is done. I'm a photographer for FitFlex. You'll be seeing our team around. We're photographing some athletic wear."

Shaking his head, Hank jerked a chin to the lake. "This isn't p-paradise. Y-you don't want your p-pictures taken h-here." His lips trembled either from nervousness or the stuttering.

"Not my call. I just work for the company who likes the view."

He slid his trembling hands into his pockets. "Well, I hope y-you folks keep this area c-clean. The previous v-visitors left a bunch of t-trash. Took me d-days to clean. It's n-not even my j-job."

"Is this your vacation home?"

"My permanent h-home."

I could understand his annoyance. "Sorry to hear about the trash. I'll let everyone know to clean up after themselves." I gave him a thumbs up, which earned a small smile from him.

"Don't w-wander out too f-far. W-Wild animals are every-where. Can g-get dangerous."

"Thanks for the heads up."

"I'll be w-watching over y-you." He saluted me.

Uh, no thanks.

"That's unnecessary, Hank."

"I d-do that for all the y-young ladies. You be c-careful." He narrowed his eyes, looking over at the lake.

The last thing I needed was a weirdo freaking me out.

"I'll be careful. Okayseeyoulaterbye." I rushed into the cabin, shut the door, locked it, and pressed my back against it. My heart thudded loudly in my ears as I waited for him to leave my porch.

When footsteps descended the stairs, I blew out a breath I didn't know I was holding, then went to the window to ensure he was gone.

Retrieving the phone from my purse, I punched in a reminder to stop by the hardware store to get a can of pepper spray. Part of being aware was preparation. A girl had to arm herself for emergencies.

I took a few moments to gather myself and checked the interior of the cabin. Polished wood beams supporting the ceiling, and rustic hardwood floors extended through the entire space. Floral curtains and casual furniture added a dash of charm. I didn't see any other racy carvings while I walked through the bedroom, bathroom, kitchen, and living room. There was a big screen TV attached to the wall with a fireplace. A ceiling fan and an air conditioner would keep the living room and bedroom cool. Satisfied with my temporary home, I dropped onto the floral print couch, closed my eyes, and tried to relax.

This vacancy would've been perfect if I didn't have a creepy neighbor. But life was like that. It tossed you unexpected lemons, as though testing your patience. I wasn't going to let one guy ruin my trip. I was going to make pink lemonade and a lemon cake from any goddamn lemons flying toward me.

I opened my eyes and glanced at my phone. It was only four in the afternoon, but I was exhausted. I didn't have to work until tomorrow when the rest of the crew arrived.

After checking on my mom and pleased that she was doing fine, I unpacked my clothes and toiletries, preparing for a quick shower, but a knock sounded at my door.

I walked over to the window by the front door and pushed the curtains aside to see who it was.

An attractive man stood on my porch. This had to be the "hunky" man Nora had talked about.

I opened the door to an attractive man that should have stirred me up, but he did *nothing*. He was tall, built, with a strong-boned face, short dark hair, and olive skin that made the aqua polo shirt stand out. The khaki shorts showed off toned legs. Was he a new model for FitFlex?

"Hi. I'm Bruno Barbosa. You must be Kiera." He offered a sexy smile that would make most women weak in the knees.

No effect on me, though. What was wrong with me?

"I am. Are you with FitFlex?" I asked, trying to figure out why I wasn't the least bit attracted to him. Perhaps my sexuality was shut off like a button on my phone.

Kiera Ford—a woman who loved sex and appreciated hot guys—was now devoid of all senses.

Help me, God.

"I'm the coordinator, replacing Stephanie. She's staying at the headquarters to work on another project. Nice to meet you."

He offered me his hand. His handshake was firm, which suggested a skillful man both inside and outside the bedroom. If that was how I'd judge men, then I had a serious issue.

Of course, that wasn't how I scaled the men I'd been with. I wasn't that shallow. It was just that when I shook a handsome man's hand, there was usually a tingle of acknowledgment, sort of like seeing a beautiful landscape. The body would react with a soft sigh or something.

With Bruno, I sensed nothing.

Stop looking for a replacement, Kiera! Why are you still trying to forget a man who's out of your league?

I didn't want to answer that question. To answer it would be to acknowledge something I wasn't ready to face. Not only that, the answer would open up an insecurity I hadn't experienced until recently. I hated feeling unworthy.

"We're heading out for dinner in a few hours. Do you want to join us?"

"Who's us?" I asked.

"Olivia and Nate just arrived. They came earlier than expected. Steven's scheduled to come tomorrow morning. We're all staying at the main lodge. I heard you checked in, so I wanted to introduce myself." He smiled, revealing perfect white teeth.

Bruno reminded me of a man I knew—a gorgeous man who had been occupying my mind too much these days. A man I thought I saw pass me on the road earlier today. Though stunning, Bruno couldn't compare to him. No one could.

I couldn't even think of his name without sending my thoughts into a tailspin. Every photographer had to beware the bokeh effect. I didn't want parts of my life to be out of focus. Any distortion—even if aesthetically beautiful—was bad for someone trying to live in reality.

Maybe if I surrounded myself with gorgeous guys, I'd slowly forget about *him*. Bruno was real, with no special effect, and standing in front of me.

"Sure. I'd love to join you," I said, feeling hopeful.

"I can give you a tour of the campground. I checked in two days ago and have done some exploring. Lots of trails and streams."

An attractive tour guide sounded like a wonderful idea that would keep my mind off a man whose name I couldn't mention.

CHAPTER FOUR

My body stiffened at the frustration and anger radiating from the woman. I rushed over and stood between her and my grandmother.

"Is something wrong?" I stared down at the woman, shielding my grandma from this awful woman who looked like she wanted to hurt someone.

She was testing the wrong person. I was in no mood to deal with her.

Grandma stepped away from my protection and greeted the woman with respect she didn't deserve. "How can I help you?"

"Your herbs are fake—this shop is a fraud!" the lady fumed.

Grandma's lips thinned, and the respect was gone. "You need anger management. Sorry, but we do not offer that kind of therapy here."

Yolanda stood on the other side of my grandma, looking like she was ready to strangle the customer. This was why I loved my cousin.

Grandma didn't tolerate people who abused customer

service. She would rather lose the sale than see her employees endure that kind of ill treatment.

The woman tugged at her bag, pulling out a small jar and several sealed paper bags of herbs. I was surprised the jar didn't crack from the way she tossed it on the counter.

"Your herbal concoction made me sick." She shot a hand in the air. "I was in the hospital for two weeks!" She shook the jar. "This isn't medicine. It's poison. I didn't take anything other than this herbal crap from your shop. I told my doctor, and he gave it to the police. You'll be hearing from them and my lawyer very soon."

My jaw tightened as a slew of questions flew out of me. "Are you taking any other medication? What are you allergic to? When was your last physical? What did you eat before and after taking the holistic medicine?"

"It doesn't matter," she seethed.

"It *does*." I stared at her. "One allergy can turn an effective medicine ineffective instantly. What works for one person can cripple another. Now, answer my questions."

The woman glared at me, and I arched an eyebrow, waiting for her response. If she had expected us to let the questions slide, she was wrong.

"This is harassment," she said, straightening her spine.

"No. This is getting the facts," I replied.

"Harassment is accusation without facts," Yolanda added.

"An educated person like you wouldn't stoop to that level, correct?" I said, gauging her. Was she authentic or was this a ploy? "I'm a doctor, and I'll be happy to educate you with any misinformation you've received."

I didn't know what had gotten into me. I'd dealt with more stressful situations than this little trouble maker. Perhaps it was the frustration of not locating the leader of the Anacondas, the growing loneliness of dealing with the vengeance, or the caution I had to take because of The Trogyn that had tipped off my equilibrium.

This woman incited my anger, and I didn't like it. "I need to know your symptoms."

Sensing my frustration, Grandma placed a hand on my lower back.

Yolanda swiped the jar from the counter, examining it, probably making sure it was purchased from Full Circle Apothecary. "We take pride in our work, and we've healed many people who keep returning. This is a healing center, and that's all we do. We heal." She showed my grandma the jar. "There's nothing potent in here. Just basic herbs you can find in any tea packages."

Grandma looked at the woman. "What kind of 'poison' did the doctor say this was?"

I grabbed the jar from Grandma's hand and checked the ingredients: jasmine leaves, dandelion, rose, and ginseng. Nothing about these contents would hurt anyone. As an immunologist, I was well-versed in infectious diseases, poison, and other things that could harm the human body.

There was no way these herbs poisoned her.

The need to protect my grandma spiked. I studied the woman who appeared to be in her mid-fifties wearing bright red lipstick. She stood straight and proud, portraying someone who didn't waver much. Her luxury clothing showed she preferred to shop at boutiques. She didn't seem like the kind that would make trouble for a payout. She already had money. But from my experience with the wealthy, I'd encountered snakes and vultures who would do anything for money.

What was going on here?

The woman kept darting her eyes away from my gaze, making her seem even more suspicious. Had The Trogyn sent her here? I didn't know why that thought intruded my brain, but I couldn't dismiss it.

However, Grandma's apothecary wasn't a corporation that could affect them. Unless they were targeting me. Had they somehow linked me and my friends to the destruction of their businesses? No, they hadn't made the connection yet. If they had, I was certain they wouldn't send one woman into a shop; they'd send an army. I had to be extra cautious because they could be anywhere. That was another level of anxiety hovering over me.

"Some scientific name. I don't remember it." The woman shrugged. "It affected my heart and intestines."

With concern straining her face, Grandma composed herself. "I'm sorry you had an unpleasant experience. I'm sorry you were sick and had to go to the hospital. But I assure you, all of my alternative medicine—and everything else I sell in the shop—is meant to heal, not hurt. Have your lawyer speak to mine. I have nothing to hide." She took a deep breath. "However, the next time you step into my shop, I expect the same courtesy I'm giving you. If you come in here and disrupt my business again, there will be another lawsuit. And that won't have anything to do with herbs."

The woman huffed. "This shop is a scam. I'll make sure everyone knows about it."

"If you do that, expect to lose everything you own." Anger pulsed in my veins but my voice remained calm. "What's your name?"

No one threatened my family. If she wanted to play in court, I was game. She didn't know who she was dealing with.

"Patricia Gallivan." She met my eyes and probably saw the threat I could impose on her, and her temper dimmed slightly.

Good. She needed to know this wasn't her place to say or do as she pleased.

Despite my dismay, I put on a polite mask and said, "If what you say is true, let the court decide. My defense team will require a sample of your bloodwork before and after you took the liquids. We'll scour your medical history to ensure that you don't have any ailments and aren't taking any prescriptions that would have interacted with the holistic medicine. My team of doctors will analyze *everything*."

She stared at me, likely weighing the pros and cons of my words.

I needed her to understand her threat. It wasn't something that could be swept under the rug.

"There could be several reasons you were sick. Perhaps you love wine, and that caused an adverse reaction. Perhaps you inhaled a scent with an allergen your body didn't like." I tried to explain in the most basic terms so she'd understand. "Or maybe you touched something that carried traces of 'poison.' You could've caught a virus that churned up something already in your system."

Her lips thinned, and her cheeks turned pink. "My lawyer will sort this out. You people don't know what you're doing." She pointed to Grandma Morena, Yolanda, and Cara. "You shouldn't be allowed to operate a business here. I'll warn the city about the dangerous stuff you're selling!"

"Once you calm down, perhaps you can think clearly. I suspect your blood pressure is dangerously high. I don't want to see you collapsing in my grandma's shop. Do what you will, but we will defend the truth." I stepped closer to her, my voice low but clear. "If you ruin my family's business from hearsay, I'll make sure you pay for the damages. Defamation is a different lawsuit." Stepping back, I pointed to the cameras in the shop. "And we have proof of your ill intentions on record."

"I could have died from that crap!" She swung an arm at the herbal tubes at a nearby display.

"Did anyone force you to buy it?" Cara asked.

"No."

"Did anyone force you to drink it?" Yolanda asked.

Patricia opened her mouth, but I lifted my hand to stop her. "You've said enough already. Get. Out."

Grandma, Yolanda, and Cara gestured to the door simultaneously.

"You *will* regret this," she huffed.

"Don't trip on your nasty personality," Cara muttered. "That was probably what landed you in the hospital."

Yolanda gave her the middle finger as Patricia disappeared from view. "Let me check in the system to see when she bought the herbs. That kind of concoction had to be purchased from the special sessions that required a registration."

I placed a hand on my grandma's shoulders. "Don't worry. It's going to be fine. I'm taking Patricia's returned items for review."

Grandma nodded. "Let me know if something is off."

I hated that woman for placing doubts in Grandma's mind.

While Yolanda searched the computer with Grandma, I sent my lawyer an email asking him to assist in this matter. Henry Traynor was a top-notch attorney, and his firm worked in various states. He wasn't cheap, but I wanted the best for my family.

My phone rang just as I emailed.

"What's up?" I asked Levi Dispenza, a friend I'd met at a business convention during medical school at Harvard University.

Levi was a wealthy man developing and selling computer software and now diving into AI. He was the other reason I was here in Texas. He had invited me to attend a banquet at the elusive club. It could be another angle to destroy The Trogyn.

This organization profited from human trafficking,

gambling, selling drugs, racketeering, and other illegal activities at a level that involved the most powerful people across the world. We had to take it down before it destroyed us.

"Got some interesting updates. Let's meet up tonight. How about seven at Taco Haven?"

"See you then," I said, wondering what he'd discovered about the club.

CHAPTER FIVE

KIERA

I hopped into the back seat of the black Jeep, sitting next to Olivia Bauer. She had gorgeous curly blonde hair and a voluptuous body that made women envy her, including me. Bruno Barbosa slid into the driver's side with Nate Ruggs in the front passenger seat. He was a preppy male model with short light brown hair, and he made suits look amazing.

"What are you guys in the mood for? Mexican food?" Bruno glanced back, meeting my gaze. "Italian? Chinese, Vietnamese, or Middle Eastern? They also have Ethiopian and Cajun."

I studied his handsome face. But right now I wasn't the least bit attracted to him. Not an ounce of attraction. I didn't know what was wrong with me. The things that used to turn me on fell flat these days. It wasn't just with men. My life seemed like it was missing something I didn't understand.

I was a snake that had shed its skin, leaving the old me behind. And yet this new version of me made me feel both lost and excited, which didn't make sense.

Olivia shrugged her shoulders. "I have no preference.

Gotta watch my appetite because I need to squeeze into that tiny swimwear tomorrow." She elbowed me. "Make sure to Photoshop any unnecessary excess out of my pics, please."

"Trust me, you don't have any excess," I said.

I'd worked with Olivia on a few photo shoots before, and the camera loved her. At twenty-three, she was seven years younger than me. Olivia couldn't resist the stunning male models and had developed several relationships with them, all of which ended in heartache.

I winced at the similar mistakes I'd made. External beauty could hypnotize, blind one to the truth. When I thought things were going well, the veil was lifted, and I was faced with the reality that I'd been cheated on. My sense of security and self-worth took a nosedive. Any woman would suffer from that. What everyone wanted was to be loved, safe, and happy, right? It was hard to find an honest and communicative relationship. Trust was rare these days. Did I have to go to a different planet to find it?

Maybe I was doomed to be single forever, which was fine. I didn't want to depend on anyone for my happiness. Perhaps this was the stark lesson I had to learn to move forward.

"Been here a few times on business," Bruno said, rolling down the window. The sun still shone at seven in the evening, and the air had cooled a bit, but the humidity sucked. The frizz probably made my brown hair look like a bird's nest that had been tossed around by a tornado. I reached up and released the hair band, letting my hair tumble.

"How about Taco Haven? I heard great things about it," Nate said. "It has spacious outdoor seating and the temps have gone down, so it should be nice for us."

I'd also worked with Nate twice before. Though he had a girlfriend at home, that never stopped him from flirting or hooking up with strangers during his travels. It wasn't my place to intervene in his business, and I didn't know any of the female models he'd been with. Now, if one of those women had been my friend, then his balls would have been bruised. Just saying.

Some men viewed women as accessories. I was no damn belt or watch that could be bought.

Keep your heart safe. Don't give it out too easily.

When things seemed easy, people didn't see their value.

Despite my values, there had been one event that took me on a winding path I wasn't familiar with. One detour I vowed to never embark on again. I wasn't a one-night stand kind of girl. It was too risky and made me feel . . . unworthy and out of place. Yet I forgot about that when I hooked up with *him*. The powerful attraction made me lose my sense of logic. Because it wasn't with a stranger, the aftermath became awkward. At least for me it did. The onslaught of embarrassment and confusion was too much for me.

I didn't know if he had a girlfriend, and I'd been foolish, letting my wild hormones decide instead of thinking things through.

From that day on, I had set hard rules for myself again. One, no more one-night stands. Two, aim for an honest long-term relationship. Three, focus on my dreams without worrying about the money factor. Four, be happy.

Simple, right? Nope.

I liked rules. They provided structure, but they were difficult to adhere to.

When I'd made that list, I also sent a wish out to the sky that night: I wanted to be happy with a man who valued and loved me. I'd waited for a shooting star to confirm, but it never showed up. One day soon.

The rules I had in college were too pliable, too unsubstantial. But I'd been young and clueless. When I got my fashion photography job, the glamor of it mesmerized me. I'd dated businessmen and stunning models, but like the glamor, the initial spark faded over time, and the ugly truth revealed itself.

Women had to look out for each other. Being the "other woman" was like being an accessory that was easily replaced. My mom had been one, and it hurt her. She said I was the gift that came from her temporary relationship, and she didn't have any regrets. But I often wondered if that was the truth.

Don't get me wrong—my mom loved me, and I loved her. Still, I wondered if she wished she'd never met the bastard. My father was a good-for-nothing sorry excuse for a man. To love someone only to be tossed aside without remorse cut deeply. I'd seen her cry when I was younger. That stayed with me, and I hated him even though I'd never met him.

In some way, I was repeating the same mistakes as my mother: dating men who didn't value me. I had to break this generational trauma. The men I'd been with were to fill a void caused by something I didn't quite understand. Perhaps women needed a sense of belonging and fell for anything that seemed to offer that security.

But no more. Kiera Ford was done expecting a man to make her happy. I didn't want to depend on anyone. I didn't want that pain or disappointment, so keeping my distance in relationships was my technique. Though I wanted a long-term relationship, I was terrified of it. Where did that leave me? Nowhere. I had no place to stand.

Stop being so negative.

Nate blasted the music louder as he rolled down his windows.

I checked my phone to see how my mom was doing. I told her to text or call whenever she needed anything. No text appeared, so I sent her a message.

Hope you're doing well. The scenery is spectacular here. Rest up. Love you.

She was probably sleeping because of all the medications she was taking. The news of my mom's illnesses pulled the rug from under my feet. Two years ago, she contracted Hepatitis B, a liver disease, from an accidental needle stick at work. She was a nurse, and these kinds of accidents occurred no matter how careful she was. The weak liver made her tired all the time. Mom used to have a full head of hair; now she feared she'd go bald. She couldn't take walks around the neighborhood like she used to because of the muscle pains. My mom and I used to get our nails done together. But now, she was too tired.

Though she was suffering, she never complained about anything. I admired her strength and resilience. She believed that she'd get well one day soon and did her best to stay positive.

Last year, she was diagnosed with the inflammatory muscle disease known as dermatomyositis. There was no cure for it, so the doctor had been prescribing her various medications to ease her muscle pain.

Mom's illnesses made me realize that life was too short. I had to get my life together. To do that, I had to know what I wanted. And what I wanted was to live a fulfilling life—to be happy. We had planned on taking a mother and daughter trip around the world, and I prayed she'd get well enough for that to come true. I didn't want to think about the alternative. It would devastate both of us.

Out of habit, I checked my email and saw a new message from her doctor, and my heart sank.

Kiera,

. . .

I wanted to update you regarding our conversation about the new medication that could help your mom. I spoke with a team of doctors working on a special prototype for Hepatitis B and dermatomyositis. Of course, like any new medications still in the works, the insurance company won't cover an experimental treatment.

I'm sorry I don't have better news. If you're still interested in treating your mom with the cutting-edge medication, please let me know. I'd reserve a place for her. We can try it in increments, perhaps every three months instead of every month. There are also payment plans to help you if you choose this path.

Please find enclosed the financial breakdown for your reference. Take your time and let me know your thoughts.

Best Regards,
   Dr. Samuel Schaeffer

I opened the attachment, and anxiety knotted my stomach. My appetite vanished, replaced by nausea. How was I going to pay for my mom's treatment, never mind the new medication? Right now she couldn't afford this so-called prototype, even with my help.

My mom raised me all on her own. She didn't deserve this. She deserved a life filled with love, abundance, and great health. I stared at the amount of money only the wealthiest could afford. All those zeroes after the dollar sign sent me into panic mode.

Even if I sold my condo and used up my savings, I wouldn't be able to afford it. The healthcare system was a scam. Why were medicines so expensive? Why did the insurance companies pick what they wanted to pay? They should pay for everything, considering all the money we had put into it. I didn't understand it.

Anger melded with my anxiety, making everything worse. I wanted to return to my cabin, where I could be alone. Socializing wasn't going to help me.

Calm down, Kiera. You can only solve problems with a clear head.

Maybe I could take out a loan? Or sign up for more freelance gigs?

Audri and Michelle would lend me money, but I couldn't ask them. Shame and pride squirmed in me.

Don't puke. Not in front of everyone.

"You okay?" Olivia asked. "You're pale."

I didn't know these coworkers well enough to dump my personal issues on them. Shoving my problems aside, I inhaled a breath, placed a hand over my tummy, and forced a smile. "Just hungry. I'll be fine."

Needing fresh air, I pressed the button, and the window slid down, sending in a whoosh of air. The warm summer breeze usually brought me ease—summer was my favorite season—but right now I didn't know if there was anything that could remove this anxiety.

The car stopped at a red light, and a couple strode in front of us at the crosswalk, hand in hand, looking comfortable and in love. Another wave of sadness rolled over me. Would I ever connect with anyone like that? Why was I being so sensitive?

I didn't understand this loneliness inundating me. Stress did several inexplicable things to the body and mind.

My stomach growled, and everyone laughed.

"We're almost there," Bruno said.

The aromas of freshly cooked tortillas, grilled chicken, chilis, and the pungent and earthy smell of mezcal teased my nose, making me hungry again. The hunger and the lively atmosphere snapped me out of my depressed mood.

When I return to Providence, I'd sit down and make an action plan, reevaluating my finances. Seeing everything written down would help me understand the next steps. Unlike photography, which captured a moment in time by snipping away what wasn't seen in the entire image, real life was everything in between.

I had to look at my problem from various angles so I could pay for my mom's medical needs. There was always a solution to a problem.

A full stomach would help me think, and a drink would loosen me up.

Bruno pulled into a parking lot with a side patio with strings of lights crisscrossing under the large awning. Customers crowded the outdoor seating, and some even spilled onto the steps. I liked the casual environment. Samba music echoed through the chatter and laughter.

We got a table by the corner and ordered a tray of tortilla chips, guacamole, a seven-layer black bean dip, and mango habanero salsa. These appetizers alone satisfied me just fine. The guys ordered burritos and margaritas while Olivia and I got chicken quesadillas. I got a cantarito and Olivia got her chelada. Comfort food and cocktails were exactly what I needed.

I dug into my food and smiled. I had skipped lunch in place of unpacking and replying to emails to confirm my other freelance projects for the next six months. Editing photos was my forte, and repeat clients kept me busy. Though my schedule was full, I could still squeeze in a few minor projects. I needed the extra cash now more than ever.

I made good money as a fashion photographer, but not enough to shell out over two million dollars. That was how much it cost for a year of monthly blood transfusions and the medication trial to ease my mom's pain. It was fucking ridiculous.

Did doctors just let patients die if they couldn't afford to pay?

Stop thinking. Just eat and enjoy yourself. Worrying isn't going to make you fast money.

As I finished my quesadilla and sipped my cantarito, my skin tingled. I ignored the strange sensation until I looked up, and all the air in me evaporated. My heart toppled over, rolled, and melted into the abyss. I locked eyes with the man who could make me feel more in one night than all my previous boyfriends combined.

The tingles intensified as they skipped down my spine. I took a slow inhale, and my heart recuperated and returned to its position. A hand went to my chest as though protecting my heart from some unseen threat.

Forrest Navarro was a gorgeous beast of a man who was every woman's dream. Based on the curious stares from the women at the nearby tables, my speculation was spot on. He stood tall, with an athletic frame, and shaggy dark brown hair, looking sexy as hell in light-washed jeans. He wore a T-shirt with the word "$Ba_7M_5Bu_{88}$" printed across it. The design looked like a chemical formula, but I wasn't sure. Underneath the bold letters was the phrase: Nature Heals the World. I didn't know why, but I made a mental note to check out the $Ba_7M_5Bu_{88}$ Project.

Everything about him intrigued me. If he wore the shirt, it probably had some significance.

You don't have time for this stuff, Kiera. Especially no time for infatuation.

It was weird that he stood a few tables away, staring at me without saying a word or waving a hand. Why didn't I smile or gesture his way?

Because the intensity of his eyes froze me in place.

Bruno came back from the bar, sat down, and draped an arm around my shoulder. His touch broke the trance, and Forrest's expression changed from indifferent to murderous.

A stunning murderous beast, indeed. He looked like he could kill someone right now. Or was I drunk and imagining things? A single cocktail had never done anything to me. Maybe Forrest was having a bad day, just like me.

"You want another drink?" Bruno nudged me with his elbow.

"No thanks."

Forrest made his way over to my table. There was a ruthless menace in the way he walked and commanded attention. A BaMBu beast ready to crush his mortal enemy. I didn't know why, but it thrilled me. The memory of us tangling in his bed flashed in my mind, making me shiver from head to toe even though the temperatures were in the mid-eighties.

The closer he got, the more the air thickened, making it difficult for me to breathe.

Arriving at the table, his potent energy swirled around me. He stared down at me with his sage-colored eyes that appeared dangerously darker than usual. Maybe the cocktail did something to my vision. God, he was a green-eyed beast that wielded power with one look, and I felt like prey that wanted him to devour me.

Why the hell did I keep referring to him as a beast? I shook my head from whatever spell I was trapped in.

"Kiera," he said in a guttural tone.

What was it about my name coming from his mouth that made the muscles in my core feel like they were being struck by lightning?

Gather your wits.

"Forrest." I smiled courteously. "What are you doing here?"

"Eating."

Duh, Kiera. Why else would anyone show up at a restaurant?

Where was the hole in the floor when you needed one?

CHAPTER SIX

FORREST

When I entered the restaurant, I sensed something was different. Then I spotted Kiera, and the displeasure I'd felt earlier vanished, followed by a massive boost to my heart as though someone had used a CPR machine on it.

Bruno's appearance by her side irritated me more than it should have. Someone like him shouldn't be with someone like her. She was in my circle of friends, and it was only natural to be protective of her, right?

How long had they known each other? Were they dating? The frustration sunk into me like serrated fangs.

I had no claim to her, even though I hadn't been able to keep her off my mind. The taste, scent, and feel of her still lingered in my system, making me wonder about too many things—too many what-ifs. What if things hadn't ended the way they did between us? What if I had reached out to her the following days, weeks, months? Why had she left before I even woke? These were unanswered questions that begged to be explained.

Another time. Not tonight.

My interest in Bruno stemmed from his association with dangerous people—people who could lead me to The Trogyn. This is why I'd volunteered to be a model at a fashion event he worked at. I hadn't expected to see him here in Texas, but life often carved out unseen paths. As a visionary, this was an opportunity to further my investigation.

Why was Bruno here? Were his friends here too? What were they planning?

A waft of Kiera's perfume slithered up my nose like a snake, seducing my entire body. Standing beside her, energy sizzled between us. If it hadn't been for the crowded restaurant, I could probably have heard the electricity snap in the air. This had never happened with anyone else.

"Are you here with one of the boys?" she asked, looking more nervous than usual.

Before our encounter, Kiera never acted nervous around me. She was striking, funny, and smart. She could whip out sarcasm like none other. But things had changed after our intimacy. It had ruined our friendship. I'd tried to forget her by avoiding all the social gatherings. I didn't want to make her feel uncomfortable.

Stop lying.

Seeing Kiera would only make me yearn for something impossible. And here I stood, drowning in the attraction, making me feel like an idiot.

"No. Just me," I replied, studying the fatigue on her face.

What was bothering her? Why should I care? I should focus on my purpose in Texas. Kiera had already distracted me enough for the past six months.

"Good to see you, man." Bruno got up from his seat, offering his hand. "What are you doing in Texas?

Bruno's voice popped the bubble that enveloped Kiera and

me from other people at the table. I looked around, finally acknowledging them, and nodded.

"Business." I shook Bruno's hand. "What brings you to this scorching state?"

"Another photo shoot." Bruno turned to the guy next to him and a pretty blonde. "This is Nate and Olivia."

"Nice to meet you both," I said.

"Nice to meet you too." Olivia smiled, examining me.

At a glance, Bruno appeared like a decent event coordinator, but there was more to him. How did he know men who ran illegal businesses? Did he work for them? Or was he a client?

The fashion industry had its own darkness with drugs and shit that could make you famous one night and destroy you the next. Money, power, drugs, and women were requirements for elite clubs. In order for me to get closer to the elite members, I had to wiggle my way in by befriending their associates.

Bruno and I weren't friends, but we could be acquaintances. I had to keep a closer eye on him for Kiera. Though a strange wall stood between us, I still considered her my friend. I didn't want anything to happen to her.

If he had any inappropriate intentions with her, I'd skewer him.

Bruno pulled over an extra chair, placed it next to him, and gestured to me. "Join us."

If I didn't have a different agenda for tonight, I'd certainly accept his offer. But there was something else I had to take care of first.

"Thanks, but I'm meeting a friend tonight. Enjoy your dinner." My gaze slid over to Kiera, whose brown eyes fixated on me. My heart thudded, remembering how she'd looked when I took her in my bed. Was she thinking that too? "See you later, Kiera."

"Later," she said.

I took my time walking away and trained my ears on their conversation.

"Who's the hunk?" Olivia asked.

"A friend."

"Is he single?"

"Probably not." The sound of Kiera's voice warmed and prickled my back.

Curious, I peered over my shoulder and met her gaze. She darted her eyes elsewhere, but not before I caught a glimpse of wonder . . . or was it longing?

It couldn't be lust and longing, could it? The Kiera I knew wasn't afraid to go after what she wanted.

"Forrest, over here!" Levi called.

I ambled over to him at a table that still offered a view of Kiera and Bruno.

"Scoot over." I shifted my chair to ensure I could see them.

"Why?" Levi asked, making room for me.

He had short brown hair, like my former clean-cut style, and a flirty smile. He wore a yellow polo shirt and khaki slacks, looking like his preppy software developer self.

"I like the view. Never been here before," I said, as a pretty waitress with a red clip in her hair arrived.

She introduced herself as Trish and tapped her pen on the pad. "Y'all ready to place your order?"

"What's the special for today?" Levi looked up from the menu and raked a gaze down her curvy body.

Levi loved women just as much as I did. But my preference was now reserved for the one woman who didn't seem interested in me.

My boys called me a flirt, but we were all flirts in our own right, especially when we were single men. But that had changed for Remi, Royce, and Grayson, who were now attached to their significant others.

As a single man, it was a requirement for me to flirt with the opposite sex. It was human nature to do so. However, after one night with Kiera, my flirtatious behavior changed. I hadn't had the urge to flirt with any other woman. What had once enticed me no longer had the same effect. It was as though when she left, she also took away something primal in me.

I should probably sit down and analyze this further, because no man wanted to be transformed without his knowledge. That was a dangerous game. I liked to have control over my life. I liked knowing when something happened, how it happened, and why it happened. Goals could only be achieved with clear vision, and muddiness led to a dead end.

I'd worked too damn hard to walk into a roadblock.

Somehow my life had gotten complicated, and I didn't know how to untangle that area of my life that involved Kiera. Perhaps leaving it alone would clear up the snarl. When she left me, she tossed me into this repetitive loop of desire, denial, and doubt. The last two were signs of weakness, which I couldn't afford.

The waitress burst out laughing at something Levi said, and I jumped back to the moment. Trish took my order of a shrimp taco plate to go with my Whiskey Smash. I pretended not to see that the waitress had slipped Levi a napkin that probably had her number written on it.

Good for him.

He had a great mind, but his personal life was chaotic. Dating two women at once meant trouble.

I watched as Levi added Trish's number and sent her a message.

"Now you have mine." He smiled and didn't even bother hiding his endeavor. "Call me sometime."

My gaze darted back to Kiera while I asked, "You're not afraid that your girls might find out?"

He shrugged. "I'm in an open relationship with them. They knew what they were getting into when they hooked up with me."

Levi came from a wealthy family, but he made his own money in software development. I admired men who made it on their own. His flirting brought him to several elite clubs, so when he invited me to a private gathering, I couldn't resist. My eyes and ears had been open for any links that could help me take down The Trogyn.

"What do you have for me?"

"The party I told you about has been moved."

"Why?" I'd rearranged my schedule to ensure I could make it to this party that was supposed to happen in three weeks. If they moved beyond that time, there was no way I could stay. I had other commitments back in Providence.

Levi shrugged. "Beats me. I heard someone couldn't make the set date, so they're moving to an earlier one. It's just a few days from the initial date."

Relief settled in me as I reorganized the calendar on my phone. "How did you hear about this party anyway? Who's attending? Where is it being held?"

"I know someone who knows someone helping with the party. It's hush-hush. He's not supposed to tell me. It was a slip of the tongue. He owes me money, and I told him he didn't have to pay me back if he got me and a friend into the party."

I leaned into the table. "How do you know I wanted to go to the party?"

I'd never told Levi anything about the crime organization. The less he knew, the safer he'd be.

"Educated guess. I knew you'd be here in Texas, and you're a wealthy, single man. I figured you'd enjoy it. Besides, you took care of my little brother when his specialist didn't have a clue about his condition. You saved him."

On top of a staph infection, Cole had an underlying issue that was overlooked by his doctor.

Dinner came a few minutes after our drinks. Three stunning women entered the patio, walking toward our table.

"Fancy seeing you here, Forrest." Yolanda bent down, gave me a one-armed hug, ruffled my hair, and introduced me to her friends. "This is Belinda and Amanda."

Her friends were hot and dressed to impress. Levi and the guys at the nearby table stared at them. Belinda had curly blonde hair and wore a strapless dress that showed off her attractive figure. With her brown hair in a braid, Amanda looked fabulous in a low-cut floral dress that made a man imagine too many things.

Yolanda stood out from her friends with her long, dark hair and an off-white dress that showed off her bronze skin. She'd never have trouble dating.

She glanced around the packed restaurant. "Mind if we join you? I don't see any empty tables, and I prefer not to sit at the bar."

"Please do," Levi said before I could suggest they sit elsewhere. I had more questions to ask him about the party. Apparently, he wanted to talk to the women more.

Levi brought over two extra chairs, and everyone squeezed in. Yolanda sat beside me and draped an arm around my shoulder.

While Levi chatted with Belinda and Amanda, Yolanda whispered, "Do you like one of my friends? I showed them pictures of you. They're interested." She patted my back. "I told them you were visiting, and they wanted me to introduce you."

"Don't set me up with anyone. I don't have time. They'll just be disappointed."

"You work too much." She patted my cheek. "You're a handsome man who needs to enjoy life."

"Not interested."

"Why not? Are they not hot enough for you?"

I flicked her an amused look. "Don't you have more important things to do than interfere in my personal life?"

She scowled. "What's wrong with that? I'm only doing that because I care. Grandma wouldn't want her grandson to be lonely for the rest of his life."

"Who said I would?"

"Based on your boring routine, I'd say you'll be a lonely old man missing out on life's pleasures."

Laughing, I finished my Whiskey Smash. "I have other interests that are more important. Besides, how do you know I'm not with anyone right now?"

Her eyes widened with curiosity. "Who? Are you seeing someone in Providence? Why haven't you shared the news with the family?" She smacked my arm. "Is she pretty? What makes her special?"

"The prettiest." My gaze slid over to Kiera's table. "I guess you could say I can't stop thinking about her. That's a unique trait."

Yolanda narrowed her eyes at me and grinned. "You're lying."

I didn't want to talk about this anymore. Knowing Yolanda, she'd go on and on and report back to my grandma, who would then call me with questions.

"You're paying too much attention to my life." The waitress came over to take their orders, and the conversation changed to something else.

Thank God.

While they chatted, my gaze kept wandering back to Kiera,

who met my eyes, sending an electrical circuit straight to my cock.

Yup, that was her specialty. She could command my body from a distance.

CHAPTER SEVEN

KIERA

Stop twisting. Stop squirming.

Though Bruno, Nate, and Olivia were having a conversation about the model Steven who was supposed to arrive tomorrow, my thoughts were on Forrest.

I scolded my body to stop reacting to Forrest, looking at me from across the restaurant. Even though there were crowds of people separating us, I felt his presence as though he were still standing beside me. Tingles ran up and down my body as though he were doing it to me with his eyes.

He had a magnetism I couldn't resist. He was the freaking black hole in space that would swallow me up if I got too close, and yet I couldn't stop myself.

I shivered, remembering that event I should forget.

Let it go, Kiera. Just let it go.

If only it were that easy. I thought about my mom's illness. If the human body could release stress that easily, we would all be happy and healthy human beings. Perhaps that was the lesson to living life—to find the perfect balance, find the answers on dealing with stress.

Or hot guys.

I cursed at myself for using my mom's illness as an analogy for my problems.

Dear God, please forgive me. I'm just having a hard time right now. Please don't punish my mom for my mistakes.

If life were a photograph, I could tweak it by adding more light, contrast, or by removing things that didn't fit. But life couldn't be edited that way.

Stop staring at me.

Stop staring at him, my logical mind countered, irritating me.

I broke the stare and focused on the conversation Bruno was having with Olivia about Steven. Since I was only half-listening, I didn't catch what they were talking about.

My thoughts were on the attractive woman sitting next to Forrest. Who was she? They seemed close. My stomach knotted every time she touched him. If I kept this up, I'd probably need to go see a doctor.

Not him, of course.

"So what are we going to do?" Nate asked. "I'm already modeling the swimwear. I can't do the active too. We need a variety of models to showcase the collection."

"What's going on?" I asked.

Olivia smirked. "Earth to Kiera. Steven Dulles can't make it to the shoot. He was injured in a triathlon and won't be flying in tomorrow."

"Oh no. I hope he's okay." I'd worked with him before. He was a nice guy, and no, I didn't date him.

Bruno swiped at his phone, his brows bunching together. "All the models we normally use are booked. Fuck." He placed his phone down just as laughter burst from Forrest's table.

Apparently, something was extremely funny. The pretty woman rested her head on Forrest's shoulder, and he smiled at her. My insides twisted. I swore I might end up in the hospital for abnormal intestinal knots.

There was something going on between them. The gestures were too intimate.

Perhaps witnessing this was a good thing for me. I could give up on this longing, wondering, and yearning—all the things I'd never felt for anyone.

I hadn't dared to admit it until now. He could provoke me with his mere presence. That confused and fascinated me. All those powerful feelings made me feel more alive than I'd ever been. I hadn't felt anything like this before him.

"Why hadn't I thought of that?" Bruno rose from his chair, looking hopeful.

"Thought of what?" Nate and Olivia asked simultaneously.

He jerked a chin toward Forrest's table. Why was it that every time I looked over, Forrest was looking back at me?

"I've got the perfect replacement. Let's hope he doesn't turn me down."

Oh no. But . . . No!

Confusion and excitement warred within me. Part of me feared being with him. The other part wanted it so badly. If I worked with him, it would only make it hard for me to eliminate these feelings. I had to move on and not become stuck.

But he's with someone.

That meant there was no chance for us to be together. It should make things easy, right? No. It only made me jealous of her.

Bruno strode over, greeted the table, and spoke to Forrest. I watched Forrest's expression, but I couldn't read his lips. Bruno nodded at the attractive woman sitting beside Forrest and she smiled back. Did he know her, or was he just being a flirt? When Forrest gave all the other women a nod and smile, jealousy overwhelmed me.

Then Forrest looked right at me, and I could see his lips forming the words. "Sure. You owe me."

Oh, God.

CHAPTER EIGHT

KIERA

The next day, I woke early from the noises outside my cabin or somewhere in the campground. I wasn't sure, but it could also have been a dream. The anxiety of photographing Forrest later today and the concern for my mother's health had me on my last nerve already.

I needed to clear my head so I could do my job properly. A walk around the campground to get a feel of the landscape would help me narrow down the location and gauge the best angle for light and contrast.

Before we headed home last night, Bruno had stopped by the local market for me to pick up some food for the refrigerator. After making a pot of coffee, I grabbed the box of Special K Red Berries cereal and poured milk into it. It had been my go-to breakfast since college.

College had been where I met Audri. She had taken a few jewelry classes during the summer at the Rhode Island School of Design, where I'd studied photography. Audri had been enrolled at Boston University, but took jewelry classes when she had time off. I modeled her jewelry shows, and she became my muse for my assignments. We became best friends from that moment on. Though Audri came from a wealthy family, she never made me feel less. Based on how hard she had worked, I didn't even know she came from money.

Would I have been a different person if I had grown up with money? Money had been scarce for my family of two, but we lived a comfortable life. My mom was a single parent working as a nurse. She gave me everything I needed, and I hoped to give her what she needed now.

As I ate, I browsed the FitFlex website and reviewed their current activewear collection. All the male models the company had used paled in comparison to Forrest. Though he wasn't a professional model, he had everything required to be one. The stunning look, the magnetism, and the charm were qualities the camera couldn't refuse. The first time I saw him wearing a luxurious suit, my heart dropped. His hair had been shorter back then, rendering him an intelligent, sophisticated, and powerful man. Not that I minded the shaggy hairstyle. It was sexy in its own way.

Everything about the man was heavenly, like a picture-perfect landscape where all the colors, hues, shadows, and light aligned to leave you breathless.

Fashion photography paid my bills, but I also delved into landscape photography when I needed a change of pace. One reason I loved landscape photography was that I could escape into the peaceful sceneries. They represented the various forces of nature—the gentle, the mysterious, and the powerful.

Forrest was a force of nature. At least to my body. One thought about him sparked something in me. The muscles in my sex quivered as I remembered all the things he'd done to me, and how his length had filled me.

My mouth went dry at the shock of my body's reaction to him. He'd moved on. So why hadn't I?

I gasped when I felt my panties go damp. *Ridiculous.* Maybe this was just a sign that I needed a good lay.

Irritation bloomed in me as I changed into a new pair of underwear. I already had too many issues to deal with. I didn't need him to trouble me even more.

You don't need a man to make you happy.

My mom's words rang in my ears.

You don't need a man to survive, and you don't need a man to be successful. Happiness isn't measured by a penis.

I admired my mother's diligence. She raised me all by herself and held high standards for the men she'd dated after my father. She had a long-time boyfriend who passed away three years ago from prostate cancer.

With my mom's words bouncing in my head, I grabbed my backpack, tucked the water bottle into it, and grabbed my camera.

Using the wide dirt path, I walked around the lake and came to a beach area with massive rocks. Some had incredible texture that would be a wonderful background for photographs. Several rocks poked out from the shallow water, adding mystery and dimension to the atmosphere.

I snapped photos of the area, capturing the peaceful reflection on the lake. On my way back, I took a smaller trail and came to a patch of mushrooms growing on the bark of a fallen tree. Covered in moss, it looked like a little world. Unable to resist the adorable image, I snapped some pictures, knowing they'd make great postcards and even greeting cards.

I loved fashion photography because I was good at depicting a mood with people in clothes and accessories. But there was something about capturing nature's beauty that spoke to my heart. Despite that, I couldn't live on selling pictures of trees, mushrooms, and moss. People knew me as a fashion photographer, and that was where the bread and butter was.

We often had to do things that paid the bills so that we could escape to our hobbies when time permitted. That was life, wasn't it?

Crouching, I ran a hand over the soft moss, admiring its texture and interesting color. This moss was a meadow green, different from the bright green embracing the nearby limb. The moss on the ground was a shade darker. So many aspects of the same organism.

Sort of like a collection of shoes in multiple colors. I loved my Jimmy Choos, Manolo Blaniks, and Christian Louboutins, thank you very much. As a fashion photographer, I'd gotten amazing discounts from high-end designers. But in this quiet area, I didn't need any of those accessories to make me feel whole or pretty.

I took a picture of the moss and a cute white mushroom, standing away from the patch.

"Why are you here all by yourself, little one?" I tapped its white cap.

"It's not g-going to talk b-back."

I jumped at the voice as my heart slammed into my chest. Looking to my right, I faced Hank, who had on a backpack and binoculars in his hands.

Nerves stirred in me. I shouldn't be here alone with him. I didn't know him, and there was something off about him, which I didn't want to find out though.

"Okay," I said and prepared to walk back toward the campground.

"N-not safe to walk around by y-yourself." Concern brimmed in his eyes. He reminded me of a classmate in high school with a speech impediment. The kids at school always made fun of her. She lived near me, so sometimes we walked to school together.

Empathy rose in me as I remembered Amber's difficulty

trying to fit in at school. Hank was different, but that didn't mean he didn't deserve kindness like everyone else. We were all looking for a place to belong, weren't we?

Perhaps my reservations about him stemmed from not knowing him. I had to be cautious, but that didn't mean I had to be unfriendly.

"Thank you, Hank. I'll keep that in mind."

When I got home, I showered and created an agenda for each of the outfits Forrest would wear. Nerves continued to stir inside me. I checked my menstrual calendar. Nope, not that time of the month. I couldn't blame it on my cycle. I should've known because my period ended right before I came here. During menstruation, I was supersensitive to everything, but right now, I was feeling all kinds of emotions for no reason. Trusting myself these days was difficult. I didn't know what was real and what was just fear mixing with confusion.

My phone buzzed, and I smiled as a message from Audri popped onto the screen.

Audri: *Hey! What's happening in Texas? Any cute cowboys?*

Kiera: *None yet. We'll catch up when I get back.*

Audri: *...*

Kiera: *What?*

Audri: *This isn't you. No hot models to dish on?*

With my friends I could tell them anything, so why was I hesitant to tell them about Forrest? Because he had affected me like no man had. So the more I talked about him, the more he would take over my life.

Kiera: *Hot guys are here. Just worried about my mom.*

Audri: *Oh, honey. Don't worry. Michelle and I are stopping by to visit her tomorrow. We'll send pics.*

Kiera: *Thanks for everything.*

My friends didn't need to help me, but I was grateful to

have someone check on my mom. How could I tell Audri that my mom's rare illness required a new medication to survive? That this new medicine would cost me millions. Just talking about the absurdity of that made me angry. Who in the world could pay that for medication? I had done my research on expensive medications, and there were more out there than I realized, especially the kind that was still in a trial phase.

The thought made me nauseous, so I shoved it away.

Kiera: *Forrest is here.*

Audri: *He is? Doing what?*

Kiera: *Business.*

Audri: *Something going on?*

Kiera: *Why do you ask?*

Audri: *Best friend radar. (Smile emoji)*

Maybe it was time I told her the truth. *Okay, here goes.* I released a tense breath.

Kiera: *I slept with him.*

Then I tossed my phone aside as though I'd just released a secret too heavy with sin to keep in my hand.

My phone rang, and I cursed at my ridiculous behavior as I picked up the call.

"When?" Audri's voice soothed my nerves. "Deets, please."

"Six months ago."

"Oh my God. And you kept it from me?"

Guilt tore through me. I'd always shared my dates with her before, but I didn't understand why I kept my one time with Forrest a secret.

Just face it.

It was the fact that I'd actually had a one-night stand—something I'd heard people talk about but never done.

"It's not a crime to be attracted to a gorgeous man," Audri said.

"He was one of the models at the shoot. We were drinking

at a hotel, and after two drinks, my hormones took over and I lost my mind."

Stop blaming it on the drinks.

"Oh, Kiera. Do you like him? Or it's just a one-time thing?"

"I don't know." A heavy sigh escaped me.

"He's flustered you. That just means . . ."

"What?"

"That he's got what it takes. Guess what?"

I could hear the mischief in her voice. "Yes?"

"You need the SSG to rescue you!" Excitement thrummed in her voice, making me smile.

"I don't think so."

"I know so! Let me gather up the girls and see when we can all hop in on a call."

"Just wait until I get back."

"That's too long of a wait. A man has you feeling upside-down, so we need to help you find answers. You did it for me, Michelle, and Natalie. Now it's your turn, babe. Besides, how often do we get to do this?"

After agreeing to a chat with my SSG, the call ended with Audri full of excitement.

Feeling drained, I dropped down onto the couch and welcomed the memory of that night.

Sitting on an elegant loveseat in the luxurious hotel lounge, I sip my second Cosmopolitan. Everyone is celebrating the completion of a successful photo shoot. As I drink, I try to subdue my attraction to Forrest.

He sits next to me, his thigh touching mine. Heat blooms through the silk fabric of my dress, and my nipples harden.

I've seen him many times at our friends' houses, but I haven't sensed this powerful attraction until now. I mean, part of that was me keeping a respectful distance from a man who is out of my league. It's not just his captivating looks. He mostly dates doctors, women in his field. I'm not a doctor.

"How long have you been photographing fashion models? What made you take this route?" Mesmerizing green eyes look at me, and my heart races.

He has short brown hair, a square jaw, regally high cheekbones, a straight nose, and a sexy masculine mouth that makes me wonder about inappropriate things.

He studies me with inquisitive eyes I can't break away from. Sitting so close to him, I see his eyes transform before me. What has been a meadow green darkens into a mysterious forest. How appropriate, given his name. What's behind the name anyway?

His gaze intensifies, and his irises shift. Spears of blue-green —almost a mint color—burst and hypnotize me. Unable to control myself, I release a sigh. His eyes flick to my mouth, and I lick my lips from the dryness developing in my throat.

The stress from the past few weeks fades as we stare at each other.

"Dare play a game with me?" I blame my brave—or stupid— challenge on the alcohol loosening me. Maybe I'll regret this spontaneous urge, but I'll deal with it later.

"That depends." His voice is low, his face mere inches from mine.

The crowd and the noise in the lounge disappear from my vision. Even the lights seem dimmer. We're in some kind of magical bubble. His intense stare tosses me into a whirlwind of wild fantasy.

"You're very handsome, you know that?"

His lips tilt at the corners.

"You're exquisite, you know that?" he counters, angling his face to look at me. "What's the dare?"

"Rock, paper, scissors," I blurt out the game I've played with my friends before I can analyze it further.

What am I doing? I have no idea. All I know is that I want to kiss him. Just one kiss.

He laughs, and the room brightens, making him more stunning. "What are you trying to achieve with this game?"

I lean in to inhale his scent, but also to make sure no one overhears what I'm about to say. "An answer to a curiosity. Do you know the rules?"

God, he smells so good.

"I do. Let's go for it." He whispers into my ear, his warm breath sending heat to my core.

He lingers around my face and takes a deep inhale before drawing back.

"Do you know what I want if I win?" I ask.

"I'll risk it for what I'm going to win." He smirks.

"Arrogant much?"

He's an abundance of arrogance, magnetism, mystery, and brilliance, all dressed in an expensive tailored shirt. His pants show off his muscular legs and attractive height. The longer I sit beside him, look at him, talk to him and smell him, the more I want the package.

"It's confidence . . . and determination."

"On a count of three," he says. I shift in my seat, my knees touching his even more.

"One. Two. Three!"

I shoot out my clenched fist and gasp. "No!" I scowl at his open palm.

He grins like a fool. "Paper beats rock."

Before I can retort, his mouth slams into mine, and all thoughts leave my brain. He devours my mouth; his tongue spearing through my lips and tangling with mine. He cups the back of my neck, angling my mouth as he kisses me, leaving me quivering for more.

I place a hand on his chest, feeling his thundering heart.

He drags an open mouth to my ears. "Ready for another dare?"

I press my thighs together and meet his challenging gaze, desperately trying to find coherent words after that mind-blowing kiss. My expression probably gives him the answer he needs, because he yanks me to my feet, and grabs my hand, leading me to the elevator.

Another couple is already in the elevator, otherwise we would've acted on this incredible energy between us. I'm in a daze at what's happening, but it also mesmerizes me. Before I know it, we're inside his hotel room. His mouth crushes into mine. Sensations explode in me, sending liquid heat pooling to my center. I love the way he ravages me.

We break away to strip off our clothes. My body shivers not from the lack of clothing, but from the anticipation I'm feeling. Then it heats from the way his eyes rake down my body.

"You're beautiful," he says in a husky voice.

My breath trips in my throat.

"Same goes for you." I smirk, admiring his taut body and the massive arousal that looks like a sexual weapon, wanting to take me over.

Like wild animals, we both attack each other with kisses and moans. He lifts me up, and my legs wrap around his hips. My tongue ensues a playful battle with his until my back presses into the cool sheets. Desire darkens his eyes as he claims a nipple while his other hand palms my wet center.

"Fuck, Kiera."

I love the sinfulness in the way he says my name.

His mouth leaves my breasts, and he kisses his way down to my sex. When he licks me, my vision goes white. His mouth is amazing. His tongue is spectacular. His fingers are . . . magical. Skillful. The pressure in my core erupts, and an orgasm tears *through me, blinding me. For the first time in my life, I see stars. They sparkle in my vision.*

Holy shit.

"Do you want more, baby?"

"More," I beg.

My brain disappears somewhere. My inner muscles are still contracting. My body is still reeling.

"I've got plans for you all night."

He fucks me sideways, from behind, and in other positions that make me thankful for my yoga teacher. I don't know how my body can bend that way.

I'm not sure when we both fell asleep, but my phone rings, and I pick it up.

"Hello?" I say, still half-asleep.

"Is this Kiera Ford?"

The serious tone jerks me awake. "Yes, what is it?"

"Your mother's in the hospital."

A knock on the door yanked me away from the memory. With furrowed eyebrows, I got up from the couch, looked through the curtains at the window, and saw Forrest looking back at me, smiling.

Shit. I'd been daydreaming and lost track of time.

I opened the door. "Hi. Come in. Sorry. I just need to gather my stuff and we can head out."

He stepped into the cabin, looking delicious as always. His height made the cabin appear small. "Did I interrupt something?"

CHAPTER NINE

FORREST

Shutting the door, she looked disturbed by my presence. Had she been napping?

My heart thumped erratically as I stood close to her. This wasn't normal. A doctor like me knew this reaction was a side effect of something that required more than medication.

We stood in her quaint living room staring at each other as though we were gauging how to act or react so that we didn't mess up whatever this was between us.

Was there anything between us? Not really.

It had been one night. I'd had a few of those in my youth. Those experiences had just been an infinitesimal moment in my life that had come and gone, like a passing seasonal allergy.

But my time with Kiera wasn't a damn cold that could be treated easily. She'd become a virus, infecting my mind and body.

I'd have given up an organ to know the thoughts playing out in her mind. Was she thinking about our time together like I was? Her stunning face was flushed as caramel eyes studied me. I remembered how those powerful eyes had darkened to a sinful brown during ecstasy. Her pink lips made my dick yearn for something it shouldn't.

She wore khaki shorts and a light green T-shirt, clothes that shouldn't turn me on, but I was having trouble shutting down that part of my brain. I should've known agreeing to this photo shoot was a bad idea.

You're a sex-deprived fool.

She broke the trance and gestured to the couch. "Have a seat. It'll just take me a few minutes."

"Take your time." Instead of sitting, I browsed the tiny cabin.

"No. I'm late." Kiera raked a hand through her hair.

"Did I catch you at a bad time?"

"No."

It was a lie. Based on the surprised look on her face when she peeked through the curtains, I knew she hadn't been expecting me.

Had she been expecting someone else? The thought of another man being inside this cabin with her or even touching her bothered me more than it should have. But I had no claim to her. Had she forgotten about our shoot?

She bent over to a bag on the floor and rummaged through it, giving me a view of her beautiful backside. My fingers itched, remembering how firm and perfect her ass had felt against my hands and body. Heat sparked in my chest and traveled to areas that had no business being turned on at the moment. This was a professional meeting, not some sexual rendezvous. Despite that, I couldn't stop my body from reacting the way it did. When I was around Kiera, I wasn't the man I used to be. She could command my body without saying a damn thing.

Right now my dick was trying not to burst from the way her hips shifted from side to side. I felt like I was suffering from some kind of ailment that turned me into a crazed man with untamed sexual energy threatening to be released. She drove me crazy.

Needing to do something, I dropped into a chair at her kitchen table where a box of Special K Red Berries cereal greeted me, bringing back memories of my college days. Cereal, chips, and fast food had been my preference at that time. This brand of cereal had been the healthiest thing I'd eaten.

Opening the box, I poured some into my palm and snacked.

She eyed me with an arched brow. "Hungry?"

Yes, I'm starving for you.

"I haven't had these in years. Forgot how they taste," I said.

She tossed a few things into her shoulder bag and slung it over her chest. Looping the camera strap around her neck, she offered me one large garment bag and a small duffle bag. "Can you carry these?"

I popped the rest of the cereal into my mouth, got up, and grabbed the bags from her hand. "Anyone else coming to the shoot?"

The last time I modeled, there had been several assistants. But that had been in a studio with many models, brands, and people running around trying to stay on schedule. Today's photo shoot was just FitFlex, more casual, which meant I had more time to stare at her.

"No." She closed the door and locked it.

I wasn't sure if I liked this impersonal treatment. Something had changed after that night. I wanted to fix it, but I didn't know how. Did I want things to be what they were before our escapade?

Hell, no.

But could we be anything more? What did she want? She'd left my bed without a word.

It was the best night of my life. Had the evening been that

awful for her? Several theories came to mind, and I didn't like any of them. It did nothing for my ego.

No women left my hotel room that soon unless I kicked them out. Why had she left? Why hadn't she spoken to me after that?

"Good," I said, glad that Bruno wouldn't be around.

She gave me an inquisitive look. "Why?"

"Because I like having you all to myself." I watched her reaction.

Something flickered in her eyes, but then it disappeared. Ignoring my comment, she walked down the porch and dragged over a wagon. "You can put the bags in here. One has clothes for you, the other has shoes and sandals. We'll be walking to the location. It's near here, just down there. You okay with that?"

"Okay with what?"

"Walking." She'd tied her hair back into a ponytail, looking fresh and casual, like a Sunday afternoon.

"Why wouldn't I be?"

"Because wealthy men like you are used to luxury. It's hot and humid out, so you're going to get sweaty. It's going to get uncomfortable."

Did she assume I lived in some ignorant bubble? What kind of person did she think I was?

I stepped closer and tucked an errant strand behind her ear. "I'm comfortable being uncomfortable. Just part of life. Heat and humidity do nothing to me compared to a particular person."

Her lips opened slightly.

I pushed on, trying to confirm my hypothesis. "Do I make you uncomfortable, Kiera?"

Her pulse throbbed on the side of her neck. It made me want to lean in and kiss it.

I couldn't help the smile that crept onto my lips. "You don't need to answer. I already know."

"How?" She narrowed her eyes.

Before I knew it, my lips landed on her pulse, and I licked it. God, the taste of her skin ignited the desire that was already on a tight leash.

I nibbled on her skin. "Your throbbing vein is showing your increased heart rate." I drew back and brushed a finger across her cheeks. "This blush proves I make you nervous. We have some unfinished business to discuss, Kiera."

She licked her lips, and my dick twitched.

"Not right now," she breathed. "I have work to do."

I took her response as a win, considering how we'd been avoiding this topic for months. It surprised me I let it go on for as long as I did. A man who had vision, understood process, and valued action didn't like to wait around for things to happen. But my patience became flexible for her. Perhaps it was because I had faced nothing like this.

It was about time I got answers.

She was right though—this was her job. I wanted her to complete her assignment. I had signed up to model for FitFlex under the specification that the company double my fees, which were more than the other models. My time was precious, and given the short notice, I deserved whatever I wanted because I had to shift my schedule around to squeeze them in.

I hadn't expected this minor detour during my visit. But to see her here was a bonus that I couldn't give up. I clasped the handle of the wagon, dragging it down a wide dirt trail. The wagon bumped along the pebbled path. In the shade, the air cooled, but not by much.

"You don't need an assistant to help during these outdoor shoots?"

"No," she said, but didn't look at me.

"What about in the studio?"

"I can Photoshop out anything that doesn't work."

"Then there shouldn't be a problem with my photos at all. It'll be a breeze for you."

She turned to me. *Good. Let me see your beautiful face.*

"Save the arrogance and charm for your girlfriend." She walked faster, then whirled around. "Why did you agree to the shoot anyway? Aren't you supposed to be busy treating patients or something?"

"I *am* busy. But you seemed desperate for a model, and I like to help when necessary."

"When necessary?" She rolled her eyes. "What does that even mean?"

"When I get something out of it."

"And what is that? I'm sure you don't need the money."

"What I'm after has no price." I stared at her. "Since you're a friend in need, I figured I'd help you out."

She snorted. "Thanks for your *friendly* gesture."

When we made it to the location, I placed the wagon beside a rock. Kiera opened the garment bag, handing me a short-sleeved knit top and patterned shorts to wear. Then she dropped a pair of black sandals on the ground. "You can change over there." She pointed to a group of boulders. "No one's around, so you don't need to worry. Plus we're not doing an underwear shoot."

I didn't go to the boulders. Instead, I took off my clothes, sneakers, and socks, and tossed them into the wagon. Then I changed into the new stretchy shirt and shorts and slipped on the sandals. "How many underwear shoots have you done?"

I didn't like the image of her with male models in nothing but underwear. A woman like her would arouse any man.

She turned her back to me as though she hadn't seen me naked. "A few times . . ."

My question was geared toward her taking photos of men in underwear, but her answer incited a new image in my head.

"You've posed in underwear too?" I wanted to strangle whoever he was.

The doctor in me—the part that was supposed to care for and treat a person in need—vanished.

Kiera turned around. "It's called boudoir photography. And yes, I posed for a friend."

"Male or female?"

She narrowed her eyes. "Male."

"Can I see the photos?"

"No."

Her quick response knifed me in the gut. "Why not?"

"Because we need to resolve our 'unfinished business' first."

My mood soured for the rest of the photo shoot.

Who got to see her in all those poses? What had she worn for the bastard?

CHAPTER TEN

KIERA

Why did I have to say that?

I didn't want to discuss any "unfinished business." That would mean bringing everything out in the open. Was I even ready for that?

Ugh. I didn't like how my brain forgot how to function properly when he was around.

I should have concentrated on finishing the session quickly so we could both depart and return to our own lives. And yet my brain held the "unfinished business" in place, demanding to be addressed.

What was unfinished about our business? We'd slept together once and never saw each other again. I hadn't seen him at any of our friends' gatherings. He'd been avoiding me. But I suppose I hadn't tried to reach out to him either. Especially not after the way things had ended.

What could I have said even if I had reached out? *Hey, thanks for a fabulous night. Sorry, I took off without a word, but how's life?* Awkwardness flared like a swollen foot, no longer suitable for that designer shoe.

We had a spontaneous one-time thing that changed the dynamics between us. Even my body couldn't stop itself from wanting him.

"How many photos are in your boudoir album?" He pursed his lips, crossed his arms, showing off the thick muscles and looking grumpy for no reason. "I want to see them." This was no longer a question, but a firm statement from a man with a mission.

Why was he so curious about my boudoir photos? I'd done it in my last year of college as part of a personal project. Somewhere deep inside me, an ember of hope sparked, warming up everything around it. Could the scrunched face and curiosity be signs of jealousy?

But he had a girlfriend. She'd been all over him at the restaurant. She was probably another doctor, something like a prostate specialist, or whatever they were called. Don't ask me why that specialty came into my head.

"Why?" I wasn't his normal highly educational type. I went through four years of college, and that was enough.

"Why not?"

"I can't imagine someone like you sitting around browsing a black-and-white photo album of women in lingerie."

He moved in closer, and the waft of his aftershave did amazing things to my lady parts. "I've suddenly developed a keen interest in boudoir photography."

Stay focused.

Gripping my camera, I walked closer to the water's edge and pointed to a spot near the rocks with pretty trees in the distant background.

"Stand over there and pretend you're looking at something extraordinary."

He walked over to the spot, looking relaxed and sexy in the athletic top, shorts, and sandals. The shaggy brown hair lightened in the sunlight. Even in casual clothes, he made my heart sigh. How could someone be that gorgeous?

"I don't need to pretend." He stared right at me, and my core tightened.

"Turn your face slightly toward the water." I jerked my chin toward the lake.

He did as I asked, and the camera loved him. He was a beautiful man, with a natural ability to pose.

For the next twenty minutes, he wore several activewear and footwear collections. We only had a few styles left to be photographed. Part of me was relieved, while another part wanted to prolong the session further. I didn't understand myself. Moments ago, I wanted to rush this photo session so I could rush back to my life—even if it was filled with anxiety. At least right now I wasn't thinking about responsibilities and paying medical bills. This man was making me think about inappropriate things, which was the perfect escape.

Every time he looked into my camera, I felt as if he were looking right *into* me, seeing all my dreams, secrets, and flaws. My heart shifted a little. This man could speak with one look. I wasn't immune to him.

He has a beautiful girlfriend, Kiera. He probably had ten of them waiting for him in different hotels. Women threw themselves at rich men—handsome rich doctors.

But why was he flirting with me?

Because you're number eleven.

Hating the thought, I bit the inside of my mouth. I didn't want to throw myself at anyone.

You had one night with him.

That didn't qualify as throwing myself at him. We had been influenced by inexplicable passion incited by a little alcohol, an elegant setting, and the need for relaxation after several stressful days of hard work.

It meant nothing.

I sighed, knowing I was lying to myself. It had meant more than I expected.

Wanting a different angle of the scenery, I glanced around and landed on an idea. "Can you walk along the shore and head over to that big rock? Act as though you're enjoying the outdoors."

"I love the outdoors. There's no need to pretend," he said as he walked slowly for me to snap several pictures.

I felt like I was intruding in his private moment with nature. There was an interesting rhythm between us as I followed him along the shore with my camera. He walked along the edge of the lake, kicking up water, admiring the natural scenery. When a bird flew by, he glanced up, staring at it. I didn't know how many times my fingers clicked on the button and the shutter went crazy in my camera. I got more pictures than necessary.

When he turned to look at me, contemplation and mystery radiated from his face, mesmerizing me. I couldn't wait to get back to my cabin to download all the pictures onto my computer. I'd probably spend all night ogling the images.

There was something about his contemplative look that tugged at my heart. I saw sadness, hope, and something I couldn't decipher. A picture could capture a thousand words, and in this moment, he gave me a story I wanted to know more about.

I couldn't deny my attraction to him. But right now, he called to me from a different place.

FitFlex wanted me to capture him in their new shorts, made of cutting-edge fabric that allowed the body to cool faster than the other brands. So I had Forrest remove his shirt. *Bad idea. Very bad idea.*

My heart knocked against my chest at the marvelous sight.

The olive skin glistened from the sun. His pecks and abs made him look like some warrior god. The muscles in my inner thighs flexed, and tingles skipped around my body in celebration. It should be illegal for someone to have abs like his. How many hours had he spent at the gym? My mouth watered from the well-defined body. During our first encounter, I'd been busy doing other things and didn't get to examine his fine body.

I wanted to touch his abdomen and run my fingers along the grooves that held secrets and sin. Yes, this man held a story I wanted to hear.

He smirked as though he knew I was touching him with my eyes.

"Who taught you how to pose?" I asked, trying to distract myself from ogling.

"Observations. Magazines. Why? Am I not performing well for you?"

I'd worked with new models who needed a little guidance here and there, but Forrest just picked it up as if he'd modeled for years.

"You're a natural at this. Hold that look. Just one last photo and we'll be done." I snapped more than once.

"No, we're not done." His expression shifted, the lust in his eyes clear through the camera lens, and my heart jolted at the impact.

In just a few steps, he stood inches from me. Dropping my hands down beside me, I held onto my camera as I tilted my head back, looking up at him. Even with my average height, I had to take a step back to look up at him. He stood like a warrior, well over six feet tall, with eyes that captured my reflection. I didn't know why, but I liked seeing myself in them. When the sage color around his eyes became a forest green, my heart felt like a new sprout bursting to life.

With his thumb and finger, he gripped my chin and examined my face. Our eyes locked, and the restraints I'd held against him snapped free, releasing me to all these feelings. If there was ever a moment in my life where I had an out-of-body experience, this would be it.

Time stood still. If I were watching a movie, it would be the scene where the dust motes rose into the air like magic. A butterfly hovered around us, and the birdsongs became a gentle hum as the scenery faded into a blur.

"I'm also a natural at this." His mouth pressed to mine, and my body automatically fell into the hard wall of his body. Unlike the urgent kiss at the hotel, this one was slow and attentive. Like he wanted to savor me.

My body sagged into his, but I kept my grip on my camera because it contained precious pictures of him. What was it about him that could disarm all my senses and ignite them at the same time?

The power of his presence shifted my organs. I wouldn't be surprised if my kidneys swapped places and my liver flipped upside down.

I pressed a hand to his bare chest, moaning. "Forrest." My lips opened to welcome his skillful tongue. It twirled around mine, igniting fire running along my skin.

Pebbles crunched somewhere, and brought me back to reality. What was I doing?

I drew back, breathing like I'd hiked up to Mt. Everest.

Licking his lips, he grinned at me. "You're a natural too. No one kisses better than you."

"It shouldn't have happened."

"Why not?"

A branch cracked, disrupting the space, startling me. I released my hand from his bare chest and looked toward the noise.

Hank stepped into view, looking flustered. "The p-police

are looking for y-you." His hand was trembling a lot more than usual. "Y-you should go back to the l-lodge. They're w-waiting for y-you."

"Is everything okay, Hank?" I asked.

He shook his head. "A c-criminal is on the l-loose."

What the heck was going on?

"Hurry b-back." He scanned the area and stared out at the lake. "Not safe h-here."

Forrest and I exchanged an inquisitive glance. I should have been nervous around Hank, because I didn't know him well. But Forrest's presence soothed my unease.

Without being asked, Forrest packed all the clothes and shoes back into their appropriate bags, arranged them into the wagon, and got ready to go.

Forrest clasped the handle of the wagon and turned to Hank. "You lead the way, buddy."

The friendly gesture surprised Hank, but also relaxed him. Though it was a subtle difference, it was there. Hank studied Forrest for a few seconds, nodded, and hopped back onto the trail. He walked faster than I imagined.

I had to speed walk to keep up with him and Forrest, whose long legs ate up the distance quicker. Though Forrest didn't say it, he slowed his steps for me to keep up and called out to Hank. "Let's slow down, okay? We're not used to this rocky path."

Nodding, he slowed his pace.

If it was an emergency, why hadn't I heard any sirens? Maybe they did blast them earlier, but I'd been trapped inside a passionate bubble that prevented me from hearing anything but my heartbeat against his.

I stole a glance at Forrest's captivating profile. I wanted to study the way light and shadows played across his face as sunlight streamed down between the openings in the trees. I shouldn't be staring at him, considering the urgency that Hank had described. But I couldn't help it.

Forrest's expression hardened at something ahead. I looked and saw Olivia sitting at a picnic table while Bruno chatted with two police officers nearby.

What crime could possibly occur at a luxury campground?

CHAPTER ELEVEN

FORREST

I should have known seeing Bruno meant trouble was nearby. One camp representative spoke on the phone while Nora—the friendly receptionist who had told me where to find Kiera—spoke to a female police officer.

A few other occupants stood around, who probably already had their interviews. From my quick research, people considered this campground first-rate because of the breathtaking views. It offered exceptional sceneries along the hiking trails and lake. Some cabins were owned by residents who lived here year around.

"There she is." Olivia gestured to Kiera. "Maybe she saw something that could help find the asshole."

Kiera rushed over to her peer. "What happened?"

"Someone ransacked my room while I was out. Bruno also got attacked from behind. He has a huge bump on his head."

I placed a hand on Kiera's arm. "Be right back. I'll check on Bruno."

As I walked toward Bruno, Hank stood with an older

woman wearing a headband in her gray hair. "Everything's going to be fine, dear."

A bearded police officer wearing a cowboy hat sneered at Hank. Hank squirmed into the woman's arm. Then the officer made a face, frightening him.

What the fuck?

"Leave my son alone," said the woman. "Let's go, honey. There's nothing to be afraid of."

The officer rolled his eyes and tipped his hat. "Y'all have a good day."

"Why are you traumatizing him?" I asked the officer as he walked past me.

"It was a joke." He smirked.

"Do you see him laughing? Is an assault a laughing matter? Do you find people who are frightened or injured amusing?" This man was supposed to serve the people. "Is that what they teach you at the police academy?"

He flicked a dismissive glance at me and strode over to join the other police officers chatting with Bruno.

As a doctor, I had treated all kinds of patients. Trying to empathize with people and see things from their perspective made me a better doctor. I'd dealt with people like Hank, who had a disability obtained either from birth, trauma, or brain injury. These people had a tough time comprehending and explaining things to others. And this asshole—who should defuse the situation—made it worse.

I walked up to Bruno, who rubbed the back of his head. "What happened to you?"

If I were a nice man, I would've asked to look at his injuries, but I didn't feel so generous. Besides, it appeared like the EMT had already taken care of him.

Maybe Bruno brought the assault on himself.

"Some asshole hit me with a rock and ran off. I tried to

chase after him, but then I heard someone scream from inside the lodge."

An officer with sharp blue eyes turned to me as a bug flew and landed on the rim of his cowboy hat. "I'm Detective David Donnelly. Are you camping at the lodge?"

"No."

"He's working with FitFlex," Bruno chimed in.

"Do you mind if we ask you some questions?"

"Not at all," I said as the bearded officer who had harassed Hank earlier approached Bruno. He met my eyes for a second before looking away.

"How long were you here? Did you see anyone suspicious?"

I answered his questions as truthfully as possible. The attack seemed odd to me. I had to be extra cautious now, especially with Kiera staying here.

The criminal could return. What did he want? I assumed it was a man because to knock Bruno in the head required height and strength.

Shifting my feet, I positioned myself so I could see Kiera still chatting with Olivia.

"Are these crimes normal for this campground?" I asked Detective Donnelly.

"Three years ago, a few girls went missing, but that's about it. It's quiet here. There's not much to do but relax, go swimming, fishing, and hiking." He tapped his pen on the notepad. "There are all types of crazies these days. We'll have the officers do a walkthrough before they leave. Y'all hear anything, give me a buzz." He offered me his card.

"Thanks." I jerked my chin to the asshole officer. "How long has he been on the force?"

"Bruce's been with us for five years. Why do you ask?"

"Well, that should be long enough to know that you don't

harass people with special needs. Life is already hard. It's especially hard for those who have trouble fitting in."

"Who?" Detective Donnelly's busy eyebrows came together.

"Hank appeared traumatized by the assault, but your man taunted him."

"I'll speak to Bruce about it. Hank's a twenty-three-year-old loner. He has issues, but they got worse after his sister went missing. His mom lives in Austin, but they own a cabin here. Hank stays at the cabin because there's fewer people around. Mrs. Peterson visits her son once a week to take him to therapy."

"Your men should always consider the citizens and their needs. A stressful situation like this doesn't need provocation or mockery. Hank will probably need extra therapy during his next session."

I wasn't a psychiatrist, but I'd treated enough patients to know that certain patients require more attention. Being of service to the community required a special skill because you had to deal with a full spectrum of people and personalities.

I glanced over at Bruce, speaking to Bruno. "In my humble opinion, Bruce needs more training."

Detective Donnelly quirked his eyebrow, probably wondering why I dared tell him how to manage his team. No man liked another man interfering with his business.

"I'm a doctor," I said, easing his curiosity. "People like Hank need extra care, and your officer lacks empathy. As a public servant, empathy is required to communicate with the people."

I couldn't tell if he appreciated my feedback or hated it.

"Excuse me, officer." A woman wearing a straw hat, a pink top and jean shorts walked up with a young boy about ten years old. "I was told to look for you. My son, Jason, saw a figure dart through the woods by the creek." She tapped his shoulder. "Go on, honey."

Jason sported shaggy brown hair that made me think of my own. "I was down by the creek looking at frogs when I heard noises. The man was wearing a camo hoodie and camo pants. It stuck out 'cause I thought it was too hot to wear that outfit. His top caught on a branch, but he broke it off the tree and took off." He tucked his hand into his cargo short pockets.

"Show me the location." Detective Connelly turned. "Bruce, come with me."

When they left, I studied Bruno. He wasn't a small guy, a couple of inches shorter than me, but he had muscles too.

"How in the hell did he manage to hit you with a rock?"

Looking embarrassed, he replied, "From behind. If I hadn't heard the scream, I would've run after him to kick his fucking ass."

"Who screamed?"

"A resident found her room in shambles."

"Did he attack anyone else?"

"Not that I know of, but several rooms in the main lodge were broken into. Probably some stupid thief." He scrubbed a hand down his face. "How did the photo shoot go?"

"It went well."

Fantastic, actually. I got to see Kiera, kissed her, and confirmed she was still attracted to me. Now I just had to figure out what to do next. "Catch you later."

"Thanks for subbing in. If you need any more modeling jobs, you know how to find me."

I offered a nod and left.

You're a natural.

Her words flowed through my mind. Since male models surrounded her, I took her compliment to heart. Despite that, my modeling venture was over unless it was to help Kiera.

Or to make sure Bruno stayed away from her.

I lugged the wagon back to Kiera's cabin, parking it in its original spot. "You should get a room at a hotel just to be safe."

I followed her to the front door.

"Why?" She shoved the key into her door. "The police are looking for the thief. I doubt he'll return."

"Stop." I grabbed her hand, pulling her back. "Stay here."

Stepping into her cabin, I surveyed the area. The living room looked as it had before we left for the shoot. The bedroom, bathroom, and closet appeared fine too. Satisfied, I turned around and bumped into her.

"I told you to stay out there. You don't listen, do you?"

She scoffed. "Not when someone barges into my place and doesn't explain what he's doing."

"Just making sure that criminal isn't hiding in here." I placed a finger on the crease between her eyebrows and rubbed. "Don't stress. He's not here."

"I'm not stressing about that."

"Then what?" I could feel the anxiety pumping off of her.

"It's nothing," she huffed.

I didn't like that she didn't trust me enough to tell me what was bothering her. Why should I care? I had too many things on my plate. The last thing I needed was to add to it.

She's a friend, and friends care for one another, don't they?

"Okay. Just be careful whenever you go out." I didn't pressure her to answer the question. Some other day, but not today.

I added a new goal to my list: Kiera Ford would one day trust me enough to tell me all her secrets. That was my mission. I wanted to know all of her secrets and fears.

Kiera and I were friends within the same circle, but I'd never made a move or anything like that. My friends were family to me. I didn't want to do anything that could ruin that dynamic. Besides, I'd heard she dated mostly fashion models, and I wasn't in that arena. Would she have even considered me as a lover? A doctor and an entrepreneur didn't seem her type. Just thinking about that bothered me.

Which was why you turned into a damn fool and tried to be her type.

Idiot.

I'd never been this irrational about anything.

She got herself a bottle of water from the refrigerator. "Do you want something to drink?"

"No, thanks. I still think you should go to a hotel."

Irritation flickered in her eyes again. Or was that anxiety?

Great job, Forrest. You sure know how to irritate a woman.

"We're done with the shoot. I have a lot of photos that need editing. That's all I'll need from you."

The early dismissal was probably due to my comment, but I wasn't ready to leave yet.

"Can I see the pictures?"

"When I'm done editing."

"How long are you staying in Texas?"

"Until the end of next week."

She was here for two weeks. I flipped through the calendar in my mind. My schedule was tight for the next few days, but I didn't want to dismiss this rare opportunity to get answers. What had happened that night that forced her to leave without a word? Was there a chance we could start a relationship?

I didn't think she'd be my type, but she was the only woman who made me feel and want more than any other woman. I used to date women who spent hours shopping at boutiques, who wanted to attend fashion shows and charities, but they all lacked substance.

No woman had hooked me for this long. No woman had made me yearn for her long after she left. I'd been careful about obstacles along my path. But somehow, Kiera had become the biggest obstacle I had to face. She wasn't just some business endeavor or a holistic medicinal venture I was after. She provoked things in me that weren't there before. And if they had been, I hadn't noticed them until now.

A man who spent too much time pondering lacked vision and purpose. But I needed to focus and not get sidetracked. Otherwise, I could inadvertently detour down an unfamiliar path that would eventually lead me to a cliff.

Despite the risk, I *needed* this second chance with her. I needed answers only she could provide.

"Let's have dinner before you head back to Providence. Okay?"

She stared at me for a while. The air in the room thickened, stirring up sexual energy.

I stepped closer and used my finger to wipe the drop of water clinging to the bottom of her lip. "Unless you're afraid of me."

That did the trick. Her eyes flashed with a challenge. "I'm not afraid of you."

Again, I placed my finger on the throbbing pulse in her neck. "This tells me otherwise." My lips hovered close to her ear, and she shivered. "Your heart rate is telling me I'm affecting you. Your heavy breathing shows you want something, but you're trying very hard to stop yourself."

"I'm terrified of you," she confessed.

"Why?"

"Because you make me want something that's out of reach." There was sadness in her voice. "I have a lot of baggage I need to deal with before I can think about relationships." She placed the water bottle on the counter. "I'm not interested in another one-night stand or casual sex."

Her humble admission held so much power. I brushed a finger down her cheek. "Thank you for your honesty."

I hadn't been attracted to anyone since her. That one night with her was like some drug I'd never experienced. She was the mystical potion that had alchemized me. Nothing about me remained the same. My body only wanted her. My mind only saw her. Her scent still lingered in my blood. My heart pounded every time I remembered the passion in her eyes when she'd come for me.

Kiera was a new medicine that entered my senses and affected me slowly. I didn't know what had happened until it was too late. She'd already seeped into every cell, every molecule. She was the only one who could cure me.

"Don't you have a girlfriend you can have dinner with?" she asked with annoyance.

"I'm not seeing anyone. Are you?"

"Don't lie to me." Kiera pursed her lips. "She was all over you at the restaurant."

I had to think back for a moment. When I realized who she was referring to, a smile formed on my lips. Nothing mattered but this simple joy I hadn't felt before. I was probably losing my mind, but I didn't care. She'd been watching me, looking at the surrounding women just as I had been observing her.

"You were watching me?"

"I'm a photographer. Details matter. I enjoy watching things."

Anyone could spot the obvious lie.

"Do you have a lot of images of me in here, Special K?" I gently tapped her forehead.

"Special K? Is that like a nickname you give to all the women on your roster? Do you have nicknames for nurses and doctors with specialties?"

She had been checking out whom I had dated. This conversation revealed more than I thought.

I gripped her adorable chin. "You're better than that cereal. You taste good, and you're good for me."

A laugh burst out of her. "Cheesy, Forrest. So cheesy."

"It got a laugh out of you. So I call that a win." I dropped a kiss to her lips. "If you must know, that woman is my cousin, Yolanda. We grew up together. She's like a sister to me."

"Oh." Embarrassment flushed her cheeks.

I reached for the box of cereal and tapped at the Kellogg's Special K. "I'm going to call you Sexy K. There's just something about you that stirs me up."

"Is that a new tagline for your cereal brand?"

"Now that you mention it." I folded my arms over my chest, contemplating. "That could probably work."

Smirking, she shook her head. "You're officially a weird BaMBu Beast."

I laughed at the unique name. "Coming from you, anything you call me is sexy."

My phone rang and Levi's number popped onto the screen. I let it go to voicemail and continued my conversation with Kiera.

"I have a proposal for you."

"Okay." Her brown eyes glinted with curiosity.

"There's a powerful attraction between us. We need to face it. We can start off with just dinner and hang out. See where things go. Maybe the attraction will fade in two weeks, or a month. But we need to resolve this."

"What if we get sick of each other sooner than that?"

"What if we can't get enough of each other?" I retorted. "Whatever the case may be, at least we'll get some answers, and our friendship remains, okay?"

"Our friendship is no longer what it was."

"You're right. Our friendship just escalated into a territory that neither of us understood. But we're finding answers now, right? It's like when you catch a cold, you take certain meds to ease your symptoms."

"Or you don't take anything at all and let it run its course." She narrowed her eyes at me. "Are you calling me an illness? It's not very endearing if you're trying to impress a girl, Dr. Navarro."

"You're not an illness at all. You are the remedy—the magical cure for all my ailments, Sexy K."

Her smile stretched wide.

My phone rang with Levi's name again. "I need to take this."

"Go ahead. I'm going to unpack."

"What's up, Levi?"

"Can you meet me in an hour?"

"For what?"

"You need to get an ID pass to the secret party."

CHAPTER TWELVE

KIERA

When Forrest left, he took something with him. The cabin felt empty, like it was missing something.

Today had been an interesting day. I'd experienced a wide range of emotions, starting with jitters before and during the photo shoot with Forrest. Then arousal from being so close to him, followed by desire from wanting more than the kiss. The attack and break-in at the campground left me more than unsettled.

What was the thief looking for?

I didn't want to move to a hotel because FitFlex wasn't going to pay for it. They'd already spent a fortune for the occupancy here. Forrest kept suggesting I get a hotel room, but I had to save money for my mom's treatment. I also didn't want him to know about my financial situation. Our relationship wasn't on that level yet.

My mom wouldn't have liked my decision to stay at the cabin given the frightening situation, but her recovery was more important to me. Nora had called to confirm that extra officers would be around for the next few days. That eased my nerves.

When I returned to Providence, I'd sit down, review my finances, and come up with a concrete plan before I called the doctor about the payment options. There was still time to think it through.

With that issue set aside, my mind wandered to the noise that had woken me up this morning. Could that have been the attacker sneaking around? Or had it been an animal? A campground wasn't the place for expensive jewelry, cash, or fancy electronics. It didn't make sense, but I couldn't read a criminal's mind.

Pushing the distraction aside, I sat down at the kitchen table to start on the photo edits. If I could finish everything for FitFlex early, I'd have a couple of days to explore before the next gig. Olivia had hooked me up with a job at an event where she'd be modeling. Right now, I'd take any job that would grow my medical fund. A few hours of photographing models at a charity event would earn me more money than what FitFlex paid me this week.

I opened Forrest's files and clicked on the images. His face and body populated my screen, and I sucked in a breath at the sudden impact. A chill caressed my skin. I didn't know if it was because I was alone or that my body's reaction to him had intensified. But dammit, the feeling that surged in me was undeniably robust. It was as though today's session increased my sensitivity to him. I sensed him everywhere, even when he wasn't here.

I stared at the photos and felt a new intimacy with Forrest. I loved his varied expressions. He was a beautiful man standing in the water as the setting sun glowed behind him with nature witnessing his spectacular presence. He brought the clothes to life by telling a story.

Come join me. Wear these clothes. Immerse yourself in the beauty of nature.

If I could sense that, others would too. This collection would be a bestseller. I'd bet my money on it.

I clicked on the exclusive photo I took of him for myself. He'd never know. The way he looked at the camera made me feel like he was looking at me, whispering secrets and stories about himself to me. My heart had skipped so fast, my fingers snapped his picture before my brain could analyze what I was doing.

I developed powerful feelings for him as the days went by, and we weren't even dating. How was that possible? Was I living an imaginary life where my bubble would pop at any moment, leaving me to fall flat on my face?

Color me confused.

I was attracted to him. Who wouldn't be? But I also knew where I stood. Even if we started a relationship, how long would it last before some hot nurse or doctor caught his eye? Where would that leave me?

I was too tired to be roped into some dating game that didn't make me feel like I was the only one. None of my past relationships had made me feel worthy or complete. I didn't even know what would make me feel those qualities. Was it normal to be this confused? I'd been picking the wrong guys all these years.

Stop worrying. Stop overanalyzing.

I cropped images, adjusted their contrast, and uploaded half of them onto the shared drive for FitFlex's marketing team. On cue, my stomach growled. It was ten at night, and I hadn't eaten dinner yet.

I should have tried to finish the entire collection today, but I was exhausted and hungry. If I didn't take care of myself, who would? My mom needed me.

Shutting down my computer, I walked over to the refrigerator, took out a Caesar salad I'd gotten at the local market, and plopped down on the couch. I turned the TV on to see a news report about the rising crimes in Austin and nearby towns. People had been going missing, and mass shootings were rampant.

Crimes had increased all over the country—all over the world. The news reported nothing joyful anymore. I was certain there was good news out there, but bad news got better ratings, and ratings meant money.

The world was so messed up. I hardly turned on the news nowadays except to get the latest weather forecast when I didn't feel like clicking on the weather app. I was too fatigued to switch channels or even turn it off.

The red-headed news anchor continued her report. "With the unprecedented crime rates in Austin, Senator Mitch Kramer is working closely with local officials to fix this problem. Here's what the senator had to say."

Nausea rose in me as I listened to his hoarse voice and cringed as he spoke about training more police. Kramer's silver hair and his expensive tailored suit made his promises seem appealing, but I knew better. Politicians always rubbed me the wrong way—Mitch Kramer rubbed me the wrong way. Did they ever tell the truth? Did they really care about the people? Or was everything just a photo op for a personal agenda?

The more he spoke, the angrier I got. Kramer was a man wearing too many masks. Didn't people know he was a liar? How could they want someone like that to represent them? He was a ruthless man who only saw money, power, and status. Everyone else could go to hell.

How could I like a man who had abandoned my mom and me?

Growing up, it was just me and Mom. I told everyone I

didn't know my dad, and that was the truth. Though I knew he existed, he didn't know about me.

He was a stranger to me, and that was how I wanted it.

Not all men are like your father.

That sore spot kept me from having stable relationships. I didn't have a good male role model growing up, and questions about my irresponsible father only brought on shame and unworthiness. Trusting men to be truthful and responsible had been difficult. It was my weakness, and I didn't know if I could ever overcome that.

When my relationships went through a rough patch, I ended them quickly. *I* had to do it first because the other option was unbearable. I didn't like the feeling of abandonment, so I'd rather be the one to abandon. Despite that, there had been a couple of instances where my exes had cheated on me. That had been a version of disregard as well.

Shame collided with resentment, giving me a stomachache. My appetite was now ruined. Though I had shoved Kramer from my mind, I hadn't expected to see his face on the TV screen while working here.

Thank God that I'd only be here temporarily, because seeing more of him would make me sick. Was the universe testing me with a barrage of things I didn't want to see?

I hadn't expected to see Forrest in Texas either. Each of these men provoked a different emotion in me. One made me feel like shit, while the other ignited hope in me. I refused to let Mitch Kramer dictate my life.

What did I have to lose by going on a few dates with Forrest? I'd been thinking about him nonstop, so facing my problem head on would solve the issue, wouldn't it?

Fine. I'd give him two dates and see where things went.

CHAPTER THIRTEEN

FORREST

Levi took me to a local pharmacy called Wellwise for my picture ID. The place was filled with over-the-counter medication, household items, packaged foods, two rows of beauty products, some clothing, and a little section that sold fresh flowers. The merchandise was well organized, portraying the pharmacy as nothing more than what it was supposed to be. But I knew other transactions occurred here that had nothing to do with the pharmacy.

How was this local pharmacy connected to an exclusive and elite party? Was the owner an attendee? Or did the banquet organizer own this pharmacy?

Questions swarmed my head as Levi led me to the back room with a space for photographs and two large printers. A sales associate wearing black-framed glasses, ripped jeans, and a logo polo shirt glanced up from the computer, recognized Levi, and nodded.

"I'll be right with you," he said while assisting an older woman. "We'll have your passport photos printed in a few minutes. Jackie will get them ready for you." He gestured to a girl wearing a cherry print dress.

"Did you get your picture taken already?" I asked Levi, who was texting on his phone, smiling like he was going to get laid.

"Yup," he said without glancing up.

"Sir?" The sales associate waved me over. "You can stand right here."

While I waited for my identification, I scanned the store, surveying the incoming and outgoing customers. Nothing stood out except for a few men in suits who also entered for their photos. Their tailored suits told me they had money.

What kind of social gathering was I attending? Why did they need a photo ID?

The banquet had to be linked to The Trogyn. Their presence was a threat to me and my friends. I'd put too much effort into building my career, wealth, and status. No one and nothing had the authority to destroy that.

I'd been doing my research on this crime organization, and my friends were investigating as well. The Trogyn's associates were everywhere, hiding in the dark corners of the city. We had to be extra careful to avoid inadvertently revealing ourselves as their enemies.

The sales associate emerged from the back room and offered me a black envelope. "You're all set, sir."

"Thank you."

I took a seat beside Levi, who was texting. I opened the envelope, pulling out a shiny black card. The back had a holographic image of me with another image overlapping it. A gold strip ran across the bottom of the card along with a series of numbers, which I assumed was my identification number.

The information I'd filled out on the online form only showed my initials. They didn't need to know my full name. I'd paid a hefty sum to attend, and that was all they needed to know.

"Mine looks better." Levi glanced at my ID, smirked, and withdrew his from his wallet.

The cards looked the same except for our faces. "I guess your plastic surgeon did a good job."

"Fucker." Laughing, Levi rushed off to a date.

I headed back to Pine Tower Hotel, wondering what Kiera was doing.

During the drive, my thoughts wandered to Bruno's associates. These men cheated their way up the ladder. Their family name had bought them a space in high society, and they had no issues bragging about it. They had no shame bedding other men's wives either. I could use that incriminating detail as a powerful weapon one day.

I'd witnessed Bruno slapping his date at an after party. He'd been drunk, but that was no excuse to hurt anyone. I'd hauled his ass away from her, and she dashed off. If she were smart, she had stayed away from him.

My research on FitFlex didn't reveal any illegal activities or ties to Bruno's associates. He worked for several clothing brands, organizing photo shoots for them. Was he doing something else for those men? Did the attacker at the campground want to hurt him, or had it been random?

My last encounter with him was at a photo shoot for Heal the World, a nonprofit organization that supported health clinics in third world countries. I was a board member of that organization. That campaign had sold T-shirts, caps, backpacks and other accessories, which brought in millions of dollars and helped open two new clinics. One was in Ethiopia, and the other in Ghana. This organization differed from others in that it also introduced holistic medicine for patients who had an aversion to western medicine.

The human body was unique and a mystery all on its own. It evolved, and medicine needed to adapt to that change. Keeping an open mind allowed me to welcome in new changes.

I recalled how the doctors had refused to treat my father because we didn't have enough money. I'd only been six years old, but I remembered it clearly. The doctors closed the door on us, literally *slammed* the door. They weren't medical professionals; they were monsters. Those fucking doctors saw money as more important than a human life. All my dad needed were antibiotics. My mom had already taken the bullet out of him, but he was bleeding too much. The herbs my grandma had used didn't stop the bleeding, and he'd developed an infection. This was where western medicine could assist. East and West could co-exist.

The man with the red birthmark on his neck had shot my father while his two thugs laughed. Fucking assholes.

"No!" Mom screams.

My dad crumples to the floor of our house. Mom drops beside him, placing her hand on my dad's stomach wound.

I join Mom and squeeze my dad's hand. I'm trembling with fear and anger.

Who are these evil men? Why are they in my house? Why did they shoot my dad?

"You live on my turf. You follow my rules, fucker. You steal my drugs, you die. Simple." Birthmark Man approaches, staring at me and my mom. "Those are the rules of the Anacondas. You got issues, you find me."

My heart races at the name. I've heard about the gang terrorizing people in my village.

"He can't move." One man laughs and mocks my dad.

Dad faints, and blood pools on the ground, looking like a red monster.

I hate those men. Something snaps in me. I glare at them, memorizing their faces.

When they leave, Grandma returns from the market and wails when she sees Dad unconscious. Grandma and my mom remove the bullet and patch the wound with dry herbs, but the wound is so deep he needs more care.

I watch their every movement. It all happens so fast. There's not much I can do except to help with little things whenever Mom or Grandma needs something. I'm so scared.

They rush him to a nearby clinic, but the two doctors ask us to pay first. They look like husband and wife. The male doctor has a mean face. Maybe he's friends with the Anacondas.

"Please help us," Mom begs. "We don't have enough money, but I promise I'll gather enough funds to pay you later. Please."

My mom and grandma beg, but the man says no. Mom even goes on her knees, pleading, but they slam the door on her. I jump from the loud noise. I've never seen mom beg like that.

I'm angry, and I don't understand. Doctors are supposed to help people, aren't they? Mom and Grandma help the villagers all the time with free herbs and the bitter drinks. They even help people who don't have money. Why are these doctors different?

My dad wakes that night, but he's so pale. He's not getting better. Mom and Grandma cry uncontrollably as they sit on the chairs watching me and Dad on the couch.

My hands are small in my dad's palms. "Don't cry. Go somewhere safe." He grips my hands tight. "Take care of your mãe *and* Vó.*"*

Nodding, I promise to take care of Mom and Grandma.

He looks at me, and I can see the love in his eyes. "Seja um bom rapaz."

My dad wants me to be a good man. But right now all I want is to kill those men who had hurt him. I also want to hurt those doctors too. I don't like to be mean. I don't want to be mean, but I can't help it.

The word "good" had so many meanings. Men had twisted that definition to suit their needs for centuries. Some wore a "good" mask to do "good" things for society, but when no one was around, they let the monster inside loose. I had encountered this in both business and medicine. I was an adaptable man, so I'd learned the flexibility of the word "good." A man had to protect himself and his assets.

But my deepest desire was to be the good person my dad had wanted. If he were watching me from above, he'd know I'd skated on the thin line between good and bad. Those liminal spaces were necessary to get shit done while protecting myself.

Why were these old memories surfacing now? Maybe it was the visit to my grandma, or the photo shoot in the woods that triggered it all.

As a child, I'd spent a lot of time in the forest behind my home, learning about plants and fungi from my parents and my grandma. We had a little vegetable garden and often shared what we grew with our neighbors. Mom and Dad also worked in this cottage by the stream. Being out in nature had made me feel comfortable, congruent, and secure.

Now, as an adult, money and power provided those things. In some way, I had lost touch with that connection to nature I once had as a child. Though I had several businesses involving nature, I didn't feel its powerful pull until this shoot with Kiera. She brought something back to me, and she didn't even know it.

I pulled into my parking spot at my hotel and sat there for a moment, trying to collect myself. My life changed the day my dad died. I'd never forget it. My dad had been at the wrong place at the wrong time. A rival gang member had stolen drugs from the Anacondas and hid them in my dad's groceries.

The past had a way of driving a man's ambitions. I let the dark memories flow like magma in my blood, igniting all the reasons I strived for success. With money and power, I could do so much.

The air of freedom smelled different when your life had been polluted with fear and blood. No one would leave their homes unless their lives depended on it. To start over in a foreign country had been hard for my mom, Grandma, and me. We had to adapt to a new way of living, a new culture, and new rules. That hardship shaped me. It allowed me to empathize with the diverse community I served.

I was grateful to have learned English as a child because it helped me adapt quickly. Mom had traded the English lessons for free holistic treatments to the students and faculties at my school.

Sighing, I took the elevator up to the suite. I'd purchased this hotel when my grandma moved to Texas. It was a prime location and had profited since my ownership.

When I got into my suite, the weight of the past pushed me down onto my couch. I stayed that way for a while, letting everything fall away. When it did, Kiera's face appeared, making me smile.

I pulled up the calendar on my phone and reviewed my agenda for the next two weeks. I had a seminar to attend, virtual conferences, and updates on my alternative medicine development. The deadline for my Level Four demo for Water-Fyre Rising was due soon. Dinner with Grandma wouldn't be until the end of next week.

Where could I squeeze in a date with Kiera?

I moved things around and sent her a text. It was late, so she'd get the message tomorrow. Exhaustion weighed on me. I yawned, scraped a hand down my face, and hopped into the shower.

As I toweled off and pulled on a pair of boxers, my phone rang. Could it be Kiera? I'd been thinking about her during my shower, but it was midnight, so she was probably asleep. No one liked getting calls at this late hour. It could only mean bad news.

The Barton Creek Police number flashed on my screen. I'd reached out to the Police Chief Jack Wheaton asking him to alert me about the case regarding the Sabian Creek Campground. My grandma had treated his wife's insomnia with an effective herbal prescription a couple of years ago.

"Hello," I said.

"Hi, Forrest. This is Detective Donnelly. Chief Wheaton asked me to update you on the case."

"Great. What do you have for me?"

"We found a body about an hour ago. It's on the other side of the woods from the campground. A truck driver had pulled over to relieve himself when he saw the body on the side of the road. Looks like some animals got to him."

My molars ground together as questions sparked in my mind.

Could he be the attacker? Did they find anything else on him? Who was he?

I would've been happy to hear about the news, but it came too quickly for me. Something about this incident felt off.

"Please keep me posted on what you find out about the man."

"Why are you interested in this case?"

"Kiera is a close friend of mine. I want to make sure she's safe." That was the truth.

"Y'all have a good night. We have extra men on patrol, so don't worry."

"Thank you."

I knew the drill. Once they identified the man, they'd pull

back their officers for other duties. I didn't blame them. Why waste the manpower on a trivial matter like robbery?

I had to convince Kiera to stay at Pine Tower with me.

CHAPTER FOURTEEN

KIERA

Lying in bed, I smiled as I read his text message that had been sent last night.

Forrest: *Dinner tomorrow? I want to see the photos.*

I checked my calendar and moved my online yoga session to another day. I'd paid for the virtual classes, which helped motivate me during my travels. Skipping a week wouldn't kill me, especially since I'd been hiking around the campground.

Staring at my phone, I tried to figure out how I should reply to Forrest. If it had been anyone else, I wouldn't have hesitated. Dinner with a friend was normal. But we were more than friends, weren't we? Friends didn't sleep with one another. Despite that, we weren't dating either.

This dinner was the catalyst that could break down the strange wall between us. I didn't know where this thing with Forrest would lead to, but I was curious. What happened to the fearless Kiera who went after what she wanted?

I couldn't hold back my frown. The fear probably stemmed from me liking him more than I should.

But he likes intelligent women in his field.

Shut up. I had to stop sabotaging myself.

Intelligence was subjective, wasn't it? One person could measure intelligence from a damn test created by a bunch of people who had nothing better to do. Another person could see intelligence as an immeasurable ability to see, hear, feel, touch, taste—the ability to understand and honor the senses. It wasn't just one's personal capacity for logic and knowledge.

There was a group of "intelligent" people with money and power cheating the world right now. Like the health insurance companies who didn't care if you could afford treatment or not. Did I want to be roped into that ugly category?

Absolutely not.

Kiera Ford was in a category all her own. What was better than intelligence? Wisdom. Yup. I'd set my own rules on worthiness, and if he didn't want me, then screw him. I was no doctor, and had no interest in becoming one. I may not have had a doctorate but I considered myself intelligent and wise, thank you very much.

With renewed optimism, I replied to him.

Kiera: *I could rush the photo edits.*

Forrest: *Thought I was a natural. Why the edits?*

He remembered my comment. What else did he remember? I lied about the edits. The camera loved him. He had been perfection in all the photographs, but I wasn't going to share that detail. A man like him didn't need his ego inflated even more.

Kiera: *Natural at posing. Edits required for other things.*

Forrest: *Not my fault about my bulge.*

Heat bloomed on my face, remembering the sight of him in those shorts. Though FitFlex wanted people to promote their amazing shorts, I didn't think they'd have appreciated the extra accessory. The female crowd would have loved it, but a part of me wanted to keep that image to myself. After all, I was the reason for his reaction, and that had made my day.

Kiera: *Not my fault either.*

Forrest: *ALL your fault. (like right now)*

An image flashed in my mind, and my mouth dropped. What was he doing? It was only nine in the morning. Wasn't this too early for a sexy chat?

Never too early for that.

I bit my bottom lip, trying to imagine what he was wearing. This was one time my inner voice was on my side.

Kiera: *Shouldn't you be working? No billionaire meetings to attend?*

Forrest: *HARD to concentrate.*

I giggled as my inner muscles twitched. That one word sent liquid heat pooling to my core, making my throat dry. I sucked in a breath, remembering the way his cock had thrust into me, claiming me. I sat up in my bed, trying to tame this arousal that wanted his hands to resolve.

Kiera: *Nothing too hard for Dr. Navarro to cure.*

Forrest: *Are you immune to me?*

I wasn't sure what he wanted me to say or what that question was referencing. But I gave him the truth.

Kiera: *You're a cold that keeps making me sneeze.*

Regret hit me after I replied. Could I be any cheesier?

Forrest: *You're a rare virus affecting every part of me.*

This conversation took an interesting turn. The word virus never had a good connotation, but coming from Forrest it reshaped my perspective. Or maybe that was my "intelligence" shifting things to suit my needs.

Kiera: *People usually dislike viruses.*

Forrest: *The literature on them has evolved. Rarest is Kiera Affectingmeeverydae.*

I snorted at my viral name—something I'd never considered

in a million years. Something was wrong with me for finding that provocative. I wanted to know all the ways I affected him. Did he think about me all the time? What was I doing in his thoughts?

What was happening to me? Maybe I was the one catching the Forrest Flu.

I'd never been attracted to men in the sciences because I didn't consider myself a science girl. I didn't need to see proof to believe in something. I didn't need to know how a rainbow was created to love it. Sometimes beauty couldn't and shouldn't be defined or explained. To me, that took away the mystery and beauty of it.

Forrest was a unique science guy. He was more than just a doctor.

From my research about him and his $Ba_7M_5Bu_{88}$ Project, I'd gained new respect for Forrest. I had no idea that there was a wide selection of bamboos in Brazil. I mean, I knew how important the Amazon forest was to Earth, but not the importance of bamboos. Hell, I only thought bamboos existed in Asia. That showed how much I had to catch up on about the world. The project sold apparel and accessories made from bamboo where the proceeds provided medicine to poor sections of South America. I'd bought a T-shirt, which was set to arrive today or tomorrow. I should check with Nora to see if any packages came for me.

Forrest was science, art, and nature. He possessed all the aspects that captivated me, making me pause and wonder. He was a perfect photograph with enough ambient light and color temperature, delivering a perfect image. Perhaps science and art made an indescribable union. There was hope for the logical and the illogical side by side.

God knew some of the things I did made no sense. Right now I should've been working, finishing my edits, but nope. I was having an interesting conversation with a man that was teasing my body and my brain.

I had questions about illnesses I wanted to ask him later. His opinion on my mom's treatment would help me decide what was best.

Kiera: *Thought I was Sexy K, "good for you."*

I left out the part about me tasting good.

Forrest: *My perfect remedy . . .*

Did I dare ask the question blazing in my mind? Why the hell not?

Kiera: *What are you doing?*

Forrest: *Trying to fix a HARD issue.*

Heat burst from my cheeks, and my nipples grew hard with aching need. Was this why people enjoyed phone sex? I'd never had one of these sexually-driven conversations via text with any of my previous relationships.

Kiera: *You're a doctor. If you can't fix it, no one can.*

Forrest: *YOU can.*

Kiera: *How?*

Forrest: *If you were a doctor, what would you do?*

I was no doctor, but I had a wild imagination. In a fantasy world, I could do and be anything. Magic had no boundaries there. He hadn't been specific about what kind of doctor he wanted, so I'd take the lead.

This was going to be interesting, and I was in desperate need of new panties soon.

Kiera: *Step 1, describe your condition.*

Forrest: *Throbbing pressure in my stalk.*

Sexual tension practically throbbed in me. A surge of desire slithered up my spine.

Kiera: *Step 2, stroke the stalk slowly.*

Forrest: *You're evil. (devil emoji)*

I grinned like a wicked goddess. He had no idea what he'd asked for.

Kiera: *Dr. Sexy K at your service. (smile emoji)*

Forrest: *Pressure is increasing. Help me.*

The muscles tightened in my sex, and I wanted him inside me. That would help *me* right now.

Kiera: *Step 3, think of my hand caressing your stalk.*

Forrest: *You're killing me.*

Kiera: *Squeeze. Squeeze. Squeeze.*

Forrest: *So evil. (three devil emoji)*

Kiera: *Feeling better?*

Forrest: *(water burst emoji)*

Oh, my God. I clamped a hand over my mouth. I'd never made a man come via text. After a few moments of silence—in which I imagined him cleaning up after himself—I sat there dumbfounded at what had just happened. I didn't know what to say.

I just made Forrest come! There was no subtlety there. We both knew what we were doing. Did he think less of me because of that? Why did it matter? This was who I was—a woman who enjoyed a playful conversation with a man who turned her on.

Forrest: *You're wicked! I want to be YOUR doctor now.*

I stared at his request while my heart thundered in my chest. Every part of my body screamed yes.

No. It would be too inappropriate. But inappropriate just flew out the window. What did I have to lose?

Kiera: *Please, Dr. Navarro.*

For the next twenty-minutes, Forrest and I exchanged text messages infused with so much heat I was surprised my phone didn't explode in my hands when the wicked orgasm rippled through me.

A reminder chimed on my phone, popping our little lust

bubble. It was a reminder for me to check in about a conference call with the marketing team regarding the recent batch of photos I'd sent them.

Kiera: *Need to go now. Be good, BaMBu Beast.*

I didn't care if he thought it was cheesy.

Forrest: *Why that nickname?*

Kiera: *You're a beast on a humanitarian mission. That makes you cute.*

Forrest: *The beast is hot and bothered.*

Kiera: *Dr. Sexy K will make all your booboos go away. (rolling on the floor laughing emoji)*

Forrest: *Got lots of booboos for you. (bandage emoji, needle emoji, blood emoji)*

Kiera: *Blood is my enemy.*

Forrest: *Blood is my ally.*

A cold chill skimmed down my body at the thought of blood. He was a doctor. He had to love and understand it. I switched my thought to the pleasure he'd just given me, which was a lot more appealing than blood.

Forrest: *Need new appointment for treatment.*

Still trying to recover from the massive orgasm, I smiled as the same thought crossed my mind. But I needed time to evaluate my life. Things were moving too fast. The sudden reconnection in Texas and the burst of sexual energy when we were together—even while texting—made me dizzy and nervous. I needed to think clearly because there were things that needed my careful attention. I couldn't get lost in lust, when practical matters like my mom's health and paying for her medical bills were my priorities.

Kiera: *TBD.*

Forrest: *You're the best doctor I've ever had.*

Charm was a scalpel that sliced away my barrier. I knew what he meant, but that comment also brought on questions I couldn't avoid. How many woman doctors did he have? Before I could stop myself, my fingers punched at the letters on the keypad.

Kiera: *Liar.*

Forrest: *The truth. I don't allow examination via text like this.*

Warmth burst inside my chest. As if he knew what was colluding in my mind, his text message made me smile like a fool.

Forrest: *Dr. Sexy K is the only doctor allowed to treat me.*

Kiera: *Next text appt. is tonight. Time TBD.*

Forrest: *On my calendar. You made my day. (happy emoji)*

Kiera: *FYI. There's a fee for cancellation.*

Forrest: *Time with Dr. Sexy K is too special. No cancellations. But if you cancel on me, there WILL be a punishment.*

What did that mean? And why did I find myself wanting to cancel just to find out? This conversation could have gone on all day, but I had work to do.

Kiera: *See you later.*

With a huge smile on my face, I changed into a new pair of underwear and prepared for my conference call and the photo shoot with Olivia and Nate scheduled for noon.

CHAPTER FIFTEEN

Fuuuck.

I couldn't believe I had sexted with Kiera for over an hour. It was my first time sexting and most definitely not my last. Especially if Dr. Sexy K was hosting. *Christ.* My cock hardened at the mention of her name.

I know you want her. But you have to wait.

I was going insane because I was talking to my dick as though he could hear me. He hadn't listened to my demands whenever I was around her. He grew and throbbed as though she, not I, had power over him.

Raking a hand through my hair, I gathered myself and prepared for my conference with the boys. I was already twenty minutes late. Dammit. I hadn't been expecting her text while reviewing updates on my clinic and the alternative medicine undergoing thorough evaluation.

Why hadn't the meeting reminder popped up on my screen? Wait, it did, but I'd swiped it away, not wanting anything to disrupt my conversation with Kiera.

She'd turned me on so fast, I'd lost control of my brain. I

remembered jack shit about what I was doing, never mind my agenda for the day. All I could think about was the blood rushing to my cock, begging for attention. I had no idea Dr. Sexy K was this lewd but I loved that about her. Her curiosity and sense of adventure were irresistible qualities.

I logged into the virtual conference. "Sorry, guys. I lost track of time."

"Don't sweat it." Remi gave me a nod. His dark hair had gotten shorter. "Everything good over there?"

Looking like a Viking with his silvery blond hair, Royce tapped his cheek. "Getting too much sun there? You're flushed."

Was I? *Fuck.*

Arrow gave me a weird look, leaning into the screen and narrowing his gray eyes. "Too much heat with the Southern babes? I hear they're hot."

I rolled my eyes. "It's like an oven in Texas. You try walking outside and see if you don't bake."

"It's definitely a woman." Grayson laughed, looking happier these days now that he was in love with Natalie. There had been a time when my boy had delved into the darkness and didn't want to come out.

"And?" I just had the best orgasm in the universe, and I couldn't care less about what they thought about me. "Are we going to waste time talking about the Texan heat or our Water-Fyre Rising games?"

Shaking his head, Remi said, "We've got two more investors. They have money and influence. We have more than enough investors to secure the success of our video game."

"I have no doubt of its success. But the more investors, the better," I said. "I'll have a demo for Level Four next month. I'm busy with seminars the next few weeks."

Royce relaxed into his chair. "Anything new on The Trogyn?"

We were all working on various angles, trying to find out who the elite members of this crime organization were. They used elite clubs to carry out their illegal business.

"I've got some astrological aliases you can check out." Arrow shared the list on the screen.

Orcus, Andromeda, and Black Moon Lilith were on the top of the list.

"Do you guys know what these names are referencing?" I asked.

"Andromeda is a galaxy, but that's all I know," Royce said.

I'd need to do some research on these names later. Details mattered. They made up the big picture. Like the thymus and bone marrow that had critical roles in defending the body against diseases, the tiny white bloods cells carried an important function in the immune system as well. Every little thing had its purpose.

"The date to the party might change. I'll keep you posted. Not sure if we'll find anything, but I have a hunch we will."

"We'll have to make sure our plan is errorproof," Remi said.

Grayson folded his arms over his chest. "Things have been quiet after the explosion of Club Diablo. Maybe they're still reevaluating their next steps."

Grayson had planted bombs inside an underground club that had served as a meeting place for this crime organization. The Commissioner of the Department of Public Works for Providence and his wife had been members who were killed along with others. I knew this organization was trying hard to figure out who had damaged their moneymaking business.

"Just keep your eyes and ears open," Arrow said. "I've outlined a strategy. Once I have the documents ready, I'll share with you."

Arrow had been working behind the scenes on creating a powerful network that would strengthen us against The Trogyn and any other crime organizations who threatened us.

After a lengthy discussion on The Trogyn, our conversation turned to our video games, which lightened the mood.

"Are the new investors local?" I asked.

"Attikus Mount is one of them. The other investor is based in Boston," Remi replied. "I guess you could call that local compared to some of our other investors."

"I'm renovating Attikus's museum. He's bought the adjacent lot, and the new museum is going to be huge," Grayson said. "The man's got money."

The more allies we had on our side, the better off we'd be. For the next half-hour, we reviewed the ad campaign proposal and discussed companies in other countries who could help promote WaterFyre Rising. I'd also downloaded the list of elite members Arrow had compiled. The unusual aliases all had ties to astrology or mythology.

When the conference call ended, I pulled up a file to prepare for a seminar later that day. But I kept checking my phone to see if Kiera had texted me. I was horny as fuck, thanks to her.

My phone rang, and Yolanda's name flashed on my screen.

"What's up?" I said, putting her on speaker as I maneuvered files on my computer.

"You busy?"

"Yes, but what do you need?"

"We had another customer in the store complaining today. Something's wrong with Grandma Morena's herbal remedy. Do you have time to stop by?"

I glanced at my watch. "Yeah. I'll be there in two hours."

That gave me enough time to review the herbs I'd gotten from Patricia and do what I had to for the seminar, swing by the shop, inform my lawyer, and attend the seminar. I'd been meaning to follow up with him, but time had been an issue.

"See you soon. Are you supposed to be working at the office today?" Yolanda only worked at Full Circle Apothecary a few days a week to help Grandma.

"Yes, but since you're making time, I figured I'll stop by to get the latest information," she said. "I don't get to see you often, so I consider this visit as a mini family reunion."

I didn't know what I'd do without Yolanda. Knowing she was there to look after my grandmother allowed me to focus on other things in my life—things that doctors shouldn't be doing. Things that could absolutely put me in prison. But that dark part of my life was for no one to see or hear, especially my grandma. I hadn't even told my friends about it. If Kiera knew the other side of me, would she even want me?

I flicked that thought away before it could wreak havoc on my focus.

"I'm having dinner with you and Grandma next Saturday. That's a reunion. Me coming over to ensure the business is protected is family responsibility."

She sighed. "That's why Grandma loves you."

"And you don't?" I teased.

"I'm offended you had to ask."

A chuckle spilled out of me. "Gotta go finish up some work if I'm to make it there in two hours."

After reviewing the herbs that Patricia Gallivan used, I concluded there was nothing wrong with my grandma's herbal remedy. Jasmine leaves, dandelion, rose, and ginseng could be found easily online or any grocery store. Ms. Gallivan was probably allergic to one of the herbs. But to be certain, I'd send it to the lab for verification. They could break down the properties and see the chemical reactions for each herb and pair them up for various effects. They could use that data and analyze it further with the global database on people who were allergic to them.

When I got to Full Circle Apothecary, the parking lot was packed with cars. It must have been the herbs class night. I entered, and the noise from the herb room confirmed it.

Yolanda saw me and gestured for me to follow her to the back room. She wore a dress with a low neckline and high heels that would probably hurt her feet by the time the shop closed.

"Are you going on a date tonight?" I asked.

We ducked into the back room filled with inventory neatly organized. Baskets of dried herbs sat waiting to be separated.

Yolanda twirled, and the skirt flowed around her. "Do I look pretty enough for a date?"

"Always." I leaned against the table. "So what's the deal with the new complaint?"

She stood beside me, twirling a lock of her hair around her finger. "Some woman said the herbal prescription made her nauseous. She wanted her money back."

"Did you give it to her?"

"I didn't want to, but Grandma said we should."

"She's right," I said. "We want to defuse the situation, not make it worse. Did Grandma pull the product off the shelves?"

Yolanda nodded, staring at the ground. "I don't know what's going on, Forrest. No one has ever had a problem with any of our herbal prescriptions until now. I hope the complaints stop because it's stressing out Grandma." She nudged me with her elbow. "Do you want to stay longer in Texas until the lawsuit is over?"

"I can't. I've sent out the herbs left by Patricia Gallivan to the lab. They'll confirm if the recipe was safe, which I know it is. But having an official document is extra ammunition in court. My lawyer is working on the case." Pushing off from the table, I took out my phone from my pocket, scrolling for

Henry's number. "I'm going to get an update from him. Where's Grandma, by the way?"

"She went to the market down the street. It's her daily exercise when we have enough coverage here," she said, and I heard a hint of sadness in her voice.

"You okay?"

She lifted a shoulder. "Just relationship issues. Nothing big."

"Is your boyfriend treating you well? If not, you let me know, okay?" I placed a hand on her shoulder. "I mean it. You deserve a man who loves you."

She smiled at me. "Thanks. I'm going to head out front to help Cara."

When Yolanda left, I called Henry for an update.

CHAPTER SIXTEEN

KIERA

Wearing my new $Ba_7M_5Bu_{88}$ T-shirt in soft yellow and some comfy shorts, I took an Uber to downtown Austin, wanting to explore. Though anxiety still stirred around me, I pushed it aside. Thinking about Forrest helped keep the worries far away. He'd become the perfect distraction.

It had been a while since I felt this kind of inspiration. Forest said I made his day with a fantastic orgasm. But he was the one who shifted my mood completely. I'd never experienced such bliss from a text message, but it seemed Forrest had opened up new adventures for me to explore.

Tingles tickled my spine as I remembered our chat, yearning for his touch again. Delight skipped inside me like a child full of wonder and invincibility. I was going to put this positive attitude to good use.

I walked up to The Southern Belle boutique, stopped, and stared at the window display. The sage maxi dress on the dress form caught my eye. It reminded me of the color of Forrest's eyes. I didn't bring a lot of dresses on this trip, because I didn't think I'd be going on a date or wanting to feel feminine and attractive. I had packed my luggage with mostly T-shirts, tank tops, and shorts. The lost luggage had finally arrived, but it was more casual clothing.

I could still wear a T-shirt and shorts on my date, but the simplicity of the dress with the thin straps called me.

Save money.

The anxiety bit me like a yappy dog—an annoyingly constant reminder of my glaring issue. My financial situation stopped me from making an impulse buy. I didn't *need* the dress.

Perhaps I could come back and buy it after I finished the side job. I could treat myself to one dress from the extra income.

The self-talk made me feel better. I really didn't need any new clothes. I had a closet full of dresses from all the designers I'd worked with, but none of them were in this beautiful sage color.

Touching the dress would be enough for now. I entered the boutique with elegant fixtures and lighting. They carried a wide selection of menswear, which differed from boutiques I'd visited. Most boutiques carried women's clothing with one or two racks of menswear. But half of the display was for menswear, including shoes.

A pretty girl wearing a black dress and a side braid smiled at me. "Welcome to the Southern Belle. Y'all need help with something specific?"

"No, thank you. I'm just looking."

"Take your time, miss," said the associate, who went to help a couple who had just entered.

I lost myself in the racks organized according to color. I touched the sage green dress, and the silkiness was to die for. Taking the dress off the rack, I placed it against my body and glanced in the mirror. It was beautiful and would feel so lovely against my skin, especially in this hot, humid weather. But I couldn't.

An image intruded into my mind—Forrest slipping this dress off of me, one strap at a time. I walked over to the three-way mirror beside a seating area with elegant couches.

"I like the other cufflinks better," said a hoarse voice that stiffened my spine.

I turned toward the seating area across the room with a display of menswear clothing. Mitch Kramer sat in a loveseat, his face hidden from view because of the angle of the large chair. I cringed at his red dress shoes. He needed a new stylist.

Of all the years I'd spent photographing fashion models and high-end brands, I'd never seen red men's dress shoes. Wealthy men usually preferred black, brown, gray, or white dress shoes, which were muted and classy.

What would happen if he saw me? Would he notice my resemblance to my mom?

He got up from the chair, and nerves churned in me. I stood behind my clothing rack as he walked by while talking on his phone. He glanced at me, and no recognition splashed on his face. He returned to his call as he walked up to sales counter. "See you soon, sexy."

I couldn't help the disappointment and sadness that followed. This man didn't deserve an ounce of feelings from me. My father didn't know me, and that was how it was going to be.

Being so close to him soured my mood and the desire for the dress. I returned it to its track just as my phone buzzed with a reminder of the medical convention—another reason I was in this area today. With my mom's new condition, I'd been trying to figure out ways to help her. I saw an ad for this convention that would showcase new and innovative medication. I'd never been to one of these conventions before because they hadn't interested me. Now, my interest shifted because of a life and death situation.

It was interesting how life changed your perspective on things. The medical convention was free to those who just wanted to browse and not attend the seminars. It was only two blocks away from The Southern Belle, so I walked there. By the time I arrived, crowds of people had already formed around a booth for some new medication.

I picked up the agenda and browsed through the directory. Mom had a bad liver and muscular issues that made her weak. I had to look for something that could aid those conditions. I spotted a booth with a liver medication and another that eased muscle ailments.

The booth with the liver medication was too crowded. Health professionals lobbed questions at the two representatives, who appeared overwhelmed. I didn't understand the science jargon. I needed layman's terms on medication. Most of the time, I couldn't even pronounce the drug's name.

I grabbed a blue promotional bag and a flyer from the stand. There was no way the representative would have time to entertain my questions. I'd review the flyer and email them with questions.

A headache bloomed. I just wanted some easy-to-understand language that could answer all my questions. Anxiety, hunger, stress, and the commotion coming from the crowd swarmed like mosquitoes. I had to get out of here.

As I headed down the hallway to exit, hoping to find a sandwich shop, my body shivered for no reason. Then someone called my name.

CHAPTER SEVENTEEN

FORREST

Ignoring my peers, I strode toward Kiera. When I stepped out into the hallway, I hadn't expected to see her amongst the crowds, but my body sensed her. Even though I only saw her back, I knew it was her.

When she turned, my heart skipped several beats. She wore one of the new $Ba_7M_5Bu_{88}$ T-shirts in a soft yellow. Seeing her supporting my project did something strange to my insides, but I didn't want to think about it. The women I'd dated before weren't interested in my project, never mind buying a T-shirt.

"What are you doing here?" I approached her, remembering our sexy chat from early this morning. Unable to resist, I leaned in and whispered, "You look beautiful in my T-shirt."

A beautiful pink dusted over her cheeks, and I lifted my fingers to brush it. A spark hissed between us, and Kiera sucked in a breath, making me wonder if that had been her reaction during our seductive text exchange.

"You joining us for dinner?" David asked, intruding on our

little world. I'd forgotten why I was at the conference and who I was with.

Turning to him, I said, "Kiera, meet Dr. David Botting."

"Please call me David. It's a pleasure to meet you." He smiled, shook her hand, and held it too long for my comfort.

Julie appeared and stared at Kiera.

"This is Dr. Julie Allen," I introduced her to Kiera, studying her reaction.

"It's very nice to meet all of you." Kiera gave them a warm smile, revealing nothing.

"Join us for dinner," I said.

Hesitation sparked in her eyes. "Oh. I was just heading out."

Her stomach growled, and David smiled. "I think your tummy is trying to tell you something. As doctors, we can force you to eat so you don't pass out."

"You might be disappointed in what I eat. I'm not always a salad girl." She smiled at him.

Why was she smiling at *him*? I was the one who asked her to dinner. I couldn't wait for our text appointment, though she hadn't specified a time. I'd ask her later.

David laughed. "Then you'll fit right in. Contrary to what people believe, not all doctors practice what they preach."

"Speak for yourself, David," Julie said. "I love salad, and I can eat it all day, every day."

I held her eyes. "Join us and see what doctors eat."

We walked to an Italian restaurant around the corner. I pulled out two chairs for Kiera and Julie. Out of all the places I imagined seeing her, I didn't expect it to be at a medical conference. I wanted to ask her what she was doing here, but held back based on her hesitation for dinner.

I sat down beside Kiera, and we gave our orders to a waitress wearing big hoop earrings. Under the table, my thighs touched Kiera's. Heat radiated from the point of contact. Instead of moving her thigh away, she pushed it closer, as if testing how far I'd go.

Vixen.

My Sexy K was more potent than any virus. She had slowly snuck under my skin and took over my body and mind, destabilizing my defensive mechanism. That should have alarmed me, and yet I couldn't resist the urge to be closer to her.

I brushed my thigh back and forth, creating more friction.

When the waitress arrived with our food and drinks, Julie yanked the tie from her blonde hair, ruffled it, and turned to Kiera. "Do you work in the medical field? What brings you to this conference?"

"I'm a fashion photographer." Kiera lifted a shoulder. "Saw this conference while I was shopping in the area and wanted to check it out."

That could be true, but the Kiera I knew—the one before we slept together—wouldn't be interested in a medical conference.

I slid my hand to her thigh and squeezed. *You're lying.*

She grabbed my hand, and a war of fingers ensued under the table while a conversation about fashion and the arts exchanged between Julie, Kiera, and David.

"It must be easy work, huh?" Julie asked. "Not like the stress that doctors have to endure."

I sensed Kiera tense. Her fingers strangled mine as though punishing me for Julie's unnecessary remark. I was about to interject, but Kiera removed her hand from mine and straightened her spine.

"That depends on your perspective and definition of easy. Photography is like any artform. Just because it looks easy doesn't mean it is." She shot Julie a sharp look. "I've met people who work two jobs to make ends meet, but they're always smiling and helpful. I wouldn't say their lives are easier or less stressful." She organized the knife, spoon, and fork in front of her slowly, as though preparing for something that might require medical needs to her enemy.

David looked at me, feeling the tension at the table. I shook my head, signifying for him to just watch the scene play out.

"We all have different limits." Kiera sipped her cocktail, peered at Julie over the rim, then placed it down elegantly. "We can define 'easy' as something one wishes for after a long day of work. Or we can define it as how a person presents herself." She smiled and slid her gaze to Julie's low-cut dress.

Julie's eyes lit up with indignation.

I squeezed Kiera's thigh, and she intertwined her fingers with mine. I liked how she pissed off Julie in style. My woman could handle herself. She didn't need me to interfere.

Julie squared her shoulders. "Four years of college isn't as stressful as ten years or more. Being responsible for someone's life isn't the same as snapping pictures. I treat patients with heart conditions. That's a life and death situation."

David cleared his throat and drank his Martini, while trying to avoid the women's strife.

"People—even doctors—who are narrow-minded need a kind heart first before they can treat others. Just saying. It's common sense if you ask me." Kiera shrugged. "But what do I know? I just zoom in and out with my camera. It's not a life and death situation, but I enjoy it."

"You capture the life and death of moments," I said.

Where the fuck did that come from?

Julie sneered, looking like she wanted to strangle me. Looking back, I didn't understand why I'd dated her. It had been a short-lived relationship that had kept my mind off of things back then. Sex was a great distraction.

But these days, I wanted more than just sex. I wanted someone who could touch me from the inside.

Looking uncomfortable, David pointed to Kiera's shirt. "Isn't that Forrest's baby?"

CHAPTER EIGHTEEN

KIERA

"It is." I glanced down at my T-shirt.

Julie shot Forrest an irritated look. I squeezed his hand, appreciating his poetic line. I'd never heard him speak in that way. This was a new side to him that I loved.

"What do you mean it's Forrest's baby?" Julie asked David.

Interesting that she didn't ask me since I was the one wearing the shirt. I should've just gone back to my cabin. Sitting at the same table with his ex-girlfriend didn't soothe my anxiety. It added to it.

"It's his humanitarian project that produces holistic medicine for needy areas around the world," said David. "I've donated to the BaMBu Project."

"Oh, that thing." Julie made a face and a disgusted sound that made me want to dump the salad right on her head. "You're still working on that? Alternative medicine isn't effective. It's been proven time and time again. It's a waste of money."

"I am, and I love it." Forrest offered her a smile that earned him an eye roll.

"I disagree, Julie." David held up a hand. "The world is changing. New ideas are popping up left and right. Before we know it, we'll have forgotten the basics—back to nature. Soon, robots will be examining patients. Look at all the artificial intelligence that are performing human tasks. Our jobs could be replaced in our lifetime." He placed a hand on Julie's shoulder. "Alternative medicine isn't bad at all. It's another way of treating patients. I welcome it."

"Good for you, but I'll pass." She poked a fork into her salad.

I wished I had magical powers that could turn the fork into a snake to bite her.

"Aren't doctors supposed to be open-minded to new ways of healing? New diseases emerge every day, and most of them don't have cures. Some of the current medications cost an arm and a leg. If you can give your patients the care they need with something noninvasive and affordable, isn't that your duty to do so?" I didn't realize my voice had gotten louder.

I couldn't help it. My mom's condition had been stressing me out. I was sitting across from a narrow-minded doctor who was stuck in her idiotic ways. Maybe she was secretly on the board of some health insurance company who voted to jack up the fees for everyone so she could benefit from the kickback. That would make more sense to me because I didn't understand why health care was so expensive.

"Don't keep the mind too open, otherwise stuff will fall out," Forrest said, probably trying to defuse the situation but failing.

I pinched his thigh, and he winced. He tried to grab my hand, but I didn't let him.

Julie smirked at his comment. "Very perceptive, Forrest. You've always had a knack for seeing the truth."

"But if you don't stretch your mind to new ideas, then you'll never see its potential, right?"

Julie pursed her lips and narrowed her eyes at him. Forrest wasn't getting any brownie points from me. The comment came five seconds too late.

I reached for a piece of bread, added butter, and bit into it. Did he regret inviting me to dinner? I wished I hadn't agreed, but I'd been too curious about his ex-girlfriend, and now I was paying for it. She was as shallow as the muddy puddles kids stomped in.

Forrest and David were probably thinking this dispute was just women being catty. They had no idea of the real reason. Julie was still hooked on Forrest, and I was a threat.

I didn't blame her. He was a fabulous catch. If I were honest with myself, I was jealous when I first saw her. She was pretty and had a voluptuous body. I assumed her intelligence was somewhere up there too, but I was so wrong.

It didn't matter what she thought of me because Forrest was making abstract symbols on *my* thigh, not hers. Was she comparing herself to me the way I was studying her?

At one point in time, I'd feared I wasn't good enough for him. He'd dated doctors who were supposed to be intelligent, but after tonight, I had to revisit my doubts. Julie may have been a doctor with years of education, but she lacked empathy, compassion, and common sense. Shouldn't those be requirements for doctors to communicate with their patients?

Was Julie one of those people who only wanted the title and didn't care about what came with that responsibility? To some people, status equaled worthiness.

David switched to a conversation on his upcoming agenda. He talked about his work schedule when he returned to Dallas and how he wanted to be updated on the $Ba_7M_5Bu_{88}$ Project. He seemed like a decent guy—a decent doctor.

Julie tossed me a look laced with poison. "Since you're into alternative medicine, Kiera, what have you learned that was useful?"

I knew she wasn't genuinely curious about me. She only wanted me to look bad in front of Forrest, but since my mom's illness, I'd been doing more research and had gained some knowledge.

"Well, I've learned that certain mushrooms are good for you, like the reishi, chaga, shiitake, turkey tail, and lion's mane —which is a *brain booster*. You should try it. I hear it clears up brain fog." I pasted a lovely smile on my face.

David cleared his throat again as he reached for the glass of water since he'd already finished his cocktail. The poor guy probably had never felt so uncomfortable sitting at a table with two women who disliked each other. I didn't have a problem with Julie until she started insulting me.

"I loved knowing that penicillin is fungus. It just shows that cures for diseases can be found in nature." I looked at Forrest, and delight flickered in his eyes.

I continued on about what I'd learned, and how the medical community should all work together to find the best remedies by trying novel approaches. Forest and David kept quiet as they listened to me talk. Julie probably regretted asking me about my knowledge.

"You should be a doctor," David said. "The passion in your voice is awfully convincing. I bet you could join a research team and you'll end up finding all the cures. Do you agree Forrest?"

Forrest drew the words "Dr. Sexy K" on my thigh.

"David's right. Are you interested?"

I snorted, and didn't care that it was unladylike. "No thanks, I'll leave that to the experts."

"I can hook you up. I work with several research labs, but I also have my own. There's one in Providence, and I think you'd be a great fit." He smiled at me, and I could tell he genuinely wanted me working in his lab.

"She'll need all the prerequisites, otherwise anything she does is meaningless," Julie chimed in.

What a bitch.

A part of me wanted to join just to spite her. But I had no time and didn't need more stress.

I made a mental note to send Dr. Julie Allen a curated self-care package with the phrase. It would include a bottle of lion's mane mushroom to help her small mind and a package of chocolate-covered laxatives to help her release that toxic behavior. Because my mom raised me well, I'd add a gift card so she could get a salad on my behalf. But if she continued with the rude remarks, I'd toss in bar soaps after I rolled them around in a bush of poison ivy.

You're evil.

Sometimes you've got to treat evil with evil, right?

I was a nice person—when people didn't step on my toes. Dr. Julie Allen needed a character cleansing.

"I'll think about the offer, but as of right now, my schedule is packed with taking pictures of hot guys."

Julie grinned as though my answer settled her nerves. I was too tired to say anything else.

Underneath the table, Forrest kept squeezing my hand. The strong mass of his palm made my small hand feel safe and secured. I extracted my hand from his grip and drew the word "trouble" on his thigh with my index finger.

He drew: "What time is sexy text appt?" Then he added a smile too close to my inner thigh. The tickle soon bloomed to arousal. The corners of his mouth inched up as he sensed the change in my body.

I didn't know if I had the energy for any sexy text exchange tonight. It might have to be postponed.

The waitress came and asked if anyone wanted dessert. We all declined. This entire situation was strange. It was like we were making out under the table while his ex-girlfriend glared at me.

When it was time to leave, David offered to give Julie a ride back to her hotel. She ignored me while she told Forrest to have a good night.

I told Forrest, "I took an Uber here. I can take one back."

"No, you're not," he said. "You had a cocktail. Let me be a gentleman by taking you home."

The look in his eyes told me he wanted something inappropriate, not gentlemanly at all. Heat flared in my core.

Inside his Tesla, he asked, "Since I'm already with you, there's no need for a sexy text appointment. We can reschedule that for another day. But I'd like to spend quality time with Dr. Sexy K tonight."

How many cars did he have? I'd seen him drive a Maserati and an Aston Martin in Providence. Remi, Royce, Grayson, and Arrow all had several cars. I supposed when you were a billionaire, you didn't have to worry about money and could spend it on cars as though they were toys.

"Yes, let's reschedule." I was too tired anyway. "My plan for the evening is to watch a movie. That's my diagnosis. If that sounds good to you, then okay."

"Works for me."

I leaned back in the seat, enjoying its comfort. "Don't you have other plans?"

"I did. But plans are adjustable. Being with you is an *urgent* matter I can't ignore. I'm in dire need, and my mind isn't functioning properly." He pulled into the parking lot. It had gotten dark, but at nine in the evening on a summer night, it wasn't extremely dark.

"I didn't realize I had a very sick patient." I laughed, taking out my key from my purse.

"Me either." He opened the door for me, took my hand, and walked me to my cabin.

I stared at our joined hands and had questions. It seemed like our relationship was developing faster than I expected. The sensor lights came on, casting a glow around the cabin and the porch.

I stepped onto the porch, and my heart raced. "Is that a dead raccoon?"

The large pool of blood appeared like a monster with angry red limbs reaching for me. I couldn't breathe, move, or say anything. Panic suffocated me, and the world spun. My body trembled as I blacked out.

CHAPTER NINETEEN

FORREST

Kiera collapsed into my arms, and I grabbed her keys before they fell to the floor. I unlocked the door, carried her inside, placed her on the couch, and positioned two throw pillows under her legs so they were above her heart level. Then I rushed to my car to retrieve the emergency kit I always had in my trunk.

The blood pressure machine showed her low blood pressure, which was a sign of unconsciousness. Her pulse felt fine, and she was breathing. She was cold, and I found a sheet to throw over her.

Panic had splashed across her face when she saw the dead animal. Did Kiera fear dead animals, or was it the sight of blood?

Who the fuck had left a carcass on the front door? Did this have anything to do with the attack? Or had a fox, coyote, or bear left the carcass? But something told me it hadn't been an animal who left the raccoon.

Kiera had to move to the hotel. If she didn't want to, I'd camp out here with her whether she liked it or not.

While she slept, I alerted the camp officials and the police, who said they'd send someone over to retrieve the dead animal. I walked outside with the flashlight on my phone, investigating the area surrounding the cabin. The night made it hard to see anything, and I didn't know what I was looking for.

Was the fucker still around?

I heard a noise by the large tree. "Who's there?" My fists clenched, ready to pound someone's face for making Kiera faint.

Hank stepped out in a tank top and shorts, looking frightened with a bruise on his face. "Is s-she okay?"

How did he know?

"Did you see something, Hank?"

Police lights flashed, but the sirens were off. Hank jumped at the sounds of slamming doors. Saying nothing, Hank rushed back to his cabin.

Detective Donnelly approached with Bruce. I relayed the incident and informed them Kiera was fine and that I was a doctor, monitoring her.

"It was probably Hank," Bruce said, looking toward Hank's cabin.

"Why do you say that?" I asked, watching another officer remove the carcass from the porch.

"He's strange. I've seen him play with dead squirrels. Should we talk to him?" He turned to Detective Donnelly.

"Based on the last incident, you should talk to him with his mother present," I said.

Had Hank seen the person? Or had he done it and felt guilty?

CHAPTER TWENTY

KIERA

Noises woke me, and I blinked, recognized my surroundings, and pushed myself up from the couch. The last thing I remembered was seeing that raccoon in the bloodbath before blackness swallowed me. I hadn't fainted in a long time. That was because I hadn't seen this much blood in a while. I tried my best to avoid seeing blood, which was why I hadn't had a physical in a while. My doctor's office had stopped calling me for appointments.

Did I bump my head on anything? I ran a hand over my head, my face, and my body. Nothing felt sore. I'd collapsed once and bumped my head on the edge of my sofa that had knocked me out for a while.

Who had left the dead animal on my doorstep? The poor thing.

Where was Forrest? I glanced out the window and saw the flashing lights. Did something happen to him?

I ambled over to the door, yanked it open, and jumped when Forrest stood before me.

He placed a hand on either side of my shoulders, examining me. "What are you doing up? You should rest and take it easy." He turned me around, guiding me back to the couch. "Sit."

Standing in front of me, he gripped my chin, lifting my face up to him. His touch made my skin sizzle.

"How are you feeling?" The concern in his eyes warmed me.

The way he looked at me differed from any other man. Was he seeing me as a patient in need of medical attention?

"I'm fine," I told him the truth.

He caressed my cheek with his thumb. "You're lucky I was with you. You could've hit your head or scratched up this exquisite face."

His voice was low, and his eyes darkened as he studied my face. Goosebumps bloomed on my arms. I was afraid he could make me want something too far-fetched. The men who had entered my life never stayed long. Their interest in me reflected my interest in them—something fun and temporary.

That had been the safe choice back then—date a hot guy for a few months, have great sex, let the passion fizzle, and move on with my life. No strings attached meant no trouble. Temporary meant I didn't delve deep into my heart or face my flaws. But now I wanted something long-term. That was my wish, but maybe he wanted something fun and short term.

I couldn't afford any heartache or getting lost in some fantasy. My mom needed me. Reality was where I needed to be instead of a dreamland that would only end.

"I've fainted before." I shrugged. "It's nothing unusual. I feel fine."

Still looking worried, he folded himself on the couch beside me. The cushion dipped, causing my hips to fall against his.

He shifted to face me. "Want to tell me why you fainted?" Warmth emanated from his eyes. "I want to help you."

Was I ready to share it? It wasn't a big deal. The two other people who knew about my blood phobia were Mom and Audri. Audri only found out because she'd witnessed my panic when we were hanging out on a beach and the kid beside us had a bloody nose.

Everyone had fears. We all dealt with them differently. I ignored my hemophobia because I didn't know what else to do. Therapy didn't work for these kinds of things. It was a mental block that needed time to resolve. I was just waiting for its time to be up.

"What happened to the carcass? What did the police say?"

"The carcass is gone. Your porch is clean. The police will investigate. Now stop trying to dodge my question."

For some stupid reason, I was nervous about telling him. What if he thought I was weak? What if he diagnosed me with something worse than hemophobia? I couldn't afford any treatments right now.

"It's nothing serious, Forrest. There's no need for you to be concerned. I'm sure you have plenty of patients to take care of."

"Actually, I don't. I'm only a part-time immunologist. Besides, you're my priority patient right now."

"Then what do you do with your free time?"

He arched an eyebrow. "My $Ba_7M_5Bu_{88}$ Project, video games, and holistic medicine development and other investments that interest me." He tapped my nose. "And I'm very interested in you. Now stop stalling. *Tell me.*"

I'd just recovered from a drop in blood pressure, so I shouldn't be this aroused. My body shouldn't be able to shift from one extreme to another. My lady parts yearned for him.

As an attempt to distract my body from being aroused, I said, "You might see me differently."

"We all have fears and issues, Kiera. I'm a doctor, but I'm still human. That means I have flaws too. I want to know about your blood aversion. How did it start? When did it start? What are your symptoms? Have you gotten help? Has it gotten worse over the years or stayed the same?"

I smiled at the flood of questions. "I never thought I'd be attracted to a nerd."

"I'm always attracted to a beautiful woman with a brilliant mind, a kind heart, with a collection of schemes to take out her enemy in the subtlest way."

"I don't know what you're talking about." My lips twisted into a smirk as I looked everywhere but at his knowing eyes.

"Yes, you do. Julie didn't know who she was dealing with when she challenged you. I could see the wheels in your head churning at dinner. Want to share what you were thinking?"

"No. Because I don't want you to be called to the stand as a witness for any crime," I teased. "I'm only thinking of your wellbeing."

"You're so thoughtful . . . so *devious*. That's sexy. That's my kind of girl." A wide smile spread across his face, making him more attractive than minutes ago.

He saw me in ways other men never did. I could almost feel my heart blossoming layer by layer.

"It's late. Shouldn't you go back to your hotel? We can discuss this another time."

"I'm not going anywhere tonight until you tell me what I need to know."

"Fine. You asked for it. It could be a long night, BaMBu Beast." I jabbed a finger, mimicking the three syllables of the nickname into his hard chest.

"You're the only one allowed to call me that. That project is important to me. You give the T-shirt and my mission more meaning."

How was I supposed to react to that?

I leaned back into the couch because I might pass out

retelling the story. Inhaling a deep breath, I released it slowly, making room for whatever emotions would emerge.

"This might help." He placed a throw pillow in my lap. Then he leaned back into the couch, propping his long legs onto the coffee table, looking too comfortable.

I didn't know why, but the casual gesture eased my nerves.

"Thanks," I said and told him my story.

"Mommy, can we eat first? I'm hungry." I skip along the sidewalk, happy that I'll be starting second grade in two weeks and three days. Yup, I've been counting.

Today is Mom's day off from work, so she's taking me shopping at the Providence Place, a mall with a bunch of stores. We're taking a break for lunch and will do some more shopping later. She already bought me two Chococat T-shirts and matching shorts.

Mom's a nurse at the Alliance Hospital. Sometimes she takes me in to work to meet her friends, and they give me yummy crackers.

"Wanna go to Food & Fun?" Mommy asks as she carries the shopping bag.

"Yes, please!" I love their grilled cheese and fries. "Can I get the strawberry shake too?"

Mom wraps an arm around my shoulder. "Anything for you." She pulls me in for a big hug.

"I love you, Mommy." I beam and hug her tighter.

She taps my head. "Love you more."

A little boy runs past us, laughing. A girl with pigtails chases after him.

"Slow down, kids!" their father warns.

I wince as they almost bump into a deliveryman pushing a big cart on the sidewalk. The kids run back to their mom and dad.

The dad ruffles the boy's head. "Be careful. There's a lot of people around. Don't want you getting hurt."

"Okay." The boy pokes at his sister, and she pokes him back. They giggle loudly.

My chest hurts. Would my dad love me the way this dad loves his kids? I don't know what it feels like. What does my dad look like? Why doesn't he want me and Mom?

Mom says she and Dad broke up before I was born. It makes me sad sometimes, but I have the best mom in the world.

We walk up to the crosswalk, and I press the button, waiting for the walk signal to appear. It's a bright and sunny day, and I can't wait to stop by more stores after lunch. Mom says she's going to buy me dresses, a new backpack, and a pair of sneakers that light up when I step. Some kids at my school have them. They're so cool.

The walk sign appears with the countdown. "Mommy. Let's go!"

A big truck flies past us and whams into a car. Boom! The loud noise makes me jump. The car flips a few times, and my heart pounds as two bodies are tossed out of the car.

I freeze from the scary accident.

Mom takes me to a nearby bench. "Stay here so I can see you. Don't go anywhere. I need to help them." She gives me the shopping bag to hold.

I nod and sit while Mom speaks into her phone and rushes to help the two people on the ground. There were two other people in the car, but they look asleep. The man from the truck is on the phone, looking stressed as people crowd around him.

So much stuff is happening. Noises from people crying and cars honking echo around me. But then the ruckus stops when I see the blood pooling from the boy and the woman. My body shakes as the pools of blood grow. The red is so bright in the sun. I try to look away, but I can't.

There's so much blood. It's so red. Are they okay? Tears fall down my cheeks. I don't know why I'm crying. I can't move my hands to wipe my tears. I'm scared for them.

Mommy can help them. She's a great nurse. She always makes me feel better when I'm sick. The boy and the woman will be all right.

I should close my eyes, but they won't listen to me. My eyes stay on the boy with blood surrounding him. Mom checks the woman, and she looks sad as she turns her attention to the boy. There's blood all over my mom too. She's wiping the boy's face with her hand.

I don't know why, but I walk over and give my mom the bag of clothes. "Use this, Mommy."

Mom looks up at me with tears in her eyes and nods. She uses my Chococat shirt and presses it into a cut on the side of his head.

I stare at the injured boy and the woman. She has scratches on her face and arm.

Blood is everywhere. My shoes have blood on them. I shiver as the blood darkens like it wants to crawl up my legs. Something's wrong with my body. I don't know why my legs are wobbling. I try to call for my mom, but no words come out. She looks blurry. Everything looks blurry. I can't hear any sounds. Everything spins, making me nauseous.

The pool of blood looks like a giant monster that gets bigger and bigger. I'm so scared. Then everything spins and turns sideways. I can feel the monster pulling me toward it.

I hear my mom calling my name as the blood monster pulls me into its bloody blackness.

I didn't know I was crying until Forrest dabs my eyes with a tissue.

"Thank you." I took the tissue from his hand and finished the job.

A relief settled in me, allowing me to breathe easier as though sharing this traumatic experience opened up space inside me.

My mom knew I'd developed an aversion to blood, but she didn't know the extent of my fear. Not wanting her to worry, I'd kept it from her.

"So now you know." I felt embarrassed. "This fear has kept me from going to the doctor's office. I hate getting my blood drawn. Closing my eyes never helps."

"How do you react to seeing a drop of blood? What are your symptoms?" There was so much understanding on his face that my embarrassment faded.

"Usually a slight chill runs through me, but that's it. The big trigger is seeing a lot of blood. I think my body remembers that event. I can't seem to remove it from my head."

"Maybe you were meant to remember it," he said in a low voice as his finger caressed my cheek, making me shiver.

It baffled me how he could shift my body's mood so easily.

"Is that your analysis, Dr. Navarro?" I teased, unsure of what he meant. Nobody suffering from a phobia or trauma would agree with that reasoning. "Are you saying that based on proven research? How am I meant to remember that devastating event?"

"No." Forrest stared at me, looking into me as though he wanted to jump into my mind and experience my pain firsthand. That was my fuzzy brain interpreting the way his sage eyes shifted. What was he thinking?

"Do you think I'm weak for not overcoming that fear after all these years?"

"You're anything but weak, Kiera. You were a child who witnessed a life-and-death situation. Trauma changes a child's mind and his or her perception of the world. I can attest to that."

I wanted to ask him what he meant, but he kissed me on the lips, and all thoughts scattered elsewhere. Though it wasn't a passionate kiss, it made me warm inside. Heat swirled in places that shouldn't be aroused right now.

When he drew away, empathy and something I couldn't identify swam in his eyes. "Thank you for listening. I feel better talking about it. That event changed my life."

"That moment changed my life too," he said.

CHAPTER TWENTY-ONE

KIERA

"What do you mean?" I asked.

Was he trying to be poetic by saying he felt my suffering? His expression was something I'd never seen on Forrest. Pain and vulnerability were rare on this man, who normally portrayed a powerful and magnetic exterior. I'd noticed him whenever we hung with our mutual friends. How could any woman ignore a package like that? He was like a warrior fighting an endless battle.

The intensity in his eyes made me think about the power of an interesting photograph, where it could pull you into its story simply by being itself.

"I should thank the owner of the Chococat T-shirt for comforting me that day."

No way.

I sucked in a breath, trying to absorb his words. "That little boy . . . was *you?* From the accident?"

He asked me about the date, and I rattled it off. I remembered it vividly because the following day I had a birthday party, but I never went to it because I'd been too traumatized.

"My mother died that day." The corner of his eye twitched. *Oh my God.*

"I'm so sorry about your mom."

What were the chances? Fate was an indescribable wonder. Sometimes I cursed it, and other times, I relished in it. Right now I wasn't sure how I should react to fate for connecting me to Forrest. Part of me loved the idea of meeting him when I'd been a child. But the other part wished it had been under better circumstances.

Would I have remembered him if I had met him at a playground? Would he have stood out to me? I didn't know.

I threw my arms around him as though I was hugging the injured boy from my memory.

He tightened his arms around me, and we stayed like that for a while. Our heartbeats spoke to each other while questions formed in my head.

"You witnessed my trauma, Kiera." He ran a hand down my hair, comforting me when I should be the one comforting him.

If I had been traumatized by seeing it, how had he experienced it as the boy who had gotten hurt—the boy who had lost his mother. It must have been worse for him.

Unlike me, who feared blood from that incident, he became a doctor.

Drawing back, I studied his face. "Did you become a doctor because of what happened?"

"No." He tucked a loose strand of hair behind my ear. "But it motivated me to work even harder."

"Where was your dad during that time?"

"He died when I was six."

I couldn't imagine losing two parents. I had more questions, but I didn't think he wanted to discuss it. If he had wanted to elaborate, he would've said something already. Taking the hint,

I didn't inquire further. There was only room for so much trauma tonight.

"Your T-shirt stopped my bleeding. I owe Chococat immense gratitude. I'll buy you all the T-shirts you want."

My heart flapped. "I'm too old for that now."

"Never too old to love what makes you remember your childhood, right?"

I had Chococat stationery and pens at my apartment, but I wasn't going to share that.

Thinking about the other people from the accident, I asked, "Were your grandmother and Yolanda seriously hurt too?" I noticed the scar on the side of his neck. "Is this from the accident?"

Nodding, his lips tilted at the corner. "You're acting like my Dr. Sexy K."

"I'm being serious." I swatted his chest and realized I'd somehow gotten onto his lap, straddling him. Had it been the hug? I didn't remember anything except embracing him.

I tried to wriggle free and return to my seat on the couch, but his hands gripped my hips in place. His thighs widened, and my butt settled into him even more. His hard length was proudly prominent against me.

"Don't go." He gave my hips a squeeze. "You're perfectly fine here, Kitty K. That's my new pet name for you now that I know you're the owner of the Chococat T-shirt." His eyes gleamed with mischief, reminding me of our time in his hotel room. There had been a lot of friskiness that night.

"I thought I was Dr. Sexy K."

"You're that and more." There was a wealth of promise in his husky voice. "Dr. Sexy K is the naughty version of you that can make me come via text. Kitty K is the frisky woman who will show me all kinds of misconduct in bed." His fingers skipped up and down my spine, igniting a fire that grew too fast.

How could a serious conversation about trauma end up like this? I had questions about his grandmother and Yolanda, but the desire in his eyes pushed those thoughts aside for now.

"You're just BaMBu Beast to me."

His eyes focused on me intently. "The only beast, right?"

I ground my hips in a circle, feeling his arousal increase. "Maybe."

The smile faded, and his jaw tightened. With two hands, he cupped my butt and thrust his hips forward. His cock slammed against my shorts as a feverish urgency lit up his eyes.

"I don't share, Kiera." His mouth crushed mine, and his tongue speared through, lashing mine.

"Neither do I," I panted as I tugged at his shirt, untucking it from his pants.

"No strings attached." His eyes locked with mine. "Just sex. While you're sleeping with me, there's no one else. Understand?"

My long-term idea was pushed aside for now as need and passion overwhelmed me, making me disregard my set of rules. I smiled, neither agreeing nor disagreeing. "Stop talking and fuck me."

He gave me a wicked grin. "That's what I've been wanting all night."

I palmed his bulge, and the heat singed my hand. A sly smile crept onto his face as he removed my T-shirt and bra. My breasts spilled out on his hands, and my nipples peaked. "God, I've missed them."

He stroked my aching nipple with his tongue. Sensations swirled, and I couldn't think or talk or breathe. When he sucked on a nipple, energy zipped through me, and my back arched, offering him more of me. His sexy mouth adored my breasts by licking, sucking, and pulling at my nipples with incredible skills. My head fell back as the bliss rolled through me.

A loud moan escaped me. Was that even my voice? Or was that his?

His mouth left my breasts, moving up to kiss me again. Then he dragged it along my jaw and scored the column of my neck. He smelled of cedar, musk, a hint of citrus, and earth—a man of endurance, freedom, cultivation, and preservation. He was like the conservation land that was protected by some sacred force of nature. In his existence, he offered more than he realized. My heart quivered as his lips pressed to the pulse pounding on my neck. He sucked the spot, and I whimpered in satisfaction.

I felt my body shift as his hands supported my ass. "I'm going to fuck you all night. Purr for me, Kitty K."

I was already purring for him now. Somehow he carried me to the bedroom as though I were feather-light. One powerful arm wrapped around my back, while the other supported my ass. My legs tightened around his waist as my arms looped around his neck.

"I've got a frisky ailment, doctor. Please help me." I nipped his earlobe.

"And I've got the perfect remedy for you." A devious smile appeared on his face as he tossed me on to the bed and yanked off my shorts and underwear. "I'm going to spoil you with my tongue."

I watched as his clothes dropped to the floor to join mine. His body was gorgeous, and I held a breath to take him in.

"Wait." I held a hand over my heart. "Don't move. I need to stare."

During our time at the hotel, I didn't have time to appreciate this godly body. He was built with broad shoulders, well-defined pecs and biceps, and an abdomen that could make a slab of stone jealous. Not fair at all. His muscular legs looked unreal. How could anyone have distinct muscles on such long legs?

I crooked a finger at him. "Come here. I need to examine something."

He arched an eyebrow, but stepped toward me anyway. I ran a hand over his thigh and squeezed. "Okay, they're real. You have legs that belong on a warrior, not a doctor."

A laugh bubbled from him. "Says who?"

"Says Kitty K. She's seen many muscular legs, and your legs —your body—could win epic battles."

"I plan on giving you an epic adventure tonight." He leaned down, placing a hand on either side of my shoulders, while his gaze seared my sex.

My eyes were on his remarkable erection. It was thick, throbbing, and thrilling. It perked like a warrior in its own right. The heavens gifted me with this gorgeous man, and my sex contracted, remembering how it had filled me.

"Great minds think alike." My hand gripped his cock, and the heat spread into my palm.

When I stroked, he sucked in a breath and straightened to his full height, which made him a spectacular spectacle for my lustful eyes. As I pumped his rod, he gasped, and his chest heaved. I loved how his erection reacted to my touch, and I stroked harder and faster.

"Slow down, Kitty K," he demanded between gritted teeth.

I wasn't in the mood to obey, so I ignored his order and tightened my grip, pumping faster.

"Fuck, Kiera," he moaned. "You don't listen. You're going to get punished."

I loved seeing what I did to him, how I affected him. My

other hand played with his balls, and his body jerked, letting out another curse.

"You have a filthy mouth, doctor."

The vein on his neck pulsed, and I knew he was on the edge. Though he stood like a god, I could make him weak. That made me feel powerful.

A drop of moisture appeared at the tip, and I bent down to lick it off. He sucked in a breath as my tongue circled his crown.

"Fuck, you're killing me." He gasped. "I ordered you to stop. You didn't listen. Now you're gonna get it."

I bit my bottom lip, loving the threat. Licking my lips in a slow motion, I taunted, "Show me."

He shoved me down onto my back, pinning my wrists above my head. "There's a special treatment for misbehaving patients."

His body pressed against mine as he devoured my mouth. Our tongues clashed, and my hips bucked, loving the way his cock brushed my sex with each contact. I felt helpless with my wrists being banded by his powerful grip. I loved that I was at his mercy. His other hand slid down my body, spread my legs wider, and found my center.

"I knew you'd be wet for me." He growled as a finger parted my slit and entered. "God, I love the way you feel." He added a second finger, thrusting hard and fast.

Liquid heat burst in me as he continued to tease my body with his skilled fingers. He hooked his long fingers in my channel, and I moaned his name. My body writhed from the seductive examination.

I met his eyes as his fingers plundered into me with a rhythm that shot heat and pleasure coursing all over my body. The sounds of his fingers entering me, along with our heavy breathing, became a provocative meditation that soothed and electrified.

When his fingers slowed, I begged, "More."

He pulled his fingers out of my throbbing core, leaving me yearning for their return.

"Evil!" I protested.

Offering a wolfish smile, he lifted his fingers to his mouth, tasted me, and released a raspy moan. "You're just as delicious as I remembered."

How long had he been lusting for me? Did that one night change him the way it had changed me? More thoughts formed in my head, but vanished when he lowered his face, lifted my legs above his shoulders, and blew at my sex.

"My beautiful Kiera, I'm going to take my time with you tonight," he said, while kissing my inner thigh.

When he pressed his lips to my straining sex, my muscles tightened, and my body jerked. He secured my hips with his hands while his tongue discovered me with meticulous precision, making me dizzy. I knew he had skillful hands and fingers, but his tongue? It was a magical tool. He licked between my folds, and pleasure rose, blinding me. I wanted to surrender to the explosive sensation, but I wanted to see him. *Needed* to see him.

I shoved onto my elbows, and the sight of his handsome face between my thighs almost made me come. He met my gaze, and he flattened his tongue, licking me up and down. "This is mine. Every inch of it."

Then he sucked my throbbing bud. The decadent pulls sent a powerful burst through my body. My legs trembled from its force, and I felt an impending orgasm.

"You taste so good, baby. I could eat you all night." The long, greedy strokes of his tongue intensified, and I braced for a massive orgasm.

My inner muscles pulsed with greedy desire, and my fingers tugged at his hair. He fluttered his tongue over my bud and slid two fingers into me. The combination of everything tossed me over the edge. The orgasm tore through me, my hips shooting off the bed, and pressed into his mouth.

"I love how you come on my tongue, baby. I can feel your orgasm." He growled and continued licking me through the bone-shattering release.

CHAPTER TWENTY-TWO

FORREST

She tasted like a secret remedy I'd been searching for—the perfect antibody to the virus threatening my soul. Sweet, tangy, and savory just for me.

What the fuck are you talking about?

Since when had I waxed poetic while having sex? This woman was turning me to mush.

The first time with her at the hotel had been sensational, but this time was *extraordinary*. Unmatchable. Cosmic. Being with her took me to another world, and I relished the thrill.

What made tonight even better was the desire growing between us since that one night.

That fate had linked us together when we were kids made it even more special. It was all leading us to this moment—a slow burn that eventually became a bonfire we couldn't resist.

That first time was merely passionate fun. Tonight's union was an intoxicating slow burn that blazed through my body, one cell at a time. The power of it alone could probably eliminate the world's deadliest diseases.

I wanted to know every secret of her body and remember

all the details. She had a cute freckle on her inner thigh and two on her left butt cheek. With a kiss and suck, I also made them mine. One night with Kiera was never an option, but I settled for a no-strings-attached relationship because it made things simple between us. I had baggage that was better left in the dark. She didn't need to be close to danger around me. Keeping this physical was the best solution for the both of us.

Then why did it feel off? And why did my chest hurt?

I didn't want to think about it anymore. I just wanted to enjoy this woman who had affected me more than any other woman I'd been with.

"Forrest," she moaned, her hands fisted into the bedsheets.

Her body still trembled from the orgasm I'd felt on my tongue. It was a mini earthquake and the most beautiful sensation I'd ever sensed.

"Yes, baby?" I swirled my tongue against her swollen bud, and she writhed.

"You got a doctorate degree in giving orgasms?" She breathed. "I think you just singed all my internal organs. I can't move my body." The blissful look mesmerized me, and I wanted to see that look on her over and over again. It was my mission to achieve that.

"That's the idea. My sex degree only applies to you."

She looked at me, and I could see the doubt in her eyes before she dropped back down to the bed. I didn't like how she thought I was tossing out meaningless words to her.

"I mean it." To prove it, I lifted her ass up and ravaged all of her, licking and sucking until she cried out my name again.

"Oh, God, Forrest! You're a maniac!" Her entire body quivered, and I swore I could tell when the orgasm started and descended. I was beginning to understand her body, moans, and sighs.

"I've never wanted anyone the way I want you, Kiera." I licked and loved every drop of moisture from her.

She had no clue how she'd affected me. Her scent and her taste had seared into my blood—into my cellular structure. She had penetrated my mind in unimaginable ways, and that analogy was the best way to describe it.

The way she gasped out my name in ecstasy did something strange to me. Her moans were magical cures for any man in pain. Kiera could make me forget my problems. I could fuck her all night just to exist in a better world.

Needing to see her face, I rose over her, adoring the woman beneath me.

"You're a beast in bed." She purred and cupped my face, yanking my mouth to hers, and kissed me like a lioness in heat.

Our tongues collided in a seductive tango. She sucked my tongue while her nails scored down my back. I craved the bite of her nails on my skin. She was branding me with her signature.

"My cock is begging to be inside you."

"I'm waiting." She nipped at my lip, opening her thighs wider.

I rose from my position between her thighs and clasped my throbbing cock, stroking it.

She stared at me, her lips opened, and she swiped her bottom lip with her tongue. I wanted her mouth on me, but that had to wait. I wanted to come inside her tonight.

I reached for a condom in my wallet, which was in my pants pocket on the floor. With swiftness, I rolled on the condom and paused a moment to take in her beauty. The sated look, the swollen lips from my kiss, the full breasts still pebbled from arousal, and the alluring center with the swollen bud painted her a goddess in bed.

I positioned the crown of my cock at her entrance and teased her.

"Don't be mean," she said.

I plunged into her and watched her face. She let out a groan as her muscles tightened around me.

Tonight meant more to me than I could ever explain. Beneath me was a woman who had been present on the day my mother died. She'd seen me injured on the ground and had offered her T-shirt to help me. Because of me, she'd developed a trauma that still haunted her. I'd do everything in my power to heal that part of her. With each thrust, I wanted to erase her pain and fill her with love and wonder.

She tightened her inner channel, and I drove in harder, the pressure intensifying with every second. "Look at me."

Our eyes connected and held. I pumped and pumped, watching the pleasure play out on her face.

"You're a wild animal, Forrest." She moaned, arching her hips into me. "I love it."

With one mighty thrust, the tension snapped, and the orgasm exploded and ricocheted through me. It tore me into a million pieces of blissful agony of wanting more. *Holy fuck.* The growl that came out sounded like a wild beast. I'd never made that kind of barbaric sound before.

My body trembled as she smiled with darkened eyes. I took a few moments to gather my brain cells. When my body connected to other parts of me, I brushed the beads of sweat from her face and kissed her on the forehead. I pulled out and rushed into the bathroom to clean up.

I brought her a towel to clean her up, and she smirked. "Definitely a beast."

Tossing the towel aside, I gathered her into my arms. "You bring out the beast in me. How are you feeling?"

"A lot better, thank you." She rested her head on my shoulder, and warmth blossomed in me.

We stayed in bed chatting about mostly nothing. This was new to me. I didn't enjoy conversation with other women I'd been with and usually fell asleep after the deed was done. But with Kiera, I wanted more of her. To understand her.

I discovered she loved to eat strawberries and chocolate ice cream. Her favorite color was green, and she loved to watch romantic movies and weird documentaries. And of course, Chococat.

I didn't understand why we hadn't connected sooner. Perhaps that was how the universe worked. We all had our own lives to live, and certain things occurred at their own time. She'd been busy with her endeavors and I with mine. I'd suppressed my attraction to her because I knew she dated male supermodels. How pathetic was that?

As though understanding my thoughts, she looked up at me and tugged at my hair. "I've only seen you with short hair before. Why the long hair now?"

I sniffed her hair. *Christ.* What was wrong with me? When had I cared about the smell of hair? Kiera had a scent I loved.

"So you've noticed me." I played with a lock of her long, brown hair.

"Of course, I have." Her hand slid down to my abdomen, kneading it. "But I knew your type. You've only dated nurses, doctors, or girls from wealthy families. I'm none of those. But I enjoy looking at pretty things, and that's what I did."

"You preferred male models. Most of them have long hair," I confessed.

She blinked, sat up in bed, and dragged the sheet to cover herself. I smiled at the modesty given what I'd just done to her.

"You grew your hair out for *me*?" She studied me keenly. "Really?"

Hearing her say it out loud made the reason sound ridiculous. Had I changed my looks because of her?

Fuuuck.

"I got lazy and canceled my hair appointments." I dismissed it with a wave of my hand.

Laughing, she raked a hand through my hair, ruffling it.

"Oh yeah? I can't see you as the forgetful type." She styled my hair with her fingers. "You have a gorgeous head of dark brown hair. It makes me feel special that I inspired this look."

Kiera tilted her head, studying me. "The shaggy style looks good on you." She kissed my cheek. "But I also love the clean-cut look. You look fabulous regardless of what style you choose. You're the hottest nerd I know."

Her words blazed through me like sunshine on the Equator, irrevocably searing.

I flipped her onto her back, loving her softness against my body. "Are you saying you'll still find me attractive if I'm bald?"

I nuzzled her neck, inhaling her floral scent.

She giggled and squeezed my cock, rubbing her thumb over the crown. "I find *him* extremely handsome, and he's bald." He twitched, loving her touch.

"I can fuck you all night." I brushed her hair away from her face and studied her gorgeous features. Those brown eyes could see into me, and those lips were made for me. "How are you feeling? Still dizzy from fainting? I'll help you fight the fear."

"Thank you." She offered a warm smile. "I'm dizzy from the orgasms. I don't remember anything about today other than them." She pinched my ass playfully.

There was one question that never left my brain since our first night together. "Did you faint that night at the hotel and then wake up? Was that why you left suddenly?" Maybe she hadn't wanted me to see her in a vulnerable light.

She twisted her lips. "Are we going to talk about this now?"

"We have to, Kiera. It's been bothering me."

Resigned, she touched my face delicately. "It has nothing to do with you. That night with you was unforgettable. You ruined me for other men."

Joy burst in me. "Then my deed is done. I can die a happy man." I buried my face in her throat, wanting to feel her pulse. "You ruined me for other women too."

"We're each other's ruination . . . a destruction so that something new can be built."

I cupped her face in my hands. "I love that mind of yours. So if I wasn't the problem, what happened?"

"I got an urgent call that my mom was admitted to the hospital. Her health took a nosedive during that time. She's my only family, so I left. I didn't want to wake you. It wasn't your problem."

If anyone knew what it felt like to have a family member ill or on their deathbed, it was me.

"I'm sorry to hear that. Why didn't you contact me after?"

"I was scared." She chewed on her bottom lip. "I'd never had a one-night stand before, Forrest. It was a detour from my normal dating routine. So that was something I had to come to terms with, and the stress of my mom's health made it worse. I assumed we both got what we wanted that night, and that was that." She paused for breath and looked at me. "You didn't reach out to me either."

"I had a lot going on too. I had to deal with an old enemy. Besides, I'd assumed you weren't interested, so I dropped the idea even though I couldn't stop thinking about you."

"What kind of enemy? Do you have a lot of enemies in business? The medical field?"

Fuck. I hadn't meant to share that detail. She'd been so honest with me, I forgot I had to filter my answers regarding my personal vendetta. The second enemy I'd been after was caught the day after we'd hooked up. Like her, my mind had been on other things. Despite that, I didn't want her anywhere near the darkness surrounding me. She was too bright and innocent for that kind of world.

I had to craft an answer that was the truth, but also kept her safe.

"It doesn't matter what field you're in. Success comes with enemies." I smoothed out her hair. "We've lost so much from assumptions. Let's not do that anymore, okay? I want you to share anything that concerns you with me."

"Same here." A hint of sadness gleamed in her eyes. It wasn't my intention to ruin the mood for tonight.

A question swam in her eyes, but she didn't ask.

"I'll share everything with you." I kissed her. "My mind has filthy plans for you tonight. After that, I want you to tell me about your mom's illness. Maybe I can shed some light and help you understand it better."

"Thank you." Her face lit up. "I've been meaning to ask for your opinion."

"The only pressure I want you to feel is this . . ." I palmed her sex and slid my finger into her. "I'm taking advantage of a sexy patient waiting for me."

She tickled my ribs. "No, it's my turn. I want to take advantage of you. You've got some booboos here." She ran her finger down my length, and I shivered as my sense of control slipped away.

I tried my best to form coherent sentences. "Please take care of it, Dr. Sexy K."

For the rest of the night, Kiera showed me how talented she was from the way her hand, mouth, and tongue "took care" of me.

CHAPTER TWENTY-THREE

KIERA

The following day, after I finished the swimwear shoot, I returned to my cabin wondering how people survived in the constant heat and humidity. Even though I wore a tank top and shorts, the heat still got to me.

Or maybe it was the thoughts about last night that kept swirling in my head. Forrest had stayed overnight and woken up early to rush back to his hotel for a conference call. I smiled, remembering all the things we did to each other. Our relationship had shifted last night. It was now at a dangerous place for me. We were more than friends, but not a couple. A couple meant commitment. A couple meant attachments—all the things that fell into my dream of a long-term relationship.

But he specifically wanted a "no-strings" engagement. For now, I was okay with that. As long as I kept my heart tucked away, I should be fine, right?

When I reached my cabin, I saw Forrest sitting on the step of my porch. He rose and walked over to me, wrapping his arms around me.

"What are you doing here? I thought you had work today."

"I did." He drew back, staring at me. "Things got delegated or shifted because I couldn't stop thinking about you."

Something beautiful and warm spread inside me like a sunrise that brightened everything. I sensed the heat blooming on my cheeks.

He rubbed a thumb over my cheek and made me blush even more. "Don't be shy. I love this reaction from you."

Couldn't a girl feel embarrassed in private? I swatted his hand away.

Smiling, he said, "Let's go. You should bring your camera."

"Why? Where are we going?" I asked as I zipped the camera into the bag, then entered my cabin to retrieve my purse.

He followed me. "It's a surprise." The spark in his eyes told me he was up to something mischievous.

As he drove the Tesla out of the campground, I studied his profile. Gorgeous. He wore an aqua T-shirt with ripped jeans. His hair was tousled with casual sexiness, and my heart melted as I took him in.

"Are you done staring?" he asked, keeping his attention on the road.

"No." I smiled. "By the way, I spoke to my mom. She's going to get me copies of her health records and diagnosis. When she emails me, I'll forward it all to you."

"Thank you."

"No, thank *you*." I touched his arm. "It means a lot to me."

He turned and smiled. "I told you, I don't want to see you stressed. Besides, your mom helped me and my family on that fateful day. This is nothing."

If I were alone in the cabin, I'd sit and think about life's mysteries and interconnectedness. No one could plan their life the way God did. It made me wonder if everyone's lives were predestined. Maybe we were all given a broad map when we were born, and we got to fill in the details like an artist coloring it in.

Being with Forrest made me think deeper about my life, and the more I thought about things, the more I wanted the forever that romance novels promised. I stole a glance at him.

Would he want that with me?

You already know, so stop wanting the impossible.

I shut off the annoying voice, switching my attention back to the moment. "Can you give me a clue to where we're going?"

"Why don't you just sit back and enjoy the ride?"

"You're being cryptic, so my curious mind wants to know. Is that okay?" Irritation from my inner thoughts flowed into my voice.

He gave me a doubtful look. "Why the sudden mood change?"

I didn't want him to know. "No mood change, just extreme curiosity."

"I don't want to ruin the surprise by telling you. You might develop an image in your head from now until we get there and destroy the power of a first impression."

His smile was liberating, brighter than a sunny day. I'd never seen him smile like that before. The irritation melted away knowing the happiness on his face was because of me.

"All of that information ran through your head?" I asked.

"Your mind churns through the same complexity. Most women's minds do. Drives the men crazy."

"I thought men like women who drive them crazy."

"I can't speak for other men, but *you* drive me insane, Kitty K." He walked his fingers up my thigh, and a different heat zinged through me.

We were acting like a couple, and I was having fun with

him. I tried not to think about wanting more. I didn't need more confusion muddling my brain.

"Here's a hint," he said.

My eyes widened. "What is it?"

"Mushrooms." His lips slanted into a smirk.

CHAPTER TWENTY-FOUR

KIERA

I quirked an eyebrow, still unsure of what he'd planned.

"Mushrooms. Just trying to be your 'fun guy.'"

"Are you serious?" My shoulders shook from laughing.

"Of course," he said with a straight face. "I don't joke around when it comes to your perversion about my body."

I couldn't believe he remembered our conversation when we'd taken a moment to cuddle before the third round of sex. We'd talked about how nature mimicked human anatomy, and I called him a "fun guy," showing him an image of a mushroom that looked like a penis. Then I showed him an image of a Peter pepper, which looked more like a penis than the mushroom did.

I'd never had these kinds of conversations in my other relationships. It was intimate, weird, and nerdy at the same time. But with him, it felt right.

"I'm afraid of what's waiting for me," I said with a smile.

"You're the first woman to compare me to a mushroom, so I take that to heart. What I'm about to show you is something special to me, and something you already love."

When I met his gaze, I expected sarcasm, but only sincerity greeted me. What could he possibly plan to show me?

He drove down the street, with no homes or buildings in sight. Woods lined both sides of the street. The car turned down another road where garden beds were being cared for by several people wearing sunhats and aprons. Beyond the garden, fields of crops spread into the distance. Several windmills stood like guardians in the fields. A massive building—or a fancy warehouse—with reflective glass gleamed in the sun.

Forrest pulled into a paved parking lot beside several cars. He got out and opened the door for me.

"You're taking me to visit a *farm?*" I got out, glancing around.

"Because you have 'farm girl' written all over you." He winked, knowing full well I wouldn't last a day working on a farm. I didn't have a yard at my apartment. A few potted plants on my balcony didn't make me a gardener, never mind a farmer.

Forrest placed his hand on my lower back, guiding me to a garden full of little flowers. A man from a delivery truck dropped off two boxes by a vegetable garden bed with other boxes stacked on a palette. He waited for the employee to sign the document and left.

An older Asian man wearing a straw hat and an apron came up to us, offering an infectious smile. "Mr. Navarro. What a surprise!" He spoke with a slight accent.

Forrest patted him on the shoulder. "Call me Forrest, Hieu. It's good to see you. This is Kiera."

"Glad to meet you, Kiera." He held my hand with his two hands, and I could feel his rough palms.

Hieu turned to Forrest. "Your friend is pretty."

"She is." Forrest smiled and asked, "How's Trang?"

"Doing great. She's visiting our grandkids in California. I'll join her in a few days. I wanted to prep the ginseng before I go. The bamboos are flourishing. The mushrooms are doing wonderful too. Let me show you their progress."

"You should've gone with her. There's plenty of help here."

"I know. But this is family to me too." He threw his hands out. "It saved me and my wife."

Forrest sighed. "I appreciate the hard work, but I want my employees to take care of themselves too. Take care of your family because you never know when it'll be their last day." He followed Hieu over to a shed with flourishing seedlings.

An image of the car accident flashed through my mind. Forrest's past had shaped him to be a leader who had compassion for his workers. He had lost his parents at a young age, and that trauma could either make a person bitter at the world or give them empathy. I liked seeing this side of him. He wasn't just focused on profits, but the people who helped him gain those profits.

Glancing around the other sheds, I noticed a world of mushrooms. I walked over and browsed the various beds.

"What do you think?" Forrest stood beside me while Hieu assisted a worker with something.

"Amazing. What's this mushroom?" I pointed to a section set apart from the others.

"The Lingzhi, also known as the reishi mushroom. It has fantastic medicinal properties."

It looked different from the pictures I saw online. "What about the Venus Flytrap?" I inquired.

"The juices from the pressed fresh plant stimulate the immune system."

All of this fascinated me.

Forrest noticed Hieu lifting something heavy, shouted for him to stop, and walked over. A younger employee intercepted before Forrest could take over.

While the men discussed something, I admired the mushrooms and other oddities. Crouching, I snapped pictures of the mushrooms and the other plants with my phone. I spotted a rack full of Venus flytraps, a plant that looked like a mouth with teeth. I didn't know this plant had medicinal properties. With every new thing I learned about Forrest, my admiration and respect for him only grew.

Forrest was both a wealthy billionaire doctor and farmer. The sentence sounded like an oxymoron, but somehow I found it sexy. Being with a farmer had never crossed my mind, but I couldn't help envisioning Forrest in sexy overalls looking all rugged and sweaty for me.

A smile curved my lips as I followed Forrest into the warehouse. The interior was like a high-tech greenhouse with plants growing under special lighting. At the far end of the warehouse was an entrance to another forest. I could see a dirt path with trees and shrubberies.

An intricate irrigation system nourished the trees and plants on the ground. A programed spray mist moved along the top, sprinkling water on the seedlings. I inhaled a deep breath of fresh air, and it invigorated my lungs.

"Wow." I released a sigh.

Forrest smiled and introduced me to some workers before he went to help an employee with something. I wandered to an area filled with herbs organized according to geographical regions. The Earth was truly amazing. It was as though the herbs were saying, "Look at what we can do for you. Take care of us."

I didn't know why, but tears streamed down my face. I thought about my mom and those in similar situations, feeling helpless and stuck. When you were sick and trying to heal, stress about payments didn't aid in the healing. It made it worse.

There was something wrong here. It didn't make sense to me. I would have thought the health insurance would want people to get healthy fast and remain that way, so people didn't need to keep visiting doctors. But that would prevent doctors and hospitals from charging the health insurance companies.

To me, it all seemed like a scam. But what could I do about it? I couldn't even begin to fix my own issues.

"What's wrong?" Forrest stood in front of me, looking worried.

Feeling embarrassed, I looked down, avoiding his eyes. Apparently I'd wandered away from the racks of herbs to an area of trees, pebbles, and moss.

He tipped up my chin, forcing my gaze to meet his. "Why are you crying?

"It's nothing important." I didn't want to burden him with my issues.

"People usually cry for a reason. Tell me."

His eyes bore into mine, and the sage green shifted, searching for the reason for my emotional distress. He looked like a green-eyed God who had absorbed the color, power, and beauty of the surrounding vegetation. Not only did he possess their essence, he also possessed their mysteries.

"I'm just worried about my mom."

"Don't worry." He cupped my face. "I'll look at her records as soon as you have them. Do you trust me?" His eyes searched mine, and I couldn't think of trusting any other man.

"Yes," I muttered.

He tapped my nose. "I'm good at what I do. I'll do my best to help her."

"Thanks." Emotion clogged my throat as I took him in with the background of trees, pebbles, and moss. A question popped into my head. "What's the significance of your name?"

"Let me show you around first." He grabbed my hand and

took me through the indoor forest with a super high, glass ceiling. It connected to an outdoor setting filled with all kinds of plant life. Massive walls secured the space, keeping it private from the public view.

He led me through a bamboo section where the tall stalks and leaves painted a peaceful scenery like the one I'd visited in Hong Kong years ago during a work trip.

"That bamboo section over there is reserved for Arrow." He gestured to an area separated from the rest of the forest.

"What's he doing with them?" I asked.

"He's working on a new product."

I admired Forrest and his friends for having so much vision and ambition.

"What are you doing with all the bamboos?"

"Lots of things. They can be eaten, or used to build furniture, homes, and materials for clothes."

I remembered the soft $Ba_7M_5Bu_{88}$ T-shirt I'd purchased was made from bamboos.

We came to a large gazebo with a table with outlets for computers. A modern house made from a combination of stone and bamboo sat nearby. It was one story with wide windows and a wraparound deck that was like houses on the farm but a lot more contemporary. The area felt like an innovative living space that used the natural world and modern amenities.

"You should stop surprising me."

CHAPTER TWENTY-FIVE

FORREST

Seeing the gleam in her eyes at the sight of this place did something to me. I'd never brought a woman here before. Grandma and Yolanda had visited the gardens when the farm first opened, but they hadn't been to this extension of the indoor and the outdoor forest. The gazebo and the research center hadn't been visited by anyone but me. Once in a while, Hieu would stop by to ensure it was dust-free for me. But he was a trusted employee, and I needed someone here to monitor my property.

Kiera walked around the ground area, and I followed her a like a puppy. "It's beautiful."

"I'm happy you approve. It's my research center," I said. This was where I'd discovered the connection between plants and the human body, especially the immune system. Their communication with each other was like an alien language that they both understood.

She angled her head, studying me acutely. The honeyed irises churned a different color as she searched my face. I was a lucky man to be examined by her.

"Do you have a life?" Her mouth gave a sardonic twist. "Do you know how to have fun? Do you ever take a break to enjoy life?"

I have no trouble taking breaks to enjoy you.

"Your statements are about seventy-five percent flattery and twenty-five percent dislike. Am I right?"

"It's more like the other way around." Her eyes narrowed with a spark of amusement. "Men like you forget the meaning of life if you're immersed in work all the time."

Her statement was accurate to an extent. It described work that lacked passion and vision. But my work was the opposite.

"The fun lives inside the passion, Kiera. When you're passionate about something, you're lost in it." I tucked my hands into my pockets and rocked back on the heels of my shoes, watching her analyze my words.

"Yes, it does. I suppose it all comes down to choice—how you choose to live." She sighed and looked away. "Sometimes circumstances narrow your choices."

Her words almost seemed sad. She possessed wisdom that could only come from experience. I wanted to find out what narrowed her choices. She deserved to live the life she dreamed of. But if I asked her questions about what her choices were, would she ask me questions about the enemy I took care of? I wasn't ready to discuss that yet. She already knew too much. Anything more would put her in danger. I couldn't have that.

So I switched to a topic I could discuss. "My friends and I have been working on the WaterFyre Rising video game for years. We do it on our own time because we *love* it."

"I've heard about it from Audri. You and the boys are a bunch of nerds, you know that?"

"There's nothing wrong with men with goals. We all need something to work toward. It takes courage to recognize what inspires you. Sometimes the thing that motivates you also confuses you. *Scares* you." I paused, stretching out the moment to emphasize how she had motivated me to change. "That kind of motivation is powerful, complex, and has no actual answer."

A soft blush bloomed on her cheeks, and I'd cherish that adorable image for the rest of my life.

She stepped closer, looked up at me, and placed a hand on my cheek. "You're a smart guy. If anyone can find the answer to a difficult problem, it's you." There was no hint of amusement, just pure honesty in her eyes.

Her confidence in me shifted something in my chest—as though a locked door had miraculously opened. I'd never needed acknowledgment or validation from anyone. I knew my worth. I knew what I was capable of and where I was going. But Kiera's belief was extra fuel to something I didn't know I needed. She gave more meaning to my work.

My chest tightened at this influx of awareness.

She turned and stared at the house made of stone and wood. Close to the house were bins used to collect rainwater, which aided in the irrigation system around the property.

I took her hand. "Let me show you."

We stepped into the hallway and sensor lights flicked on.

"Wow. Doesn't look like a research center. Looks like a homey space with a laboratory, an office, a kitchen, and a living room that somehow belong together."

The house had an open space design where I could stand in one place and see most of the rooms.

"That was the idea. I worked with Grayson on the house design. Over here is another office, conference room, and the bathroom. Down that hallway is my library, bedroom, and second bathroom."

"You sleep at work?" She placed two hands on her hips, reminding me of my grandma reprimanding me with gestures alone.

"I told you, it's not work when there's passion in it." I guided her into my laboratory. "I study all kinds of herbs. It takes time to see how each of them can heal the human body. This is a side project."

She walked up to the mushroom poster on a wall and smiled. "I didn't know there were so many healing herbs in the world."

"The human body reflects everything in nature. The inside of the walnut looks like a brain. Plant roots are like veins and arteries. A flower or an oyster resembles one of my favorite parts on your body."

Her cheeks bloomed again. I'd never seen her blush this much.

"I like how you said *one* of your favorites. Your charm is dangerous, farm boy. I can see how you charm all the women around you."

I didn't know why, but I felt the need to defend myself. "No one's been here."

She looked at me, and something passed between us, but neither of us said anything. It was as though an odd truth pulsed in the room, with no need for confirmation.

She broke the trance. "Have you discovered something worthy in this lab recently?"

"I have, and I sent the data to two research centers—one in Boston, the other in Providence. I have teams of trusted doctors and scientists who will expand on my research to ensure it's safe for the public."

Kiera placed her camera and purse on a stack of papers on my desk and wandered around my lab. She studied the large picture frame of various herbs, their scientific names, and their healing properties. The herbs represented the diverse world. Different herbs were found in different countries, and each offered a unique healing approach.

When she turned around, curiosity flickered in her eyes. "Why are you doing all of this? You're already an established doctor and businessman, making tons of money. What inspired this hobby? Or is this a venture that would add to your billions? Explain the 'passion' you keep referring to. I'm interested in how an entrepreneurial mind works." She tapped her temple.

There was no hint of amusement in her eyes. This was a serious question that demanded the truth.

I'd never dated a woman who asked me these questions. Most of the conversations I'd shared before were simple preferences like where to go for dinner and what parties or medical conferences I had to attend. None of those women ever asked me *why* I had this hobby.

Hobby was an interesting word. It was defined as something a person did for fun.

Before I knew it, words flowed out of me. "I can connect to myself . . . and to my heritage. My parents were herbalists. When I work here, I can sense them. I think they're proud of what I've done."

When I cured a patient, their joy and gratitude made me forget all the ugliness in the world, and I could imagine my parents nodding their heads in approval.

Her eyes warmed as she wrapped her arms around me. "Of course, they're proud of you. You've accomplished a lot, Forrest. I'm in awe of what you've achieved. *I'm* proud of you."

Her embrace was fuel and fertilizer for my journey—my ambition, my vengeance.

I had no idea I needed this propellant—a nourishment that worked on a soul level.

You didn't need anything until you met her.

That epiphany sparked in my chest, like a sacred meiosis cell division where one cell became two, and the two multiplied to more, creating new life. The profound feeling made me pause for a moment. I'd just discovered something serious about myself. Kiera was a new discovery under a microscope—finding her was finding myself.

"This is your dedication to them in your unique way," she spoke into my chest.

I tightened my arms around her, inhaling her scent. How could she know so much about me?

Like WaterFyre Rising, the $Ba_7M_5Bu_{88}$ Project and the Holistic Farm were my ongoing ventures—all of them took time, dedication, and energy. Things worth having never came easy.

An innovative approach to medicine for the world and making it available to all at an affordable cost couldn't happen overnight. For those who couldn't afford it, there was a fund reserved to help them. Getting great healthcare shouldn't have to be so costly. If there had been this kind of program, my dad would've survived, living happily with his family.

Kiera had reached into my soul, touching things no one ever could. I knew there was more to our relationship than just sex. But no complications meant no one had to get hurt. I had a vendetta to fulfill, and dragging her into my world meant dragging her into danger. What if I never made it back out?

"You're so sexy and wise, Kitty K," I said, trying to bring amusement to the conversation so I didn't have to think about the ache in my heart.

Coward.

Ignoring the internal thought, I focused on the softness of her body against mine.

"And sometimes moody, irrational, and demanding," she said. "But you're smart for being right, farm boy." A thought glittered in her eyes. "Oh, I have a riddle for you. It's farm related, well, sort of." Her smile showed excitement. "I read it in a magazine at a doctor's office. Don't ask me why I remember it."

"Okay." My eyes studied her every gesture.

"Why do cows have hooves and not feet?"

"I'm not that kind of farmer, and I don't have farm animals. I'm more of a researcher."

"Farmer. Farmer. Farmer." She jabbed a finger into my chest. "Give up?"

I had no clue. "Yes."

"Because they *lactose*." She laughed; her shoulders shaking as though she'd been waiting for years to ask someone that stupid question. "You want another riddle?"

"No." I couldn't help but grin at her amusement.

"Why not? The *steaks* too high for your intelligence, doctor?"

"What kind of magazine were you reading? More importantly, what doctor's office were you visiting? A psychiatrist?"

"It's a magazine for intelligent women," she said with a sexy pout. "I was visiting a doctor of philosophy."

That taunting mouth of hers needed to be punished with kisses. I wanted to see it wrapped around my throbbing cock. Maybe then I'd have stupid jokes to tell her.

She offered a wicked smirk that made me want to toss her onto the table and show her how irrational and demanding she made me feel.

Kiera made her way past the rack of tubes, an automated incubator, a refrigerator, and other research equipment. She ambled to the counter with my microscopes, two computer screens, and stacks of folders.

When she saw the crystal table, she placed a hand over her heart and gasped, "Wow. What kind of crystal is this?" She ran her fingers along the uneven edges, acquainting herself with the smooth surface. My dick pulsed as though her fingers were roaming my stalk.

"It's rare black opal."

Her mouth dropped open. "I don't even want to ask how much this cost."

"It's a stunning gem. I love things that are rare."

She placed her palms on the table and leaned down to examine the colors. "The bright red, orange, and even the blues and greens look like liquid fire against that beautiful black. It's so gorgeous."

I came up beside her and used a finger to trace a stream of red that ran into a cluster of orange and blue tones. "The liquid fire reminds me of WaterFyre Rising, where each color represents an aspect of me and my friends. Water and fire are opposing elements, but they create this powerful energy and beauty because of their differences."

She turned and met my gaze, and I swore I met my other half. There was an inquisitiveness in her eyes that showed her unfathomable fascination. She was wrong about me being attracted to doctors. An inquisitive mind captivated me, making me weak. Kiera Ford had me by the balls.

"What's your video game about? What color represents you?" she asked.

These were other questions no woman had cared to ask me. Maybe it was because I'd never shared my video game project with anyone except Grandma and Yolanda. But even with them, it was general information. They thought I loved playing video games just like any other guy.

"Try to guess." I crossed my arms.

She glanced around the table, moving her hands around as though trying to sense the answers. Then she tapped the table, and my heart shivered at the accuracy. "Black."

"Why that color?"

She lifted a shoulder. "Black is a color steeped in mystery. When you mix solid colors together, you get black. It reminds me of a quiet night's sky that cradles someone to sleep. It also represents security and a sophistication that's often misunderstood."

"Black also signifies an abyss. The unknown. That's scary to some."

She eyed me. "Not to me. I love the mystery in you. The deeper I venture into the dark forest, the more treasures I find." She smiled, and that gesture cast a rainbow into my heart and beyond. "Did I pick the right color?"

I nodded. "Yes, you did."

"I've always loved green, but this exquisite table makes me love all colors."

"You like them all because it's how you see the world through your eyes and your camera."

Her smile widened. "Well, aren't you perceptive and poetic?" She bent over the table and spread her arms out wide like she wanted to immerse herself into the slab of opal. Then she placed her cheek on the surface and sighed.

My gaze took her in as she embraced the table. Her ass taunted me—even in those shorts—and my cock twitched. I wanted her now.

Moving to stand behind her, I braced my hands on the table, caging her in as my mouth nibbled her ear. "The perception I'm getting is that we should christen this opal table. It has potent energy, and we should definitely take advantage of it."

"Oh, really? I feel 'hard' energy poking at me already." She giggled and wiggled her ass into my cock.

"You're driving me insane." I groaned and gripped her hips, grinding into her. "I want to perform some sexual research with you."

Prior to this moment, nothing but scientific and holistic

research had occurred in this room, but that was going to change today.

She straightened up and leaned back into me. "That sounds enticing. How much have you already done?"

"You're the first."

"Okay then." She purred and touched my face, dragged my head to her neck. "By the way, I can give you a haircut whenever you'd like." She threaded her fingers through my hair, massaging my scalp. I could stand there all day with her hands caressing my head.

That statement referred to two separate things that loved her caress equally.

She was the reason for my long hair, so it made sense she'd cut it. "Be my guest."

Hairstyling by a significant other was also another first for me. She was cutting away all my barriers, giving me so many firsts. I wasn't sure if that was good or bad. There was no time to contemplate other than tending to the pressure threatening to burst.

My hands slid up her body, cupping her breasts through the shirt. The delicious sound she made ignited a new circuitry in me. I had to be inside her. I'd never craved a woman this much.

"I want you so bad," I said, stripping off all her clothes and tossing them into a pile on the table.

She whirled around, lust darkening her eyes. Her gorgeous body was primed for me, full breasts with nipples aching for attention.

"So beautiful." I licked a nipple.

Kiera moaned as I drew it into my mouth, suckled it, and watched her watch me. God, I fucking loved the way her face transformed. She whimpered as I adored each breast with the same passion.

With trembling hands, she yanked at my shorts. "I'm in an experimental mood too."

I stripped in record time. Sexual energy circulated the room as though it was the only air for us to breathe in—to act on. At least for me, that was all I could register.

"I'm the doctor now." She clasped a hand over my cock and stroked. "Tell me if my touch increases your heart rate. Show me how strong you are." That wicked smile deserved a spanking on her fine ass.

She dropped to her knees on the wooden floor, tossed me a daring look, and licked my length up and down in a slow and tantalizing motion. My body jerked from the delectable jolt rushing through me. It felt like my body was experiencing a mini earthquake, with tremors shooting out everywhere.

Fuuuck.

This woman could destroy me.

Fearing I'd collapse from pleasure, I leaned against the edge of the opal table. Its coolness didn't last long because of the heat scorching my blood and brain. A decadent buzz zipped through my spine, making my body more sensitive than it had ever been.

She mesmerized me with the flick of her pink tongue, branding my dick. It felt like silk caressing an iron pole. This had to be the most beautiful thing I'd ever seen.

"What's the verdict?" Her curious tongue circled my crown and all the blood drained toward my aching cock, leaving me empty of thoughts.

"What?" I muttered.

She smiled and stroked. "How's your heart rate?"

I swallowed because my throat had gone dry. "Threatening cardiac arrest, but I don't fucking care. Please continue."

A smirk appeared before her mouth took me in again. The licking and sucking were almost meditative, cathartic, and addictive all in one. I gasped like a man chasing his last breath while trying to suppress the pressure from exploding.

"Baby, slow down or I'll come in your mouth."

She paused one second to acknowledge she'd heard me. "I want to taste you."

What was a man supposed to do with that kind of request?

Ignoring my demand, she took what she wanted, stroking me harder and sucking me faster.

"Kiera!" My fingers carded into her hair, yanking her face up to look at me, and my restraints burst free.

A massive orgasm rolled through me like an earthquake with 10.0 magnitude on the Richter scale. I heard energy sizzle in the room. Or was that my ears drumming from the explosive power?

I poured myself into her mouth, and she swallowed every drop of me. No woman had ever loved me like this. Nor had I ever experienced this massive climax from a blow job. The orgasm reverberated all the way inside me to the abyss of my soul—a place that hadn't been touched. I was in deep shit. I was tangled in her in so many ways that made my demand of a no-strings-attached relationship sound as false as the sun never rising again.

With her, I felt the dawn of myself emerging. That scared the shit out of me. I always thought I knew myself—had control over my life. But Kiera had just yanked the rug out from under my feet, leaving me with nothing to stand on except this raw emotion that opened my heart so wide I was afraid that everything I'd stored within it would fall out.

CHAPTER TWENTY-SIX

I'd never devoured a man the way I'd just devoured Forrest's cock. My previous relationships never went this far. I'd never wanted to please any man like this, but with him, I wanted to touch and taste him—*discover* him.

There was a mystery to him, and just now, I'd unlocked a part of him. The way he looked at me when he trembled shifted my heart too.

My body quivered from the hunger in his eyes. "Your turn," he growled.

Lifting me onto my feet, he turned me around to face the table. With my back to him, he nudged me down onto the opal surface, and the coolness shocked my flaming skin. I turned to the side, letting my cheek kiss the crystal while I admired our reflection from the glass cabinet. He stood like a warrior behind me, all muscle and man, getting ready to stake his claim. I was a willing woman, allowing him to do as he pleased. The image alone aroused the heck out of me.

I shivered when his massive rod nestled between my buttocks.

"You're going to gift this opal crystal with your superb orgasm." He spread my legs apart, cupping my sex. "So gloriously wet for me."

My hands tried to grab onto something, but there was nothing but a flat surface. I was deliciously trapped by him and loved it.

I expected his thick cock to enter me. Instead, he pressed his face between my buttocks.

"Forrest!" I gasped as his tongue swiped me up and down. Pleasure whipped me back and forth. The need to escape warred with the need for more.

He continued loving me as I cried out in pleasure. The voice didn't sound like mine at all.

"So tender." A flick of his tongue made my body jerk. He spanked my ass. "I love finding your little secrets, baby."

His skillful tongue should have its own name. It should win awards at the Olympics. It did amazing things to all my lady parts. The way I moaned his name with a plea for more should embarrass me. But powerful sensations overwhelmed all senses.

My blissful cries filled the room, which encouraged him further.

"Did I pass the test, doctor?" I breathed and turned back to the glass cabinet that showed him on the floor with his face in my ass. That image was so hot. It was now forever etched in my mind.

"Yes. There's a freckle here that needs my attention," he spoke into my folds, and his voice vibrated all the way to my heart.

My legs wobbled, and somehow I was sitting on his face while he devoured me like no man ever had.

Oh my God. Need coiled inside me. It felt so good that it blinded me for a moment. The licking and sucking sent shockwaves through me. My muscles tightened, preparing for the onslaught.

"I love the way you leak for me, Kiera. You taste so good. You're mine in every way."

Pleasure surged through me, pushing me close to the edge.

"I don't have a condom." Forrest cursed.

"It's okay. I'm on the pill. And clean."

"Thank fucking God." He rose and urged me back onto the table, positioned my thighs as he teased my core with the tip of his cock. "I don't want any barriers between us."

The words came out more like a whisper, so I wasn't sure if he was talking to me or himself.

I was so busy swimming in a daze of pleasure that my ability to listen and engage in coherent conversation was little to none.

When he plunged into me, I gasped at the sudden fullness. My inner muscles stretched to accommodate this warrior of a penis.

"You're so tight. So unbelievably amazing." He moved in and out of me, creating an addictive friction that added to the tension building in my core.

"Forrest . . ."

"You like it, baby? I'm never putting on another condom with you."

I shouldn't have been thinking about anything other this incredible pleasure, but my goal of a long-term relationship flashed in my head. Could I have that with him? Did he see all of his relationships as "sex only," like ours?

If not, then why had he suggested that to me?

He groaned and sank even deeper. I sensed the massive wave coming and curled my hands into fists. His sweaty body draped over me, and his fingers interlaced with mine.

"Come for me, Kiera." He pounded into me and broke the dam. The ecstatic flood rushed through me, and bells rang in my ears. "Forrest!"

"That's right. I'm the only one who can do this to you. You're mine." He kissed my cheek and added another mighty thrust that took my breath away.

I think he just sent an organ up to my lungs from that powerful thrust. Sex with him was raw and animalistic.

"Do you love having me inside you, Kitty K?"

"Yes," I affirmed with a contraction in my muscles. There was no replacing him.

"Did you enjoy that wild night at the hotel when I ate every inch of you?" He nibbled my shoulder, lifted me up, and cupped my breasts while still inside me.

"Yes," I moaned when he pinched my nipples delicately.

"That night changed me." He pulled out of me, the crown kissing my entrance.

I didn't like the void one bit.

"I didn't know what my type was until you." He plunged in again, pumping hard.

His body stiffened. Then he growled. A vicious orgasm that probably rearranged all my internal organs made me tremble from head to toe.

Holy shit.

Forrest banded his arms around me. "You'll be the death of me, woman." He kissed the top of my head. "But if I had to go, this would be the only way."

A loud boom roared through the area, and the ground shook. The sexual energy dissolved, replaced by something chaotic. We exchanged worried glances.

"Fucking hell." He pulled out, grabbed the roll of paper towels on the nearby table, and attempted to clean me.

"I can do it. Is that some kind of farm equipment being turned on?" I reached for my clothes and offered his to him.

"No. Something just exploded. Let's hurry. I need to check it out."

CHAPTER TWENTY-SEVEN

Rage threatened to swallow me as I stood staring at the damages to the gardens, delivery port, and storage facility. They needed major renovation. Fuck. This was a costly setback.

The police determined the explosion had come from one box that had been delivered today. Because of my visit, the deliveries were left in the storage instead of being moved to various parts of the farm to be unpacked. The employees didn't want boxes cluttering the space for my review so they'd delayed moving the packages. They'd done this every time I visited. Thank God that hadn't changed—someone could've gotten hurt or killed if they had opened the package.

I glanced around at the scattered debris while the firefighters and police officers combed the area for evidence. I wasn't sure what they'd find, but I'd be doing my own investigation. The city often took longer to do things because of protocol. I didn't have time for that shit.

I scanned the area looking for Kiera and found her sweeping the debris near the gardens. She was helping Hieu while the other workers reorganized as best they could. I couldn't hear what she said to him, but he patted her shoulder and smiled. That man and his wife were critical to the success of the Holistic Farm. They knew their herbs, especially the green tea, *Camellia sinensis*, which was a huge seller for the farm.

From this plant, I could get green, black, and oolong tea—each benefited the body differently. Their difference was in the production. While green tea leaves were either steamed or pan fried at high temperatures to prevent oxidation, the black tea was withered and left to oxidize. The oolong tea possessed a partial oxidation, so it was in between its siblings.

Hieu and Trang had owned a tea farm in Vietnam before they escaped the war and immigrated to the United States. Years ago, he'd gotten sick from Hepatitis A and had entered a special program that offered new medication that boosted the immune system. I'd met him during the program because I'd been one of the participating doctors. The program benefited some patients, but it had been temporary because the insurance did not cover the entire duration. Hieu didn't have money to continue, so I'd paid for the rest of his treatment. In exchange, he showed me how to harvest the green tea leaves.

The people who worked on my farms had families. I didn't care about the damaged facilities; they could be rebuilt. My loyal employees couldn't be replaced.

Who wanted to destroy my farm? I didn't have a lot of competitors in this field. Holistic Farm supplied herbs for several online stores. The only local store I delivered to was Full Circle Apothecary.

Though the holistic industry was growing, it differed from other businesses I'd invested in. I'd never sensed a strong competition between other farms in the area. Everyone minded their businesses. I didn't care about the guy harvesting his corn or potatoes. I wasn't competing with anyone.

Who had sent that fucking bomb?

After speaking to the detectives and getting their reports, I told everyone to stay home for the next few days until I met with the management team.

"You okay there?" Kiera placed a hand on my back, rubbing circles.

My back muscles relaxed instantly. She could smooth out my day with a simple touch. "I'm okay, but I need you to stay at the hotel tonight."

"Why?"

I gestured to the damaged area. "Right now, we don't know who sent the explosives or why. I want you where I can see you. The campground isn't safe compared to my hotel."

"I don't want to impose."

I placed a hand on either side of her shoulders. "You're not imposing. It's my hotel."

She twisted her lips, thinking. "Do you have a lot of enemies?"

"Are you worried about me?" My chest warmed.

Her eyes sparkled with amusement. "Well, if something should happen to you, I want to make sure you donate the black opal table to me. Since I christened it, it has my energy." She smirked, trying to make light of the situation, and I wanted to kiss her for that.

"I'm not a saint, Kiera. I'm an entrepreneur who also dwells in the medical world. So my enemies are extensive."

I shouldn't have said all of that because anxiety filled her eyes, along with questions. But she didn't ask any of them.

"Don't worry about it." I draped an arm around her shoulder, guiding her to the car. "My other businesses garner more profits than this farm. It could have been kids playing a stupid prank. They do shitty stuff for exposure on social media."

My statement landed on her, and she sighed. "That's true. The news said Texas's crime rate had increased by eighty percent compared to previous years. That's scary. The city officials should do something about it."

We walked toward my car. "If you want change, vote for the right people and make sure they're not easily bought by companies or other donors waiting in the wings with an agenda."

"The world is a frightening place."

We stopped beside my car, and I wrapped my arms around her, wanting to protect her. "It is. But it's not so bad if we have each other. Right now I have you in my arms, and I won't let anything happen to you."

She smiled and rested her head on my chest. "You're the sexiest farmer I've ever met. So when are you going to wear overalls for me?"

I laughed. "When you wear a sexy librarian outfit for me—a very short skirt, an oversized cardigan over a low-cut tank top, with black-rimmed glasses, and high heels."

I loved she could make me smile amid stress and uncertainty.

"Your description is clear, but stereotypical. Not all librarians look like that." Her eyes glinted with amusement.

"Then show me your version. Enlighten me."

She drew back, arching a sexy eyebrow. "I didn't know you had a librarian fetish."

"I only developed it after meeting you—after you called me a nerd." I leaned down and whispered, "I've got more fetishes that I want to show you in my bed."

"Make sure you're not delinquent on any book borrows. You'll have to pay," she said with a straight face.

"I'm willing to pay you in sexual pleasures that would make the books on your shelves orgasm. I've got a severe case of Kiera Syndrome, and you're the only one who can help me with it."

"And what do you suggest is the first step in treating this syndrome?" she asked, forming a little pout.

"I need to fuck you every night." I nibbled her earlobe. "If you're an incurable syndrome, I don't ever want to be cured."

She slapped my chest and laughed. "You're so corny."

"It made you laugh, didn't it?" I ran my finger over her lips. "Smiling and laughing are the only things I want to see on your face." I opened the car door for her.

She settled in the seat and crooked a finger, looking serious. "Come here."

Worried, I bent down. "What's wrong?"

"I'm not feeling well."

"Where are you hurt?" Concern surged through me as I checked her face, neck, and body.

Kiera cupped my face, smiling. "I have a severe case of the Forrest Syndrome. A kiss would suffice." She kissed me, and I forgot about the explosion and anything else I had to do tonight.

She broke the kiss, leaving me wanting more. "I'm ready to go get my stuff from the campground now." She buckled her seatbelt and sent me a seductive wink. Then her phone rang. "Hi, Nora."

As I drove out of the parking lot, Kiera's startled voice had me stopping. "What's wrong?"

Fear splashed on her face, and I hated seeing it on her.

"My cabin is on fire. The firefighters are there now."

CHAPTER TWENTY-EIGHT

KIERA

"What the hell happened here?" Forrest asked Nora and the facility manager named Warren, who had come in on his day off because of the fire.

"I don't know. I was busy registering a visitor when a boy came into the office shouting about the fire." She turned to me with trembling lips. "I was so worried you were inside. But the firefighters confirmed they didn't find a body. I'm so sorry about your belongings."

Forrest stalked over to the firefighter and the police officers with their cowboy hats. I recognized some of them from the attack incident.

"I can replace them," I said, my heart aching. My computer was gone. It was a good thing I only brought a spare and had saved all my files onto the company's shared drive. So all my photos were safe.

I placed a hand over my camera, grateful that I had it with me. If it had been at the cabin, it would have been gone too. Now I had to buy new clothes and luggage, which meant more money out of my pocket.

Nora left to help recent visitors, and I stood alone, staring at the sad cabin. Half of the cabin had crumbled to ashes while the other half struggled to stand. It would probably collapse any time.

Tears streamed down my face. What had caused the fire? Was there an electrical issue I didn't know about?

"I'm sorry about y-your cabin." Hank appeared beside me with tears in his eyes too.

"Thank you. I've had such bad luck since coming here." *I should go get some sage or a good luck charm tomorrow.* This negative crap had to stop. "Did you see what happened?"

Hank's shoulders slouched as he looked at the debris. Sadness swam in his eyes. He was probably used to seeing the cabin every day, but it was now replaced by destruction.

"I f-found this near the d-debris." He pointed to an area and gave me a travel-sized bottle of lotion that hadn't been damaged by the destruction.

I held it in my hand, remembering that I'd given the Uber driver a package for his wife. This brand of lotion was a high-end European brand. Very few stores carried it here because of its price. Had a recent visitor used this brand? Or had the person responsible for the fire dropped it?

"Thank you, Hank." I rushed over to Forrest, showed him the lotion, and told him of my suspicion.

He snapped a picture of the lotion, took my hand, and walked over to the police officers.

"Detective Donnelly," Forrest interrupted their conversation. "This was found outside of the cabin. Can you add that to the evidence bag?"

"Where exactly did you find that?" Bruce asked me in an unpleasant tone.

I remembered seeing Hank recoil from him the last time he was here.

Being protective, I said, "On the ground near the collapsed porch." If the police officer had done his job thoroughly, he would have found it. "Maybe you missed it."

He flicked me an irritated look. "Our work *is* thorough, miss."

"I didn't say it wasn't. Just trying to help, *officer*." I wasn't in the mood to deal with incompetent cops.

Color me confused. Weren't cops supposed to defuse a chaotic situation instead of adding to it?

"Don't talk to her that way." Forrest leveled a stare at him that would make most people scuttle away. "She's a victim. Her cabin just turned to cinders, and you're mocking her?" His jaw tightened. "You're not competent to be a police officer."

Bruce clamped his mouth shut and walked away, ignoring Detective Donnelly's disapproval. "Sorry about that. Bruce has been under a lot of stress lately. Personal issues can affect our work."

I wanted to say that I was under a lot of stress too, but decided against it. The only thing I needed was a hot shower, food to eat, and a soft bed for me to mope in and figure out what to do next. I had one more photo shoot left. A few swimsuits for Olivia wouldn't take me long.

After signing some papers at the cabin, we headed to Forrest's hotel. He was in a contemplative mood, probably worried about the bomb incident at his farm—and now this fiasco.

"I'm sorry to be another burden." I interlaced my fingers on my lap, thinking about all the ways I'd been someone's burden. My father hadn't wanted me. My previous boyfriends never cared enough to stick around.

Maybe I was born with bad luck. I'd been there the day Forrest and his family were hit by a truck. Had that been my fault too? Did I bring unfortunate incidents to those around me?

Hot tears flowed down my face before I could stop them. Why couldn't I hold them in until I got into my hotel room? I needed a good cry.

Forrest pulled over on the side of the road. "Are you okay?" He reached for a tissue box inside his glove compartment and offered it to me.

"Yeah. Just a lot to take in. I can't help but think I'm bad luck." I dabbed my eyes and squeezed the tissue as though everything were its fault. "You should stay away from me. I don't want to get you injured."

"Why would you think that? You're the best thing that's ever happened to me, Kiera."

Honesty gleamed in his eyes, and I looked away because if I stared at them too long, I'd want something I could never have. I was slowly falling for him, making this relationship more complicated than he wanted.

I was a mess.

He gripped my chin, turning me to face him. "You saved my life with Chococat, remember?"

I had helped. But now so many horrible incidents made me doubtful.

Stop the negative thoughts.

Releasing a sigh, I nodded. "I'm just stressed about a lot of things. My mom, and now this strange fire at the cabin. I need to get a new computer, clothes, toiletries, and makeup." I didn't want to look like a zombie for the new contract job.

"You need a good night's sleep." He brushed my tears away with his fingers. "Then you're going to let everything out. If you keep your worries inside, you'll weaken your immune system and be prone to illnesses."

A small smile formed on my lips. "But I'm already sick with your syndrome."

"That's the only one you're allowed to have. You don't need a new computer. I have two spare ones in my office. Take your pick. You can shop online for clothes and have them shipped to the hotel. Or you can browse the boutique attached to the hotel. Maybe you should try out the spa in the salon next to the boutique. That might help the stress. As for toiletries and makeup, there's a drugstore around the corner from the hotel."

I gaped at his clear mindset to plan out everything so efficiently. I supposed that was how billionaires made their money. They had well-executed strategies instilled in their heads at the ready. My brain wasn't wired like that. I could plan and considered myself organized, but sometimes I just wanted to leave my brain blank so I could breathe.

"Thanks for the computer. Let me know how much, and I'll pay you back."

"Don't worry about it. We'll discuss that later. Feeling better?"

The computer would be another chunk from my savings, which were reserved for my mom, but I didn't want him to know.

"How can I not when you've just helped me with your meticulous plan?"

"Having a plan helps in times of need. Besides, I'm used to it. Let's get you settled so you can rest. Everything else can wait."

Was I being hopeful, or did Forrest just put me on the top of his list? For the first time, I was a man's priority.

You're a sad and wounded woman, Kiera.

Was it wrong to wonder if I mattered that much? I knew I had abandonment issues, but so did many people in this world.

They grew out of theirs.

I wished my inner voice were friendlier to me, instead of brutally honest.

Maybe Forrest had no intention of saying those words the way I had understood them. Maybe it was a general statement with no hidden messages. Whatever it was, his words slathered a healing balm over my aching heart, and I was grateful for it. At least now I knew what it felt like to matter to a man.

For the rest of the ride, silence filled the car. It cloaked me like a warm blanket on a chilly night, or rather, the cool breeze of the river cooling me off from the heat and humidity of summer. The quiet wasn't awkward at all. Forrest didn't ask me questions as if he knew I needed the space.

CHAPTER TWENTY-NINE

FORREST

"I can't stay here with you." She stood in the living room of my suite, wanting to go to her hotel room.

"Why not?" I retorted.

"Because." Her lips thinned.

"That's not a suitable answer, Kiera."

"You can't make me stay here."

I crossed my arms, staring at her. "Try me."

Her elegant eyebrows pushed together. "Why are you being so difficult?"

Based on what had occurred in the car, she was under a lot of stress. It wasn't just the cabin fire. Though that was probably what had her the most on edge now. All the more reason for her to stay with me.

"Because I need you safe."

"Why?" Her eyes flashed with heat.

"Why not?" Didn't she understand that I just wanted to take care of her without having to explain everything?

"That's not a good reason, Forrest." She mocked me. "I need my space. And you need yours."

What exactly did she want me to say? We stood staring at each other, and the energy in the room pulsed.

I stepped closer. "I do like my space, but I don't mind sharing it with *you*. I have three big bedrooms. It's been a stressful day. We should stop this ridiculous argument."

My emotions were high, and part of it had to do with her. I was feeling too much and too fast. I didn't know what to do about it yet. Her defiance wasn't helping my impatience either.

"You can stay in that room." I gestured to the one across from mine. "It has its own bathroom. You don't even need to step out of the room."

Kiera closed her eyes, sighed, and opened them again. "Why do you care so much? We're not dating. We're just two people having sex. People like us go our separate ways after the fun is over, right?"

Her words knifed me in the chest. Was that how she perceived me?

I didn't have time to reply because she continued, "Staying here with you would complicate things, Forrest. I know you're trying to be nice, and I appreciate your kindness. But let's not complicate things . . . I might not survive it." She grabbed the new luggage we just got from the store and turned toward the door.

I clasped her arm. "What do you mean? Explain."

She turned around and looked me in the eye. "Things are getting very complicated for me. You're sending mixed signals by being attentive and caring. I might get the wrong message and think it's something when it's not." She chewed on her bottom lip. "I want more, but I know you don't. You made it clear before this 'thing' started, and I agreed to it. So just let me stay in my room, and we're good. Okay?"

The beautiful words landed and seeped into my skin like a healing ointment mending an unseen wound. Each word was a beam of sun that brought light and hope to the darkness I'd lived in for so long. A way out of the mire.

Kiera wanted me just as I wanted her.

I didn't let go of her arm. Instead, I pulled her flush against me. "It was never just sex to me."

Her brown eyes brightened like topaz. "But you wanted—"

"It was a protective mechanism." I brushed the hair away from her face. "You're a danger to my heart, Kiera. I couldn't stop thinking about you after that first time. So when I saw you here, I knew it was my second chance." My hand slid to the back of her neck, massaging it.

Her body relaxed as her anxious expression softened.

"I thought keeping it casual with only sex would give me time and help me understand these feelings for you," I said. "That maybe it was just infatuation, but I was wrong. The more time I spent with you, the more I wanted you." I dropped a light kiss to her lips.

Her arms came around me in an embrace as she peered up at me. "It's my second chance too. I turned down dates because I couldn't stop thinking about you. My sex drive dipped for every man, but spiked when I saw you."

I grinned like a fool. "You were born for me."

Her face flushed with the adorable pink I could never get enough of. I didn't know where our relationship would go, but it felt right to be with her. At first I'd wanted to keep a distance to protect her, but it seemed that decision created more pain for both of us. I'd do whatever I had to in order to protect her from the vicious world lurking around me.

The human heart wasn't something that could be tested with logical variables for a specific outcome. Instead, it was ambiguous, powerful, and magical. Studies had shown that the heart was intelligent. That it emitted a magnetic frequency five thousand times stronger than that of the brain. No wonder emotions were life-changing.

I kissed her forehead. "You're the electrical charge my heart needs to survive."

Her lips slanted into a smirk. "You getting poetic on me again?"

She had inspired me to look at things differently. "Every cell in the body holds an electrical charge known as millivolts. A healthy charge is between seventy and ninety millivolts, whereas cancer cells hold a charge below twenty millivolts." I tapped her heart. "Being with you enables my heart to stay healthy."

Her expression warmed, and she chuckled. "I'm your recharging station, and you're mine."

I smiled at how she'd turned a science fact into poetry. "We're dating, starting right now."

"I don't remember you asking." She skipped her fingers along my ribs, tickling me.

"I thought it was understood." I did the same to her, and she squirmed away with a squeak, but I caught her again.

"Women need clarity and not assumptions, Dr. Navarro."

She was right. The same method applied to conversations with patients. Assumptions often led to miscommunication.

"Okay." I tipped her back and scored her gorgeous neck. "I want to fuck you all day and night and have you scream out my name over and over again. I want you as my lover and my hot librarian, who will organize all the books in my office wearing nothing but a see-through thong and stilettos. I want to take boudoir photos of you for my personal collection. Wanna be my girlfriend and fulfill those requests for me?" I kissed her for a long moment. "Is that clear enough for you?"

She patted my butt and squeezed. "How can I refuse such an ass?"

"I appreciate a clear and concise woman too."

Yawning, she said, "I need a shower, but I need to get new clothes."

"Wild Flower boutique will have something you like." I took her hand and led her out to the elevator. "You should sleep in my bed tonight. It would save me a trip from sneaking into yours."

"Maybe," she said, leaning her weight into me.

"Maybe is not a clear answer. And will only get you spanked."

The boutique was busier than usual because of two banquets in the hotel. While Kiera browsed, I sat in the lounge area with two other men, probably waiting for their women. I sent a text message to the PI, who had been hired by Remi initially. But he'd proven his skills and integrity, so he now worked for all the boys. I'd given him an important project to work on, but I needed him to investigate the explosion at Holistic Farm first.

My fingers curled thinking about how my dad had died, how other families had been executed by the same people. Seeing that kind of violence had instilled fear in me as a kid. I understood how Kiera had developed her trauma, and I planned on helping her recover. I no longer had fear. Vengeance had replaced it.

Would Kiera see me differently if she knew the dark side of me? Would she still want me? I didn't want to think about it. She was here with me now, and that was all that mattered.

PI: *What do you need?*

Forrest: *Any video recordings of delivery trucks near Holistic Farm. I want all their info.*

The PI used an encrypted number, which made our business transaction safe and untraceable.

Three women stood nearby chatting about missing people

and other crimes on the news. The news was depressing. They include mass shootings, violent deaths of innocent citizens, political corruption, or some other shit that scared people. I understood these terrifying things were real. But the media could distort the truth and make someone believe the devil had been reincarnated as their neighbor.

I scoured for Kiera and saw her browsing the lingerie section.

I waved at the sales associate wearing a black dress. "That's my girlfriend over there." I gestured to Kiera, who had moved to another section. "When she checks out, put everything on my account. She'll refuse, so just tell her I get a discount."

The sales associate smiled. "Will do, Mr. Navarro."

"Thank you." I turned my attention to a group of people walking across the courtyard of my hotel, and my stomach sank at the sight.

I stood up slowly and walked over to the glass panel, trying to see the man with the red shoes. The image brought back a memory from when I'd hidden in a garden and saw two men discussing a crime. I'd googled red shoes many times, trying to find out what company made it, but nothing had ever come up.

Men didn't usually wear red dress shoes. I couldn't see his face as other people in the crowd blocked him from my view. Was it the same man I'd seen long ago? Or was this a different man who shared similar tastes?

My grandma would call this unexpected vision an omen. The red shoes had appeared in my life during a time I'd rather forget. Seeing them again signified something.

I sensed a storm coming and prayed I could protect those I loved.

CHAPTER THIRTY

FORREST

After Kiera finished shopping for clothes and toiletries, we returned to the hotel and she went into her bedroom to organize. I settled into my office and took a moment to gather myself before diving into work. I was behind on a few things, so it was catchup time.

Leaning into my chair, I replayed the day. The urge to protect Kiera had overwhelmed me after the explosion at my farm and the fire at her cabin.

What would have happened if she had been there? Did someone intentionally set the cabin ablaze? But why? Was this associated with the attack at the campground?

Several scenarios burned into my brain. Anxious thoughts sent chemicals to the brain, which activated the immune system's responses. The psychological immune system was another study that fascinated me. Healing the body wasn't just about antibodies, platelets, or white blood cells. Stress—the unseen illness—was the trigger for many diseases.

After a few moments, I logged into my computer, checking

my emails and saw a message from my medical clinic account with the subject line: *About the fire.*

I didn't get many emails from this account because my patients usually logged into the online portal for immediate assistance with nurses and doctors. But I had this email posted under my bio for business purposes.

I hesitated to click on the email with the address, "camping-funooo" and the initials H.P. The last thing I needed was some fucker infiltrating my computer with a virus. But I plugged the email address into a system to check for authenticity. When it passed the authentication, I opened the email.

It's Hank. I need to talk to you about the fire.

I replied to the email. *Let's meet up.*

The quick response surprised me. *Arcade Zone at Silver Field Plaza at 10 p.m. They close at midnight.*

I walked over to Kiera's bedroom, but she was in the shower. I left a note on top of the laptop I'd given her.

Need to run out for a quick meeting. Will be back shortly.

Don't wait up. Get some rest.

I took the elevator down to the garage and took one of the hotel's black SUVs used for miscellaneous things. There was no logo on it, but it had commercial plates. I didn't want to draw attention to myself with a fancy car, especially at the place I was heading to. An internet search showed it was in a plaza that needed major renovations.

Why hadn't Hank asked me to call him or meet him at his cabin instead?

CHAPTER THIRTY-ONE

KIERA

I changed into the silky pajama set I'd gotten from Wild Flower, where Forrest had an account and a discount. He'd refused my money when I wanted to pay him and told me to pay him in kisses. I told him each kiss would cost a hundred dollars, but he countered, demanding that each kiss was only a dollar and that I could spend the rest of my life paying him back.

Adorable jerk.

The boutique had men's clothing, but the majority of the shop was womenswear. I saw a rack full of Natalie's Momentum line and bought a few of her designs to support her. Not that she needed support from me. Her fashion collection was an international sensation. Stores around the world wanted her clothing in their shops.

I picked up Forrest's sticky note and my insides melted. He'd been more attentive to me than anyone I'd ever dated.

We were now dating—an official couple. I smiled as my heart skipped several beats. I hadn't expected this development during my work trip, but things had escalated at a rate I couldn't ignore. We had a powerful attraction. But now we were connected beyond that. We shared a moment in time that changed us. I'd developed my blood phobia, and he'd lost his mother during that car accident.

It was time I faced the weakness trapping me. Years ago, I'd researched ways to overcome hemophobia but hadn't tried any. When I returned to Providence, I'd look again. Maybe they had new ways to treat this phobia now.

Tonight I just wanted to relax and update my friends. Settling in my bed, I glanced at the clock. It was late, but the time difference should have been okay for texting.

Kiera: *Hello. Busy?*

Audri: *Oh no. What did you do with my Kiera?*

Kiera: *Eye roll. It's me.*

Michelle: *Real Kiera doesn't say hello.*

Natalie: *Too formal.*

Vivian: *We want her back!*

Kiera: *Okay, bitches! Happy?*

Audri: *There she is! Lol! What's up?*

Michelle: *You met a hot guy?*

Kiera: *(Smile face emoji)*

Natalie: *Ooh la la. (Heart emoji)*

Vivian: *Since when?*

Audri: *I want all the deets.*

The quick texts from so many names made my tired eyes dizzy.

Kiera: *Group call, pick up.*

"What's his name?" Audri asked.

"Do we know him?" Vivian chimed in.

"Is he a model?" Michelle inquired.

I waited for all of them to connect so I didn't have to repeat myself.

"You know what this means, right?" Natalie blurted out.

"What should her mission be?" Michelle asked.

Oh, gosh, I was afraid of what they'd plan for me.

"It's Forrest." My face and ears grew hot even though no one could see me.

"A hot guy for our hot girl," Audri said.

"Have you done the deed? Is he huge?" Vivian asked with a laugh echoed by the other girls. "He's a hot doctor. I know a lot of doctors and dentists, and they don't look like him at all."

He was one of a kind, indeed.

"Yes, and yes," I confessed.

"It was a work trip, after all. You had some late nights there." Natalie teased.

I didn't tell them about my one-night stand with him or our fated connection, because it would require me to explain my blood phobia. Only Audri knew about it. Tonight's conversation would just be light. No heavy topics.

"We're officially dating now, so there's no need for any SSG mission."

"Is that why you held off on telling us?" Michelle asked. "You got to plan mine, Audri's, and Natalie's. You're not escaping this, Missy."

"We need our fun too," Audri said.

Vivian added. "Tell us some things that stand out in your relationship."

I told them about the opal table, his $Ba_7M_5Bu_{88}$ Project, the Holistic Farm, and the medicine he was developing.

"How about Opals are Forever?" Natalie suggested.

"Love that!" Michelle exclaimed.

"We'll need to think about this and reconvene," Audri said.

I didn't mind the title since I'd fallen in love with opals, especially the black opal.

What did my friends have in mind for the Opals are

Forever mission? A part of me was afraid to find out, but another part was thrilled.

CHAPTER THIRTY-TWO

To my surprise, the parking lot at Silver Field was packed. The plaza wasn't huge, but a good size with a strip mall of five businesses, two of which had closed for the evening. A lamp post flickered as I walked toward the Arcade Zone, which brimmed with lights flashing from inside. I couldn't see much from the windows being covered with posters of new video games, Magic card tournaments, and other events happening. Next to the arcade was a laundromat, a drugstore, a beauty salon, and a diner with crowds of people. I assumed the bulk of the parked cars came from those patrons.

As soon as I entered the arcade, my ears were assaulted with a very familiar racket. Yup, I remembered hanging with my boys at our local arcade before most of our time was dedicated to the bigger picture—WaterFyre Rising.

I didn't know what I would've done if I hadn't connected with Remi, Grayson, Royce, and Arrow back then. Their friendship saved me from a very dark time. My father's death, my desire to make his killers pay, the escape from my homeland with my grandma and Yolanda, and my mom's death hounded me like a beast. My resentment grew and grew until I met these guys who had vision and purpose. They sparked hope in me. They made me remember my passion, and I understood that success yielded money and power—all the things I needed to ensure those who hurt me and my family would pay.

I watched as two teenagers stood in front of a claw machine. The guy was trying to get a Sanrio stuffed animal for his girl. He maneuvered the claw to a Hello Kitty toy, but the claw dropped it. Chococat was squished in the corner, looking trapped. I smiled, wondering if Kiera would like it.

"Hank, can you help me get this stuffed animal for Amelia, please?" asked the boy with too much gel in his hair. "I've already spent too much money on this stupid machine."

I was too busy wondering if I should try to get that stuffed Chococat for Kiera and hadn't noticed Hank's arrival. He wore a T-shirt with comic superhero on the front and cargo shorts, a different outfit from when I saw him earlier at the campground. A backpack was slung over his shoulder.

He looked at me and lifted a finger. "Just a m-moment."

"Take your time." I walked up to the machine and observed Hank helping the teens. His hand gripped the joystick and moved it with efficiency. His intense focus reminded me of my friends. The determination on his face showed nothing else existed but the end goal.

In this gaming atmosphere, Hank seemed like a new person —young, free, and more relaxed. It differed from the awkward guy wandering around the campground.

I didn't know why, but my suspicion of him lessened. With ease, he got the Hello Kitty plush and gave it to the teen boy, who gave it to his girlfriend.

The teen boy offered money to Hank, but he refused. "It's okay. This m-machine eats up money like c-crazy."

"Thanks, man! You're the best."

After the teens walked away, I gestured to the machine. "I'm going to try for that Chococat plushie stuck in the corner. If I fail, can you help me?"

He asked, "Is it for K-Kiera?"

I nodded, inserted two dollars into the machine, gripped the joystick, and went to retrieve my Chococat. The claw reached down, extracted it from the tight corner, lifted the plush, and moved toward the opening. But then it wriggled free and dropped on top of a Keroppi plushie.

"Shit." I shouted.

Hank laughed, sending me a pitying look, which should have annoyed me. Instead, I smiled and stepped aside. "Show me your skills, buddy."

Here I was, developing a multimillion-dollar video game, and I couldn't even win a plush for my woman. I should probably buy the damn thing and have it shipped to me the next day to save the money and embarrassment.

I hated losing, and this machine was primed for people like me who kept feeding it money, knowing full well the chances of winning were slim.

But that was the beauty of these games. Like WaterFyre Rising, it allowed the player to escape into a world, keeping him there until he figured out how to move onto the next level. It was a natural human condition to win, survive, feel alive. To be in control. The booming games industry homed in on those emotions.

Hank moved the handle to grab Chococat. Then he shook the joystick until the claw trembled and spun while holding Chococat tightly as it moved toward the mouth, releasing into the drop.

Holy shit. He did it.

We sat down at a booth in the back of the arcade. Noises

boomed around us, giving us the privacy we needed by making us inconspicuous. It was a great meetup place.

"Y-you want anything to eat?" Hank asked, sitting across from me. "The pizza is good here."

"No thanks, but you go ahead," I said, realizing that Hank's stuttering wasn't as bad in this environment as compared to the campground. If the camp was so stressful, why did he live there?

Hank ordered two slices of pizza with everything on it.

I paid for it along with a fruit punch for him and an iced tea for me. "It's a thank you for helping me get Chococat." I patted the plush, which sat beside me like a pet.

"Okay, thank you." He bit into his pizza and chewed.

I interlaced my fingers, studying him. When he finished a slice, I asked, "What can you tell me about the fire?"

He placed down the pizza and sipped his fruit punch, looking nervous. "I saw them torch the cabin."

"Who?" My fingers curled, itching to hurt whoever was responsible.

"Not sure. They came at different times."

They? "Have you told the authorities?"

Hank's mouth tensed. "N-no. I d-don't trust them." Fear sparked in his eyes as the stuttering returned.

His hands trembled, and I suspected something horrible had happened to him that triggered the stuttering.

"Thank you." I squeezed his hand. "You can trust me, Hank."

I wanted to know what happened to him, but he might hesitate with a stranger.

"I don't think the t-two people were working together. A woman came first when K-Kiera was out, then a man arrived a day later. He was the one w-who torched it. They both wore caps and face masks. It's hard to see because of the t-trees. My camera isn't very good."

Hope sparked. "You have videos? Can you send them to me?"

He nodded. "I'm saving money f-for an upgrade. It's hard when you work part-time here."

"Why do you trust me with this information?" I asked.

"Because you care for K-Kiera. She looks like my sister. The long brown hair." He patted his head. "If someone had cared about my sister, Nikky, she'd still be alive today."

"What happened to her?"

"Went missing two years ago. Her body hasn't been f-found. I know she's dead. The police department wouldn't tell me or my mom anything. They said they had no leads. It's a cold case. Officer St. Pierre came to my cabin once . . ." He inhaled a breath, and his body shook. "N-Never mind."

"Tell me." I held his eyes. "The best way to fight the monster is to face it. What did he do to you?"

Rage boiled inside me as Hank revealed the torture he'd endured.

"I was d-doing well with my stuttering, but it got worse after that day. Mom doesn't know all the details. I don't want to her to worry."

Bruce had threatened Hank, who was just trying to locate his missing sister. Was Bruce the person who torched Kiera's cabin? Who was the woman?

An idea popped into my head. "Can I hire you?"

"For what?"

"Keep recording what you see at the campground. I know Kiera's not staying there anymore, but I want to know what's going on. I'm ordering you a set of high-end cameras. They're small, so you can place them at various angles outside to get the best footage."

"Like a spy?" His eyes gleamed.

"Yeah."

"Okay."

"We keep this between us. Understand?"

Hank agreed, and for the next few minutes, our conversation swung to video games and movies. He didn't stutter during any of those discussions.

Fucking Bruce had traumatized Hank, sending his body into panic mode, which increased the fear and stutter.

I needed to visit this fucker soon.

"Your stuttering will improve the more you immerse yourself with people and places you love." I smiled. "I'm a doctor, so I know how the body and mind work."

He sighed. "The b-body they found on the road wasn't the man who attacked that resident and broke into the rooms."

I figured that much. "Do you know who that criminal is?"

He flicked me a look, and I knew without him having to say anything.

CHAPTER THIRTY-THREE

KIERA

I woke early with Forrest's arm around me, the other tucked behind his head. His eyes were closed, and he looked handsome and peaceful, like a warrior taking a break from a rough battle. His tan chest rose and dipped, mesmerizing me with its rhythm.

I snuggled closer, wrapping one leg over him. My thigh pressed into his morning wood, and I smiled. I didn't remember him coming home last night or when I'd fallen asleep. The last thing I remembered was the Opals are Forever mission, which made me laugh.

I loved being in his arms. I stroked a hand around his bare chest, enjoying the firmness of his muscles and the slight dusting of hair as I moved lower.

The clock by the bedside table read five in the morning. I didn't remember ever waking up this early with anyone and feeling promiscuous. My hand landed on his cock and remained there, feeling its heat intensify by the second. What was wrong with me? I should let him sleep.

"Causing trouble already?" His groggy voice startled me.

I looked up and met his gaze. He didn't have any sleep in his eyes.

"Were you awake all this time?" I pulled back my hand, feeling embarrassed.

"Yes." He smiled devilishly, clasping my hand and placing it back on his cock.

I slid my hand under his boxers and gripped his raw arousal. "Why are you up?"

"I have a lot of meetings scheduled today. Need to get an early start. But I wanted to be in bed with you a bit longer until you started teasing me."

I yanked down his boxer, setting his cock free. "Good morning to you," I said, stroking it with slow seduction.

He sucked in a breath, watching me. "What time do you have to work?"

"Ten. You?"

"Eight. So we've got three hours to kill." Flipping me under him, he pressed me down with his weight. He was a big man, and I loved the feel of him over me. He kissed me while his hand roamed south, sliding into my panties and finding my wet center.

Forrest slid his cock into me, pumping like a wild man. "Did you miss me last night?"

"Yes," I gasped. "Where did you go?"

"I got you a Chococat." He drove in deeper, and I wrapped my legs around him, loving the connection.

"Sure," I replied at the unbelievable thought.

I couldn't think as my body tensed, preparing for the impending orgasm.

"You don't believe me." He smirked and pumped faster, deeper. "Let me show you all the things I'll do for you."

"Forrest!" The orgasm rippled through me, sending a wave of bliss that made me want to stay in bed forever.

He studied my face. "Do you believe me now?"

"It's hard to think when you're doing that."

"Maybe this angle will help, baby." He flipped me sideways and plunged deeper.

Two hours later—after a steamy shower that gave me another unforgettable orgasm and a quick haircut that made him appear sexier and more sophisticated—I got ready to head to the campground for my last FitFlex photo shoot.

"How are you getting there?" he asked, dressed in a white crisp shirt with his sleeve rolled up to his elbows.

I loved his longer hair, but there was something about the clean-cut look on him that made him even sharper, more dangerous, like a blade that could cut through anything. It was my second time cutting a man's hair. The first time was at a charity event. I'd learned the skill from a hair stylist.

"Bruno and Olivia are picking me up," I said.

He growled. "Why do you need Bruno?"

Bruno was the FitFlex organizer, so he could attend all the photo shoots if he wanted to. But Forrest wasn't looking for any explanation. He was a man being possessive, and I was the woman who caused that.

My lips curved into a smirk. "Actually, he's not."

"Are you testing me?" His eyes flickered with heat.

"I just want to see your jealous face." I patted his cheek. "Still very handsome."

"That's a dangerous game, Kiera." He clasped my hand and looked me square in the eye. "I'm not a fan of any man who looks at you like he wants to strip you."

"You're the only one allowed to do that," I assured him.

His eyes softened. "Be careful of your surroundings. Let me know when you get there and when you leave, okay?" He kissed my forehead.

"Okay." This overprotective gesture stirred something deep within me.

Forrest opened a closet and pulled out a gift bag. "For you."

I opened it and gaped at the four-inch-high plush. "You actually went out to get me Chococat? Are you crazy? It was so late at night."

But the adorable plush warmed my heart. It was a good size that would look wonderful on my desk or in my car. I nuzzled it against my cheek, and he smiled.

"I'm crazy about you."

I threw my arms around him as tears threatened. "Thank you for the gift."

Though it was a simple stuffed animal, it meant the world to me. The little things in relationships mattered. I didn't need an extravagant shopping trip or dinner at a fancy restaurant. I could plan those myself. Small gestures that showed he was thinking of me—of how it had connected us—touched my heart. I squeezed him, letting out a long sigh.

He drew back. "What's wrong?"

"Nothing's wrong. Everything's right." I kissed his cheek and dropped Chococat into my bag, which gave him plenty of room to lounge around. "He's hanging out with me today."

Forrest smiled, and my heart fluttered at how gorgeous he was. He was blessed with insanely good looks. But there was something in his eyes that worried me. He had a lot on his plate and yet he got me a plush.

I had an idea to help him relax, but that had to wait until after my photo session.

His face turned serious as he led me to a couch. "Have a seat. I need to tell you something."

I sat down on the edge of the cushion. "What's going on?"

"Hank's cameras caught people around your cabin before the fire."

"Have the authorities seen them?" Fear squirmed in my stomach.

Shaking his head, Forrest explained Hank's fears of the police because Bruce had mistreated him. Hank didn't trust the police, and I didn't blame him.

Anger spiked in me. "He shouldn't be a cop. He should be in jail."

"Hank's protective of you because you resemble his sister."

"He greeted me on my first day at the cabin," I said, remembering his awkwardness and stuttering. I was grateful he had recordings to help with the case. "Have you reviewed the videos?"

"Not yet, but I will." He paused a moment. "Hank saw a man torch your cabin."

I hated the way fear nibbled its way inside me. It shouldn't have this kind of power over me. "I don't understand why. I don't have enemies . . . well, at least I'm not aware of any."

"Maybe it has nothing to do with you. The fire could've been aimed at the campground owners. A bitter resident could've returned and picked your cabin because it's set away from the main lodge, making it an easy target. Regardless, I want you to be aware of your space."

My phone pinged. "Olivia's downstairs waiting for me." I got up from the couch, grabbed my bag and camera, and headed to the door.

"Are you forgetting something?" Forrest asked from behind me.

I whirled around to find him standing with his hands tucked inside his pants, looking hot and sexy. Smiling, I stepped closer, got up on my tiptoes, and kissed him on the lips. "Is that what you wanted?"

"Damn right."

CHAPTER THIRTY-FOUR

FORREST

After Kiera left, the air in the suite changed. An emptiness rushed into the room, making me feel uncomfortable even though I'd stayed in this suite since I bought the hotel seven years ago. I stood in place, trying to acclimate myself to this new realization that she meant more to me in ways I couldn't understand yet.

When we'd connected all those months ago, something profound had been planted. And now that seed was germinating, growing faster than I could anticipate.

Kiera made my life brighter, more vivid. The sun shone brighter. The air smelled fresher. The earth felt more fertile. As these additional aspects illumined in me, fear also surfaced. No woman had mattered this much to me until now. Well, my mom and my grandmother mattered, but they were different. Kiera pulled at my desires and tied them into one complicated knot.

Initially, I had intended to wake early to start my day. I needed to reply to emails that I'd neglected yesterday, review the status of my holistic medicine, touch base with the director of Vitality Health Clinic in Providence, check in with the lawyer regarding the lawsuit with Grandma's shop, and follow up with Hieu at Holistic Farm, including other members of my management team who were overseeing the $Ba_7M_5Bu_{88}$ Project. Though my management team was competent, it was my enterprise. A snapshot of the big picture was one way to avoid major pitfalls.

Aside from this, the threat of The Trogyn loomed over me. What were they planning?

In addition to everything, I was searching for my father's murderer. I didn't know his name. All I knew was that he was part of the gang called Anacondas. I'd put in a lot of effort, time, and money searching for him and his real name, but nothing had surfaced. A couple of years after killing my father, he'd gone under the radar after killing another gang leader. But I knew I'd find him. People like the Anacondas didn't deserve to live.

I felt like I was walking through a storm, trying my best not to get battered by flying debris.

Despite the long to-do list, it all faded when Kiera woke in my bed like an adorable kitten seducing me. The stuff on my list transformed into things I wanted to do to her. Her magical touch sent electrical currents coursing through me. When a man experienced this kind of exceptional bliss, nothing else mattered. The skim of her elegant fingers over my skin illuminated nerve endings that shot straight into my dormant heart, waking it up. Because of the potency, I knew what true desire felt like, and there was no going back.

I wanted more. The "more" meant something I wasn't ready to admit yet.

Putting everything aside for now, I ambled to my office and got ready to work. I checked on the status of the new security cameras I'd purchased last night before hopping into bed with

Kiera. They were due to arrive before five this evening. I'd forwarded the details to Hank's email. I shipped the cameras to the local warehouse for Hank to pick up to avoid any suspicion, in case the person responsible for the fire was still around. It could be a campground worker for all I knew. It was safe to consider everyone as the enemy for now. Hank said he'd send me the recordings from his camera this morning.

True to his word, I saw a link to a shared drive and downloaded the files. I appreciated dependable people—those who kept their word. The world was a bleak and dangerous place, and a man who kept his word was rare.

I reviewed Hank's files and sighed. He was right; the quality sucked. They were too pixelated. I could barely see the figures around Kiera's cabin. For someone who lived there and was used to the surroundings, he could make sense of the blurry sections better than someone like me. Despite the low quality, I made out two figures around the cabin at different intervals. When the fire occurred, the smoke blocked out everything. I fast forwarded until I saw another figure peeking into the dumpster.

Who was this person? What was he or she looking for? Was this the same person sneaking around Kiera's cabin, or someone new? Or could this be the person who had attacked Bruno and stole items at the main lodge?

The fire department had deemed the cabin fire was arson. An idiot could have told them that. The stove, microwave, and refrigerator were still standing. I was no fire investigator, but one glance told me the flames didn't start there. It was in the living room, the wall that faced Hank's apartment.

Intuition told me something dangerous was at play here. Was the person searching the dumpster as a thief hoping to find treasures he could sell? Or was there something hidden in the cabin that he wanted?

The PI would have smart software that could enhance the quality of the videos. I sent the PI the email with the link. Maybe I could see more with a better resolution. Regardless of clarity, these videos confirmed that three individuals were around Kiera's cabin. One of them had burned it down.

With that task crossed off my list, I spent an hour replying to work emails and made some phone calls to my management team. When that was done, I turned my attention to Bruce St. Pierre. I'd done research on him last night but didn't find anything useful, so I'd asked the PI for assistance, and he delivered. As I skimmed the data, a skewed character formed in my head. Bruce was a follower, not a leader, though I was certain he'd object to that. He barely graduated from the police academy and worked as a security guard for a large law firm in Dallas before becoming a cop for the last five years. He was married with two sons and had been reprimanded a few times by the department.

I smiled when the information got interesting. Juicy developments were the wild card in a negotiation. The things he did —or was still doing—should put him in prison for a long time.

Bruce had booked a few days at a fishing resort about an hour's drive from here. Today was his first day there. It was time Bruce and I had a conversation. If he didn't give me honest answers, I'd make sure he knew that although I was a doctor who healed people, I was excellent at killing them too.

CHAPTER THIRTY-FIVE

Despite losing my belongings, I quickly regained my balance thanks to Forrest. The way he took care of things—*took care of me*—made me feel that everything was going to be all right. I couldn't remember the last time I'd experienced this much anxiety.

He didn't want payment for the computer and asked for kisses instead. I didn't know what to do with this man. He resolved my financial issues without even knowing it.

I'd received a text from Bruno asking if I was interested in photographing an Australian fashion brand in Sydney. Though I appreciated the opportunity, I'd declined because—thanks to Forrest—my financial anxiety wasn't as acute and the job would take me across the globe, far away from my mom.

The photo session with Olivia finished quicker than I expected. We only had a few swimwear ensembles to photograph, and I took more than usual. Since she brought her laptop, I used it to download the photos from my camera's SD card and uploaded them to the shared drive. I could access them tonight or tomorrow for some edits. Olivia took fabulous pictures, so there wouldn't be a lot of edits.

"That's a wrap, Liv." I logged out of her computer. "Thanks for letting me use it."

"Anytime." She tucked it back into her bag. We brought all the clothes back to the car and headed out. "I'm meeting up with a friend for lunch. Want to join me?"

I already had plans to go shopping. "Thanks for asking, but I'm going to pass. I want to check out the area and get a souvenir for my mom. We have that second gig in two days, and I'm flying back to Providence right after."

"Yes, go shopping. I can drop you off at the shopping district. Do you need me to pick you up after?"

"No, I'll be fine."

Olivia pulled over to the street parking. "Y'all have fun, babe!"

I chuckled at her attempt at a Southern drawl, got out, and waved. "Thanks for the ride."

The shopping district was two blocks away from Forrest's hotel, so I could walk back if I didn't melt from the blazing sun. With my camera bag and purse in tow, I strode down the sidewalk in my sandals, admiring all the little shops that illustrated the community.

I stopped by a window with an assortment of cowboy hats, boots, and leather accessories. An image of Forrest in jeans, a T-shirt, cowboy boots, and a cowboy hat sparked in my mind, making me shiver. *Sure would like a ride on that cowboy.* Though the image was hotter than the current temperature, Forrest was no cowboy. He was a polished and sophisticated man who preferred to bathe in luxury and propriety—though he showed me plenty of impropriety in bed.

Despite that, he was also a hot farmer who got his hands dirty by growing medicinal plants. So, although he wasn't a cowboy, he was my incomparable farmer, doctor, forward thinker, and entrepreneur. I made a mental note to place an order online for a cowboy hat and cowboy boots and have them shipped to Providence.

My stomach growled, and I entered an eatery with a pink awning to get a turkey sandwich. With my lunch and lemonade, I went to the outdoor patio and sat at a table with a large pink umbrella.

I'd spoken to my mom before the photo shoot and she'd sounded tired but well. She hadn't gotten any worse, but she hadn't gotten any better either. Mom had forgotten to send me her health records because she'd had some friends visiting. But she'd promised to send them today.

I checked my phone, found her email, and forwarded it to Forrest. Like me, he'd been under a lot of stress, so I told him to review them whenever he got a chance, and that it wasn't a rush. I didn't want my burden to become his.

A text appeared in my group chat with the girls, and I grinned at the mission they'd come up for me. The Opals are Forever mission required Forrest to say the L word. I replied, saying they could be waiting a long time. After a quick chat, they all had to go, and I returned to my lunch and solitude.

While I ate, I watched people on the sidewalk going about their day. Some rushed along, while others took their time. Everyone had their way of approaching life. I had to admit that I was one of those who had rushed along until my mom got sick. I had to slow down so I could appreciate my time with her. What was the point of rushing when I'd miss all the little things that mattered?

It didn't take me long to finish my sandwich and lemonade. The quiet solitude relaxed me a little. I took out my Chococat, who had fallen to the bottom of my purse, and placed him on the table.

I patted his head. "Enjoy the sunshine." I found a tiny heart pin in my purse from some event I didn't remember and secured it on Chococat. "Let this heart give you love and happiness."

Smiling at how perfect the pin looked on my adorable plush, I snapped a pic with my phone and sent it to Forrest with the caption: *Missing you meow.*

Then I stuffed him in the front pocket of my purse, which was a perfect size to secure him in place. From that position, he could see the world instead of being inside a dark purse.

I double checked the address for the apothecary and made my way there. As I walked, I noticed a car driving past me in the other direction. Was that Juan, my Uber driver from the airport? He was driving a red SUV instead of the Honda Civic he'd picked me up in.

My gaze followed him, but I couldn't make out the plate number. Juan had seemed like a nice guy. I remembered him telling me he was working two jobs to support his family. My heart had gone out to him, which was why I'd gifted him my precious spa kit. Had he given the bottle of lotion to another passenger?

I'd been wrong about some people in my life, so I wouldn't have been surprised if my hunches about Juan were incorrect. I supposed I always saw the good in people first. How could I live thinking everyone was my enemy? That would stress the hell out of me, making me not want to continue living. Deep down, I believed people forgot how to be nice. It should have been a simple gesture, but life was hard, and sometimes that turned a nice person bitter.

Photography had taught me that. When I looked back at older pictures I'd taken all over the world, I saw the transition of time in the expressions on people's faces. As technology advanced, making it more convenient for people, I noticed they became more disconnected with themselves and the natural world. They were more connected to their devices.

This was one reason I was drawn to nature photography. Plants, moss, and mushrooms, these things told a lovely story about their evolution, all while being connected to everything around them via their roots. They were in touch with what gave them life—the soil, the water, the air, the sun, and the rain.

I often wondered what kind of amazing life existed beneath the soil or in the forest when no one was watching. Like something magical. These curiosities made me happy, but they didn't pay my bills. Fashion photography did.

Maybe I was drawn to Forrest because he was connected to nature and, at the same time connected to the advanced technology. He had a good balance between both worlds. That wasn't easy. Was he aware of that?

A car honked and yanked me back to reality. I'd digressed and lost track of where I was going. I should stop analyzing and just enjoy this time to myself.

More people filled the streets as I made my way down the sidewalk, passing stores and restaurants. Someone darted out of a shop and knocked into me. The force pushed me into someone else. Her groceries scattered all over the sidewalk. I couldn't regain composure and fell onto my ass with my palms scraping the sidewalk.

"I'm sorry, ma'am!" A teen boy looked at me in horror.

I pushed myself up and helped the elderly lady gather her groceries.

"Jason! You need to watch where you're going!" The mom emerged from the store and turned to me. "So sorry."

"It was an accident." I smiled at them even though my butt hurt like hell. "Apology accepted."

As the mom and son walked away bickering about him

needing to pay more attention, I gave the bag of groceries back to the lady with a warm face and sharp eyes.

"Are you okay?" I asked, surveying the older woman. "Sorry about that."

She took the bag from me and smiled. "No need to apologize. It wasn't your fault. Thank you for your help." She tapped the bag. "These are for a special dinner tomorrow for my grandson."

"Nothing beats a homecooked meal. My mom used to cook a lot for me when I was younger."

"Taking care of family is very important. My grandson is a hard worker. Successful people often forget one thing—no one remembers you worked late except your children, your family."

Those words dropped into my heart like pebbles into a well of wisdom. That statement was true. How many times had I worked my ass off on a project only to have them not renew my contracts or ask me for a lower rate? The only people truly affected were my loved ones.

"Thank you for that," I said. "It was nice to meet you. I hope you have a fabulous dinner. I'm heading to Full Circle Apothecary to get some gifts. Have you been there?"

Her green eyes sparkled. "You're in luck. That's my shop. I can help you choose."

I needed the luck. Delighted, I followed her.

CHAPTER THIRTY-SIX

I spotted Bruce on a pier with two guys wearing tank tops and shorts. He wore a red baseball cap, a black T-shirt, and camo shorts. Another group of people cheered further down the lake. A cool breeze blew in from the lake that glistened from the bright sun. I wouldn't mind the Texan weather if it were temporary.

Even in my T-shirt and shorts, beads of sweat formed on my head. I walked over to a shaded area with picnic tables and sat down. Beside me was a table filled with food, packages of beer, sodas, plates, napkins, and utensils.

An older man strode up wearing a cowboy hat, tipping it at me. "Howdy. You fishin', son? Which group are you with?"

"No, I'm here for moral support." I jerked a chin toward the pier. "Meeting up with my friend Bruce."

He turned and shouted, "Bruce! Your buddy is here. What you doing over there?" He smiled, revealing a missing tooth. "Enjoy your day."

The man strode off to join a group of women and children.

Bruce looked at me once, then twice, and something passed

over his face. He said something to his buddy, handed over his fishing rod, and walked toward me.

I got up from the bench and met him halfway.

"Can I help you?" Bruce asked suspiciously.

Only someone with a criminal past would suspect everyone. His enemies could appear at any moment.

"I have questions that need answers, and you have them. It's best we discuss this elsewhere."

"I'm not going anywhere." He glanced around. "Whatever you need to ask, do it here."

The heat was getting to me, and Bruce's inability to cooperate added to my frustration.

Stepping closer, I placed a hand on his shoulder, squeezed hard, and whispered, "I can certainly do that if you want people to know about the beating deaths of two men." I named them for him. "And the recording that showed you with a fifteen-year-old girl. Her father is on the city council in Dallas. Do you want me to call him, Officer Bruce?"

Shock splashed on his face as he swatted my hand away and stepped back from me. "There's a brook down this way. Come with me."

The beast in me wanted me to kick his ass right now. With my years of training in Brazilian Jiu-Jitsu, I could easily drop him, but martial arts wasn't about attacking. It was about discipline and self-defense.

I inhaled a deep breath and followed Bruce down a hiking trail, away from the people. We arrived at a brook, surrounded by shrubberies and tall trees.

He glanced around, probably making sure no one was within earshot. "How in hell did you find this information? It's all just rumors."

"Then why are you scared? Photos and videos don't lie."

His mouth dropped open. "What do you want?"

"Did you torch Kiera's cabin?"

"No!" His eyes widened. "Why would I do that?"

Because you're an asshole.

"Do you know who?"

He inhaled and exhaled, stress clear on his face. "They'll kill me. They're dangerous."

Hank and I both thought Bruce had been responsible for the fire, but things were more complicated than I realized.

Could Bruce be part of The Trogyn?

"Who left the raccoon on Kiera's porch?"

His eyes darted away from me. "They told me to scare her."

"Why?"

"I don't know. They told me to do random shit without giving me a reason. If I ask too many questions, they'd think I was being disloyal."

"Who are they? Why are you working for them?"

Bruce paced around, tugging at his hair. "I needed money to pay off gambling debts. They helped me at first, but then it turned into a large amount of money I couldn't pay back. So I started working for them, doing all kinds of shit. Drugs messed me up bad."

I wanted to say so many things to him, but I needed answers. Insulting him—even though it was the truth—wouldn't benefit me right now.

"You shouldn't be a cop."

"I didn't want to be one!" He shot out one hand into the air. "I was fine working as a security guard, but they wanted me to work in the police department . . . maneuver stuff around." He kicked a rock, and it flew into the brook.

"Drugs?" I asked.

He nodded. "Big money. I hear they own some cartels."

Money had a way of talking loudly. I had no doubt The Trogyn managed the cartels.

"Why the cabin? What's in there?"

"They got intel that the drugs were at the campground, so they searched around."

"But why *that* specific cabin?" He was hiding something.

"Something happened in that cabin before."

I went on a hunch. "Does it have to do with Hank's sister?"

Bruce's body tensed, and he paced again.

"Think carefully before you answer," I said. "Those people might be dangerous, but so am I."

He braced a hand on the tree trunk and looked at me. "Who are you? Some kind of private investigator?"

"I'm a man on a quest to find out what happened to my girlfriend's cabin. She could've died." My lips thinned. "The way Hank cringes around you piqued my interest. You can say I'm a guy who likes to right some wrongs."

Balance was needed in everything, including the human body. Equilibrium boosted the immune system, strengthening the person. When out of balance, diseases emerged.

I was not God, but I believed those who committed crimes should be punished.

Then you should look at yourself too.

I ignored my inner voice because I didn't have time to argue with it.

Bruce stared at me for a while, probably trying to weigh if he could trust me. If I were him, I'd be doing the same thing.

"I want to stop working for them," he blurted out. "But I can't. They know too much about me and my family."

"You should have thought about the families of those you've killed and raped. Start repenting by telling me the truth."

His body sagged against the tree trunk, looking like a cornered creature. In some way he was, he had to choose a side now: me or The Trogyn.

"We have a common enemy, Bruce," I said, trying to shed light on his dilemma. "This conversation will stay between us and these woods. Unless the trees and birds can talk, no one will know about what you tell me."

He licked his lips and took in a deep inhale, followed by an exhale.

"Nikky Peterson stayed at Kiera's cabin, right?"

"Yeah, with two other girls. The men came and took them one night."

"They're dead, aren't they?" I asked, and his eyes confirmed my suspicion. "Where are the bodies?"

Tension formed a deep crease between his eyebrows. When he told me the truth, I wanted to drown him in the brook, but it was too shallow.

Before I left the fishing resort, people assumed Bruce and I were good friends discussing a handy work project. There was a lightness to Bruce after his confession. Though he didn't kill Hank's sister, he was involved with the people who did. I didn't always believe in second chances, especially for criminals who kept repeating the same crime. But after meeting Kiera and reconnecting with her, I believed in it. She was my second chance at happiness.

Even though Bruce deserved jail time, I gave him a second chance. He needed to give me information on The Trogyn and where they kept trafficked victims and the locations of their drug operations. He told me he didn't know, and I believed him because he didn't even know the crime organization was called The Trogyn. Someone on his level wouldn't be privy to top information, but he could get creative if I was his ticket to salvation.

I could be the compassionate devil who gave him this second chance.

I also discovered the person who had attacked Bruno was some guy named Bo, who had orders to make it look like a robbery. Bruno happened to be at the wrong place at the wrong time and took the hit. I smiled at the thought and asked if Bruno was part of the organization. But Bruce had never seen him at any of the meetings.

Had I been wrong about Bruno? Or was he part of another crime organization?

Inside my car, I leaned back into the seat and breathed. The conversation with Bruce drained my energy. I had to inform my boys of this recent development and compare notes with them.

After a few moments, I checked my phone and smiled at Kiera's photo of her Chococat with a little heart pin, enjoying a lunch date. Her text message lightened my mood, rejuvenating my body instantly.

I typed a reply. *I love that you're my girl-fur-end. You're purrfect fur me.*

A laugh escaped me, followed by shock and embarrassment.

I'm so fuuucked. Since when did I send out that kind of text? Even thinking in such a silly way was beyond me. But now I was capable of that and more.

I had it bad for her.

With renewed energy, I sent out a conference request to all my friends. My phone rang with Levi's name flashing on the screen.

"What's up?" I asked.

"The banquet has been moved to Sunday evening."

The day after dinner at Grandma's. I didn't know why they kept changing the date, but I went with the flow. Something was happening here in Austin, Texas, and it was bigger than I could ever imagine.

"Just give me the address, and I'll be there."

"They'll send a text to let us know twelve hours before the event. I don't know why they're being so paranoid this time. The last few gatherings weren't this secretive."

This was a tactic used to weed out people who weren't in close proximity. The ones who were serious about the event should have already been here in Texas.

"Okay. I'll keep an eye out for it. If I don't get it, I'll be calling you."

"Sounds good. It's a black-tie event, so don't come in jeans," he teased.

"Do you know anyone new who's attending?"

"I haven't been asking, and I'm not going to. Why?"

I didn't want to disclose anything that could hurt my friend. The less Levi knew, the better. "Just curious. I mean, there could be a celebrity attending. Maybe that's why they're being extra careful."

"I didn't think of that. Maybe a celebrity is performing for us like a halftime show."

The organizer knew me as a wealthy man who was looking to spend money and have fun. Men like me shouldn't care who attended because spontaneity was the heart of any party.

"Well, gotta go now. I have a meeting."

"See you later."

After I hung up the phone, I headed back to the hotel for a conference with my friends.

CHAPTER THIRTY-SEVEN

KIERA

As we strode on the sidewalk, I discovered Morena was an herbalist. She showed me various shops I should visit and shook her head at the businesses I should avoid.

As we approached Full Circle Apothecary, a couple was leaving.

"Thank you for treating me to this, honey. I love you." The woman kissed her beaming lover on the cheek.

The Opals are Forever mission seemed impossible to me. Forrest and I were just getting to know each other on a different level. He wouldn't say the L word first. Would he? Did it matter? Most men feared that word like it had spikes around it. They'd ignore that idea for as long as possible. Male and female brains worked differently.

This mission could last a year or two before completion. Would we still be together? I didn't have a great record with long-term relationships. A nugget of doubt surfaced. Would my relationship with Forrest end up the same way?

Stop the negativity.

I wished there were a button on my body that I could just

press to delete all these negative thoughts forever. But that would make life too easy. I think God wanted all of us to learn lessons.

But we need a break now and then, don't we? I glanced up at the sky as though someone were listening to me—maybe even laughing.

I stood and admired the beautiful apothecary from the outside. There were apartments on the top floors. Cars filled the parking lot on the side. Lovely pots of plants decorated the front door, while a sales display occupied the space near the entrance.

I opened the door for Morena.

"Thank you," she said.

As soon as I stepped inside, my body immediately relaxed, as though an invisible shower of serenity poured down on me. A lovely scent drew me to a basket of dry lavender on a table with organic soaps. Glancing around, I absorbed the peaceful setup. I'd expected a mystic-themed display, like the stores I'd visited decorated in dark colors and filled with a mishmash of trinkets. But everything in Full Circle Apothecary was well organized, making it easy for the customer to appreciate every item.

The ambiance in the shop was like heaven on Earth, and the soft colors tones of green, teal, and aqua welcomed me in. Along with those pretty colors were brown and gray accents, presenting this shop as the most unique apothecary I'd ever encountered.

The clothes Morena wore described her sense of style and personality. This shop cemented her as a wise woman who could tap into a person's somatic senses. I didn't know why, but I felt so at home here. My body calmed, and my mind opened up, and the stress in me dissolved with no effort on my part.

Morena introduced me to Cara, a sales associate and herbalist with a friendly face, who was preparing for a class.

A customer approached Morena with a question.

Morena turned to me. "Take a look around, and let me know if you need any help."

"I sure will. Don't worry about me. Do what you need to do."

I walked over to a section with books and small pots of live plants. Pulling out a curvy chair, I sat down on the soft cushion and flipped through a book of herbs. Pictures of live plants and their dried samples showed their transition. When I finished reviewing the plant bible, my eyes darted to another book titled *Finding Your HeART* by Nadia Han. It was a journal with prompts, activities, and mesmerizing art. I had a journal when I was younger, but stopped writing as I got older. Life got in the way.

I flipped through the book, and it stopped on a page that had my heart bursting with joy. The word "Imperfect" stared at me. Next to it was another version of the same letters that read "I'm Perfect." One word became a powerful statement. I blinked at the profound truth of it, and how the author conveyed it with simplicity by adding a heart-shaped apostrophe. She was right. All it took was one shift in perspective to change the power and meaning of the word.

I held the book to my heart, and felt the energy of the book seep into me, unlocking my emotions. What came through were raw images of my past, present, and future. I was an imperfect woman dealing with many things. I juggled abandonment issues, the blood phobia, my mom's medical condition, and being honest with myself about my dreams and desires.

I'd suffered from trying to be perfect, but I didn't really know what "perfect" meant. Was I chasing after it for me, or was it a validation to belong somewhere?

I flipped to the next page, smiled, and glanced up at the ceiling. Yup, God was watching me, for sure. The word "Impossible" blazed on the page, and "I'm Possible" winked at me on the next.

The Opals are Forever mission is possible.

Anything was possible with that statement. Instead of buying one copy, I'd purchase four more, one for each of my friends. They'd love it.

Filled with optimism, I got up and browsed the herb room where a class was taking place. I snapped a picture of the schedule for reference. I wouldn't mind taking a class to create an herbal drink at home. This could help my mom too. Maybe they had online courses that I could sign up for.

As I passed a display of greeting cards and postcards with dried flowers on them, an idea bloomed in my head.

What if I created greeting cards from my nature pictures? I had a ton of images of mushrooms, ferns, and other plants that would make exceptional greeting cards and postcards. A thrill rushed through me as the idea expanded into a full concept in my head. This could be a thriving side business for me. I could use all those images I'd taken over the years. They would serve a purpose instead of hiding in a file on my computer. They'd get to see the world like Chococat.

"The world is filled with possibilities, right Chococat?" I tapped its head.

"I see you've found some things already." Morena appeared beside me, smiling at the books in my hand. "Excellent choice. That book just released, and it's been selling like hotcakes."

"There's definitely magic in it."

"I don't carry a lot of journals, but when I saw a copy, I knew it would resonate with many people."

"That's why I'm giving it to my friends. We all have stuff to heal. I love everything in this store. Maybe you can help me find something for my mom." I gave her a brief description of my mom's Hepatitis A symptoms and the extreme fatigue that prevented her from enjoying life.

Morena went to the herbal counter and opened a bag. Then she walked up to a wall of compartments and picked out herbs from various containers, weighed them, and placed them in the bag.

"This is a soothing drink with ginger, cloves, dandelion, a bit of ginseng, and magnolia bark. It helps rebalance her immune system. This won't interfere with any of her current meds. Here are the directions for the brew." She added the note.

Morena packed three bags and tied them up with a nice ribbon, placing them aside on the counter. I put the books next to them, freeing my hands to continue shopping.

"Let me know how she likes it," Morena smiled. "Is there something else you need help with?"

"Yes, please. A good luck charm. I've been experiencing bad luck recently, so I'd like to clear that energy and protect myself better."

"Come right this way." She showed me a display of interesting amulets. My eyes went to a dish with floral amulets made of woven willow branches. They were small enough to fit into my purse. I could even hang one on the rearview mirror.

"These are gorgeous." I choose two circular designs, one for me and my mom. The diamond-shaped design was for Forrest.

"A local artist and shaman made these exclusively for this store."

"He must love your shop."

"I helped him lower his cholesterol and blood pressure, so he's now a happy and healthy man."

I brought the items to the front desk and saw that more customers had entered, keeping Cara busy.

Morena placed the items in the shopping bags for me. "You don't owe me anything. It's my gift to you."

"What?" I blinked at the unexpected gesture. "Of course, I do. You're running a business. Please let me pay."

"This isn't just a business to make money. It's just as much a business to help people heal."

I didn't know what to say as I stared at the shopping bag. I wasn't just getting one thing from the store—I bought a lot of stuff.

"Also, it's my gratitude for your help with the dropped groceries. Some people would have just ignored me. I appreciate your kindness."

"It was really nothing. Just common sense and human decency, you know?"

She sighed. "You'd be surprised how many people lack those things. I was glad no one took the opportunity to rob me. With all the violence lately, it's always good to meet genuinely nice people."

I decided right then and there that if I had known my grandmother, I hoped she would've been someone like Morena. My grandmother had died before I was born.

A thought sparked in me. "Thank you, but I want to do something nice for you too. I have this idea for some greeting cards and postcards. I can print out a small supply and send them to you to sell at your store. They're my gift to you. You keep the profits. If they sell well, would you consider carrying them in your shop?"

I explained my concepts, and her face beamed.

"Would you like to come to dinner tomorrow night and discuss this idea? My little family would be there. They'd love to hear it. It's a yes for me."

I checked the calendar on my phone and didn't see anything planned for the next evening. Olivia and I were supposed to start a new job tomorrow, but I should be done before dinner.

"I'd like that."

After waving goodbye to Cara, I exited the shop and walked toward the hotel when Yolanda walked by with two of her friends. She wore a pretty yellow sundress. I didn't know if she recognized me, but she didn't say hello when we made eye contact. I didn't blame her. We didn't know each other. I only saw her sitting with Forrest at Taco Haven. I couldn't believe I'd been jealous of Forrest's cousin in the beginning. But all of that was in the past. He was with me now.

As I walked, I swung the shopping bag containing the willow amulets and my mom's herbal mixes like a gleeful girl who had gotten everything she wanted. A plan formed in my head for when to give Forrest his amulet. I'd tell him I had a dinner date planned but wouldn't tell him with whom. Would he be jealous?

My visit to Full Circle Apothecary was the adventure I needed today. I felt rejuvenated just being in that tranquil atmosphere. It was like taking a stroll inside the woods, where every nook and cranny had things to discover. The incense, herbs, live plants, lotions, soaps, perfumes, and essential oils healed me indirectly. I had enough energy to take over the world.

My phone rang, and I stopped by a bench.

"Howdy, Olivia! What y'all up to?" I asked, trying out the Southern accent.

"Why are you so cheerful?"

"I bought some cool gifts. What's up? How was lunch?"

"I just got a call from Yvette, the manager hosting the fashion show. She said the stage and showroom are all set up now. She invited us to check it out. Want to look at it with me? I want to see the space and the clothes I'm going to wear. The images in the email looked gorgeous, but I'd rather see and touch them myself."

I always preferred to familiarize myself with the setting before taking photos. Paying a visit would save me time trying to gauge the angles, shadows, and light.

"Sure, let's go. I have my camera with me." I told her my location and waited for her car.

Twenty minutes later, she arrived. I put my shopping bag and the camera in the back seat and buckled into the passenger side.

The GPS took us down a small residential street. A murder of crows flew out from a tree and across the car windshield, startling us.

"Shit!" Olivia shouted as she screeched to a stop.

An uncomfortable feeling squeezed my stomach. "Are you sure this is the way?"

When the crows left, she continued on and came to an intersection. "GPS is usually reliable. I'm just gonna call Yvette to double check." She pulled over to a parking spot.

I could see industrial buildings across the street.

A black van drove up and parked beside us. Two men wearing white masks got out from the side door and aimed a gun at us. "Get out. Keep your mouths shut, and keep your hands up or I will kill you."

Oh my God! Olivia's hands shook as she dropped her phone.

Fear spiked in me, and for a moment, I remembered that day when I saw Forrest's bloody body on the ground. I snapped myself out of it because I wasn't a little girl experiencing extreme fear for the first time anymore.

"Let's get out," I said to Olivia. "Do as they say, okay? If they wanted to kill us, they would've done it already."

Olivia nodded and squeezed my hand.

I pushed the fear down, and it sat in my gut, churning and churning. I had to be strong to survive.

Looking at the men, I said, "You need to open the door if you want our hands to stay up."

One man yanked my door open while the other went over to Olivia's side, dragging her out. I considered using the self-defense moves I'd learned in Vivian's class, but I hadn't been practicing enough. Fear had numbed parts of my body, so my chances of escaping two huge men were slim. Not to mention, I had Olivia with me.

I tripped on something on the ground, stumbling into the man in front of me. He turned and grabbed my breasts and squeezed. I slapped him, and he slapped me back. It stung and infuriated me. I'd never been hit before.

Olivia screamed, "Leave her alone, you asshole!"

He slapped her too, and tears gleamed in her eyes.

I clasped Olivia's hand, pulling her into me.

Who the hell were these guys? What did they want with us?

They shoved us both into the van that had bench seating. One guy got in, sat down on the opposite bench, and aimed his gun at us as though we were dangerous. The other man slid into the driver's seat and sped off.

I prayed that *someone* had witnessed this and called the police.

CHAPTER THIRTY-EIGHT

FORREST

After an hour of chatting with my friends about Bruce's confession, we'd discussed the status of our individual investigation into the elite clubs.

Arrow had organized the growing list of aliases we had to check on. Some might pan out; others could be meaningless names that were thrown around at parties. Regardless, we had something to go by. Organization gave us a snapshot of the big picture. The Trogyn was linked to underground clubs all over the world, but we wanted to focus on the local clubs that were more accessible before looking into foreign countries.

To rest my brain, I played the demo version of Level Four. My video game world was set in a magical jungle where the trees became portals to other worlds. Some connected to parallel modern worlds, while others took the players to fantastical places. The rare plants offered bonus lives and boosted life force.

As I played the game, I thought about Kiera, and an idea percolated in my head. I stopped playing and switched to creative mode. It would be cool to have a goddess with the ability to grow rare blood plants named Agoona. The plant produced the Agoona fruit, which contained magical blood that healed diseases and boosted the body's life force. It would upgrade the WaterFyre Rising energy for skilled players who could obtain it.

Enthusiasm rushed through me, and I knew adding Kiera to Level Four was the perfect addition. I'd been stuck on the plot for a while until this moment. She came into my life and made sense of everything, so it was no surprise that she unraveled the plot for my game too.

When I finished rendering her face and body, an avatar of Kiera looked at me—my perfect Goddess K. Outside of the game, she was my Sexy K, but in this fantastical world she was the sorceress that held all the power.

What would she think if I showed her this?

I looked at the time on the computer, and it was already seven in the evening. Where had the day gone? Where was Kiera? Grabbing my phone, I checked for new messages and didn't see any new texts or a voicemail from her.

The last text message I received from her notified me she was going with Olivia to visit a showroom for her job tomorrow. That had been three hours ago. She should've been home already.

An uncomfortable feeling stirred in me. I called her number, and it went straight to voicemail. Icy knots twisted in my gut.

I called Hank. "Are you busy? Can you help me?"

"How can I help?"

"Go to the main lodge and let me know if you see Olivia's car."

"Something wrong?" he asked.

I was too concerned about Kiera, otherwise I would've pointed out that his stuttering had improved. It motivated people when you acknowledged their progress, but I didn't want a waste a single moment right now.

"I can't reach Kiera."

"Okay. Stay on the phone," he said, and I heard a door open and close.

Fear clawed at me as wild scenarios played out in my head.

The sounds of footsteps and heavy breathing filled the other line. I prayed Hank would tell me Olivia's car was there. Maybe Kiera was hanging out with Olivia and forgot to tell me. The cellular reception around the campground wasn't the best, so she could've missed my calls.

Something in my gut told me she was in trouble. I didn't know how I knew that, but I did.

"The car isn't h-here." I could hear the stress in Hank's voice. "Maybe they took her. The same people who took Nikky."

Fuck.

"If anything strange happens at the campground, let me know. I'm going to make some calls."

"Do you need me to d-do anything else?"

I didn't want to drag Hank into this mess. Stress would make his condition worse, and he'd been more than helpful.

"You help me by monitoring the recordings. Call me if someone comes around again."

After I hung up with Hank, I called Bruce. After our conversation earlier, he would tell me everything he knew.

"I don't know. I swear." Fear made Bruce's voice waver. "The only time I know something's up is when they contact me to do something for them. No one has called."

Silence filled the conversation as I waited to see how much Bruce wanted to get out of the organization by helping me.

"Normally I get a call a few hours before a job is needed. But I can call around and ask."

"You do that and let me know. Text if you have to." I'd given him a burner phone to communicate before I left the fishing resort.

Who had taken her? Why?

I paced around my office as thoughts pounded my head, trying to figure what to do. I didn't have Olivia's number, otherwise I'd call her too. Should I reach out to Bruno? Was he or his associates responsible for Kiera's disappearance?

My phone rang and interrupted the silence in the room. I grabbed it, thinking it was Bruce, but it was Detective Donnelly.

Terror escalated, and my body tensed. Receiving a call from a detective at this moment wasn't a good sign.

"Yes, Detective."

"Sorry to bother you, Forrest. But we just discovered something disturbing. We need your help."

Fifteen minutes later, I arrived at a residential street that overlooked the industrial section of town. Olivia's car was parked crookedly along the curb, which told me they'd probably pulled over unexpectedly.

Kiera's camera and a shopping bag from Full Circle Apothecary were in the back seat. She went to Grandma's shop today? I should've gone with her and introduced them.

Detective Donnelly gestured to the house where the car was parked. "The resident claimed he heard crows and went to the window. He saw men push the girls into a black van and drive off. He didn't get the license plate number because his vision is bad."

The detective handed over Chococat with the heart pin. "This was in the street near the car."

"Thank you." I clasped the plush tightly as a sharp pain stabbed my heart.

I dusted the dirt from the stuffed animal and prayed Kiera and Olivia were safe.

Clenching my free hand into a fist, I vowed to find these assholes.

"I'll have my officers review all the cameras around the vicinity and let you know if we find anything." He pointed to the car. "We have to tow this for further examination."

After speaking with Detective Donnelly for a few more minutes, I took Kiera's and Olivia's belongings with me and drove around the area, hoping to spot her. It wasn't the most efficient idea. I knew I wouldn't find her, but I had to look. Just being in the area where she'd been abducted made me feel closer to her.

Was she afraid? Was she safe? Did they hurt her?

So many emotions roiled inside me, and I couldn't think clearly. Though I wanted to destroy the world to find her, I knew she needed my clarity and stability. She was waiting for me, and every second counted.

An hour or so later, I pulled over on the side of the road and called the campground, asking them to connect me to Bruno.

"I don't know man," Bruno said. "I've been trying to reach them because I need to return the rental tomorrow."

I sensed the truth in his voice. "Let me know if you hear of anything."

"Okay. I'm due to arrive in Providence for another photoshoot, so I won't be around. You can reach me at this number anytime. Keep me posted on Kiera and Olivia. I'll alert FitFlex."

Next I called the PI. "Can you get all the video recordings around this area ASAP?" I rattled off the location. Waiting for the police to get back to me would take too long. My baby didn't have time. "Track my girlfriend's phone too. She's missing." After I gave him her number, I headed home.

I took a quick shower, hoping to release the stress and to clear my head. My phone rang again, and I rushed to pick it up.

I wasn't in the mood to talk to Grandma because she'd have sensed something was wrong. I didn't want to worry her, but I couldn't ignore her call. What if she needed my help?

Grandma was the only other woman who worried me right now

I took a deep breath and pretended everything was fine. "*Vó*, you need something?"

"Do I have to need something to call my grandson?"

"No."

"I just want to remind you about dinner tomorrow."

Shit. I'd forgotten all about it. I couldn't cancel on her, no matter what. It would crush her. Maybe I'd hear news about Kiera before dinner, and I could take her to meet Grandma.

"Yes, I remember. Do you need me to bring anything?"

"No. Just come ready to eat. I invited a new friend. She's really pretty—"

"*Vó*, I already have a girlfriend." I had to interrupt her because I didn't want to discuss another woman while the woman I loved was missing.

Fuuuck.

The emotion I'd been avoiding glared at me. I loved her. I'd been so afraid of the truth that I kept shoving it to the side. She gave meaning to my life. She brought a new sense of wonder and amusement—all the things I was missing.

"What? You didn't tell me?"

"I was going to introduce you to her before I went home. You'll get to meet her soon." Then something occurred to me. "You never invite strangers to our family dinner, *Vó*. What happened?"

"I'm not sure either. But she has a business plan I'm interested in, and I need your input."

A new business plan was the furthest thing from my mind, but I didn't want to disappoint my grandma. "Okay. I'll see you tomorrow."

I walked over to the counter and poured myself two fingers of Scotch, hoping it would ease the tension in my body. As I swirled it around my mouth, I thought about Kiera and how she'd changed me. She made me believe in fate. I was angry with God for a long time. Because if there were a God, why didn't He or She save my father and mother?

Even when I worked at the hospitals, I was used to seeing people suffer when their loved ones passed. I saw the grief on their faces. They were probably asking the same questions as me.

Where is God?

Grief and pain demanded we look inside of ourselves for strength, but I couldn't wait for God. He was probably too busy trying to fix the messed-up world as best he could.

I got my strength back because of Kiera. Love inspired, motivated, and healed people better than any medicine.

Love was the only medicine that could save a dark and unsalvageable heart.

But loving her meant she had to be close to me, and being close to me meant danger. Was *I* responsible for her abduction? Had the leader of the Anacondas caught up to me? I'd already eliminated the other two men who had been present the day my dad died. Only one was still missing.

Intuition told me it wasn't the Anacondas.

What if I never got a chance to tell her how I felt?

Don't think like that.

Too tired, I dropped into bed and closed my eyes. I just needed a little rest before I conducted more research on Kiera's whereabouts.

But my body had its own plan, and exhaustion dragged me into a nightmare.

CHAPTER THIRTY-NINE

KIERA

Olivia and I clung to each other when the driver's phone rang again. The man sitting across from us lowered his gun and looked toward the front seat.

The driver held up his phone while he stared out into an empty parking lot, listening to the distorted woman's voice. "You can bring them back now."

Earlier, she'd told them to drive to another city and stay there until her call. I didn't know how long we'd been sitting in fear, but when the call came, the men were relieved. I'd taken that time to study the men from their conversations with one another. They'd done this many times before. There were other women being abducted in a nearby town. Were they transporting us to some holding place? The driver said he had to drive around until he got the approval to go to the master destination.

I was certain this was a sex trafficking ring. I'd heard about them on the news, but never imagined I'd find myself in this situation.

The terror numbed me. If I wanted to survive, I had to be smart and calm.

"It's fucking hot." The man aiming the gun removed his mask, fanning himself.

Another wave of fear skittered down my spine. He was the homeless man who had cleaned the windshield on Juan's car the day I'd arrived in Texas. He didn't look homeless right now. Why had he acted like that? Were all the homeless people part of some underground crime organization?

Would Olivia and I be some of those missing people who would never be found again? Bile crept up my throat, but I pushed it down. I didn't want them to see how vulnerable I was right now.

I wanted my phone, which was in my purse, but he'd grabbed it and shoved it into a box behind him. Chococat had fallen out of my purse. That plush meant so much to me and Forrest. Olivia had left her belongings in the car.

Did anyone see the abduction? Did Forrest know I was missing? Would I see him again? Would I be able to see my mom? She needed me.

Various emotions stirred in me like a bad soup that gave me a terrible heartburn. Fear swirled with anxiety, outrage, confusion, and the need to survive. Survival required me to calm down so I could think.

Was there a proper reaction to dangerous situations like these? This wasn't a TV show. I'd seen enough of them to know Olivia and I might die tonight. Even if we could escape, we might not be the same person . . .

Stop it. You need to stay positive.

I agreed with my inner voice. Freaking myself out wasn't going to help anyone but the enemies.

The van took a sharp turn, and Olivia and I slid into each other. I was grateful they hadn't tied us up.

"I remember you. What do you want with us?" I asked the fake hobo who had grown a mustache.

He smirked. "Excellent memory."

He ignored my other question, and the van stopped. The driver got out and opened the door. Another man stood beside him, looking like a mean bear with curly brown hair and a bushy beard.

Bushy Beard looked at Fake Hobo. "Bo, take them to room fourteen and get them showered and fed to prepare for tomorrow night. They should be in pristine condition—that's Yvette's reminder. We're expecting a very generous crowd."

Ice formed in my stomach. What did that mean? A crowd of what? Realization dawned and terror chewed up my intestines, giving me horrible cramps.

"Got it." Bo shoved my shoulder, and when I didn't move—couldn't move—he shoved his gun into my back. "Move."

"Yvette." Olivia looked at me, and I could see the fear in her eyes.

"Bitch," I mouthed. She'd lured us by pitching a too-good-to-be-true job.

I was angry at her and myself for not thinking clearly. My financial situation had blurred the truth. How many other girls had fallen for her scam?

"Be strong," I whispered to Olivia, who nodded.

We couldn't let fear make us weak if we wanted to escape.

Bo shoved me again, this time harder. I willed my strength, and somehow the stomach pain subsided. Or rather, my need to survive added to my anger numbed it. I straightened up and walked faster toward a brick building surrounded by many other buildings like it. Could I be in the industrial area that was close to where the car had parked?

With his gun, Bo gestured for me and Olivia to enter the side door. The sound of another car had me turning back to see another black van stopping to let out three more frightened women.

What the hell was going on?

We entered the building, and Bo led us down a dimly lit hallway. A thought flared in my head. Why hadn't they tied our hands? I'd watched too many crime shows to know that most abductors tied up their victims.

They should be in pristine condition.

Tying us up would force us to break free, which would leave lesions.

Bushy Beard's words echoed in my head. The idea of being sex-trafficked appeared more real by the second. I'd preferred being murdered over being a sex slave to someone.

The recent news on TV about the missing people in Texas blazed through my head. Indignation rose in me, blocking out my warning to stay calm and cool.

"You're responsible for all the missing people, aren't you?" I glared at him, wishing my eyes could shoot out fire into his chest.

A smirk slithered onto his face, irritating me even more. "Your perception's gonna get you killed, pretty girl. Now shut up and keep moving."

Olivia gripped my hand, reminding me she and I had to escape safely. I needed to be more careful and stay quiet, no matter how much I hated these people.

The dim hallway opened to a spacious floor of an industrial building. The massive room had high ceilings. Stacks of cardboard boxes lined one wall. What was in them? Probably something illegal. The space reminded me of a wholesale store with rows of stacked merchandise on palettes. The opposite side showed a series of metal doors with numbers on them. An office was occupied by men dressed in black working on several computer screens. Bo and Bushy Beard greeted the men.

A lanky guy with creepy eyes walked over from his desk and surveyed me and Olivia. "Looks like we'll be making bank tomorrow night."

"Yvette's got a good eye for girls," Bo said.

Another guy said something to Creepy Eyes, who sat down and resumed working. The multiple computers made me think of stock traders managing a lot of money simultaneously. Was that what they were doing?

Could these people be part of that crime organization Remi and Forrest had spoken about? I wished I'd paid more attention to their discussion during gatherings.

A litany of fear swarmed in me.

Bo stopped by door number fourteen, opened it, and shoved Olivia and me into the room.

I wanted to say something, but I feared for our safety. So I bit my tongue and imagined hurting him in other ways.

"Rest, shower, and food will be delivered." He raked a gaze down my body. "Act up and you'll regret it. Don't make me have to hurt you, because I won't hesitate. The last girl who misbehaved died, and her body parts were burned to cinders." He smiled as though he was talking about the weather. Then he winked at us and shut the door.

What an evil asshole.

A surge of violence overcame me, which was better than fear. Fear made me feel helpless, whereas anger made me want to do something. I wanted to claw that smile off his face. I wanted to poke out his eyes with my nails and cut off his hands for groping and slapping me and Olivia.

"God, Kiera, did you hear him?" Olivia's lip quivered, and the blood from her face drained.

I hugged her. "He's just trying to scare us. He's supposed to make sure we're in 'pristine' condition, remember? Do as they say and we'll be fine for now." I rubbed circles on her back, soothing her and myself. "Let's check out the room."

It had two beds, each flush on opposite walls. A couch sat on the side with a coffee table covered with fashion and lifestyle magazines. The irony of it almost made me laugh. What kind of fucking lifestyle did they think this was? No woman would want to give up their freedom to be controlled by a group of fucking insane men. There was also a bookcase with all kinds of books, a side table with a lamp, and a TV screen attached to a wall. The room didn't have any windows.

The comfortable atmosphere didn't comfort me one bit. Did they think the fake prison would make me or Olivia comply? A camera blinked from the top corner of the room.

I turned to Olivia and whispered, "Camera. Let's pretend we're behaving. We need to preserve our energy to survive."

Olivia met my eyes. "Okay."

I didn't know where I was getting this adrenaline from, but I was wired, and survival mode made the body do all kinds of abnormal things.

Where did they take the other women who had arrived after us? Were they in the adjacent rooms? Were there more rooms in other parts of the building? What was happening tomorrow?

"This is insane," Olivia whispered. "What do they want with us? I'm scared, Kiera."

"Me too." We sat down on the couch and turned slightly so the camera didn't have a full view of our faces. No lip reading for them. "How did you meet Yvette? What does she look like?"

"I've only spoken to her on the phone. I saw a modeling job advertised in a social media beauty group. We chatted via text before the actual phone call. She has an AI avatar and said she knew Bruno, so I assumed she was a coordinator like him." Tears streamed down her face. "I'm sorry I got you into this."

"Don't apologize. It's not your fault."

Wanting to wash the filth off of me, I got up and walked to the stack of clothes on the bed. A long white T-shirt, underwear, and no bra.

I walked over to where Olivia checked out her clothes and leaned in. "I'm not sure what's going on, but we have to stay alert. Be extra careful and pray that help is on the way."

Forrest should know I was missing by now. What was he doing? Did he miss me? I shouldn't be thinking about him because that only made me feel worse. I didn't want to acknowledge that I might not see him again.

I reined in my emotion and asked, "You want to shower first?"

"I guess." She shrugged. "After that, I'm going to read a fucking book about how to kill kidnappers." She didn't keep her voice down as she headed to the bathroom and slammed the door.

I smirked at her sarcasm because there was no such book on the shelf.

While Olivia showered, I grabbed a magazine and pretended to read while a plan to escape formed in my head. They would eventually take us out of the room, so I had to look for a second escape route other than the main entrance. Was there a fire alarm I could pull? That would alert the fire department, wouldn't it?

When it was my turn to shower, I didn't spend nearly as much time as I normally would. Water soothed me, but I didn't know if there were cameras in the bathroom too. So I was quick about it, facing the blank wall whenever I could. As long as I could calm myself and escape safely, they could look at my ass.

Olivia and I sat side by side on the couch, flipping through fashion magazines while wondering what was happening to us.

The sound at the door drew our attention away from the

magazines. Bo entered, pushing a cart of food to the coffee table.

"Eat and go to bed," he ordered. "Don't worry, there's no poison in here. We need you healthy."

Why did he sound like a rabid fox trying to be a harmless bunny?

He probably saw my thoughts because he said, "If you don't eat it, we *will* come in here and shove it down your throat. You want that?"

We gaped at him. He didn't wait for an answer, leaving the room and locking the door.

Olivia and I stared at the roasted chicken thighs and drumsticks in a large porcelain bowl. They smelled so good, and my mouth watered looking at the side dishes of string beans, red peppers, and broccoli. There were two garden salads with several bottles of dressing. A plate of brownies and cookies completed the meal.

I was thirsty, but didn't know if the bottles of water, juices, and sodas were safe to drink. There were also two cups of tea, but no coffee. Not that I drank coffee for dinner, but the setup told me someone meticulously planned out this meal.

Our stomachs growled at the same time.

"I'm hungry," Olivia said, took a fork and filled up a plate with food. "If I'm going to die, I'm going to die on a full stomach. Besides, pristine condition, right?"

I was hungry too, but worry gripped me. Filling up my plates, I ate the salad. I got some salad dressing on my arm and went to the bathroom to wash it off. The water from the faucet gleamed in the light, calling me. I didn't know why the water made me think of Forrest. The photo shoot I'd done of him at the lake with the waterfall backdrop was one of the most tranquil places I'd ever visited. His presence had made it more special for me.

It made me realize how much I'd yearned for him, but was too afraid to admit it. It was always easier to push your issues aside until that issue stood in front of your face, demanding you respond.

How was he doing? Was he sleeping all right? Was he thinking of me?

My heart tightened, and I placed a hand over it, acknowledging the truth—I was in love with Forrest. When he brought home Chococat, that did it for me. The other gestures mattered too, but that sealed the deal. Chococat had linked us together during a traumatic moment in time, and when he gave me that adorable plush, he was offering me a way to heal myself. He probably didn't know the depth of his gesture, but I knew, and my heart swelled profoundly.

I hoped the good luck charm found its way to him. I hoped it protected him and removed all obstacles in his way. He was a man with vision, and the world needed to see his brilliance. Why was I thinking as though I wouldn't see him again? I should have taken the amulet and placed it in my purse. Maybe it would've shown me a way out of this danger.

Tears blurred my eyes, and I couldn't keep my emotions in check. I gripped the edge of the sink as my body shook from the release. I didn't care if those bastards were watching me. There was nothing new about a woman crying. All the women before probably wept in the bathroom too.

Despite the chaos, I also felt hope. I wanted more time with Forrest to see where this relationship could go. I gathered myself and splashed cold water on my face, shifting my mindset as best I could.

Though I was hungry, I could live a day without food. I drank more water from the faucet, filling my stomach, and returned to the couch. Grabbing my fork, I moved my food around to make it appear like I'd eaten a lot.

After we finished dinner, we watched an old soap opera. I wanted to see the news, but there was no news channel. These criminals probably blocked them out so we wouldn't see our faces on the screen as missing persons.

After a moment, the room chilled. Olivia giggled at a sad scene in the show about a sudden death of a girl's pet.

"Are you okay?" I asked, not understanding the humor.

She yawned. "Yeah. Just tired. I'm going to bed."

The clock on the table read ten in the evening. The room had gotten colder from the increased air conditioner. I slid into bed too, but noticed a strange smell. It had a sweet aroma like an herb. "Do you smell that?"

Olivia answered with a snore. My body felt relaxed, too relaxed. I didn't want to fall asleep. What if something happened to me or Olivia while I was unconscious? Though I tried my best to stay awake, my body eventually succumbed to the heavy drowsiness.

CHAPTER FORTY

FORREST

As I sat on the couch in Grandma's living room, waiting for her to finish cooking, concern for Kiera inundated me. With her missing, every second dripped like molasses. I felt the walls of my world collapsing brick by brick, and there was nothing I could do about it.

I'd been doing so well all these years, making sure I had control of everything. That was how I'd succeeded in running my empire. I'd taken careful steps to ensure my success because success equaled power, and power allowed me to take down my worst enemy. An enemy I had envisioned killing in details. When I caught Red Birthmark, I'd shoot him several times in areas that wouldn't kill him instantly. His wounds would bleed out, and he would endure the pain he'd bestowed upon my father. After that, I'd pour acid onto his wounds and watch it destroy his flesh centimeter by centimeter. Then I'd toss him to the alligators, or the sharks. The last portion could be adjusted accordingly.

I'd lived this moment in my head too many times. My goal

had always been vengeance. Nothing else had mattered—until now.

Right now the most important thing was finding Kiera. I'd lost sleep and appetite in the past couple of days. I didn't want to attend dinner with Grandma and Yolanda this evening, but I couldn't disappoint her, so I pushed my fear away to have dinner.

How could I rest when my woman was in danger? Was she all right? Was she cold, hot, scared, or hurt?

Something clattered in the kitchen, and I turned in that direction. "Are you okay? Do you need my help?"

"No need. Just dropped a lid," Grandma replied.

She'd insisted I stay here because my minimal kitchen skills would only hinder her. Yolanda had been helping Grandma, but she had darted into the guest bedroom to take a phone call.

I worked on the computer compiling information about the area where she'd been abducted, including trying to find the fuckers who had taken her. Something popped onto my phone, and I grabbed it to check, thinking it was the PI or the police giving me an update. But it was about a conference call I'd cancelled yesterday. Fucking hell. I'd somehow rescheduled it for tonight instead of cancelling it. What else had I done wrong? I was losing my shit.

With swiftness I sent an email to my secretary and management team, asking them to cancel all my appointments for the next two weeks and requesting they take the lead on ongoing projects.

I scrubbed a hand down my face, blowing out a frustrated breath.

The fear of not seeing Kiera again forced up anger and vengeance—all the emotions I'd felt as a child when my father died. I'd been young and helpless and had succumbed to the dark monsters. But I wasn't young and helpless now. I could do something.

My soul was bruised and torn in so many directions. I'd dwelled in the dark for a long time, and I didn't know how lonely, sad, and angry I was until Kiera entered my life. She'd brought love, hope, and medicine to my wounded soul. Because of that, I now saw an alternative to vengeance that still satisfied me but allowed me to keep my soul. It was something I'd think about later.

I didn't want Kiera anywhere near the darkness. Yet the darkness got her anyway.

I'll find you, baby. I'll make them pay.

I browsed through the information on Kiera. The PI didn't locate her phone. Her last location showed the abduction spot. He got some recordings from the street cameras, but someone had erased the recordings for the day of the abduction and the days before it. However, he'd hacked into the residential security cameras along that street and got me what I needed.

Fury had coursed through me as I studied the recordings. I'd ensure the asshole who put his hands on her would die. It was difficult to see the license plate number, so I'd asked the PI to locate the two men for me. He had advanced facial recognition software that could find people easily.

I didn't give a damn how he did it if I got results. Rules must be bent or even broken to get things done. I'd done many things that would make most people cringe. But certain bad actors required certain methods to get to them. My father's killers and Kiera's kidnappers were no exception.

Kiera was waiting for me. I didn't have time to play by the rules and wait for the police to give me answers. To them, she was just one of many kidnapping cases. Did she know I was doing my best to find her?

"Come on over." Grandma placed plates of food onto the round wooden table.

I got up from the couch. "You should've told me you were finished, *Vó*. Do you have more plates in the kitchen?"

"I'm all set. Just sit and enjoy the meal."

I sat down on the chair with my phone beside me at the ready in case a call or a text came in regarding Kiera's abduction. The longer she was missing, the more likely she wouldn't be found alive. My chest tightened just thinking about it.

The commotion in my head made it difficult for me to focus, but I tried my best. I glanced at the food that normally made my mouth water, but it did nothing at the moment.

"You look like a zombie." Grandma stared at me. "Have you been eating and getting enough sleep?"

I didn't want to lie, but I couldn't muster up words to explain everything.

When I didn't answer her, she filled my plates with her special *farofa*, which was fried tapioca flour mixed with pieces of bacon. She scooped a side of rice onto my plate. Then she gave me some *feijoada*—black beans cooked with chunks of meat. The table was set up for a party of ten or more. She also had *joelho*, a bread pastry with cheese and ham on the inside. This was a much-needed comfort food for right now. I grabbed one with my fingers and popped it into my mouth. I chewed and swallowed, and my stomach rejoiced.

How will you find Kiera if you don't have any energy left?

For a few moments, I let the food distract me. My eyes went to a dish of *quindim*, a pastry made from egg yolk and ground coconut. My mom used to make these for me when I was a kid.

"You went overboard, *Vó*." I stared at the tray of steak and chicken kebabs. "How are we supposed to eat all this food? There's plenty to eat without the kebabs."

"I didn't know if she'd like the traditional Brazilian food, so I made kebabs." Grandma sighed, looking at the clock on the wall, which showed seven twenty in the evening.

"Who's she?" I asked, eyeing the steak kebab.

"She told me she would come. She seemed really excited about the project."

Oh, right. I'd forgotten about her guest.

Grandma had never invited anyone over for dinner, especially not a stranger she'd just met. Family dinners were just family, so I was curious who this guest was that had charmed Grandma.

"You made all this for a stranger you met yesterday? What kind of project did she sell you?"

"Her name is Kiera. She said she had an idea about—"

"Wait." My heart leaped, and I cursed at myself for not connecting the dots when I saw the Full Circle Apothecary shopping bag. My mind had been in panic mode. "Was anyone with her? Did you see anything strange?"

"You know Kiera?" Grandma's eyes beamed.

"Of course, I know her. She's my girlfriend."

"*What?* When did you get a girlfriend?" She stood up from the chair with hands on her hips. "Why didn't you tell me?"

"I wanted to, but she's missing."

"What are you talking about?" Grandma's eyes switched from being angry to concerned. I loved that she liked Kiera enough to invite her to dinner.

I didn't want to worry her, but I also knew she wouldn't stop hounding me with questions if I didn't share some information.

"Oh, dear." She placed a hand to her heart and told me how she'd met Kiera in the street.

Grandma even saw Kiera crying while reading a journal. I'd like to check it out later.

"Are the police out looking for her?" Grandma stalked over to the window, looking out as though Kiera was there. I'd done the same thing many times at my hotel suite.

"Yes. Don't worry—I'll find her," I said. "Let's eat before the food gets cold."

"So this is why you look like you've just seen ghost." Grandma walked over to me, cupping my face in both hands. "I've never seen you like this, Forrest. Tired, worried, angry. It's not good for you. She needs you to be strong for her."

She shifted to stand behind me, massaging my shoulders and at the base of my neck. She'd taken several courses on acupressure methods, and right now, each pressure point she pressed felt like a miracle. Her fingers moved up my neck and head.

After a few minutes, she walked over to her herb counter and took out a bottle, bringing it over to me. "Sniff it."

"What is it?"

"Thieves oil."

"Oh, gosh, I can't stand that smell."

"I know. But it's a boost to your immune system. Stress is taking a toll on you whether you feel it or not. You're not a machine, Forrest." She placed the bottle under my nose, waiting for me.

Thieves oil was a combination of cinnamon, clove, eucalyptus, lemon, and rosemary. I didn't mind these herbs by themselves, but the fragrant blend wasn't for me.

"Did you know that during the Black Plague people lathered themselves in this oil to keep the germs away?"

That had been a rumor.

"Just sniff it. It'll make me feel better. If you don't, I'll pour this all over you."

God, no. I sniffed right away. "There. Happy?"

She smiled and returned the bottle back to the counter.

Then she returned and continued massaging my shoulders. I knew she'd snuck some oil onto her palms to lather on my neck, but I didn't say anything. Despite the unattractive smell, the oil and Grandma's touch soothed me, bringing me back to a place where I could see how unstable I was. Grandma had always given me comfort, and I'd forgotten that until today. She was my second mom.

After a few more minutes, she sat down across from me.

"Thank you," I said.

"You're welcome. Now eat. You'll need energy to find her."

"She's important to me," I confessed.

"Okay, I'm ready to fill my tummy! The food smells so good." Yolanda entered the dining room, sniffing the air and rubbing her hands together. "Why is the food still untouched? You're not waiting for me, are you?"

"The guest who was supposed to show up is a missing person," Grandma said while scooping food onto Yolanda's plate and then her own. "She's actually Forrest's girlfriend."

"You have a girlfriend? Since when? Were you going to introduce her to the family?"

"Yes. She was at Taco Haven that day you came with your friends and intruded on my dinner meeting," I teased.

She narrowed her eyes at me. "Oh, that one. She's pretty."

"Beautiful." Grandma added. "And genuine. That's the energy I got from her." She looked at me. "I was going to play matchmaker."

I couldn't help but smile, knowing my grandma approved of her.

"*Vó*! You've never believed in that stuff before. You always told us to find our significant others on our own."

Grandma smiled, lifting a shoulder. "Something about her changed me."

We ate and discussed trivial things. Then silence filled the room. No one knew what to say, fearing the wrong words would make things worse for me. Even the plants in the dining room looked sad. The color of the food lacked vibrancy. Grandma's shoulders stooped, looking tired.

Yolanda met my gaze, and she offered a small smile. "She'll be okay."

"Thanks."

Yolanda's phone rang, and she glanced at her screen, muttering, "I guess today is one of those days where nothing is going right."

"What's going on? I asked.

"Work. Just annoying. I have to get it." She got up and went to the window. "I'll help with it to expedite the process. I want this done right, so I'll be there." She hung up, looking angry.

"Everything okay?" Grandma asked.

"Yeah. I'm working on an extensive project with a giant bonus if all goes well. I don't want to jinx it. I'll see you two later."

"Do you want to take some food home?" Grandma asked.

"Yes, please."

After Yolanda left, Grandma and I finished dinner. She packed me some food to go. Talking with her helped me find my stability again. Personal matters made everything worse. I hadn't told my friends about Kiera's abduction either. I wanted to wait until after the banquet tomorrow.

"Did you know that Kiera's mom helped our family the day mom died?"

"The car accident?"

I nodded. "Her mom was the nurse who came to help our family." I also shared about Kiera's Chococat T-shirt.

"The next time I fly up to Providence, I'd like to meet her and thank her." She leaned against the kitchen island, staring at something on the table, thinking. "I'll never forget that day.

Yolanda and I were barely hurt in the accident. Anita took the hit for us."

"And you took care of us." I wrapped an arm around Grandma.

She rested her head on my shoulder. "It's the least I could do for my daughter-in-law. It was just bad luck for us. When the EMT got me out of the wreckage, I saw a Good Samaritan holding your mom's hand. The tears in her eyes told me your mom was gone. It comforts me to know she had an angel beside her when she left this world." She lifted her head and looked at me square in the eye. "You must find Kiera."

"I will." That was a vow to myself and the universe.

CHAPTER FORTY-ONE

FORREST

As I left Grandma's apartment, Hank called me. "Can y-you come over? I have something to show y-you."

The stuttering told me he was stressed about something. Though he had improved from when I first met him, he still needed a lot of time to recover.

When I got to Hank's cabin, he showed me a plastic bag filled with pills. I held a pill between my fingers and examined it. It was circular, reminding me of painkillers I could get over the counter at the drugstore. But I didn't recognize it.

"Where did you find this?"

His shoulders slumped. "I wanted to h-help find Kiera, so I went to the d-dumpster. Part of her luggage wasn't d-damaged from the f-fire. The bag of pills was in a small makeup b-bag."

My eyebrows furrowed, wondering who could've hidden it there.

"Thank you." I looked over at him. "We'll find her. I don't want you risking your life, though. She wouldn't want that. If you see something out of the norm, discuss it with me first, okay?"

He nodded. "Dumpster is gone now. The truck removed it today."

"See anything on the recordings?"

He shook his head. "Just raccoons, rabbits, squirrels running around."

"I'll let you know as soon as I find Kiera." I tapped his shoulder and left with the bag of pills.

I could have brought the pills to my lab at Holistic Farm, but I needed to dedicate my time looking for Kiera and focus on the banquet tomorrow. Any scientist could decipher these pills for me. I also had to research those aliases to prepare for any unexpected encounters. What if an elite member came up to me to ask an astrological question? I didn't want my ignorance to ruin everything.

I made a call to a friend at a local pharmaceutical research laboratory and asked for a favor. What were these pills? Once I knew what it was, then I'd know its value.

Was the person who had burned down the cabin trying to destroy the evidence or retrieve it?

CHAPTER FORTY-TWO

KIERA

My body felt icy one minute and hot the next. I curled into the blanket and then kicked it off. I could tell my body was fighting something, and it was exhausting me. All I wanted to do was sleep.

I'd dreamed of Forrest just now, and sadness overwhelmed me. God, I missed him. Was my mom feeling better? What were my friends doing right now? Did they know I was missing? I hoped my mom and my friends didn't know. It would stress them out.

Voices echoed from outside my door. I didn't dare move because someone could be watching me. So I closed my eyes and concentrated on the voices. I made out Bo's voice and a woman's voice. They were whispering about something, but I couldn't hear them.

A blast of cold air came through the vents. I could tell from the noises the vents made. A sweet fragrance snuck up my nose and before I could focus back on the conversation, I'd fallen back into a deep sleep.

CHAPTER FORTY-THREE

FORREST

The following day, my emptiness and anxiety were only worse as there was still no news on Kiera. The whirlwind of emotions paralyzed me on so many levels. I'd almost brushed my teeth with soap instead of toothpaste. My mind and body were two detached items instead of working together as one entity.

Keep yourself together. Kiera needs you.

Deep in my heart, I knew she was alive. But was she hurt? Had they done anything to her?

Fucking hell. I hated this helpless feeling.

I tried to keep busy, but everywhere I turned, I saw Kiera. Heaving a frustrated breath, I went to the guest room where the shopping bag from Full Circle Apothecary sat on the desk. The protective willow talismans looked pretty, and I brushed my fingers around them, silently asking them to keep her safe. I was doing whatever I could to get her back. If I had to pray to a rock, I'd do it.

What was the point of having all this money and influence when I couldn't even save my woman?

She bought five journals, probably giving some to her friends. What had made her cry?

I flipped through the journal, and by the time I got to the end, I understood. I didn't journal and had no time for such things, but I understood why Kiera had gotten emotional. She went through a journey into her heart and found something worthwhile.

For me, I liked the layout of the book with the three major heart phases, which reminded me of cellular division. The "heart purge" asked you to declutter your mind. The second phase of "heart prayer" asked for your acknowledgement and choices, and the "heart promise" required an intention.

That book helped me see into my heart and soul. Kiera was the beaming light from those places. My feelings for her deepened every day. The determination to find her and punish those responsible kept me intact. Did they keep Kiera with Olivia? Or had they separated the friends to frighten them even more?

This private gathering had to yield critical information about Kiera's whereabouts. I called my friends to go over the plan for this evening once more.

When our conversation ended, they knew about Kiera's abduction. I asked them not to tell anyone yet, fearing her mother would get wind of it. With her poor health, this terrifying news would send her to the grave. Releasing a heavy sigh, I closed my eyes to let things settle before checking my emails.

Kiera had forwarded her mom's health records to me. Health and science would give my mind a break from crime organizations. As I read the records, I had questions and emailed my doctor friends in Boston and Providence, asking for their opinion on her diagnosis. I understood that medical treatment wasn't a cookie-cutter method, but something seemed off to me. The medication her doctor prescribed didn't seem to fit her illness.

Kiera's mother had played a crucial role during my mom's last moments. Not only had Mrs. Ford comforted my mom, she also gave birth to the woman I love. It was odd how things came full circle.

Dressed in a black tuxedo, I checked my ID and waited for the text message of the location. I hated not knowing where I was going ahead of time. But I supposed that was the nature of the elite clubs. Whoever organized this banquet wanted people to know that he was in control and that the attendees played by his rules.

I reined in my distaste and tried to look at the positive side. Victory often required patience, and that was the mantra I repeated to myself in order to stay calm.

I had an hour before the text for the location was due to arrive, so I researched astrology in case someone from The Trogyn asked me those weird questions like they had done with Grayson. Grayson wouldn't have known anything if his uncle hadn't prepped him ahead of time. I didn't know anything about these space objects, but I had to prepare myself. Part of winning any war was preparation. Luck favored those who were prepared.

Forty minutes later, I discovered that Orcus was an Etruscan god of the underworld and the punisher of broken oaths. Andromeda was our nearest galaxy about two and half million light-years away, and Black Moon Lilith was a virtual point in the moon's orbit around the Earth.

My head was now filled with stuff I'd never cared to know. However, the information was a pleasant distraction, and I'd learned that astrology symbolized the personality archetypes. There was an art and science to this method of looking at the stars and the gods and goddesses associated with them.

My phone rang with the PI's number, and I answered immediately. "You have news on Kiera?"

"No, but your prime target is in Texas. Will send you a current pic."

My heart thudded, but it wasn't as powerful of a reaction as I had expected.

What an interesting plot twist. This visit to Texas symbolized so much for me. I'd been searching for the leader of the Anacondas—the man who had shot my dad—for years. I'd searched all over the continents for him, but failed. Now, he was in the same state as me. This was no coincidence. It meant something.

He hadn't been on my mind since Kiera's abduction, but now he was an issue that stood side by side.

"What's his name?" I asked, looking at an image of my enemy, who had gotten older with a head of white hair. He still had a red birthmark on his neck.

"Goes by Red Venom. Some say he goes by Orcus too. Still looking for his real name."

The heavens were shining down on me. He was no god of the underworld. He should be a prisoner in hell where he could endure infinite suffering.

Red Venom was a good start. "Thank you."

My heart raced at the recent development. My search for Red Venom had lasted longer than I expected. I'd developed a charity in Brazil and used that facility as an office space to expand my search. The $Ba_7M_5Bu_{88}$ Project helped my people, the vulnerable within the small villages and those in the cities. But that branch also served as a research center for Red Venom and his crew.

My team in Brazil had monitored the crimes around the town my family used to live in. It was now peaceful, known as a place that offered organic vegetables and free medicine to the people. Despite my hatred toward the gangs and doctors who hadn't helped my dad, I didn't have anything against innocent people. As for the doctors who had refused to treat my father, they'd both died before I could confront them.

Things were falling into place in ways I couldn't have imagined. Why was Red Venom in Texas? What was his business? Or had he always lived here?

Would he recognize me? I doubted it. He probably had too many enemies to worry about one little boy who had been searching for him all these years.

A text pinged on my phone, and the address appeared on the screen. I shoved Red Venom aside for the moment, put on my high-tech Rolex, and headed out.

CHAPTER FORTY-FOUR

FORREST

I drove a rental SUV and arrived at the seven-story brick building with a sign for Quality Printing & Marketing. This was no printing business. I studied the industrial surroundings. They all looked similar.

I pulled into the parking lot and the valet, dressed in black, scanned my ID.

He gestured to the lot. "You can park anywhere." I chose the spot near the back door.

As I got ready to leave, my phone slipped out of my pants pocket, dropping to the floor. I bent down to pick it up and cursed, "Fucking hell."

I glared at my mismatched socks—a black sock and a light gray one. I'd never been this out of sorts. Leaning back into the seat, I inhaled a deep breath and released it heavily.

Get it together. Kiera needs you.

Getting out, I surveyed the lot. There was only one way in and out. A good number of cars were already parked. I didn't see Levi's car.

This industrial district was near where Kiera had been

abducted. It couldn't be a coincidence. I lifted my Rolex watch, pretending to look at the time, but I was scanning all the parked cars, getting their license plate numbers. Maybe the kidnappers had driven here in one of these cars. Right now everyone was my enemy.

The drive to this area was secluded except for a few men walking up and down the streets in T-shirts and jeans, as though guarding their territory. Were they spying for uninvited guests? Or were they looking for someone else?

I entered the lavishly decorated banquet hall. Unlike the mundane exterior, the interior portrayed marbled floors with chandeliers dripping with crystals. The men in gray suits at the desk scanned my body, took my phone, put it in a black container, and locked it.

"Don't worry, sir. No one will touch it. You'll get it back when you're ready to leave," said the man with a tattoo on the side of his neck.

"I'd better, or else my grandmother will be coming after you. There are baby pictures on that phone that she's dying to get." I smiled. "You don't want her wrath."

"There's nothing like the wrath of a determined Nana," said the guy with a scar on his chin.

"Thanks for understanding." I patted his shoulder and gave him a generous tip.

Because I didn't know what to expect at this banquet, the phone they just took was only a spare. If it got lost, they could have fun looking at a bunch of stock photos of adorable babies.

The security men didn't take my watch because it wasn't a smartwatch, or so they thought. The intricate face of the Rolex resembled an old-fashioned watch, but in reality, it possessed advanced technology. Remi had given me and each of my friends a Rolex to take down the conglomerate.

The video recordings from the watch synced to a secure

shared drive that my friends could access. For efficiency, I would alert them to access the recordings if something were off. If this banquet turned out to be just that, with no hidden agenda, I didn't want them wasting their time.

I walked into a ballroom with high ceilings and metal bars above. It was well-lit like the main entrance. The dim lighting gave off a mysterious ambience. Sheer red curtains draped stylishly between the bars, coming to join at a large chandelier dripping with sparkling crystals. The suspended red curtains looked like blood vessels, and the fabric flowing down to the ground looked like bloody waterfalls. A black rug covered the floor, making me feel like I was browsing through hell. I didn't see any cameras, but that didn't mean they weren't there.

Several men hovered around a standing table, chatting and laughing. More men browsed the room looking at Renaissance paintings.

The ballroom reminded me of the videos I'd seen when Grayson visited Club Diablo. That had been an underground club. However, this space was twice as large. Glass pillars stood in various corners, with lights glowing from within. A tray of hors d'oeuvres sat next to a wide candle.

Apart from the appetizer stands, there were about fifteen round dining tables with black covers and matching chairs. Crystal cases glowed as center pieces.

"Hey. Sorry I'm late." Levi approached, dressed in a black suit, sporting a hickey on his neck. "I had to convince my lady friend that I'd see her tomorrow. Anything interesting?" He looked around. "Wow, this is a lot fancier than the gatherings I've been to."

Everything about the setup had The Trogyn's signature on it. A thrill rushed through me. I surveyed the area, looking for anyone who could be Andromeda and Black Moon Lilith. No one stood out. Maybe those names weren't relevant to this private party.

Orcus was another name Red Venom had used. Could he be here tonight? Was he running the show? Or was he at another party in Texas right now?

"Want anything to drink?" Levi asked, gesturing to the bar with a blonde bartender wearing a white shirt, a black vest with matching pants.

"I'll take a Scotch. Neat."

While we headed over to the bar, I scanned the growing crowd.

Are you here, Kiera? Give me a sign.

Was my Kitty K still in Texas? In the United States?

Fuck. Stop thinking about the unthinkable. But how could I not?

The past few days had been an indescribable nightmare. The other day, I couldn't believe I forgot to turn off the car and left it running for hours until I had to get something in the garage. Not knowing if she was safe had driven me insane. I'd never been this lost. The unknown was a fucking monster that fed on my fear. I'd used a lot of energy battling that monster because my love needed me.

Adrenaline had become the hot fuel in my blood, helping me survive the minutes. Pain and suffering took on a new meaning—an unfamiliar edge that cut up my heart.

While Levi ordered our drinks, I ambled around, studying and memorizing the men's faces. I came to a door with the word Gambling etched across it. Farther down was a door with no label.

Levi came back with my Scotch and said he was going to check out the gambling room. "Want to join me?"

"I'll pass."

Levi entered the gambling room with three other men.

That was when I realized there weren't any women at this event. Why? Normally I'd see waitresses at these elite men's club, but all the waiters and bartenders were men.

From the corner of my eye, I saw red shoes. But when I turned, the man had disappeared into a crowd. Was this the same man I'd seen outside the boutique?

I headed in his direction, but then a voice came over the speaker. "Good evening, gentlemen. The auction is about to begin. Please take a seat and enjoy the show."

Auction? Something sharp twisted in my gut. Was the man with the red shoes attending the auction?

Something told me this auction was tonight's main event. The gambling was just a side entertainment.

I followed the men to the glowing unnamed door.

CHAPTER FORTY-FIVE

KIERA

I sat in a shabby stylist's chair so a woman could do my hair. She didn't look happy about it. Olivia sat next to me, talking far too excitedly. Three guards stood on the side, watching us. Four other women had finished with their hairstyle and makeup. In sexy lingerie, they babbled on about nonsense while leaning against the wall. They didn't act like women in distress at all.

"I'm thirsty," Olivia said, rising from the chair. She tripped on her own feet, falling to the floor.

"You okay?" I asked, wanting to help, but the stylist held me in place.

Bo approached with a paper cup filled with a pink drink. "Stay in your seat. Here's a pink lemonade for you."

I was going to tell her not to drink it, but she yanked it from his hand and gulped it down. I'd woken up this afternoon and had no recollection of the previous day. My only vivid memory was the night I'd skipped dinner and the smell of something strange coming from the vents. That had been two days ago.

Had I been asleep all that time? They must have spiked the food, drink, and air.

"Oww." I winced when the stylist tugged my hair with the curling iron.

"Sorry." She released my lock of hair into a bouncy curl.

Were these stylists also forced to work here? I didn't dare ask because Bo and his men had eyes on us. My body felt weak, and I didn't think that I could run if I saw an escape route.

When my hair and makeup were completed, they gave me a black lacy lingerie set to wear. The bra barely covered my breasts, and my underwear was a small patch. The see-through robe did nothing but make it more sensual.

"I'm not wearing that," I told the woman standing at the clothing rack.

Bo interjected, "You will wear it or I will hold you down and dress you. Then I'll let my men take their time undressing you. Your choice."

I fumed, waiting for the right moment to stab him with something.

After I got dressed, I stood next to Olivia, who appeared mellower. She glanced at me, touching my robe. "You look nice," she slurred.

Did she even recognize me?

"Are you okay?"

A man with a mustache walked up to the woman with a tray of drinks. "Tea to calm your nerves."

One girl refused, saying she felt sick, but Bo gripped her chin and forced her to finish every drop.

Goosebumps grew on my body as my heart thundered with fear. I knew the drink would make me lose control of myself. But if I refused, they'd pour it down my throat.

So I drank most of it, holding the last swallow in my mouth.

Music boomed and startled me.

The mustache guy smiled and cheered. "Time to see how much money we'll make tonight."

What did that mean? Was he gambling with us?

Olivia wobbled and dropped to the floor. When I bent to help her, I spat the liquid from my mouth into a pile of clothes inside boxes on the floor. The music grew louder, and no one paid attention to me and Olivia. I shoved a finger into my mouth, forcing myself to vomit the drink out as much as I could.

The booming music drowned out my gagging sounds.

"I got you." I told Olivia and stabilized her.

"Thanks," she muttered. "Don't know why I can't even walk right."

My mouth tasted awful, but I didn't care. I could feel my body weakening, but I knew it would have been worse if I had let the drink stay in my system.

Bo gave me a wristlet with a number on it. I was number two out of the ten.

"You listen to what the host tells you to do," Bo said. "When your number is called, you walk across the stage, turn, pause, and walk back. No talking. If you don't listen, you will be missing a limb once you get off stage. Understand?"

Everyone nodded. It was strange how my mind didn't want to listen to him, but my body was too weak to "defy" him. What kind of drink was this? It was no healing tea for damn sure.

Nerves churned in me, but my body didn't feel as scared as it should have been.

We entered a wide stage with soft lighting. Gasps came from the audience hidden in the dark lighting. I couldn't see anything in front of me. I made out a few silhouettes. Or were they mannequins?

I blinked because my vision blurred for a second. Sparkles flowed like fireflies around me. But they disappeared after I blinked a few more times. The floor felt unstable too. I knew this was the effect of the drink, so I took a deep breath and tried to concentrate by picking a spot in the audience to focus on.

A male voice announced. "Gentlemen, look at these beautiful women. They could be yours forever. Infinite pleasure for all your needs. Make your bid into the handheld devices."

Oh my God, we were being sold at an auction. I suspected we were being trafficked, but *this*? Did people really auction off humans like this? Bile rose in my throat, but I forced it down.

More recess lights lit up the audience. Men sitting at tables stared at us. I swallowed down the lump that had formed in my throat and tried to study the audience. I needed to see who was here bidding. There were fifteen to twenty men. It was hard to tell because my vision was playing tricks on me.

After blinking a few times, I flicked my gaze back out to the audience and landed on a face that had my heart leaping with hope.

Someone laughed, and I turned to a table with two men dressed in expensive suits. One of them brought on a horror that made my legs wobble.

So I turned my attention back to a man who made me feel safe: Forrest Navarro.

CHAPTER FORTY-SIX

FORREST

Shock, fear, and relief slammed into me. My first gut reaction was to run up to the stage and take her away. But I knew that action would probably get us both killed. I didn't know who was watching this auction. How many men were backstage, ready to shoot me?

Think clearly. Think carefully.

When I'd discussed tonight's event with my friends, a few scenarios came up that would require immediate attention. I pressed the button on my watch twice, alerting my friends that an urgent matter had surfaced. They knew about Kiera's abduction, and that had eased the tightness in my chest.

I gripped the handheld bidding device and made sure my watch captured all the women on the stage, including the faces of as many men as possible.

I'm here, baby. I've got you in my sight.

Right now, the safest path to her rescue would be to play along. In order to keep her safe, they had to believe I was just an attendee looking for a woman. I didn't want their men targeting me before I even got to her, and I certainly didn't want them searching for us afterward.

My fingers curled into a fist that throbbed with violence. I'd never felt so much fury and fear all at once. The people who placed her on that stage would pay. I wanted to kill every man in this room for staring at Kiera.

When the spotlight landed on her, a man made a sound, signifying he wanted her. I wanted to murder him on the spot. This surge of malice and protection coursed through me, but I couldn't act on them.

Control yourself. Get her to safety. Then deal with the fucker.

I couldn't see his face properly from the angle of his seat and the dim lighting casting a shadow over his area. As though the universe took pity on me, he turned and my blood boiled.

Red Venom.

My body stiffened as another wave of dark emotion surged through me. My father's murderer was sitting in the same room as me, but I couldn't eliminate him the way I'd dreamed of. This man had taught me the meaning of hatred and vengeance. Just because he'd disappeared didn't deter me from finding him.

The snake had finally left its cave. He may have been an anaconda, but I was the fucking black mamba.

I studied him, taking in all the details. Older, with long silver hair slicked back with a sheen. The strands glistened from the recess lighting. Wrinkles carved lines into his forehead and the corners of his eyes. He was dressed in an expensive suit, showing he'd obtained wealth and power all these years. What had he been up to? How many more families had he destroyed?

My heart stopped when I saw the red shoes. He wasn't the only one wearing them, though. Senator Mitch Kramer also wore the same shoes. I'd never been a fan of him, and now I knew why.

Red Venom and Senator Kramer had to be members of The Trogyn.

"Shit. I didn't expect this at all," Levi whispered, looking surprised as he took the empty seat. "Sorry, lost track of time."

The moderator spoke, and I turned my attention to Kiera, who wore an impassive expression. What was she thinking? Did she know I could see her? Was she afraid? Or was she play-acting out of fear?

Olivia stood near her, trying her best to maintain balance. The other women on the stage all appeared too cheerful or too mellow for being in this situation. Being sold at an auction should never make anyone happy. Had they drugged these women?

Fuck. Was Kiera drugged? My body thrummed with a viciousness that forced me to breathe in deeply so I didn't explode.

Levi glanced over. "You okay?"

"Yeah."

When the bidding began for Kiera's number, the first bid showed five hundred thousand dollars. My face twitched, hating every man who placed a bid for her. She was mine. There was no way she was going home with them. I'd die stopping them.

A few seconds later, a million-dollar bid came through.

My grip on the bidding device tightened.

"Don't tell me you're bidding," Levi said.

"I have to. That's Kiera, my girlfriend. She was abducted. I've been looking for her."

"Are you fucking serious?" Levi's eyes widened. "What do you need me to do?"

I appreciated his help but there wasn't anything he could do.

"Nothing right now. I'll be taking her home."

I flicked a sharp gaze over at Red Venom. The way he smiled and stared at Kiera told me he was the one who had placed the million-dollar bid.

Over my fucking dead body.

He would never get close to her.

I pressed a button on my Rolex three times consecutively to send an urgent code to my friends, telling them to alert the authorities. This auction had to stop, but it had to look like it came from the outside.

My friends were probably already doing this once they saw Kiera, but I didn't want to assume. Sex trafficking was a money-making business for The Trogyn. I could only imagine how deep it ran, how much money they would've made tonight. The news stations would love to cover this, and I knew my friends were already on that.

With Red Venom here in the room, I couldn't help wonder if the universe orchestrated an opportunity for me to eliminate my worst enemy. I'd envisioned his death at my hands so many times that my fingers itched to pour the acid onto his wounds and watch him die. The rage and hatred surged like a slow-moving storm. Though I wanted his death, my concern for Kiera trumped my personal vendetta.

That was something I had to contemplate later.

I put in a bid of ten million dollars for Kiera.

Gasps rang out in the room, and the bidding paused as men glanced around, trying to figure out who had placed such a high bid for a woman.

To me, Kiera was priceless.

I won the bid. When the spotlight came on Olivia, I bid for her too. She was Kiera's friend, and I couldn't leave her to the wolves. Olivia wobbled and fell on the stage, but she got back up quickly.

What the fuck had they given the girls?

People gasped when I won the bid for Olivia too.

"Lucky man," Red Venom said to no one in particular. "You gotta tell me how that party goes."

A man from another table cheered. "The more, the merrier."

Laughter erupted in the room.

My eyes locked onto Kiera, and I gave her a slight nod.

Hold on, baby. I won't let anyone hurt you.

I scanned the room for the exit doors. There was one outside of this auditorium. Another exit door sat below the stage, but a guard stood there.

"Who's the other woman?" Levi asked.

"Kiera's coworker."

"Christ." He raked a hand through his hair.

I leaned in and whispered, "Something bad is about to happen."

"No shit." He glanced around. "This is my last party."

I didn't want to reveal too much to Levi, but I didn't want him to get hurt in whatever was to come. "Follow me when something happens."

He furrowed his eyebrows, but nodded.

Alarms sounded, and lights flashed. The men looked around, shock and fear splashed on their faces.

Boom.

Boom.

Boom.

Something erupted at various intervals around the building, shaking the ground. Half of the lights in the room went out while the other half flickered. People scrambled.

I rushed down the aisle to Kiera, and Levi followed suit.

Kiera cried when I embraced her, kissing her head. "I've got you. We're going home."

"What's going on?" Olivia slurred and fell against Levi.

"We're getting out of here," Kiera told her.

A gunshot rang out by the exit door below the platform and another boom followed, and the lights went out.

"Stay behind me." Using the light from my Rolex, I walked toward the exit door. Noises erupted around us, but I pushed them aside, focusing on getting Kiera and Olivia to safety.

The body of a dead guard lay on the ground. Who had shot him? It didn't matter. I took his gun, shoved the door open, and we rushed down a dark hallway. Olivia's legs gave way and Levi carried her in his arms.

"Forrest!" A familiar voice drew me to a shiny door.

"This way!" Arrow spotlighted his face with a flashlight and gestured for me to follow him.

"How did you get—"

"Later." He was armed and dressed in black, wearing a bulletproof tac vest.

We turned down another hallway and into a room with an immense hole in the wall. Arrow probably had something to do with that. As a former Navy SEAL, my friend was used to these high-octane situations. We exited the building to an alley with dumpsters that weren't part of the lot where my rental was parked. That rental was a loss, and I'd pay for it. Sirens blasted on the other side of the building.

I helped Kiera into the back seat of the black SUV while Levi secured Olivia on the other side. I untucked my shirt and used it to wipe my fingerprints off the gun, tossing it into the dumpster. I slid in next to Kiera and wrapped an arm around her, pulling her into me. Levi hopped into the passenger seat, and Arrow drove off.

As Arrow drove away from the scene, I saw Red Venom and the senator enter a silver car on a side street.

I'll find you.

CHAPTER FORTY-SEVEN

KIERA

Two men reach for me as I back away, my back hitting a light pole. The street is dark, and no one is around. I don't know why I'm alone with them.

Where's Forrest? He was just with me.

I shout for him, but no sounds come from my mouth. I try again.

Then I feel something wet on my face. I glance up, and blood is dripping from the streetlamp. My body jerks at the blood, but then it stops when the droplets glow like little lights on the ground.

The man with the sleazy smile and a birthmark on his neck steps closer to me. He can easily overpower me, but I know he likes the fear coming from me. Psychopath. I recognize him from the audience at the auction. He's wearing ugly red shoes. He should go to hell just for that.

Why am I thinking about stupid thoughts like that at a moment like this? Where am I? Wasn't I just at the auction?

Sleazy catches my arm, pulling me close. His touch sends a chill through me. He reeks of alcohol. I hold my breath, trying not to gag.

"You're going to keep me company tonight, bitch." Sleazy slides his eyes down my body.

I kick him in the shin, and it bleeds. How is that possible? My kick can't be that strong, could it? Why am I not freaking out about the blood leaking from his leg?

Could the fear of what he's about to do to me overwhelm my hemophobia? Or is my desire to hurt him overpowering my blood phobia? The stream of blood glows bright red.

He doesn't seem bothered that he's bleeding and presses his face toward my neck.

I scream, "Help!" But a gurgling sound escapes me.

Sleazy grins. "No one is going to save you. You belong to us. We're going to sell you. But first, you're going to pleasure us. Got that?"

The bald man standing beside him laughs. I see another shadow behind him. Who is the third man?

My body is burning, and a trickle of sweat slides down my face.

Sleazy bands his arms around my waist, hurting me. "Open the van. I want to tap that ass!"

I kick him, but Sleazy's arms tighten even more.

"Be quick, so I can have my turn." The bald man clasps my legs. "Behave or we'll kill you."

Panic surges as I call for help. "Forrest!"

His name comes out muffled. I cry uncontrollably as the third man steps out to the shower of light from the light pole. He's also wearing red shoes. I hate seeing the man who doesn't know he's my father.

"You look like someone I know." He studies me as though searching for clues.

An irresponsible and selfish man shouldn't have the power to make rules for others.

Something fierce erupts in me. Hatred and violence uncoils like a viper. With all my might, I become an animal, thrashing all over the place.

"Get off me!" My voice rings out against the quiet night.

As though on command, they immediately release me. I run for my life, and the glowing blood droplets transform into a bunch of mini Chococats, guiding me down the street. I'm no longer in the dark.

Then one of the little Chocoats leaps into my arm, gives me a big hug, and melts into my body. I feel its love, warmth, and healing as though medicine has just cleared away all my ailments. My body shivers as I run, knowing that whatever blockage I've had with blood breaks apart in that moment. What has been terrifying is now replaced with by love and hope.

Somehow I know this is a dream.

I may not fear blood, but I'm frightened of those men. I can hear them laughing as they rush after me. I don't know how I'm able to run so fast, keeping pace with the multiple Chococats.

The dream feels real and strange to me. But I'm able to decide. I will my body to scream loud and clear.

"Forrest! Help me! I need you!"

When a hand touches me, I scream and punch into the air, hitting something.

"Oww."

I woke to Forrest staring down at me with worried eyes while rubbing his shoulder.

Bolting up from the bed, I gripped his shoulder, examining it. "Oh my God. Did I hit you?"

"It's okay. You were dreaming." Those gorgeous sage eyes searched my face.

I missed him so much. My handsome BaMBu Beast—a

man who made me feel safe, desired, and worthy. Whenever I'd seen my friends' lovers look at them, I wondered what it would feel like to have a man look at me the same way. Now I understood. That feeling was beyond powerful. I could feel his affection for me erase all the imperfections I'd collected over the years.

My heart palpitated with a surge of energy.

"You okay?" he asked.

He probably saw the emotions in my eyes, but I didn't want to talk about it. For now, I wanted that special moment for myself.

"Me? You're the one who got hit for no reason."

Forrest slid into bed with me, gathering me into his arms. "I'd take the hit for you any day." He kissed the top of my head. "I'm here now, and I won't let anyone take you away from me again."

I felt his promise wrap around my heart like a velvet ribbon.

A tear slipped from my eyes, but it wasn't from sadness. It was from how he was healing me. I snuggled into him, breathing in his scent, absorbing the comfort and security he offered me. "The dream felt so real. I knew I was dreaming, and I made decisions. I've never been able to do that in a dream before."

"You experienced lucid dreaming. It's when you're aware you're dreaming and have some control over the dream. Lucid dreams can be beneficial. They can enhance creativity, solve problems, and help you overcome fears."

Overcoming my fears interested me the most. I remembered being able to control my dreams by willing the men to release me, and the power of the Chococat blood drops healing my body. "How do I induce this kind of dreaming?" There was another world beyond fear.

"Spontaneously." He lifted a shoulder. "There's not an

absolute method. There are some devices that help, but I always like the natural route. Start with a dream journal. Train your brain to remember your dreams. Then it'll start happening more often for you. You planning on dreaming of me?"

"I've already dreamed of you many times."

"Were they kinky?" His eyes gleamed.

"Maybe." I wasn't going to admit it, but he knew based on my smile.

"Then I want to know about them in detail. Better yet, I want you to demonstrate them when you're feeling better." He skimmed his fingers along my arm, sending chills down my body.

He was the only man who could make me forget the trauma I'd just experienced, making it less important.

"It must have been the acute anxiety and then seeing you. How long was I asleep?"

"Sixteen hours."

"Whaaat?" I detached from his arm, straightening up. I'd never slept that long before. My body probably needed it.

Forrest placed a hand on my forehead. "You've sweated out all the toxins. You just have to wait for the body to purge and heal itself."

He brushed a hand down my hair. "While you were out, I made an executive decision and took a sample of your blood for testing. I hope that's okay."

I nodded. "You can be my healthcare proxy and decide for me when my mom can't."

"You're going to live a long and healthy life. I'll make sure of that." His eyes warmed, but soon turned cold. A complete switch in emotion like the unpredictable weather in New England, where it could rain, snow, and embrace the sun all in one day.

"What did you find in my bloodwork?"

"They gave you Ayahuasca, which is a brew with hallucinogenic properties found in the *Psychotria viridis* shrub and the *Banisteriopsis caapi* vine. It can make you drowsy or cause hallucinations. Different people react differently."

I'd never heard of that drink before, but it was now etched in my brain to avoid.

"My body felt weird, and they threatened not to give us the antidote if we didn't behave."

A muscle ticked on his jaw. "Like any medication, the wrong dosage could kill you, but your blood work showed small traces of it. They needed to control you so you'd behave at the auction. They didn't want you dead or injured because nobody was going to pay for damaged goods."

The idea of humans being sold sickened me. I'd watched the news and heard horrible stories about human and sex trafficking. Others had gone through the same, or worse. My chest tightened, wondering if someone would come to rescue them the way Forrest had saved me.

People with wealth had the power to contribute to society, and yet some of them hurt people. I'd never understand why people would choose that.

"Did you bid for me?"

"Ten million dollars."

"WHAT?" I gaped at him, my heart pounding at the number. "Are you out of your mind?"

"I had to make sure every man in that room knows you belong to me." He brushed his finger across my lips. "But don't worry, after the authorities arrived, the show became obsolete, which means there was no official transaction."

I sighed with relief. Ten million dollars was a lot of money. I didn't have anything close to one million in my savings, which were slowly dwindling. I felt guilty for having him pay that much to save me. My mom's condition flashed across my mind. That amount of money could certainly save her too.

"Will they look for me?" Concern twisted my gut.

"No." His eyes hardened. "They're not getting anywhere near you. They're probably not going to do anything rash right now."

"Who's they? I mean, I only know the men who captured me, but who runs the show?"

"Powerful and dangerous people. I don't want you worrying about them. Save your energy to recover."

A sudden fear gripped me. "Does my mom know about the abduction?"

"No. Your friends don't either. I told the boys not to say anything. It'll just worry them."

"Thank you for thinking about everything." I turned my face into his neck, inhaling his musky and masculine scent. No other scent comforted me more than his. "Where's Olivia? Is she okay?"

"She's recovering at a hospital near Levi's house. He's looking after her now."

"Olivia drank the entire drink. She wasn't herself. I'll call to check up on her soon. What happened to the other women?"

"According to the news, only two women were rescued to safety. The others were shot and killed."

Goosebumps erupted on my arms at the horror. Those evil people wanted to get rid of the evidence of their crimes.

"I tried hard not to succumb to the drowsiness. I was afraid if I fell asleep I wouldn't wake up, you know?" My body shivered, reliving the fear. Our gazes met, and the shiver turned to warmth. "I kept you in my mind."

He kissed me lightly, pulled back, and pain filled his eyes. "I'm sorry you had to go through that."

A flicker of menace gleamed in his eyes like a sharpened

blade ready to attack. But it softened when I placed a hand on his cheek. "Not your fault."

"I should have been more protective of the person I care deeply about."

Love.

Though he didn't say, I felt it and saw it on his face. We were both heading toward something marvelous, life-changing, and frightening. I knew how he felt without the words, and I only wanted to hear them when he was ready.

I struggled with the same. Did I love him because he was the security I needed right now? Or did I love him because that was what my heart felt regardless of the circumstances? I had to be sure.

Despite that, my heart inflated with giddiness. I shouldn't be feeling this after what I'd just experienced, but that was the power of love, wasn't it? To put you in a state of bliss where darkness couldn't touch you.

The Opals are Forever mission was closer to being fulfilled.

"What does 'care deeply' mean?" I drew hearts on his firm abs, loving the heat that emanated through his T-shirt.

A serious expression filled his face. Was he nervous? A smile curved on my lips as confirmation lit up my heart. This stunning warrior who normally portrayed confidence, intelligence, and fearlessness with ease was unsettled because of *me*.

A rebellious mood surged in me, and I challenged, "Define it as only you can."

"Fear of you being hurt was like a virus that attacked me unexpectedly. I wasn't prepared for this foreign invasion. So my immune system kicked into gear, producing an enormous amount of white blood cells, antibodies, and platelets, fighting something that wasn't physically found in my system. The anxiety I felt released stress hormones that told my body I was being attacked, but it was just my concern for you."

His words made the trauma fade a little, and I smiled. "Cheesy. But perfect coming from you."

"I've never been so scared, Kiera." He brushed the hair from my face. "I haven't slept well in days. You're not leaving my sight ever again."

Covering his hand with mine, I said, "I was scared too." A memory surfaced, and I jumped off the bed searching for my shopping bag. "Where is it? Where's the bag from Full Circle Apothecary?" I glanced around as another thought popped into my head. "Oh my God! I missed my dinner date. She probably thinks I'm some con artist. I have to call Morena to let her know." I rushed out to the living room. "Where's my phone?"

"Calm down," he said, gesturing to the couch. "Sit. I'll get the shopping bag from the chair that's pushed in at your desk."

I sat and waited.

He returned with the bag, handing it to me. "I informed my grandma about your abduction. She had planned on introducing us during dinner, but things got complicated."

"Morena is your grandmother?" There had been so many surprises lately, I couldn't keep up. I looked into his sage-colored eyes, and I could see the resemblance. There was an odd comfort that came from her, even though I didn't know her. Some people just radiated warmth. "She was so knowledgeable about herbs. We'll have to take her out to dinner to make it up to her."

"She'd like that." He sat down beside me, watching me take out the protective charms.

"Here." I gave him the lucky charm. "Hang it in your car. But if you're embarrassed by it, you can put it in your glove compartment. It doesn't matter. I just want it to protect you."

"Why should I be embarrassed?"

"I don't know." I shrugged. "Some guys wouldn't want their friends to make fun of them."

He laughed. "You know my boys. We make fun of each other about everything. But that's how we are." He held up the charm. "I'll keep it in my wallet."

"Really? I wish I'd bought it sooner because it could've prevented—"

"It brought me luck. Arrow wasn't supposed to be in Texas, but something came up for work and placed him here to help us. Also, a murder of crows got a neighbor's attention, so he went to the window, saw your abduction, and called the police." He rubbed the willow charm. "The intention you had when you bought it for me is powerful too."

Smiling, I held the circular charm to my heart. "We make magic and miracles happen."

He opened his wallet and placed it inside. "You should keep yours in your purse."

"I will." Curiosity piqued. "How many women have given you a protective charm?"

He grinned. "One."

My lips curled into a pout. "Who was she?"

"My grandma." His smile widened, and he wrapped his arms around me. "But I don't know where I placed her bag of crystals." He placed a finger over my lips. "Shhh. Don't tell her. It's our secret."

"Okay." I smiled and tucked my charm in my purse.

"Do you have energy to pack?" He got up from the couch and headed toward the kitchen island. "Want anything to drink?"

"Just water, thanks." I followed him to the kitchen. "Right now I have the energy to lift an elephant."

Those sexy green eyes gleamed as he opened a bottle of Pellegrino and offered it to me. "Use that energy to pack your essentials because I'm taking you on vacation. You don't have any projects lined up for the next week, do you?"

"No, but I'd planned on helping my mom resolve some medical bill issues." I sipped the water, letting the chill coat my throat, and placed the bottle on the marble counter.

He held up a hand. "I'll fill you in on that as soon as I have some news. Your mom's condition is stable right now. No need to worry, and don't ask me any more questions. I'll tell you everything later. Your mind shouldn't be too active right now. You need to rest and relax."

"Maybe take your own advice here?"

"I'm a doctor, so I know what I'm doing."

"Says all the doctors addicted to something they don't even know until it's too late."

"I'm addicted to you, but I don't care."

My anxiety lowered several notches knowing he'd reviewed my mom's medical history.

I slapped his chest playfully. "Don't you have a million better things to do than take me on vacation? Where are we going, anyway? Shouldn't we wait to hear if the authorities caught those criminals? They were selling women! We *have* to catch them."

He placed a hand on each side of my shoulders. "I *will* catch them. That's a promise. Those who tried to hurt you will pay for it." His eyes flashed with a deadly calm I wasn't used to seeing.

There was another man inside this gorgeous face staring at me. Who was he?

"You don't have to worry about Bo and Deon. They were taken care of." He released me, walked over to his bar, and poured himself two fingers of Scotch. "They won't abduct women anymore."

How did he know their names? I knew the answer, but I was afraid to ask.

While he sipped his Scotch, he kept his eyes on me, and my body burned.

I swallowed as my mind read the message between the words. "What do you mean?"

"You don't have to worry about them." He placed the glass down and walked over to stand in front of me. "Kiera, there's something you need to know about me."

Oh God. What now? I wasn't sure if I was ready to hear this.

Stop holding your breath. That's not going to stop anything except the flow of oxygen your body desperately needs.

I forced a slow inhale and exhale. "You have an arranged marriage with a powerful princess who commands an army and wants to perm your hair?"

He screwed up his face and then smirked. "No."

"You fathered five kids with three different married women whose husbands are working together to go after you?"

Amusement gleamed in his eyes as he considered me, probably wondering what happened to my brain. "You have an incredible imagination. That sounds like an exciting life, but not for me. No to that question."

He pulled out a drawer from the counter and showed me a tray of fancy knives. He held up a knife, and it gleamed in the light.

"Like a knife, medicine can heal or hurt people. Though I'm a doctor who heals, I don't have a problem hurting those who deserve it." His tone was even and cool, reminding me of a calm ocean on a lovely day, but beneath the surface was a strong whirlpool of emotion threatening to surge.

When he shifted the knife around, it caught a reflection of his face. He was the blade, and the blade was him. We made our own choices.

His words cut into my skin, but not in a painful way. They

were raw and real, and made me realize something about myself. I gripped the smooth handle of a small knife and examined it. Certain circumstances called for certain actions that no one else had the right to judge.

I looked at him. "I can't judge you for your decisions, Forrest, because I would have used this knife to save me and Olivia from that trauma. Sometimes, survival requires you to hurt another person."

His eyes softened on me.

I stepped closer and tapped my knife to his. The blades clinked with a kiss—a tribute of acknowledgment, honor, and respect.

His eyes flickered with understanding, and a smile formed on his lips. "You're a one-of-a-kind woman, Kiera."

"Because you're a one-of-a-kind man, Forrest." I took both knives and placed them back into the tray.

"We're made for each other." Forrest swallowed, and my eyes went to the motion of his throat and the scar at the back of his neck that he'd acquired from the car accident.

"I need to show you something in Brazil. You'll understand and see me in a different light. You can decide if I'm worth your affection." His gaze intensified like a dark storm. "If you think you're better off without me, I'll let you go."

I sucked in a breath. "I don't like the sound of this, Forrest. You're scaring me."

He gripped my chin lightly. "Scaring you is never my intention. I just want to be honest with you. I want you to see me . . . and all my flaws. Isn't that what a relationship is about? I'm not a perfect man, but I want to be one for you."

His honesty did something to me, and I touched his face, caressing it as though it were a cold blade begging for warmth. The motion warmed me as well, and I hugged him to prevent myself from crying. Forrest was opening himself, letting me in, and here I was being skeptical.

"Everyone has flaws, Forrest. They're what makes us different from the rest. I'll take you as you are."

"What I've learned in the past few days is that life is too short." He gazed down at me, his eyes holding so much emotion. "I could lose those I care about in an instant. I don't want it to be too late for us. So I need you to know the true Forrest Navarro."

My previous relationships lacked communication and trust. I hadn't trusted those men enough to let them in either. I'd safeguarded my heart because of a father who wasn't there for me. That sense of abandonment and loss skewed my perception with men. But Forrest was changing all of that. He was the healing I needed.

Forrest had created this sense of security that I'd never experienced, and I welcomed whatever he had to show me because my past wasn't unblemished either.

This heaviness surrounding us needed some joy, so I smiled and said, "Okay. I'm ready to see Brazil and unravel my mysterious man. May I shower first?"

"You may, but I'm joining." He didn't ask for permission.

"I'll allow it since you have dark circles under your eyes." I tapped the spots gently, wanting to erase them.

"After the shower, we're hopping on a flight on Grayson's plane. I'm going to feed you on the plane, and you can tell me exactly what happened to you before, during, and after the abduction. I want all the details of what you went through."

My brain was tired just trying to see into his mind. I looped my arms around his neck and studied him. "How do you do it?"

"Do what?"

"Manage it all. Your medical facility, the $Ba_7M_5Bu_{88}$ Project, the Holistic Farm, the alternative medicine development, and the video games with your boys. And these are just the major projects that I know of. I'm sure you have more. Seriously, how do you juggle them all, and make it seem so easy?"

He shrugged. "It's not easy." He wrapped his arms around me. "I've been organizing my life since I was a kid. It helped me see the big picture. Everything just became a habit over time." His forehead touched mine. "But when you went missing, my routine became erratic. I . . . I became lost. I had to delegate everything to my team because my emotional and mental state were disconnected."

"But I'm back now." I kissed him on the cheek and pressed my face into the crook of his neck, hugging him tighter.

This man with many plans needed my security too. I had other questions for him, but I was too tired to dig deep, so I asked a simple one. "You don't have a plane of your own?"

"I'd considered it, but since Grayson has one and graciously offered its services to his friends, I couldn't refuse. One less thing for me to manage. Why do you ask? You want one?" he asked in a casual tone, as if ordering me dinner.

I laughed at the paradox. Here was a calculated man who always knew what he wanted, and yet, he offered me a plane as though it was a cocktail drink at a bar. That either showed he trusted me wholeheartedly or that he was still "lost."

My gut told me it was the former, and my heart swelled.

Color me curious. "Would you buy me one?"

"If you want it."

I grinned at the ridiculous offer. What would I do with a plane? But I loved how he'd get me whatever I wanted.

"I don't want one, my BaMBu Beast. Let's go shower so I can show you the way home. I don't want you to be lost." I winked.

"*Coming* right up, baby." He emphasized the word as he squeezed my ass.

CHAPTER FORTY-EIGHT

FORREST

Taking Kiera to Brazil served two purposes for me. One, she needed to be away from the evil she'd experienced.

When I'd watched her sleeping in my bed recovering from the spiked drink, a surge of violence burst in me. If she had drunk more of the Ayahuasca, she would have gotten really sick. For a body that had never experienced a psychedelic drink, it would have been a powerful shock to her system.

Two, I wanted her to see the $Ba_7M_5Bu_{88}$ Project—to see me.

I loved her, and I needed her to know there were blood-stains on my hands. I wasn't the doctor she thought I was, and it terrified me that she might leave. That was why I couldn't say those sacred words to her. What was the point if the relationship was going to end?

Before I showed her the project, I wanted her to see where I grew up.

We stayed in a house I'd purchased on top of hill that gave a breathtaking view of the town. Right now, we were dressed for an adventure in the Amazon Forest. I wore a green T-shirt, camo cargo shorts, and boots with a backpack filled with hiking essentials. Kiera had on cargo capris, a light blue T-shirt, a matching bucket hat, hiking boots, and a fanny pack slung across her chest.

"Are you ready?" I asked as I sprayed us with a holistic insect repellant.

"Yup!" She took my hand, and we walked toward the dock with the awaiting boat.

Whenever I returned to the Amazon River, I often took the boat out to be with nature. The sounds and the scent of the earth reminded me of my parents.

"Absolutely." Her eyes widened as she glanced around the water and trees.

I'd secured a small riverboat instead of the larger riverboats that were offered from my tour company. The boutique riverboats were too large for us. I wanted something intimate as I showed her this marvelous river. Money could buy many things, and this part of the Amazon forest belonged to me. Nature belonged to no one. Or one could say it belonged to everyone equally. Regardless, I wanted to safeguard it as best I could. My mom and dad would have appreciated that. This was my heritage, and I had to protect it.

The riverboat had a roof with curtains on the side and comfortable seating for six people. Kiera sat down on the seat near my backpack as I steered the boat along the water. It moved slowly, allowing her to sightsee.

"I have the boat all to myself with such a handsome helmsman." She smiled, then looked at the flock of birds that flew nearby, creating a beautiful reflection in the water.

Warmth spread within me as I watched her admire the land. I didn't know how much it mattered to me to have her here—to share this part of my life with her.

I'd never cared before about bringing another woman here.

"Wow!" Kiera gasped when she spotted one of my boutique riverboats appearing in the distance. "That's like a moving condo on a river. Look at the three floors and the wrap-around deck."

I chuckled. "We can take a tour on it next time. It's beautiful inside. I'll make sure the office sets it aside for us."

"What do you mean? You don't own it, do you?"

"I do."

"Rich bastard," she mumbled, even as her eyes sparkled.

Wildlife made itself known as I steered the boat to the edge of the river. The birds cawed loudly, their calls echoing through the lush green vegetation. A parrot perched on a tree to our right and watched us as the engine hummed along. The fan from the ceiling helped ease the heat and humidity.

"Look! It's more beautiful in real life." Kiera pointed to the colorful parrot. "Everything is so . . . alive here. The air is fresher. I feel like I'm intruding on some private sanctuary."

"Nature is everyone's sanctuary. You're not intruding; you're my guest." She scooted closer, looked toward the marsh, and sucked in a breath. "Is that an alligator?"

"Yes, but no need to worry. It's just chilling."

"Until it's *hungry*," she said as her gaze stayed on it even as the boat passed.

I docked the boat, slipped on the backpack, stepped onto the pier, and offered her a hand. "Time to explore the forest."

Smiling, she took my hand. "I already know my way around a *spectacular* Forrest." She wiggled her eyebrows. "But please show me more 'wood,' sexy guide." She squeezed my shoulder.

"Who's cheesy now?" Laughing, I tapped her bucket hat.

"I'm taking pointers from the best." She kissed my cheek, looking nothing like the woman who had gone through hell. "So, where does the path lead to?"

I wanted my parents to meet her. She was the beacon of

light that seduced the darkness out of me. She gave my heart direction when it thought it knew the way. I followed that light and found myself again. The path to vengeance had been lonely and dark until her. My path had shifted because of her.

"To where I was born."

He held my hand as we walked on the dirt path. "Has this path always been this wide?"

"No. We have a team managing this area because it belongs to me. Though I love the wild look, the shrubberies need to be trimmed, and the grass needs to be cut so I can access the space."

I paused in my steps. "I can't believe you own part of the Amazon."

"Why? A lot of it is being torn down for business developments. I preserve what matters to me."

"I'm sure the animals and trees love you for it. You saved their home."

We came to an adorable house made of wood and small stones with a lovely front porch that had been updated. It was like a secret gem in the midst of the forest. A large garden sat on the side of the house.

"My parents used to work here to prepare herbs to sell at the markets in nearby towns and villages. They grew a lot of stuff in this garden. It has fertile soil. They'd rented the house from a friend, but it's mine now."

I glanced around, admiring the flower bushes along the path that led up to the house. The flower pots on the porch were filled with gorgeous red flowers. "Why did your parents name you Forrest?" He never got the chance to answer me when I first asked him at the Holistic Farm.

"Because I was born here in this house, in the middle of the forest. They loved plant life, and the sound of it in English." He opened the door and gestured for me to enter.

I looked up at him. "It's the perfect name for you."

The inside of the house had simple wooden furniture. I browsed the two cozy bedrooms and one and a half bathrooms. I walked out to the backyard where a wide hammock was secured to two trees. Fruit trees stood in the distance.

"What kinds of fruits are those?"

"Papaya."

"Why are the trees spaced out evenly? There's an empty spot for a third tree."

For a moment, he didn't speak as a storm of emotions stirred in his eyes. A muscle ticked in his jaw as he stared at the trees as though remembering something dark.

"You don't have to tell me if you're not ready." I touched his arm gently.

His eyes bore into mine. "If I weren't ready, I wouldn't have brought you here." He ran a hand down my cheek, and heat soared in me. "Besides the groundskeepers, no one has been here but me."

"What about your grandma?"

He shook his head. "She knew that I'd bought the house and had it updated, but she hasn't been here since she left Brazil."

Love overflowed in me.

He let out a slow sigh. "Each of those trees represents a man who was involved in my father's death. I'll plant the third tree when the third person is dead."

I furrowed my brows, not truly understanding what he said. People usually planted a tree as a remembrance of a loved one. Didn't he hate his father's killers?

"I don't understand."

"I didn't plant those trees to commemorate them. That would be blasphemy. With each man's death, I gained closure. With every ending, there's a new beginning. The fruit tree was the beginning for me. The fruit is delivered to the BaMBu center, and my employees include them with other food and supplies that go to the local shelters."

"You're feeding the needy. That's a beautiful gesture, Forrest."

"I can't let this fruit go to waste."

I felt honored standing beside him. "Do you know that you're the essence of your name?"

"Explain." He flicked something off my bucket hat.

"A forest provides a lot to the Earth. It's the home to animals and plants. It provides oxygen and keeps the natural cycle of life going." I didn't know why, but emotions surged through me. Tears rolled down my face as I choked, "It's a gift to the world—a gift to me."

"Oh, baby." He wrapped his arms around me, holding me tight. "The beautiful way you see me has the power to heal the devil."

"Can you tell me what happened to your father?"

He led me to the stone bench with a carpet of gorgeous moss. Pretty flowers dotted the surroundings, along with rocks and exotic shrubberies. I kicked off my boots and socks, then stepped onto the soft vibrant green moss that made my feet sigh. I loved the way it kissed my bare feet.

"Sit here with me." I patted the spot next to me.

He also kicked off his boots and socks, sitting beside me. Like kids, we wiggled our toes into the moss.

"Three thugs dealing drugs framed my father. My parents were harmless and hardworking citizens. They loved nature and offered free herbal treatments to schools, and in exchange I got to learn English for free as a kid."

He told me how a rival gang member from the Anacondas had hidden drugs in his dad's groceries. There were several local gangs trying to dominate the drug business in the small towns. His dad had been a victim of those rival wars.

"They refused my dad's explanation and shot him. I'll never forget that day. Those men were monsters. They changed my life. The people feared the Anacondas because they were ruthless. As I grew up, I searched for them." He turned and met my gaze. "I made them pay."

My breath hitched as the meaning of this admission swirled in my mind. I understood what pushed him to that level.

His gaze never left mine, as though he wanted to know my reaction. "The areas where they once ruled are now thriving. The local government saw how I'd improved the community, and they supported my business expansion, which provided jobs and affordable health centers."

"Why didn't the authorities do anything back then?" I asked.

A flash of temper lit his eyes. "Money is power. There's corruption everywhere—even in the States. If you know the right people and pay the right amount of money, they can look the other way. They won't care what happens to the citizens."

My stomach clutched. I knew what he was doing— revealing all the shadowy parts of him to me. Not only was I not afraid, I admired his courage, persistence, and his heart. He was a brilliant billionaire, but more than that, he had a good heart. An intelligent man without a heart is nothing but an empty shell, with nothing on the inside.

I stared at him for a while, remembering what he'd told me prior to making the trip. *So I need you to know the true Forrest Navarro.* This was a man eradicating evil so people could live without fear. I loved him more for it.

"You said there were three men. Where's the third?"

"He's left Brazil and changed his identity. I recently found him." He picked up a rock by his foot and chucked it into the distance.

I wanted him to have the closure he deserved. I tried to imagine his life, but my heart hurt just thinking about how vengeance had propelled him along. Studying his profile, I wanted to reach inside of him, and pull out every root of darkness, and destroy them for him. Vengeance was a prison, and he deserved to be free and happy.

"Kiera, I need you to understand the man I am. I'm not just a doctor—I'm also a killer."

Those words should have shocked me, but his honesty just made me want him more.

I placed a thumb over his lips. "No. You did what you had to do because no one else had the courage to do it. You didn't turn a blind eye to those in need. That doesn't make you a killer, it makes you a hero—*my* hero."

Forrest searched my face and relief swarmed in his eyes.

I could only imagine how many people the Anacondas had killed over the years. My man took matters into his own hands and did something about it. How could I not accept and admire him for that?

"If you didn't get rid of them, they would've continued to destroy lives. People should thank you, not despise you."

He released a soft sigh. "You don't think less of me? I have blood on my hands, Kiera."

"But it's the kind that washes off, Forrest. It's the kind that allows innocent people to live. You're doing so much for the community. I admire and respect that. Your parents would've been proud." A lump formed in my throat. "Your father sounds like a kind man who took care of his family. Mine isn't like that."

"Is he alive? You haven't talked about him."

Bitterness grew in my mouth. "You've seen him. He was at the auction wearing red shoes."

Forrest blinked. "Senator Mitch Kramer?"

"He got my mom pregnant, told her to get rid of me, and ended the relationship. He said he wasn't ready for a family and didn't want the responsibility. Mom raised me on her own. He doesn't know I exist."

His jaw clenched as he took my hand in his. "He doesn't deserve you or your mom."

Tears filled my eyes. "We all have a past that makes us who we are. I'm ashamed to be related to such a cold person. It was hard growing up not understanding why my father didn't want me or Mom. As I investigated and learned about him, I didn't want to be related to him."

"It's his loss. You're perfect, you understand me? You're not a byproduct of someone's sperm. You are defined by the person you become. Your heart, your mind, your intelligence, and your imagination are qualities I fell in love with."

My giddy heart jumped up and down. "What did you say?"

This had been a revealing day, with so many confessions and discoveries. I shifted my leg, placed it on the other side of the stone bench, and straddled it. She did the same, so we were now facing each other.

I cupped her face with my hands and kissed her gently. "I love you."

Her hands rested on my chest as she kissed me back. My vixen darted her tongue into my mouth and played with mine. Being here in this sacred space with her meant the world to me. It was like me coming home with a full heart.

"I love you too." She sucked on my tongue, and an electrical shock zipped to my cock.

"You're perfect," I muttered against her lips.

Not only did she accept me for my flaws, she admired and respected me for doing what I did. Those acts were crimes in the eyes of society, yet she understood me. How did I get so fortunate to land a woman like that?

I wanted to protect her and show her I was the only man she'd ever need. No one could love her like I did.

She was mine—a thought I sent out to the earth, the wind, the water, the air, the trees, and the animals. They were witnesses to this unveiling of my soul. If I were the devil, she was the light that made me betray the darkness. She saved me.

With every new decision I'd make, she would be at the forefront.

I drew back to look at her beautiful face and swollen lips. "I've waited for you all my life. You were right in front of me all this time."

My lips pressed into her neck, feeling her pounding pulse.

Palming my cock, she breathed, "I need you right now." Her eyes darkened.

With lightning speed, our clothes scattered the yard. I loved that I could share this place with her, showing her off to the land where I was born. We kneeled on the soft moss as our mouths connected in a slow and tender kiss. My eager hands found her breasts, so full and soft for me. I broke the kiss to claim a nipple, suckling hard. She cried out in pleasure, and the delightful sounds echoed through the forest. I could imagine the trees and river smiling as two lovers created magic.

I wanted to give her everything, devouring her breasts and loving their softness, taste, and scent.

She gripped my cock, stroking it. "I want him in my mouth."

"No. It's about you right now."

"Not fair."

"Life isn't fair, Kitty K. I'm going to fuck you so hard all the animals are going to be jealous."

Laughing, she lay down on the grass like a nature goddess, with her long brown hair fanning out around her face, making her wild and sensual.

She spread her legs apart, and her eyes gleamed with desire. "All yours."

Gloriously gorgeous.

I stared at her glistening sex and growled like a starving beast. Primal instinct kicked in, and I lowered to a prone position with the soft moss caressing my skin. This was my first time taking a woman on a carpet of moss. From the provocative image, it wouldn't be the last.

I tossed her thighs over my shoulders, cupped her ass in my hands, and lifted her sex to me. I flattened my tongue and licked her slowly. She released a moan that made me want to stay here forever. Her hypnotic scent was like a blooming flower, mesmerizing me. I wanted to absorb every aspect of her, letting her body know I was the only man allowed to touch her. I licked, kissed, and sucked, ravaging her like a wild beast who only had one goal—to satisfy his hunger.

Liquid heat slid out from her, and I lapped it up, desperate for more.

"Oh, Forest." She writhed.

"You need to come, baby?" I slid a finger between her folds, then two. She moaned when my fingers pushed deep into her channel. "Clench hard and fuck my fingers, baby."

"Oh, God," she gasped as she pushed onto her elbows and rocked.

The sexual energy stirring around us was dark and inhibited, and I loved seeing that on her face.

"So. Good." She whimpered while rocking hard against my fingers, which were soaked in delicious silk.

I clenched my jaw, loving the pleasure playing out on her face. She was fucking beautiful.

I extracted my fingers, and she protested. "No!"

"You taste like silky sin. I'm not done eating you, love." I fluttered her bud, and she screamed my name. Then I ravaged her hard and slow, loving every crevice of her body.

One of her hands gripped my head while the other clawed at the moss.

"I want you to come squeezing my cock."

"Forrest . . . I need . . ." Her body trembled.

"Hold on." I got up on my knees and prowled forward, pushing her legs up and over. I slammed into her. Her tight muscles stretched as a powerful circuit coursed through me. I pumped hard and fast, each thrust sending me deeper into her. My face hovered over her, watching each flicker of bliss that glittered in her eyes. Our moans, and the sounds of my cock sliding in and out of her wetness, echoed around us.

"I'm the only man who loves you." I plunged, and her muscles constricted. "You're mine, love." Another mighty plunge that had me scrunching my face. "Mine. You understand?"

"Only you." Her eyes rolled back in her head, and I knew the moment her pleasure arrived.

She shuddered, and the sensation choked my cock. I erupted, pouring myself into her. My dick quivered as the climax rolled through me. Our bodies trembled together in a beautiful rhythm.

"You're an absolute beast," she panted against my chest as I released her legs, covering her body with mine. My cock continued to throb inside of her.

Birds chirped, and something splashed in the river.

"I think the animals heard your sexy cries, so they're fucking too."

She turned to my neck and giggled, "Adorable perverts."

After a moment to catch our breaths, I rolled over beside her and held her hand as we both looked up at the blue sky. This was the life. Inside of this beautiful cocoon was just me and her. The outside world couldn't penetrate it. I wanted to stay like this forever. No worries, no vendetta to complete.

My phone rang, and I reached for my shorts. It was the number of a man who gave me a second chance at life.

I kissed her forehead and sat up. "I need to take this."

"Go ahead. I'm going to admire the view." She gathered her clothes and got dressed.

"How's it going, Slash?" I asked, wondering why he was calling me now.

He'd kept a low profile ever since he came back to life after faking his death to get The Trogyn off his back. Slash still had contacts within the crime organization, but due to its size and secrecy, it was hard to identify the top players who made the big decisions. Slash had been a member of The Trogyn when my friends and I witnessed their crime. Instead of killing us, he let us go, because we had reminded him of his younger brothers, who died being in the wrong place at the wrong time. Slash had become a trusted friend to us.

Because of Slash, I tried to remember that not all the bad guys were "bad." Circumstances determine how we operate in this world. Compassion is hidden somewhere deep inside of every person, but we have to find it on our own.

"Lots going on." I looked over at Kiera, who had wandered over to the papaya trees. "Is everything okay?"

"Heard you were looking for ugly red shoes. Got something you should look into. One factory is in Brazil, one in Texas, and another in Florida. The warehouse in Providence is the smallest."

I wasn't sure what to think about the timing. If Kiera hadn't been here with me, it would have been perfect. But I didn't want to risk doing anything that would put her in danger. I could send her back to Providence and stay a few days to research. She'd ask me questions, but I didn't want to lie to her. She didn't need to know these dark details.

I could have my men investigate, but this was too important

to me. Red Venom was the final snake I had to destroy. He wasn't just a threat to me but to everyone.

"What's the address for Brazilian location?"

CHAPTER FIFTY-ONE

KIERA

That next evening, he showed me around the villages and nearby towns. By the time we got back to the house, I was exhausted.

"I've got to make a stop by the BaMBu office. You hang out here, and I'll be right back."

I had a packed day tomorrow with visiting the office and taking a plane to visit Rio de Janeiro. I'd never been there and was excited to explore.

"We can watch a movie later."

"Okay." He kissed my forehead and left.

After a long shower, I perused his house, which was nestled in the woods on a hill overlooking a valley. There were neighbors around, but not close. When I looked out the window, I saw the town's lights in the distance. The location was private and yet close to everything. Settling in bed, I texted my friends.

Kiera: *Guess what?*

Audri: *Mission accomplished?*

My best friend knew me too well.

Kiera: *Party pooper.*

Audri*: Really? Was just a guess! Do tell! (Wine emoji)*
Michelle: *We want all the deets.*
Natalie*: So . . .*
Vivian: *How did it happen?*

I stared at the chat and grinned. They were like little guppies all excited about a tiny bit of bait. I loved these girls.

Kiera: *He said those words today.*
Audri: *What did you do?*
Michelle: *Did you pin him down and threaten him?*
Natalie: *While dressed in sexy lingerie?*
Vivian: *Nudity works better for you? (LMAO emoji)*
Audri: *Don't be shy. We've all done it too. (Laugh emoji)*
Kiera: *None of it.*

I told them the brief version about his humanitarian mission in Brazil and how he brought me to a place no other woman had been to.

Natalie: *When a man lets you in that way? True love.*
Audri: *How did you reciprocate?*

The image of us fucking on the moss and me screaming into the forest flashed across my mind.

Kiera: *Gave him what he wanted. (Heart emoji)*
Michelle: *(eggplant emoji) (Cucumber emoji)*
Vivian: *(Tongue emoji) (Wink and tongue emoji)*

After our hilarious chat, I promised to share more details when I returned to Providence. I went to my luggage, took out the *Finding Your HeART* journal, and began to discover myself. Halfway through the book, I felt a sense of peace I'd never experienced. It was another layer of healing added to what I'd experienced in the lucid dream. I'd work on the other prompts later.

I retrieved the blank journal I'd gotten after Forrest had suggested I try journaling to help me remove my blood phobia. I tried a different approach and wrote:

. . .

Dear Adorable Droplet,

Thanks for being in my dream. I have so much to tell me. Here goes . . .

I wrote to the Chococat blood drop who had helped me in my dream. I told it my fears and symptoms. I poured everything out, literally and figuratively. Journaling did wonders. It extracted something from my psyche.

My reaction to the mere thought of blood had already changed from before. My body didn't cringe like it used to. No nerves churned in my stomach. When I'd written out ten full pages, I closed it and smiled, proud of myself.

Too happy and wired to sleep, I browsed the TV. Apparently Forrest had set up some satellite that enabled me to watch channels from the States. Should I find a romantic movie or something with action and suspense? Or a documentary?

When I stumbled on a science channel with a documentary on blood and how it helped the body heal, I paused. I had no idea what had gotten into me, but my attention zeroed in on the blood cells. The red blood cells looked like flying saucers while the white blood cells looked like donut holes dusted with powdered sugar.

As I listened to the narrator talk, I saw blood from a new perspective. It fascinated me how technology could see into the body, showing me a busy and active world inside of me. I shouldn't be afraid of it. Doing so would be fearing myself, right?

Realization flowed into me: I wasn't afraid of the blood itself, but of the terrifying event. I had been a child, experiencing loss for the first time. Now that I knew that day had connected me to the man I love, the trauma shifted completely. What had been filled with terror was now healed with love. Our love for each other changed my outlook on that fateful day. So instead of fear, I appreciated how I had been there at the right moment and the right time just for him.

All the rules I'd set for myself were now checked off. No more one-night stands? Check. Aim for a long-term relationship? Check. Focus on my dreams without worrying about money? Check. Be happy? Check.

He was the shooting star to my wish.

CHAPTER FIFTY-TWO

FORREST

Slash had gotten me a fake alias to enter a factory that made luxury shoes for several fashion brands. The warehouse hours differed from the office, which had closed already. But the night shift manager, Ricky Lima, agreed to meet with me after I apologized about my late flight, which had made me miss the regular hours. His interest piqued when I wanted to invest in footwear and planned on opening several retail stores.

After checking my name on the visiting guest list, Ricky asked me to follow him down a hallway. He had short dark hair and a goatee. He was a short and stocky man wearing a short-sleeved button-down shirt and khaki pants.

"We only have a small crew for the night shift, so the showroom area will be quiet." He turned on the lights to a large office space with cubicles. "The warehouse is over there if you want to look later." He pointed. "Our facilities follow all the required codes. There are no children working here. We're strict about industry guidelines and humanitarian laws," he said.

"Thank you. Ricky. You speak English very well."

"I had to learn so I could travel to the States. We have another factory in Providence. It's a lot smaller and used mostly for distribution."

"Good to know. That would make it easier for me."

We walked past a sewing station with industrial sewing machines and various shoes and boots in different stages of production. The scent of leather filled the air.

"What does your company do?" he asked.

"We do women's accessories, but we're looking to expand into luxury footwear for both men and women."

His eyes brightened. "Let me show you our footwear show-room. We make a lot of shoes for high-end brands."

When I entered the showroom, my eyes went to the red shoe on display. I walked over and pointed. "That is quite the shoe. May I take a look?"

He hesitated a moment, and something splashed over his face, but he nodded. "We also have better shoes over here." He gestured to the fancy black and brown men's shoes that I had several of.

I held the red shoe in my hand, studied it, and my heart quaked.

Fuck. This can't be true. But it is.

I wanted to vomit, but I controlled myself. My hand released the grip, and the shoe thudded to the floor. I inhaled a breath, stared at it for a while before picking it up, and placed it back on the shelf.

"This red shoe isn't my preference, but it's unique. It commands attention. May I ask who owns this brand? I've never seen anyone wear this."

"It's not a brand sold in the public market. We make it custom for a client who requests this style."

"What's his name? I'm just curious who would want something so gaudy."

The guy leaned in. "I've never met him, but between you and me, I don't like that shoe either. My boss doesn't either, but he has no choice but to make it."

"Between you and me," I repeated his words, "does this man go by the name Red Venom?" I studied Ricky's face, and the fear in his eyes gave me the answer. "I don't like him either."

He pressed his lips into a tight line and nodded.

"Let's look at something I can sell to a wider audience."

His face beamed. "This way. Sir."

"By the way, you wouldn't know his address, would you?"

"I'll see what I can do."

By the time I got back to the house, Kiera was sound asleep. She looked peaceful all tucked in my bed. A documentary on blood replayed on the TV screen.

Had she wanted to watch the documentary with me? Or had fear pulled her into sleep?

I pulled up the comforter that had fallen and tucked her in better. Then I adjusted the AC. The house had gotten too cool.

After washing up, I updated my friends on the sick discovery. The red shoe wasn't made from animal skin—it was made from treated human skin.

CHAPTER FIFTY-THREE

KIERA

We flew to Rio de Janeiro, and I fell in love with the liveliness of the city. The beach was alive with colors and music. It looked just like all the tourism photography I'd seen on the internet.

We were back in the small town today, and Forrest took me to visit the $Ba_7M_5Bu_{88}$ Project, and I met his dedicated employees. It resembled the Holistic Farm in Texas with the abundant plants and dried herbs, but this center had an expansive farm in the back with a lot of fruit trees and vegetable gardens. An attached warehouse had workers sorting out the fruits and vegetables. A few people loaded up containers onto delivery trucks with the $Ba_7M_5Bu_{88}$ Project brand on it.

The employees pronounced the project as BaMBu without subscript, which was how I'd been addressing it.

We exited the office and headed down the street to the health center. We held hands as we walked down a paved street with adorable little shops. He'd told me earlier that this area hadn't been developed until he came and built the center. If there ever was a billionaire who used his money well, it would be him.

"What's the significance of the subscripts?" I pointed to the numbers on his $Ba_7M_5Bu_{88}$ T-shirt.

"Those were dates that changed my life. July fifth was when my father died. August eighth was when my mother died." He stopped on the sidewalk and gestured to the grocery store where an older woman exited with a little girl. "This was what they wanted for me—to live in a safe place where money didn't determine your worth."

I wrapped my arms around him, stroking up and down his back, wanting to smooth out all the wrinkles in his life. He'd seen and experienced too much at such a young age. His trauma could have turned him into a bitter person. And yet the man before me offered hope to people. Did he understand the magnitude of his achievement?

His desire for revenge against Red Venom had placed a veil over him, making him remember the dark things more than the hopeful things. I wanted to change that for him.

"You're doing marvelous work." I placed my cheek against his chest. "I know your BaMBu Project is making a tremendous difference in the world. Your employees must be honored to be part of this project—this movement."

He drew back, smiling. "What movement is that, Kitty K?"

"Affordable and free healthcare for everyone. Teaching people how to heal themselves by going back to basics. Reminding people to love and respect themselves and others, including nature. I think society forgot the definition of human-ity." I gestured an arm to my surroundings. "But I see it here. And it's all because of you."

Something passed over his face.

"What are you thinking?" I asked.

"You know what's strange? A lot of people, including my grandma, have told me this. But your words are the only ones that finally sank in." He tipped up my chin. "Your love and understanding of my mission means more to me than you could ever know."

My heart burst into a thousand suns, each forming their own galaxies. The joy in me was indescribable. I went up on my tiptoes and planted a loud, sloppy kiss onto his lips.

"Let's go see the health center, then we can head out for lunch."

The health center offered services based on a sliding scale. People paid what they could, and for those who couldn't, they were free. He'd gotten grants from the government and put in his own money to support the clinic. His billionaire friends also supported the cause.

My heart was full when we sat down at a local eatery facing a pretty garden. He ordered the traditional Brazilian food of papaya, coffee, ham, cheese, bread, and beans.

"I'm going to gain twenty pounds from all this food." I bit into the papaya, and it was sweet and juicy.

"More of you to love." A wicked smile formed on his lips. "I can help you burn off the calories."

I was going to tell him I had plans for him when the host came out to our table. "Dr. Navarro, you have a phone call from the States."

Forrest's eyebrows furrowed. "Be right back."

While I ate, an older woman wearing a straw hat walked by with her barking white Pomeranian. She tripped and fell, and the dog leash escaped her grip. The dog took off into the garden, chasing after something.

"Cupcake! Come back here!" The woman flinched as she tried to get up.

I stepped out to the sidewalk, helping her up.

"Thank you," she spoke perfect English as she limped. "Can you help me catch Cupcake? I think I sprained my ankle. I'm on vacation and don't want to lose my dog."

"You sit on the bench. I'll get her." I brought her to the iron bench by the tree.

"This bag of snacks will help you lure him out. Thank you, dear." She handed it to me.

With the bag of treats in hand, I rushed into the garden, calling his name, "Cupcake!"

Someone grabbed me from behind and placed a plastic bag over my head. I screamed as terror spiked. But the scream and my own heavy breathing suffocated me. But I kept at it as the bag muffled my cries. I tried to fight off the attacker by scratching his face. But my fingernails dug into a mask. Panic overwhelmed me. Was I going to die like this?

No. I kicked and punched out, but someone shoved my hands down in front of me.

"If you don't want to die, stay away from him, bitch." The woman spoke through something that distorted her voice.

A knife pricked my rib cage. "Stay still," said a man, probably the one wearing the mask.

"Kiera!" Forrest called my name in the distance.

My heart leaped, and I shouted for him. But my cry wasn't loud enough.

"Keep quiet or we'll kill him too," she warned.

The man pulled the bag tightly around me, and panic intensified. My body shook, and I couldn't breathe.

I heard Forrest calling me again, but I couldn't scream and dared not take a deep inhale.

"Kiera!"

I kicked at something on the ground, and it made a sound somewhere.

"Fuck! He's here, Yvette."

Curses erupted, and the man released me. I yanked off the bag, breathing hard.

Forrest spotted me, rushed over, and crouched. He tipped up my chin to examine me. Worry and viciousness swam in his eyes. "Are you okay?"

"Yes." Concern for him numbed my other emotions.

"You stay put. I'm going to kill them." The lethal look in his eyes told me he meant it. He glanced toward the shadow of the man running away and dashed after him.

"Don't! I'm fine!"

Fear gripped me, the sensation more powerful than the terror I'd just experienced. What if something happened to him? What if there were more attackers waiting there?

I pushed myself up and rushed after Forrest with adrenaline pumping through my blood. I followed the dirt path deeper into the garden that led into the woods. No one was around.

A scream erupted nearby, and I ran toward it. When I got there, Forrest was pummeling the unconscious man. Blood oozed from Forrest's hand.

"Stop!" I gripped his arm. "You're hurt."

My presence made him turn toward me. He stepped away, and his chest heaved. I could feel the violence pumping off him.

I stared down at the man who had tried to suffocate me. His face was now all bloodied and bruised. His head lolled to the side with the damaged mask near his face.

"Is he dead?" I asked, worry icing my stomach.

The bloody knife sat beside a tree trunk across from the man.

"No. But he should be." He grunted as he clenched his fists, and blood oozed through the seams of his fingers.

The terror that should have arrived from the sight of blood

didn't. The only emotion in me was the concern for Forrest's wellbeing. Excessive blood loss would be detrimental to his health. My legs didn't wobble, and I didn't freeze from helplessness like I used to.

I reached for his clenched fist. "Let me see." I opened his hand and saw a gash across his palm. "Oh my God. You need a doctor."

"I *am* a doctor." He smirked.

How could he smirk at a time like this?

"Are you in pain?"

"Yes, but seeing you safe makes all the booboos go away."

I rolled my eyes. How could he tease right now?

"You need to take care of this or you'll bleed to death." I used the hem of my shirt and dabbed the blood from his palm, trying not to touch the gash.

He didn't even wince when I accidentally touched the swollen flesh.

"Does it hurt?" I asked, wanting a serious answer.

"Yes."

"Where?"

"In my other hand."

"What?" I dropped the injured hand to look at the other one, but no injuries appeared.

He flexed it. "It's in pain because it's throbbing to hurt the escaped attacker."

The police and emergency crew arrived, took the wounded attacker to the hospital, and dropped us off at his health center where Forrest added ointment to the wound and wrapped his hand in gauze.

I held his palm in my hands, staring at the white gauze. Then I drew a heart at the center with my finger and kissed it. "That'll heal the wound faster."

"It certainly will." He raked a gaze up and down my body. "Are you sure you're not hurt anywhere?"

I nodded. "They just had a bag over my head. You came just in time." I was scared to death, but compared to his injury, mine was psychological. It would pass soon enough.

"The fuckers." His jaws tightened. "That was a traumatic experience you didn't deserve."

It was traumatic, and my body trembled a little remembering it. He pulled me into an embrace and kissed the top of my head.

"Do you have an ex-girlfriend who still loves you?"

"What? No. Why?"

"A woman warned me to stay away from you. Her voice was distorted though."

He stared at the floor, thinking. "I don't know who it could be. No one stands out. Maybe it's a misdirection. I'll work with the local authorities on this. Let's not think about this anymore. We need to get you back to Providence. I want you safe. There's good news waiting for you there."

"News about what?"

"Your mom will be okay."

An immense burden fell from my shoulders. "Really? How? What did you find out?"

"I'll tell you on our flight back home. I want you safe. You have three hours to pack."

He deserved a gold medal for the ability to think clearly under stress.

"No more being nice, okay?" He touched my cheek delicately. "That old lady vanished when you went after the dog. When I came back to our table and didn't see you, I knew something was wrong. The restaurant has a camera so I asked to see it. Don't trust anyone. My enemies could be after you because you're mine."

"Oh . . ." Goodness, I should be extra cautious of people.

What the hell was going on? Were his enemies using me as bait? I could tell there was more he wasn't telling me. Maybe he was still trying to piece everything together as well.

I want you safe. He'd told me that too many times.

But I wanted him safe too.

CHAPTER FIFTY-FOUR

FORREST

I'd never wanted to kill anyone as much as I did those fucking monsters who'd placed a plastic bag over her in Brazil. That image had etched itself into my mind. Though I didn't kill the prick, someone else did while he was in the hospital. That person had disguised himself as a nurse and pulled off his oxygen mask. He'd injected poison into the attacker.

Who was behind this attack? Was it a warning to me? This person knew Kiera was important to me. Or was the attack designed to distract me from something else?

Had Red Venom discovered who I was? My hunch told me no. There was something off about the attack, but I couldn't figure it out.

The manager at the shoe warehouse had given me Red Venom's business address, and I'd been looking into it. It was in Miami, which gave him easy access to the Caribbean, where he'd been living like a king. He worked with a small shoe factory in Houston, Texas, but had since severed ties.

Kiera and I returned to Providence, and I had things to take care of at the medical clinic and the research center that was experimenting with my holistic medicine. I convinced Kiera to stay with me at my home, which had plenty of room for her. I needed her in my sight. With all these recent attacks, I couldn't risk anything happening to her.

Was the darkness coming for my love because of me?

Upon seeing Kiera's mom's health records, I'd made accommodations for her mom. I wanted to make sure that when Kiera saw her, it would be when her mom was on the road to recovery. Her mom had had chronic compartment syndrome, which was caused when pressure arose in and around muscles. The pressure was painful and could be dangerous. It limited the flow of blood, oxygen, and other nutrients to the muscles and nerves. It occurred often in the legs, but also affected the feet, arms, hands, and abdomen.

Unlike acute compartment syndrome, the chronic version is easily treatable. And yet, her fucking doctor gave her extensive exercises that worsened her condition, so she couldn't tell between urgent and nonurgent issues.

"You okay?" Kiera asked as we exited the top floor of the hospital where her mother had been transferred to.

"Fine." I smiled, not wanting her to see all the things in my head.

She'd been through hell, and I didn't want her to worry about me. From this moment on, she'd live a peaceful life, and anyone who prevented that would deal with me.

I'd make sure Dr. Samuel Schaeffer would be imprisoned for his crimes. The information I'd received from my friends verified my suspicion of the false diagnosis. Further investigation from the PI revealed Dr. Schaeffer was part of a national insurance scam that made corrupt doctors millions of dollars while bleeding the sick dry.

He was a fucking shithead I had no qualms about destroying.

On top of her mom's health issue, I could only imagine the pain Kiera had gone through seeing her dad at an auction where he could have placed a bid on her. Even though they'd never interacted, the shame and disappointment still existed.

I led her down a hallway away from the other patient rooms.

"Oh, when was she placed in the hospital? I thought she was doing fine at home." Kiera looked at me, looking worried.

"It's more comfortable here for all the tests. She needs to clean her system."

Her eyes warmed as she placed a hand on my cheek. "When did you have the time to plan all of this?"

"I make time for those I care about." I opened the door for her.

Kiera entered the room and beamed. "Mom!"

Elizabeth Ford was watching TV, looking well. "Sweetheart, what are you doing here?"

"Visiting you, silly. How are you feeling?" Kiera sat down on the edge of the bed and studied her mom. "You look great!"

"I feel wonderful. Not so tired anymore." Her eyes darted to me. "Oh, you're more handsome in person, Dr. Navarro."

"You've met already?"

"We had a virtual conference with a new nurse, another doctor, and Dr. Navarro about my new treatment. He moved me to this fabulous room. I didn't even know these existed in hospitals. And it's free, sweetie."

Kiera flicked me an inquisitive look, but I swung my attention to her mother. "You can call me Forrest, Ms. Ford."

"Then you address me as Liz." She smiled.

Kiera's eyes warmed on me. "Thank you. What did you learn from the tests?"

"Your mom's condition isn't as bad as Dr. Schaeffer claims they were. He misdiagnosed her on purpose."

Her mouth dropped open. "What?"

"Your mom had already recovered from the Hep B, and her muscle pain is from an inflammation that is *treatable*."

Anger flashed in her eyes. "Dr. Schaeffer told me it was dermatomyositis, and that there was a costly medication that could help ease her condition."

"She doesn't have that autoimmune disorder. There's no need to worry."

My fingers flexed, hating what that bastard had done to Kiera, her mom, and the countless patients who had trusted him with their lives. Some of the worst humans hid behind the facade of important people. Sometimes I wondered if I was one of them. But I didn't want to think about that right now.

"He gets a huge bonus from the pharmaceutical companies developing these new medications. This has been ongoing for a while. I've alerted the authorities, and he's in hiding right now, but I'm sure they'll locate him soon."

She reached for my hand and squeezed. "Thank you for everything."

"You're welcome."

Liz looked sad and angry. "He ruined my life. He could've killed me. I'm grateful you did the extra work to find out the truth. Thank you, Forrest."

"It's the right thing to do."

She looked at me with brown eyes that were lighter than her daughter's. "May I ask what kind of doctor you are, Forrest?"

"An immunologist." I knew what she meant. I'd never mistreated patients for money. But I'd also done things a "good" doctor would never do. Doctors were supposed to heal. I guess I was healing society in my own way—a way that Liz would not appreciate. She would definitely not want her daughter to be with someone like me.

Liz nodded, waiting for me to continue.

I wanted to see her smile, so I said, "The kind who tries to do the right thing. I've never collaborated with any pharmaceutical company to hurt my patients."

Sometimes the right thing required an elimination of wrongdoers, right? To some, that might make me a bad guy. But I didn't care. I was no saint. I was just a man protecting those he loved—a man trying to preserve the quality of human life as best he could. And if I committed sins while doing so, I'd gladly accept my fate.

Kiera met my gaze, and a silent understanding passed between us. She didn't look stressed or exhausted anymore. Her eyes appeared brighter, her skin became more vibrant, her smile was wider, and her energy thrummed with hope. I could feel the joy and gratitude emanating from her. That was how I wanted to see her.

With enthusiasm in her voice, she said, "Mom, did you know that you met Forrest a long time ago?"

As Kiera relayed the car accident, Liz cried. "I'm in awe of God's will. A part of me can't believe it, but another part truly believes in the magic of the universe. I'm so happy you're here. Because of you, I'm well again."

"Because of you, *I'm* here. My family is truly grateful for your help back then."

She waved a hand. "Any person would have helped. It's just human decency, you know?"

She was wrong. Decency was just as rare as honesty. Not everyone would have stopped to help like she had, but I didn't want to ruin the moment by injecting negativity.

"How's your grandmother and cousin?" Liz asked.

"They're well, thank you. When they come to visit, I'll invite you over for dinner."

"I'd love that." She looked at me for a while, probably

preparing to ask the question all concerned mothers would ask. "Are you taking care of my daughter?" Something twinkled in her eyes. "Are you her *boyfriend?*"

Kiera interlaced her fingers on her lap and smiled at me.

"Yes, to both questions."

Tears leaked from Liz's eyes. "That's the best news I've heard in years. My baby deserves someone like you."

"Mom." Kiera clasped her mom's hand. "Your recovery *is* the best news."

Liz shook her head. "My health has been a huge burden, I know, but you can rest assured that I'll be around to see you start your own family."

"Mom." Kiera embraced her.

My phone rang, and I excused myself to take the call and let mother and daughter have their private moment.

CHAPTER FIFTY-FIVE

KIERA

Today had been one of the best days of my life. I knew good news was waiting for me, but I didn't expect a complete recovery. The luxurious hospital room was a bonus I needed to talk to him about. It must have cost a fortune.

I loved he was helping me and my mom, but I didn't want him to feel obligated. I certainly didn't want him to think I was taking advantage of him.

Despite that, my heart overflowed with love and gratitude. I went from stressing about money, thinking about selling my apartment to move in with my mom to save on costs, to not having to worry about anything. Anxiety had weighed on me for too long, that the sudden liberation left me a bit confused. I'd snap out of it soon enough.

Dr. Schaeffer's behavior pissed me off. I wished he'd get the punishment he deserved. How many lives had he ruined?

Mom squeezed my hand, bringing my thoughts back to her. "So how did you meet him?"

"I told you already—during the accident."

"You know what I mean." She smiled, her face blossoming with much color and life.

I explained how we'd been friends for a while, but had been with different people.

"It's good to know the person before you take things seriously." Mom leaned back into her pillow. "I was young and infatuated with your dad. If I had known before we started dating, maybe I would've known he didn't want the same things I did."

The memory of him at the auction made me want to puke. My dad was involved with bad people—the crime organization that had threatened Forrest and his friends. He'd been there to buy a woman. It made me sick that I was related to him.

Despite that, I wanted to know the man who had gotten my mom pregnant and left.

"How did you meet him?"

"He attended a conference at the hospital, saw me, and asked me to dinner. He was handsome and knew some doctors working at the hospital. I was single, so I didn't see any harm in a meal. We dated for six months, and then I found out I was pregnant. I was on the pill, but I'd missed a few days." She sighed, and there was no sadness in her voice. "He was a councilman working his way up the political ladder. I was a hindrance to him. A family would keep him tied down."

"Work was his life." Based on what I saw on the news in Texas, it was still his life.

"It was all he talked about. He was working on several projects that could make him millions. He said he didn't want a baby and told me to get an abortion." She caressed my face. "I couldn't do that. You were part of me. Even if he didn't want you, *I* wanted you."

I debated telling my mom about what I knew about him.

Though Mom had moved on, she should know the current affairs regarding her ex in case she saw him on the news.

"I'm happy I didn't have him in my life. He's a senator in Texas, and it seems like nothing has changed. He's still selfish and wants to climb the political ladder."

"People don't change easily," Mom said.

"I looked him up when I was eight years old."

Mom had told me his name during a casual conversation one night. She probably thought that I'd dismissed his identity long ago because he hadn't been part of my life. But I clung to the name and investigated.

I wanted to know who this man was. The truth wasn't as beautiful as I had hoped. It was human nature to find out your roots, even if they were poisonous.

"Sweetie, I thought keeping him from you protected you."

It wasn't my mom's fault. She protected me the best way she could.

"I know, Mom, and I appreciate it. I'm blessed to have you as my mother. My curious mind wanted to know. Finding out the person he was—is—didn't make me any happier. But I needed that closure. I wanted to know why he left you."

"And *you*. You didn't have a father growing up. I understand, sweetheart." Mom drew me in for a kiss on my forehead.

I patted her back. "I have closure now. He didn't deserve us. He could climb his political ladder to become president, but in my eyes, he'll always be the man who never took responsibility."

I left the part about the auction out of the conversation. She'd ask questions, and I didn't want her to know I'd been abducted. That alone could hinder her healing further.

I could share another truth that would delight her. "I'm in love, Mom."

"It shows." Her eyes gleamed.

"I also want to pursue something that has just been a hobby."

"What is it?"

I told her about my nature photography and greeting card ideas. I'd never seen my mom happier than at this moment when I went after my dreams, not because it paid well but because it made my heart soar.

CHAPTER FIFTY-SIX

FORREST

"Everything okay, Hank?" I asked, entering an empty room.

"Yes," he choked. "They found my sister. The DNA test confirmed the remains belonged to Nikky. She can be buried now." A moment of silence followed, and I let it settle, giving him the closure he needed.

When Hank told me about his missing sister and his suspicion, I'd reached out to my influential friends who got me an approval to siphon the lake for the remains of the missing people. Hank mentioned seeing people in boats out on the lake many times late at night, including the days when his sister disappeared. I'd assumed she could be down there.

The city didn't hesitate, because I paid for the entire process and they saved face by bringing closure to families.

"Thank you for your help. It made my mom happy and sad. But we don't have to wonder anymore."

"You're welcome." Closure was something I'd been working on for myself for years, so I understood the pain he'd endured.

My quest for Red Venom would come to an end soon. It had always been a matter of when, not if.

"The authorities said they found ten bodies in bags. I knew she was down there all these years, but no one listened to me."

I didn't know what to tell him to make him feel better. The corruption that existed within the city and beyond was something he didn't need to know about. The more he knew, the more danger he'd be in.

"When did they find the bodies?" I inquired.

"Last night," Hank said. "Oh, something awful happened this morning."

"What?" I prepared myself for another shocking news event.

"Officer St. Pierre got into a car accident and died at the scene."

The Trogyn had gotten to Bruce. Did they catch him searching for information for me? Or was this murder a simple discard of incompetence? He'd been doomed the moment he started working for them.

"Did you know the warehouse where they kept Kiera burned down last night?"

They were getting rid of evidence.

"I heard. Thanks for the update."

Now that Kiera was home and safe, I could dedicate my time to finding Red Venom and his connection to The Trogyn. The fact that he'd produced shoes from human skin made me want to peel his off and hang it to dry. His skin didn't deserve to be made into anything. Filth like him didn't deserve to waste an atom of oxygen.

I couldn't dismiss this unsettling feeling stirring in my gut. Something awful was about to happen, and I couldn't decipher if it was my intention toward Red Venom or something else. It could also be the accumulated stress from the past week that I hadn't fully shaken off.

"There's one more thing." Hope sprouted in Hank's voice.

I just realized something that made me smile. There was goodness in the world after all. But I'd share that with him later.

"Good news or bad news?"

"I think it's good." Rustling noises sounded over the phone. "Someone left a letter addressed to Kiera, but there's no return address. It feels like a greeting card."

"Mail it to me via next day service."

"Okay. I'll do that today."

"Thank you, and Hank?"

"Yeah?"

"Did you know that your stutter is gone?" The previous conversations with him showed a wonderful improvement, but today's conversation had no stuttering at all.

"Oh . . . Umm . . ."

I could imagine him stunned by the news. I didn't notice it at first, but as the conversation progressed, it was obvious. He also sounded more confident when he spoke.

Maybe the closure involving his sister's death also removed whatever it was that had blocked him.

"I . . . Yeah." He released a sigh, and I could see him smiling over the phone. "You're right. It's gone."

The joy in his voice radiated through the phone. I'd been waiting for the perfect moment to make him an offer.

"If you're looking for a job with opportunities for growth, I have something for you."

"Are you hiring? What do you need help with?"

"My BaMBu headquarters is always looking for talent. We're expanding and always looking for talented and hardworking people. You're excellent with details. There's a position that requires that skill and computer knowledge."

"I'm interested."

"Okay. Go to the headquarters and ask for Hieu. He'll set you up with an interview. Tell him I referred you."

After we hung up, I emailed Hieu and gave him a brief description of Hank's skills and asked him to hire the kid. Hank needed a break. He was smart, honest, and reliable. Those were qualities I liked in a person.

What piqued my interest was the anonymous letter to Kiera. Who had sent it?

CHAPTER FIFTY-SEVEN

KIERA

The next day, I sat with my laptop on the back deck of Forrest's house while he went to pick up lunch. The five-bedroom house was on a private lot surrounded by trees. I didn't know why he needed so much space, but each room felt like a secret nature sanctuary. There were plants in every room, strategically placed. Ferns, herbs, and succulents made the home feel like a breath of fresh air. He had an indoor greenhouse that connected to an outdoor one just like the Holistic Farm in Texas, but on a smaller scale.

He even had a pomegranate bonsai that bore fruits.

Aside from the lovely home, he also kept a condo in downtown Providence, close to his Vitality Health Clinic, where he only worked part time. His colleagues had kept the clinic busy and thriving.

My man was busy developing holistic medicine for the world all while developing his WaterFyre Rising video game. He said I inspired a character in his demo, which I hadn't seen yet. He'd been swamped, so I'd postponed asking him to show me.

His determination and creativity were rubbing off on me. Ideas for my greeting cards populated my head as I browsed through my extensive collection of nature photos. I had to narrow down a few plants and fungi for printing.

Earlier this morning, I had backed out on a couple of projects that didn't interest me. I'd signed up for them to supplement my mom's medical bills. Now that everything was resolved, I didn't have to.

Forrest had gotten a lawyer to represent us in the lawsuit against Dr. Schaeffer, including the hospital, for its negligence. The hospital had received several complaints about the doctor, but looked the other way.

Mom would get a large sum of money from this fiasco, including the other families who had also joined us in the fight. Let this be a lesson for doctors and hospitals everywhere. It felt good to fight back. People needed to be punished for taking advantage of the sick and vulnerable.

Aside from the chaos, Forrest mentioned that Full Circle Apothecary had dodged a potential lawsuit that could have dragged down the shop's name. Two customers had claimed they'd gotten sick from the herbal remedies, but had since recounted their claims.

I didn't understand why people would create lies just to see if the other party would settle. Forrest had been dealing with an insurmountable amount of stress, and yet he still took on mine without hesitation. He'd done so much for me, and I appreciated every bit of it.

This had been one of the most stressful times of my life. Forrest needed a break too. I smiled as an idea formed in my mind to help him release stress.

I walked into his office, where I'd seen an emergency kit. I took out the stethoscope and borrowed his white lab coat he had hanging on a hook in his closet with other medical supplies.

On my way to the bathroom, I found an unopened box of essential oils from Full Circle Apothecary. Morena had probably given it to him. I lifted the box to my nose, inhaled, and made the executive decision to open the box so he could benefit from it.

Tonight, he'd be pampered like a king.

CHAPTER FIFTY-EIGHT

FORREST

After retrieving the letter from the mailbox, I entered the house with takeout from a Thai restaurant. I placed the food and letter on the counter and walked to the back deck, where Kiera had been hanging out for the past few days. I loved that she was living in my home—our home. We'd fallen into a rhythm as though she'd always lived here.

I glanced toward the back deck through the sliding doors and didn't see her.

"Kitty K, where are you?"

"Find me." Her voice told me she was upstairs.

What is she up to?

Smiling, I made my way up the stairs. "You misbehaving while I was gone?"

"Yup," she shouted from the bedroom.

As I stepped onto the second-floor hallway, an aroma of sensuality greeted me. I wasn't sure if that was the right word, but the enticing floral scent made me think of passion with her. The soft music in the background added to the allure. What had my kitten been up to?

Pink rose petals scattered the floor in a trail that led into the bedroom. On the way, I picked up a pink thong, a pink bra, a blue T-shirt, and khaki shorts.

I inhaled her scent from her clothes, and my cock immediately hardened. When I entered the bedroom, I chucked the clothes aside, making a pile on the floor.

Kiera stood at the center of the room wearing my lab coat, which was way too big for her. Using my black tie, she'd belted herself, looking sexy and ready to be fucked.

I walked up to her and pouted. "You've been causing trouble without me. I don't like it."

"The pout tells me you're unwell," she said with a serious expression as she placed a hand on my cheek.

"How do you know?" I bent down and sniffed her neck. A hint of lavender and something else charmed my senses. "You smell so good, baby."

"Your cock is hard." She palmed me through my jeans. "Your breathing is heavy." She squeezed me. "Those are symptoms of a man in heat, and he needs immediate treatment."

I laughed and played along. "You're right. How will you remedy that, Dr. Sexy K?"

"Sit." She pointed to the velvet ottoman in front of the armchair. "I'll give you a thorough examination."

Did she know she was fucking hot in my lab coat? I wanted to yank it off her. Was she wearing a sexy set of lingerie underneath the lab coat? Or was she naked for me?

I hadn't expected this role play when I came home, but it was a pleasant surprise I didn't mind repeating. My heart thudded at the thought of coming home to her every day. My mind had never wandered into that "forever" arena before. Never even considered it . . . until now. Somehow things had shifted in my life, and there was now only room for her.

I couldn't imagine my life without her. She belonged here in my home. She belonged with me.

I sat down on the ottoman as directed. "I think I'm developing a fever, doctor. Overheated." I fanned myself with my hand.

She studied me, pursing her lips. "I'll be the judge of that."

"Would it help if I removed my clothes for you to examine?"

"You're a good patient," she said with a straight face.

I stifled a laugh at her disciplined composure. She traced my shoulder with her fingers. "There's a lot of stress on these strong shoulders."

After I took off my clothes, I felt like an eager specimen being examined by a very hot doctor.

Kiera walked around to stand at my back. She massaged my shoulders, and her touch relaxed the tension I didn't know was there. I could almost hear my body sigh. Her hands moved lower, pressing into my shoulder blades, kneading, caressing, and traveling lower and lower.

"There's a lot of tension here. You've been working hard. Got a lot of stuff on your mind?" Her hands continued to caress me, making me want to grab her and toss her into my lap to examine her.

"What are you going to do about that Dr. Sexy K?"

She moved to stand in front of me, removed the stethoscope from her neck, untied the belt, and watched my eyes as they followed the tie as it floated to the floor. My mouth salivated as the lab coat opened to a tiny lingerie set. She stripped slowly, revealing an irresistible body primed for me. I stared at the gorgeous breasts with pebbled nipples desperately waiting for my mouth, and her sex seemed to whisper secrets only I could understand. It wanted me just as much as I wanted it.

My eyes darted back to her face, which wore a fuck-me look.

"Christ, you're going to kill me." I yanked her close, pressing my face into her bosom, inhaling her scent and softness.

She smiled. "That's not what I want, my gorgeous beast with an Olympian body, the mind of a genius, and the face of a god." She nudged me back and kissed me softly. "I want you healthy so we can do this every day."

She placed the stethoscope over my chest, listening to my heartbeat. "Your racing heart tells me you're extremely excited, BaMBu Beast."

My dick twitched, and a wicked grin stretched onto those luscious lips.

When I entered the bedroom, I didn't need a doctor. But if I didn't taste her soon, I might need one to resuscitate me from an overdose of need.

I pushed off the lab coat, one shoulder at a time, and held it up to my nose. "This smells just like you." Then I tossed it over to join her pile of clothes on the floor. That lab coat was now designated for my sexy seductress.

"If you can guess what kind of essential oil I've put on, you'll get a prize."

That wouldn't be hard. I'd been around my grandma long enough to pick up the various scents. I'd used them in certain holistic prescriptions.

"Is that a bribe?" My hands slid to her ass while my open mouth skimmed the mounds of her breasts, going around and under. "What kind of prize?" I spoke over her pointy nipple, purposely not touching it.

She whimpered when I skipped around her nipples, loving the protest. I wanted her to yearn for me.

"Whatever you want. You can earn a sticker for good behavior."

My little vixen was such a tease.

I licked her nipple. "Is this good behavior?"

She moaned. "Very good."

"You're wearing lilac here." I circled her peak, loving how her body responded to my touch. Her fingers fisted into my hair, tugging with desperation.

"Excellent behavior." Her eyes darkened. "You're such a lascivious patient."

"You're a hot doctor I can't resist." I dropped kisses to her neck and breasts, lingering on her heart. "I already feel better."

My mouth closed over a nipple, loving it. Her body arched into my mouth. She met my gaze and licked her bottom lip. That image was the fuel that sent the internal fire surging to an untamed wildfire.

I kissed my way down her body, savoring every inch of her. My fingers found her sex, and I crooned at how wet she was for me.

The scent of orchid on her abdomen snapped my patience. Growling, I kicked the ottoman aside, flipped her onto her back on the armchair, and braced my arms on either side as I hovered over her. She was the most beautiful woman I'd ever met, and she was all mine.

Pressure swelled in my cock, but I didn't want to burst yet.

Her face was flushed with an adorable pink, and her eyes glinted with desire and a challenge. It was as though she understood the need in me and wondered how long I would last.

"Is this session helping with your aches and pains?" she asked, reaching for my cock.

I stopped her, gripping her wrist. "No. You've unleashed the beast. He's going to devour you." I grunted.

She opened her thighs wide, offered herself to me, and arched an eyebrow.

My glorious Kitty K.

I lowered my face to her sex and inhaled her aroma. "Rose and vanilla." I licked her, and she gasped. Another lick, followed by a ravenous feast, had her writhing against my mouth.

"Oh, God. So good." Her hips trembled as hot liquid slid out of her.

Growling, I stared at her beauty and savored every drop of her.

She jerked and groaned as I devoured her the only way a beast could—with primal need. With greed and possession.

"Forrest!" Her body bucked as she came.

I rose to my feet, lifted her ass up, positioned myself, and impaled her like a madman.

She gripped the sides of the armchair for stability as I pounded her. Her head hit against the cushion of the chair with every thrust.

"Is this how you want to be fucked, baby?"

"Yes!"

I flipped her to the side, supported her hips with my grip, and drove in deeper from that angle. She was so tight and marvelous. Sex with her was soul-destroying in the best way.

"Oh my God! You are indeed a BEAST!" she cried out, smiled, and looked at me with so much love that my heart exploded into tiny stars.

I loved her so much.

The eruption tore me to shreds as I dragged her into the rug and collapsed beside her. Her leg swung over my mine as I drew her close with my arm. We lay on the floor in silence, listening to our ragged breaths.

When my body connected to my brain again, I got up and

walked into the bathroom to grab a towel, cleaning myself. Grabbing another towel, I returned and dropped to my knees—a position I'd never been in for any woman—and cleaned her. I loved this intimacy between us.

"This is how you're going to welcome me home for the next week until our guests arrive."

"We have guests?"

"My grandma and Yolanda are visiting. They want to meet your mom."

"That would be nice." Kiera got up, took the towel from my hand, tossing it aside. "We'll need it later. I wanted you to destress today. Is it working?"

"Hell yeah."

"Want another round?" Her eyes twinkled with mischief. "I want to show you how much I love you."

She didn't give me time to reply because she pushed me down onto the rug, gripped my cock, and gently clawed my length with her nails.

"When I'm done with you, I want to make sure you have no brain cells left so you can sign your life away to me." She smirked. "You're getting ravaged by a lioness."

I had a spectacular plan for her today, but that could wait until later. What sane man would deny a sexy lioness like her?

CHAPTER FIFTY-NINE

KIERA

After our intimate shower, where he fucked me every which way, we ate lunch. When that was done, he gave me a box from a boutique. "Put it on."

"What is it?" I studied the pink box with the satin ribbon from The Style Palette, a popular boutique in Providence.

"You're going to experience a holistic healing session today. It'll remove your phobia, any residual trauma from the abduction, and when you had the plastic bag over head. These are all intense moments in your life. Sometimes, trauma seeps into our cellular memory, and we don't realize it until later. I want to make sure you're cleansed from that darkness."

Whenever I thought about the lack of air and how I'd trembled against the plastic bag, my body shook. So yes, I knew my body still remembered that event even though my mind had made a decision to move on. But to be aware of that weakness was already a step toward healing.

I appreciated his thoughtfulness more than he knew. "I don't know what to say to you."

"Say you'll do as I ask for this photo session." His eyes twinkled with mischief.

I was going to tell him I was already healing from the blood phobia, but I was curious what he'd planned for me, so I kept quiet.

My jaw dropped when I opened the box and I pulled out very provocative red lingerie where my nipples and sex would be exposed while still wearing the small pieces of fabric. I might as well not wear anything. The photo shoot he had in mind was a lot sexier than the boudoir I'd done.

"What kind of kinky healing is this?" I arched an eyebrow. "I'm not sure if I'm comfortable exposing myself in this way for pictures, Forrest."

"The camera won't capture those parts. Those are for my eyes only. We'll be strategically placing props in areas and angles that would keep those gorgeous parts out of view."

"You got props too? How long have you been planning this?"

"That's not important." He smiled. "What's important is we're going to have fun."

Being with him was fun, but I'd never imagined him to be planning a boudoir photo session. Then again, I didn't peg him as a guy who would grow his hair long because he thought I'd find him more attractive.

Even though I knew he could be lethal, I loved this sweet and adorable side of him. Perhaps a man needed two opposites to balance his energy.

He ambled over to the closet and took out a bag of props that ranged from realistic to artificial-looking flowers, mushrooms, and ferns.

"I had a healing day planned for you today, but you beat me to it with your doctor's examination. Today's holistic session is called a boudoir healing."

I laughed. "I've never heard of such a thing."

"That's because it's a new therapy created just for you, love."

He walked over to the bookcase where I'd put some of my books and pulled out my boudoir photo album. A crease formed on his forehead as he flipped through the book.

"This boudoir collection of you is in black and white. Ours will be in color. Who's the photographer?"

"My friend, Zach."

Irritation flashed in his eyes. "Where is he?"

I placed a hand on his arm and glanced at the page with me on the bed in lacey lingerie that seemed tame compared to the set he'd gotten me. "Zach's gay. He now lives in Europe with his boyfriend. Audri knows him. He'd gotten her jewelry into a fashion show in Boston when she was just starting out."

His expression relaxed. "Europe is good. He should stay there forever."

I kissed my adorable jealous boyfriend. "He was the perfect candidate when I needed someone with great photography skills."

"From now on, you have me. I'm the photographer." Heat flickered in his eyes. "I plan on a photo op."

"Wait, you want to be in it too?"

"Why not? I'm the biggest prop. You're developing these images in your darkroom. No one will see them but us."

I didn't know what to say. "Where's the darkroom?"

"Being added on to the side of the house. Grayson's firm will take care of it."

No wonder there were a few men browsing around the house the other day with him.

"When your body and mind are conditioned a certain way, you need to break that routine in order to heal. You do that by introducing something different to it—something unconventional. Something unexpected. This is how the body and mind will remember the lesson."

I wasn't sure what to expect from this photo session, but it excited me.

Once I was dressed in the most risqué red lingerie set I'd ever worn, he asked me to sit in my office at my desk and pretend to read a book. The red color reminded me of blood, which I knew was a detail he'd thought of. He'd purchased the latest DSLR camera for this photo shoot, and I said he could've just asked to use mine.

"This camera is for you. I'm just borrowing it for this session."

More gifts for me. My heart swelled. I'd never been pampered like this, and I loved it.

I got comfortable in my chair and opened the journal. I never got to finish it like I'd planned to. Reading a book in sexy lingerie had never occurred to me.

He stood to the side of the room and clicked away. I didn't know what the pictures would look like, but I trusted his vision.

The next pose was on a chaise, where he had ten poses for me to do. He'd actually printed them for me to reference. As I lay there for him to place the floral props, my skin flushed under his scrutiny. He held a big rose in his hand, ready to cover my center.

His eyes darkened as he surveyed my body. "I love seeing you like this. You're bare to me in every way." His palm caressed me before he covered it with the flower. "I see your soul and your heart."

I was lost in the wildfire of his eyes and had nothing to hide from this man. Love billowed in me as I let myself surrender to the thrill and wonder of being my authentic self in front of him.

At first I didn't understand how this photo shoot could heal me. The photography and the poses had nothing to do with my fear of blood, or any trauma. But that was it—that was the magic. I had fun doing this with him. The joy in itself was healing me from the inside. I didn't need to know the exact spot of healing. All I knew was that my body and mind found an indescribable calmness—a balance within that I could only attest to a holistic healing in process. It was something that was felt and not explained in words.

I'd never forget this moment.

More joy emanated from me when he prepared the tripod and set the camera on the timer. He stripped down to his red boxers and became a prop, covering my breasts with his head while he adored my nipple. His palm rested lovingly over my sex while his talented tongue did amazing things to my breasts. From this angle, the camera would only catch the back of his head.

"You're being incognito," I breathed.

"This photo album is about you, not me."

"That just means there's going to be more photo sessions where I get to photograph you."

"That's the plan, Kitty K." He smirked as he slid a finger into me just as the camera snapped an image of me gasping with lust.

CHAPTER SIXTY

By the time the photo session finished, Forrest had gotten over a thousand images of us. *Insane, I tell you!* It would take me forever to develop these pictures in the darkroom. I'd be sure to take my time and relive every moment.

After a late lunch, we lounged in the living room, looking outside the window at the setting sun. It was a simple evening, yet it fulfilled me. Forrest told me that Bruce had died, and that he'd left the dead raccoon on the cabin porch to scare me. I couldn't believe Bruce worked for a crime organization.

Forrest also informed me Hank's sister had been found. I was happy for Hank because he'd gotten the answers he needed. He deserved a second chance. But I was also sad for all the other bodies that were discovered. One of those bodies could've been me.

I could now understand why Hank had been protective of me. He had known something wasn't right.

"I'd like to visit him the next time we're in Texas," I said.

"We can certainly do that. He'll be working at the BaMBu center."

"That's wonderful. Do you know who sent the bomb yet?"

"The truck was found in a parking lot with no fingerprints. The authorities aren't spending time and money to look for the criminals. We've set up extra security around the premises. I've set it aside for now to deal with other pressing issues."

Forrest had a lot on his mind. Though the explosion damaged the property, it was not as important as searching for the man who had killed his father. On top of that, he was working with the Brazilian authorities to find my attacker.

I feared for Forrest going after Red Venom, but I knew he needed closure. Nerves stirred in my stomach, sensing an impending storm. Whatever it was. I'd weather it with him.

He'd done so much for me to ensure I was well in body, mind, and spirit. My mother was on her way to full recovery because of him. His love healed more each day as though he was the fresh air giving me life. It wasn't just the phobia that was healing, but also my sense of self-worth. It had taken a detour but found its way back on the right path. I'd been searching outside of myself, believing that I needed someone else's validation to feel worthy. He made me realize the opposite.

I'm worthy. I'm perfect as I am.

What I offered and how I loved was the definition of self-worth and self-love. All I wanted to do was shower him with all the beautiful things he'd given me.

Forrest straightened up from the couch, reached over to the coffee table, grabbed a letter, and gave it to me. "For you."

"What's this?" I glanced at the handwritten envelope addressed to me with no return address.

"Someone left it for you at the campground. Hank sent it up."

My heart raced as I opened the letter.

Dear Kiera,

First, thank you for the self-care kit. My wife and daughter loved it. I like the mini lotion bottle you gave me too. It was the kindest gesture I'd ever received from a stranger.

Second, I'm sorry for dragging you in danger. When I recognized Bo disguised as a homeless man washing the car windshield, I knew his people would be after me. Sometimes life makes you do bad things when you don't want to. My wife's medical bills were piling up, and I'd moved drugs for bad people so I could pay the bills.

I understood his situation. My mom's illness had placed me at a dead end where I had nowhere to go.

I'd stolen drugs from them, hoping to make extra money. Greed is a monster that can destroy you. I hid the drugs in your luggage when I took them out of the car. I was hoping to retrieve the drugs later. But it was too late. They caught up to me . . . Don't worry. I'm okay now.

I told them I didn't know your name. They searched the campground for new visitors because they knew the drugs were with a new guest. Sorry I had to burn your cabin so they'd believe the drugs are gone. But I made sure no one was inside.

A female member named Yvette threatened my family, so I no longer live in the USA. Be careful with her. She has ties to

Senator Kramer. A friend of a friend introduced me to a man with a slash on his face. He said he knows you. Thanks to him, my family and I have a new ID to start a new life. My wife's medical bills are paid. I don't have to sell my soul to take care of my family anymore.

Your kindness is a reminder that good people exist. Don't ever change.

Your driver,
   Juan

"Wow." I dropped the letter onto the table, happy that Juan and his family were safe. "I don't know a man with a slash on his face."

"I do." Forrest grabbed the letter and read it.

After a few moments, he looked up. "Slash has been helping us behind the scenes. He gave me and the boys a second chance at life when we were teens."

Forrest told me about Slash on that fateful day at the abandoned church. This crime organization was a threat to society.

"Yvette is all over this mess. Arranging the shoot knowing we'd be abducted and trafficked, coming after me in Brazil. What else is she planning?"

His jaw clenched. "I'll find her."

A grim look scrawled on his face as he stared at me. There was something he wanted to ask me but didn't.

"What is it? I'm already involved. Keeping the truth from me isn't going to help." I scooted closer to him. "Tell me what you're thinking."

Forrest swallowed. "You're important to me, Kiera—the most important person."

My heart free-fell from my chest into a pool of gooey love.

"And you're important to me too. I don't want any secrets between us. I want to know the good and the bad." I grabbed his hand—the one that had been injured during the fighting with the male attacker in Brazil—and drew a heart over the hint of a scar that would disappear soon. "That heart I just drew is my secret code for you."

He smiled. "What does it mean?"

"It means you do everything I say. I'll keep it simple and practical for you."

"What kind of code is that?" Amusement flickered in his sage-colored eyes. "Makes me feel like I got the short end of the stick."

An idea popped into my head. "How about we use it in times of urgency or something? Maybe when one of us is mad at the other and doesn't know what to say, we say it with images." I drew circles and other random symbols on his palm.

"You're just using the excuse to touch me."

"Don't burst my bubble." I kissed him again. "So, tell me what's on your mind."

The grim look faded from his face as he twirled a lock of my hair around his finger. "I don't know what's going to happen when I find Red Venom. He might point at your father for heinous crimes. Or your father might get hurt in the process—"

I pressed my finger to his lips.

"He may have helped create me, but he is *not* my father. He lost that right long ago. Mitch Kramer doesn't know I exist—he doesn't *know* me. And what I know about him doesn't make him a man worthy of any love or energy from me." I rubbed circles on his back. "Don't worry about me. Senator Kramer means no more to me than a stranger in the street."

"Okay." Understanding filled his eyes.

"I'm working on some greeting cards to show your grandma when she visits."

"I'd love to see them before she does." He draped an arm around me, pulling me into him.

"That's the plan."

CHAPTER SIXTY-ONE

FORREST

On Wednesday, I spent time at the research lab reviewing the test results on my holistic medication, which still needed a name.

We had an overwhelming number of volunteers who wanted to take the concoction made of ginseng and other natural ingredients. One ingredient was the Lingzhi, which had been used in traditional Chinese medicine for centuries. That little ingredient was the magical key.

I had seen the chemical reaction under a microscope and hoped it would be the next best thing to curing a cold. My intention was for it to boost the immune system. If the immune system was strong, then it could fight anything.

I met with several candidates who claimed one spoonful of the liquid cured their cold overnight. Another person said he'd been feeling weak after having surgery a month ago and bounced back after two days of taking the liquid.

Once the liquid proved effective, I'd develop it into a pill.

I spoke to more volunteers and discussed the results with my research team. Without a doubt, I knew this alternative medicine was exactly what people needed. It was gentle on the body, yet effective.

I called my lawyer to prepare the documents for a patent and initiate other steps for this product to go public. Full Circle Apothecary would be the first store to sell it.

It had taken me three years of trial and error, dedication, and belief to complete this medication.

When I arrived home, I was hoping to find Kiera in my lab coat again, but she'd gone out with her mom for some pampering and self-care. So I worked on Level Four of Water-Fyre. The demo only needed one more revision. When I was done, I uploaded it to the shared drive for my friends to review.

I crossed the task off my to-do list. Feeling relieved, I called Grandma. "*Vó*, what would you like to eat on your first evening here? I'll place the order."

Grandma wouldn't be arriving until Saturday evening and staying for a week. What would she and Yolanda like to do during their stay? I couldn't remember the last time Grandma had taken a vacation.

"I'll eat anything. Don't stress about it. Why don't you ask Kiera and Liz what they want to eat?"

"I already did, and they told me to ask you. I'll just get a little of everything for my favorite people."

Voices sounded in the background.

"Yolanda wants to yell at you."

I could hear Grandma shuffling the phone, handing it over to Yolanda.

"Why didn't you ask me what I wanted to eat?"

"Because I already know. Seafood and lasagna."

"Glad you remember what I like. I'm heading up there a day early for a meeting in Boston. You'll have an early guest. I hope that's okay."

"Come anytime."

"Oh, I want to bring a gift for Kiera and her mom. What do you think they'll like?"

"That's unnecessary."

"You're not them. How do you know? This is my first time officially meeting both of them."

"Get them something from the apothecary then."

CHAPTER SIXTY-TWO

KIERA

After a wonderful morning with my mom, I went in for my physical exam, which I'd delayed so many times. All was well, and I was now sitting in the chair at the laboratory, waiting for the nurse to draw my blood. My heart raced a little, but it wasn't overwhelming like it used to be.

I thought about Forrest, his love for me, and the documentary I'd watched about blood. Like his love, blood was a vital part of me, and there was nothing to fear. That acknowledgment calmed my nerves as I stared at the needle and the tube being filled with my blood.

Before I knew it, the friendly nurse got a bandage ready and said, "You're all set."

I am all set.

Smiling to myself, I drove home and glanced in my rearview mirror. A gray sedan with tinted windows was behind me. I'd noticed it when my mom and I were at the spa and shopping center. Was I being paranoid? It could've been another gray car . . .

Still, something unsettled me. I pulled over to the side of

the road, putting on my emergency lights, took out my phone, pretending to call someone. I just needed a moment to let the anxiety pass. The gray car slowed down, and a man with curly hair glanced at me before driving off. Other cars did the same. An older man in a van stopped, rolled down his window, and asked if I needed help. I graciously declined.

I was probably just spooking myself. Inhaling a breath, I called Forrest on speaker and drove home. I didn't want to worry him; he had a lot going on. Besides, I was likely being paranoid with everything I'd experienced.

Just listening to Forrest's voice made me feel better already, and I was motivated to get home to work on my greeting cards.

CHAPTER SIXTY-THREE

FORREST

The next day, Kiera met up with her friends at the Krazee Tavern, a restaurant owned by Remi in downtown Providence.

I hung out with Arrow and Remi at his house. Royce and Grayson had other engagements. We discussed the WaterFyre Rising video game briefly, and took a break for lunch before delving into information about the red shoes and Red Venom. I hadn't planned on telling them about my personal vendetta. But Red Venom was now linked to The Trogyn, and it would be wrong not to inform them. These guys were my brothers. I'd trust them with my life, and they trusted me with theirs.

I had wanted to protect them by keeping my vengeance out of our discussions, but that didn't sit too well with my friends.

"That's not cool, man." Arrow punched me in the shoulder.

"I didn't want to drag you into my mess."

"We're friends. Anyone after you has to deal with us." Remi crossed his arms from across the table.

"Well, now you know. I'll fill the other guys in later."

"And you'll get punched then too." Arrow sneered.

When all was said and done and the boys had forgiven me, we shared information about the red shoes and a shoe repair shop in Providence, owned by a law firm based in Texas. Slash's information had paid off.

My stomach twisted as the dots connected in my head: the law firm in Texas to a shoe repair shop in Providence.

My phone rang. Before picking up the call, I told Remi, "Look up Law Time Group and see if Senator Kramer still practices there."

The man had gotten his law degree and that helped him climb the political ladder. He had started his firm years ago but closed it to join a bigger one. He'd been promoting the Law Time Group recently, and that piqued my interest.

"*Vó*, everything okay?"

"Yes. All is well. I'm just calling to let you know that I finally saw Yolanda's boyfriend yesterday."

"She brought him over?"

Yolanda never spoke much about her man, and I'd never asked. I figured she'd introduce him when she was ready. I hadn't brought home the women I'd dated either.

"No. I left the apothecary early to get a few traveling items and saw them walking into a restaurant. The man could be her father! It's Senator Kramer. Maybe that's why she never brought him home. I'd spoken to him over the phone a while ago and didn't like the energy he gave off. Now I know why."

Shit. Icicles formed in my gut. Yolanda was probably working for his law firm. I should have paid more attention to her life.

"I know this sounds weird, but did you see his shoes?"

"Yes! *Horrendous!* What kind of man wears red dress shoes?" She released a sound of disgust that made me smile.

Yolanda's connection to Mitch Kramer threw me off course.

"Thank you, *Vó*. I'll see you on Saturday."

Was Yolanda planning on telling me about her man during this visit? Did she know about his involvement with The Trogyn? How long had she been dating Kiera's father?

I raked a frustrated hand through my hair. She was my cousin, though not by blood, but we'd grown up together. She was family to me, and I didn't want her to get hurt.

CHAPTER SIXTY-FOUR

KIERA

The Krazee Tavern was packed. If Audri hadn't reserved a table, we would've had a long wait. The birthday crowd created most of the exuberance in the restaurant. Another event was in the back function room, which added to the noise and energetic vibe.

I didn't mind the cheerfulness because I was in a celebratory mood. Not only did I come bearing gifts for my friends, I had something to share with them—I was in love.

Audri and I sat a table in the corner, waiting for Vivian to show up. Michelle and Natalie had accompanied their men on some business trip. When I spotted Vivian, I stood up, waving her over. She smiled and walked over, maneuvering around the crowded tables with swift elegance—her self-defense techniques. Though I'd taken some classes, I wouldn't consider myself elegant or swift when it came to fighting. I was too clumsy.

"Sorry, ladies. Had an emergency extraction." Vivian sat down, blew out a breath, and tied her long black hair in to a bun. She was Vietnamese-American, and just as beautiful as Audri, who was Chinese-American.

I loved my group of friends. They represented the world—a blend of nationality and culture. I'd learned so much from them. My heritage on my mom's side was Scottish, French, and Dutch. Kramer had ties to Ireland. I supposed I was a mutt.

"I thought today was a short day for you," Audri said.

"It was, but the office got a call about an infection. I couldn't let the kid suffer all night." She grabbed a menu. "Let's eat. I'm starving. Coffee was my breakfast this morning."

We ordered a combination plate of appetizers. I took out the books that were wrapped in shiny pink paper and gave one to each. "I hope you love it just as much as I do."

"That's so sweet." Audri opened the wrapper, looked at the book cover, and flipped to a page. "Oh, Kiera. This is perfect. I've been looking for a journal like this."

"It's more than a journal," I said. "It really opened my eyes . . . and my heart."

Vivian was glued to the pages. "I love it. This is the perfect woman's journal and activity book. The prompts make you think. I'll need to stop by the store to get a pack of color pencils. You know what? I'm going to buy this book for the girls at work. *Finding Your HeART* is a book everyone needs." She placed it to her chest and smiled.

"Kiera!" someone shouted my name.

I glanced up to see Yolanda walking straight to our table. What was she doing here? Forrest had mentioned Yolanda was coming on Friday, and Morena's flight was scheduled to arrive on Saturday. Perhaps Yolanda's meeting got shifted to Thursday?

She wore a chic black dress with a thin gold belt and Christian Louboutin heels. "I just finished a meeting and needed to get lunch. I can't believe I bumped into you here."

"Audri, Vivian, this is Yolanda. She's Forrest's cousin. Do you want to join us?" I didn't think my friends would mind me inviting her. She was going to stay at Forrest's house for a week, so I might as well get used to seeing her. She was truly beautiful.

"I'd love to." Smiling, she sat down next to me and turned to my friends. "I hope I'm not intruding."

She didn't even say hello when we passed each other outside the apothecary, so why was she acting so friendly now?

"We love meeting new friends. I didn't know Forrest had a beautiful cousin." Audri gave her a menu.

Was that a blush on Yolanda's face?

"That bracelet you're wearing is gorgeous." Vivian gestured to the gold accessory with emerald gemstones.

She lifted her arm, and the bracelet glistened in the light. "Forrest got this for me when I turned twenty-one. He's very thoughtful and sweet."

I didn't like the energy coming from Yolanda. I sensed the venom underneath the pretty cloak she was wearing.

Yolanda pulled out her cell phone, showing me a picture. "Did he tell you he had a crush on me when we were little?"

From the corner of my eye, Audri and Vivian exchanged awkward glances.

"But you're his cousin," Audri said, studying her.

"That's just wrong." Vivian eyed Yolanda like she was ready to kick her in the head. Though the image soothed my anger, jealousy and a bunch of other uncomfortable emotions clawed at me. I appreciated my friends' protectiveness.

Forrest hadn't mentioned much about Yolanda to me. Did he have a crush on her before? Did he still have feelings for her? Was that why he hardly talked about her?

"You didn't know? We're not blood related. His grandma

took me in when my parents died. I didn't have any family around."

Forrest only told me she was his cousin, but not the other details. Jealousy grew like thorns stabbing at my heart.

Yolanda tapped her phone. "Want to see pics of us?"

Not really. But I'm pissed right now, so why the hell not?

Why hadn't Forrest mentioned any of this to me?

I held her phone and noticed she had an album dedicated to Forrest. Images of them smiling and hugging. There was one image of him kissing her on the cheek. He must have been thirteen or fourteen years old in that picture. Though none of these images proved anything, disappointment and betrayal surged in me.

Did he have a relationship with her? Had they . . .

I shook my head clear of that vile image. My heart ached, and I pushed the phone back. "Thanks for sharing." I didn't like fakers. If she had an agenda, she should just spill it. It was a waste of time for everyone. "Why are you here, Yolanda? Why are you showing me all this? It doesn't matter that you grew up with him. He's my boyfriend now."

Audri shot a look at Vivian, waiting for her answer.

Yolanda turned to me, and the slow smile that slithered onto her face was like a snake rising, preparing to attack.

"There's something you should know. Forrest belongs to me." Yolanda's haughty tone sent chills down my spine. "I've loved him since I was a little girl. He just needs to be reminded of how much he needs me." She rose from her seat and placed a hand on my shoulder.

Hurry and fucking leave, before I stab you with my fork, bitch.

Our gazes met, and she said, "I'm carrying his baby."

That statement was like a sledgehammer to my heart.

Then something sharp pricked my back, but the destruction in my heart was too painful. It numbed everything else.

"Get the fuck out of here, bitch!" Audri heaved.

Yolanda sashayed out of the restaurant, tossing something into the trash, and winked at me. A man with curly hair came up to her and smiled. "The car is ready for you, Yvette."

She was Yvette?

That man . . . He was the man in the gray car following me . . .

I had to tell Forrest. I had to tell my friends . . .

Why couldn't I form coherent thoughts?

A fever rose in me, but I couldn't tell if it was my blood boiling from anger or something else. My body shook, and my chest constricted. The pain differed from anything I'd experienced before. It was like my body was slowly collapsing. I couldn't voice my thoughts. Everything seemed discombobulated.

"Kiera, are you okay? You're so pale." Vivian tipped up my chin. "You're burning up."

My body swayed, and pain exploded on my back where Yolanda had placed her hand. Wincing, I reached for my shoulder.

Vivian pulled down my shirt and examined it. "Shit. It's swelling. Call an ambulance."

My vision blurred, and my body quivered from the heat and then the chill. Then I lost feeling in my body. What was happening to me?

Vivian or Audri placed me on the floor. As I stared up at the ceiling, voices collided. I couldn't tell who was speaking.

"She's been poisoned."

"I'm calling Forrest."

CHAPTER SIXTY-FIVE

FORREST

While I reviewed photos of Yolanda and Senator Kramer, my friends conducted their own research.

My phone rang, and nerves churned in me. "Why is Audri calling me?" I asked Remi.

He shrugged, and Arrow paused what he was doing on the computer and looked up.

"Audri, is everything okay?"

"No! Kiera's been poisoned. I don't know what to do," she cried. "We called an ambulance, and they're on their way."

I bolted out of my seat, heading to the door. "What's her condition? Breathing? Is she cognizant? What happened?"

The word poison sent my nerves skyrocketing. There were many types of poison, and each body reacted to it differently. The organs could shut down quickly, and if she didn't get immediate care, she could . . .

Don't think like that. She's going to be okay. She needs you to be strong to help her.

"Yolanda did something to her. It happened so fast."

Yolanda? Why? Had she gone insane? So many questions

erupted in me, but I forced all of them aside to concentrate on the matter at hand. If I made a wrong move, it could cost Kiera her life.

She was my life, and if she was gone, then I had no purpose.

"Tell the ambulance to take her to Vitality Health Clinic," I said. "Please go with her."

I knew how the emergency room worked. The protocols and the long line of sick people waiting to be seen meant Kiera was just one of the many people in need of care. My baby had to be examined immediately. I had all the equipment necessary for emergency care.

I rushed to my car as Remi and Arrow caught up to me.

"What's going on?" Remi asked.

"Kiera's been hurt. Your restaurant is now a crime scene. Can you head over there?"

Nodding his understanding, Remi headed to his car.

Arrow looked at me. "Need me to drive? I don't want you killing yourself or anyone before you get to her."

"Thanks." I slid into the passenger seat.

My fists clenched and unclenched. I needed to do something, needed to hurt someone. Yolanda wasn't due to arrive until tomorrow. Did Senator Kramer order her to hurt Kiera to get to me? The fucker didn't even know Kiera was his daughter. Would that have stopped him? Or had Red Venom ordered the attack? Neither man knew who I was so they couldn't have known about my vendetta. Had Yolanda told him about me?

But Yolanda didn't know about my vengeance against Red Venom. I'd never shared it with her. Though she was part of my family, we didn't hang out. She had her life, and I had mine. What changed her? What had I missed all these years?

Adrenaline and cortisol—stress hormones—pumped through me. I could feel my body reacting to this dreadful news. My heart rate increased, affecting my breathing, my thoughts. Though I knew how to treat people, telling them what to do to strengthen their bodies, I struggled to listen to my own advice. When things became personal and emotions were at play, it was hard to do what was right.

Right now I just wanted to kill them all.

Stay focused. Stay strong. Kiera needs you.

My world, my responsibilities to my empire, my video game, and to taking down The Trogyn all shattered, leaving only Kiera for me to worry about. The renewed fear spiked through me like thorns. But this time they were sharper and lathered with poison. There was no unknown moment like during the abduction. I knew where she was, and I understood the complex battle that would require to save her.

"She'll be fine," Arrow said, turning down a street. "The girls are with her. Stay focused on how you'd treat any patient. That'll help you remember your skills."

I looked at my friend with gratitude for understanding the chaos within me.

The intense anxiety crippled my thoughts, but how would that help Kiera? He was right—I had to look at her as though she was a patient I didn't love. Objectivity would help me get through this. Objectivity would not make me crumble.

As I played back all the time I'd spent with her, remembering the love she'd given me, I felt like the luckiest man. She'd told me she loved me. She'd shown me her love in countless ways. I had everything I needed in Kiera.

Fear was an enormous monster taking chunks out of me right now, but I had to fight back. I wanted to be strong for her.

"You've got this, man," Arrow pulled into the parking lot. "You're a great doctor, and you know that. What's the first step in urgent care?" He stared at me with calm eyes. "You *know* what to do. Focus on your skills. This is when you can follow the rules in the books. That'll help right now."

Going by the book had never been my preference, but those academic guidelines would help me see through the clutter.

"Thanks." I dashed out, glanced at the ambulance blocking the front entrance, and entered.

"Who's with her, Patty?" I asked my receptionist, who had just gotten off the phone with someone.

"Dr. Boland and Tiffany are with her."

I walked toward the back of the large examination room. Arrow fell into step with me. We found Audri and Vivian sitting on the couch in the waiting room.

Spotting me, they got up from their seats, wanting to talk.

"We'll talk later. Every minute counts right now." I turned to Arrow.

He read my thoughts. "Go. I know what to do."

I needed him to interview Audri and Vivian to get all the details before they forgot.

When I saw Kiera lying on the examination bed, hooked up to too many machines, my heart stopped for a moment. The image was too real. The horror of it squeezed my heart until my chest hurt and my legs wobbled. I dropped into the chair beside the bed and kept my gaze on her.

"We've stabilized her for now," said Dr. Elias Boland, my colleague of many years.

"Do you know what got into her system?" I asked.

"Not yet."

"Her blood pressure was very low." Tiffany tapped the monitor. She'd been a nurse at the clinic since it opened. "I took some blood for testing. I sent it to the lab down the street. We'll get results soon."

"Thank you." I appreciated her thoroughness.

Kiera would need constant monitoring to ensure she

remained stable. What the fuck did Yolanda do to her? I needed to know everything.

A knock on the door sounded, and Patty peeked in. "Sorry to bother you, but your next appointment is here, Dr. Boland."

"I'll take over," I told him. "Go take care of your patient. Thank you."

When Dr. Boland and Tiffany left, I stood staring at Kiera. Helplessness inundated me. I had money, power, and medical knowledge. But right now, none of those things could save the woman I loved. How fucking pathetic was I?

I couldn't do anything but wait for her labs. Every second stretched out longer as frustration grew stronger.

She looked so pale, as though life were draining out of her. What kind of pain had she endured?

I took her hand into mine. Her fingers fell limp and lifeless in my palm. "I'm so sorry I wasn't there to help you. But I'll get to the bottom of this even if it means turning the world inside out." I squeezed her hand. "Stay alive. Come back to me."

Anger and frustration warred inside me, and I surrendered because I didn't know what else to do. My body sagged as a tear streamed down my face, surprising me. The last time I cried was when my mom died. Nothing had affected me this deeply until now. More tears came, and I let them flow, wishing I could take her place so she didn't have to suffer.

I couldn't lose Kiera. Life would be meaningless without her. My $Ba_7M_5Bu_{88}$ Project, the vengeance toward Red Venom, the WaterFyre Rising video game, and the alternative medicine didn't matter if she wasn't with me. Nothing mattered to me more than her.

What would my life be like if I achieved all my goals but was missing the one person who made my heart beat? It was true you didn't know how much you needed someone until you were on the edge of losing that person.

Like a cell, she was the fundamental unit of my life. Without her, I couldn't live. Without her, I didn't exist.

I'd give up everything for Kiera—I'd give up my life for her.

For the next hour, I sat in silence reading the monitors, checking her vitals, and waiting patiently for the toxicology report from the lab. Thoughts jumbled in my head. Days earlier, I'd been focused on closing in on Red Venom. Destroying him would offer me closure, but as I looked at Kiera, I wondered if my past deeds had caught up to me. I'd killed people. Even though they were society's filth, I still ended their life—some directly, some indirectly.

Was God punishing me for my crimes? Was karma coming for retribution?

Please no.

A voice sounded in my head.

Your parents wouldn't have wanted the vengeance.

No, my parents were kind souls.

For the first time since my mom died, I prayed and asked God to save Kiera. She was a marvelous person with no bloodstains on her hands. She deserved to be saved. *Let all the darkness fall onto me.*

I had a beautiful future planned with her, but that could change. The fangs of anger sank into me, and the pain seared through my senses. No one was going to fuck this up for me and her. I'd do everything in my power to make it come true.

Renewed with a mission, I released Kiera's hand gently. "I'll be back, baby."

I walked into the bathroom, dragged a hand down my face, and splashed cold water onto it. I needed to set my emotions straight so I could see this problem objectively and plan accordingly.

CHAPTER SIXTY-SIX

FORREST

Remi and Arrow brought me food as we sat at the conference table at Vitality Health Clinic. It was eight in the evening, and everyone had gone home. I wasn't leaving the clinic until Kiera regained consciousness.

"What did you find out?" I asked Arrow.

"The girls said Yolanda had her hand on Kiera's back before she left. Moments later, Kiera grew pale."

"Videos from the restaurant showed she tossed this in the trash before she exited." Remi slid over a plastic bag with a small syringe. "I hid it from the police officers at the restaurant. Do you know your cousin well?"

"I thought I did." Gripping the bag, I stared at the needle responsible for Kiera's condition. I had to get this to the lab.

"Audri said Yolanda is in love with you. That you 'belong' to her." Remi eyed me. "That she's carrying your baby." A pause, then he asked, "Is the baby yours?"

"What the hell, man!?" I shot up from my seat and slammed a fist onto the table. "I'm offended you even asked that."

"Don't get pissy. I just want to know the truth. You're my boy, and I can only help if I know what I'm dealing with."

"We're all concerned about Kiera, and we don't know Yolanda well. She never hung with us."

I tugged at my hair. This was ridiculous. "That's because she has her own group of friends. My grandma was friends with her parents. So when they died, my grandma took her in."

"So she's not your real cousin."

"No."

"Audri said she showed a picture of you kissing Yolanda when you were younger."

What the fuck? I knew my friends were trying to see the truth, but fucking shit. I felt like I was being interrogated.

"Because she asked for one when her science project won first place in the science fair in sixth grade. It was a kiss on the cheek."

Had Kiera believed her? Her heart was probably shredded. We hardly spoke about Yolanda. There had never been a reason to.

"She was like a sister to me. And now she's trying to kill the woman I love."

I remembered how Yolanda had brought up the science project incident many times during our family dinners until I told her to stop. I never understood why she kept bringing up that kiss that meant nothing and was irrelevant to my current life. When had she started having feelings for me?

"I've got news on Red Venom. You want to hear it?" Arrow asked.

"What?"

"He's in Providence attending a political fundraiser with Senator Mitch Kramer."

I briefed them that the senator was Kiera's father and also Yolanda's boyfriend.

"Wow. Just when I thought we had a handle on this fiasco, it got more complicated." Arrow blew out a breath.

"No shit," I said.

"Mitch Kramer was a councilman for Providence a long time ago," Remi said, looking at his computer. "He became a lawyer and climbed that political ladder fast. Texas loved him more than Rhode Island did."

A memory surfaced, connecting the dots for me. I'd seen two men discussing an illegal transaction the day after I'd witnessed the crime at the abandoned church with my friends. Two men had been speaking about drug money. One of them had worn red shoes—an image that had never escaped my mind—and the other wore shiny black shoes. The man wearing the red shoes had been Red Venom.

My gut told me it was him.

I'd been *so* close to my father's killer and not known it. If I had known, could I have done anything? Probably not. At that time, fear had overwhelmed me, and hearing two men speak about another crime only intensified the terror. The quest to find my father's killer had been pushed aside during that moment when I was afraid someone was after me and my loved ones.

Though I hadn't seen their faces on that day, I saw and heard enough. Kiera's father had colluded with my father's killer. It didn't matter when they'd joined the crime organization; they were members who had committed crimes, and they would pay.

The web around The Trogyn grew more intricate with every new piece of information I discovered. Somehow the people I knew were linked to them. To destroy a mammoth crime organization seemed impossible for a small group of men like me and my friends. But nothing was impossible if there was a calculated strategy incited with passion—the passion to eradicate these fuckers. Our lives had been turned upside down because of them.

We had damaged this monstrous organization in our own way. Remington had dismantled the sex trafficking ring run by Audri's uncle, Royce had tackled the corruption within the Providence Police Department, and Grayson had eliminated an elite gambling club and took over the underground tunnels used by the organization. With every attack, The Trogyn weakened.

A plan percolated in my head. Time was of the essence, and I needed all hands on deck. "I've got a plan."

"Let's hear it," said Remi and Arrow simultaneously.

***

The next day, I picked up Grandma from the airport and brought her to Vitality Health Clinic. She'd heard about Kiera's condition and wanted to come a day early. During the drive, I'd briefed her about Yolanda.

"I can't believe this, Forrest. Where have I gone wrong?" Grandma looked out the window. The sadness in her voice flooded the car.

"You did your best. Her choices aren't your fault," I said, wanting to remove the disappointment from her face. "We don't know what truly goes on in someone's mind. Maybe she hung out with the wrong crowd and made some bad decisions. She claims she loves me." I still couldn't believe it.

Grandma looked at me. "You didn't know?"

"You knew?" Why did it seem like I'd been oblivious to so many things? "Of course I didn't know. She was like a sister to me."

"I thought she'd grown out of it once she started dating, but I was wrong. The way she looks at you and talks about you should have been obvious signs that something was off. I should've talked to her." She sighed and placed a hand on my arm. "You saw her as a sister, which made her want your attention even more. Your love for Kiera probably pushed her over the edge."

Was it my fault for not noticing this issue? Could I have helped Yolanda?

It didn't matter because I was meeting her in a few hours. I could ask her all the questions.

I dropped off my grandma at the clinic. She and Kiera's mom embraced, cried, and connected like old friends. Kiera would've been happy to see that.

"Do you want us to bring you back anything?" Grandma asked, getting ready to head down to the cafeteria with Liz to pick up lunch.

"No, I have a follow-up meeting at the police precinct soon."

"Okay." Liz tapped my shoulder. "We'll be back to take over."

After they left, I checked Kiera's vitals, which appeared normal. "You need to wake up, baby. I miss you. I love you."

I checked the computer in the room and saw the toxicology report had come through. A burst of energy zipped through me as I clicked it open, reading the report.

Her blood test matched the results of the drug on the syringe, which showed traces of barbiturates and other toxic agents. But the concentration had been diluted with other solutions. Though Yolanda knew herbs from helping at the apothecary, she didn't know that mixing certain drugs together reduced the effect. I thanked the heavens for her oversight.

I had feared the report would show traces of Oxy-X, which were the dangerous pills hidden in Kiera's luggage. The destructive pills were a potent version of OxyContin and new to the black market.

Kiera's body needed time to flush out all the toxins. Not knowing how her body would react, I had to be extra careful. The human body was a mystery that still needed extensive studies. Doctors and scientists didn't know everything. I knew enough to take things slowly, but my patience was running thin with every minute Kiera remained unconscious.

It had been twenty-four hours, and I needed a sign that she was conscious before I could give her the alternative medicine I'd just developed. It didn't even have a name. Intuition told me it could help her, but I was afraid because Kiera mattered too much. What if things went wrong?

Sitting on the chair, I held her hand. "Come back to me, Kiera. I *need* you. There's so much we have to do. Remember that medicine I was working on? It's done now, and I'm proud of it. I want to share it with you." My voice choked, and I took a deep breath to gather myself. "Your mom is here with my grandmother. They want to see you."

A slight movement of her hand caught my attention, but I dismissed it as part of my hand shifting hers. But then her finger moved on my palm, drawing a heart.

Hope burst in me.

CHAPTER SIXTY-SEVEN

KIERA

I walk along a cold, dark path, looking for my way home. The trees and shrubberies have a tint of bruised red, making me think of dried blood. Where am I? Why is my body hurting so much? Is this another lucid dream?

I continue along the desolate path with only a flashlight in my hand. I don't know where that comes from. Then I hear Forrest's voice.

Come back to me, Kiera. I need you.

The sadness and desperation in his voice make me turn to my right. As I walk toward his voice, soft light illuminates my path. The redness in the trees and flowers brighten, having more life. I sense his hand on my skin, and I remember that sensation so well. The feeling of love and protection blossoms in me. With that come memories that surprise and scare me.

I feel like I've been asleep for too long.

Remember that medicine I was working on? *Forrest's words echo louder.* I want to share it with you . . . Your mom is here with my grandmother. They want to see you . . .

I flex my fingers and draw on his palm, letting him know I hear him. When he draws a heart in my hand, it feels like magic has penetrated my skin, sending his love straight into my heart, into my soul.

I want to say something, but my voice is stuck somewhere. Though I want to draw more shapes onto his palm, fatigue drags me to sleep. Despite that, I know that when I wake, I'll be okay.

CHAPTER SIXTY-EIGHT

FORREST

Knowing that Kiera was on the road to recovery was like a drug all on its own. But I needed the public to believe there hadn't been any improvement in her health. I couldn't risk anything happening to her.

While Grandma and Liz watched over her, I drove to an outdoor table at Java Jitters in downtown Providence. Yolanda and I had been there a few times when we were teens. The café had been renovated, looking more spacious.

The late lunch crowd had died down. There was a group of three sitting a few tables from me. Otherwise, the outdoor seating was empty.

Yolanda arrived wearing a floral summer dress, her brown hair was tied back into a ponytail. Removing her sunglasses, she sat down and smiled at me as though nothing had happened within the last twenty-four hours.

"I've reserved a vacation for us in Fiji for next week. You'll enjoy it."

"I'm not going anywhere." I stared at her in disbelief. "What's wrong with you?"

Her expression transformed, and I didn't recognize the cousin I'd grown up with. "She's going to die. Why are you still hung up on her? What does she have that I don't?"

I tried my best to hold my composure. I didn't know what Yolanda would do if she knew Kiera was on the mend.

"Even if Kiera weren't going to make it, I wouldn't choose you." I met her gaze. "You've always been a sister to me. I'm not attracted to you."

"You never gave us a chance." She pursed her lips. "Everything I've done is for you."

"What have you done?"

"I thought if there were lawsuits toward the apothecary, you'd stick around Texas to resolve them. I wanted you to spend more time in Texas with me and *Vó*. Love takes time to build. You just needed time, baby." She reached to touch my face, but I grabbed her wrist, stopping her.

Yolanda wasn't well. She'd gotten sick somewhere along the way.

"I'm a lot prettier than her. Haven't you dreamed of fucking me? We'd be so good in bed."

"Stop it!" I slammed a hand on the table, and she jerked in her seat. "You tainted Grandma's herbal concoctions just to get her sued? Do you know how serious that is? What if Grandma got convicted? Do you want to see her sitting in a jail cell? What the fuck, Yolanda?"

"That wasn't going to happen. I just wanted you there. I would've paid them off once you realized you wanted to stay in Texas with me and *Vó*. Besides, there's nothing to worry about now. I've paid the two women to shut up and told them it was my mistake. They agreed and withdrew the lawsuits."

"Were you responsible for the explosion at Holistic Farm?"

She nodded. "I wanted you to stay in Texas—closer to me. At all costs."

I couldn't believe what I was hearing, but it all made sense. Her twisted love for me created this disaster.

She flicked me a gaze filled with disgust. "You took her to Brazil and brought her to your private space—a place *I* wanted to go, but you never took me."

Her statement shot my blood beyond boiling. "You're responsible for Kiera's attack?"

She lifted a shoulder. "I wanted to cut up her face, but then you showed up. It was *her* fault you got hurt with the knife from Pedro." An evil smile slithered onto her face. "Pedro's dead now for hurting you." The way she smiled told me she was used to killing.

A narcissistic person always blamed others for their mistakes. Who was this woman?

"I didn't like that Grandma invited her to dinner." Yolanda fumed. "Dinner had always been us three. No strangers were allowed. She didn't even invite my boyfriend when she knew I had one."

Did Yolanda hear her own words? She had a boyfriend, and yet, she still clung on to the delusion of being with me.

The pieces of the puzzle connected, forming an ugly picture. "You orchestrated Kiera's abduction?"

"I just escalated something that was going to happen anyway." She leaned into the table. "I work for powerful people who run a successful trafficking business. Bruno was supposed to deliver her and the model, but he said he could replace them with new girls. He didn't want to go through with it. I guess he liked Kiera and Olivia. He's weak." She waved a hand. "But not me. I didn't want Kiera to join us for dinner, so I told my men to abduct her earlier."

Bruno. I always knew he was associated with criminals. When I'd called him to inquire about Kiera, he said he didn't know anything. The fucking liar.

"How do you know Bruno?"

"I work with his father. Red Venom is an elite member of the organization. Speaking of which, you should join us. They'd appreciate your talent."

What the fuck? Bruno was Red Venom's son? Now I knew why I had an inexplicable distaste toward the man when I'd first met him.

She continued to tell me how she'd threatened Juan, forcing him to burn down Kiera's cabin, blaming her for stealing drugs and stealing me from her. Yolanda had hurt so many people, and there was not an ounce of remorse in her voice.

"When did you join the crime organization?"

"When I started my job at Mitch's law firm. So right out of college. We were good at using each other. I'm hot, and I make him look good when we're out. But I don't fantasize about him like I do you." She stared at me, and I saw a lost soul. "When his face is between my thighs, I imagine it's you."

I couldn't help Yolanda turn back. She was beyond saving.

I took a moment to compose myself. Then I leaned in, smiling seductively at her, playing my part. She could assist me in apprehending Red Venom and Senator Kramer.

"If you want me to join the organization, there are questions I need answered."

"Ask away, baby. I'll do anything for you."

"Do you really think it could benefit my business? I don't want something that'll take time from my clinic or Grandma."

"You'll make a lot of money. That's a fact. They have businesses all over the world. You can attend as many meetings as you want. I'll make sure you have more time to spend with me and Grandma."

"You have that much power?" I asked.

"I've been with them for a long time." She smiled, reaching over and caressing my hand.

"How did you join the organization anyway?" I let her hold my hand. "Since you've been with them for so long, you must know the other elite members? Can I meet them?"

What would she do if she knew that Red Venom had also been responsible for her parents' death? He and his crew had killed almost everyone in her village. Would she even believe me or dismiss it as me trying to smear her colleague?

"I accompanied Mitch to several meetings and started working for them. They pay me fabulously. I don't need to work anymore, but I want to. Mitch makes me feel wanted."

"He got you pregnant, didn't he?"

She slid me a bitter look. "That could've been you. We would've made beautiful babies. But you can take care of me now."

Unable to reply, I offered her a smile.

Yolanda was carrying Kiera's half-sibling. I wasn't going to share that information, because it could drive Yolanda even crazier. Yolanda's flat stomach told me she was in the early stages of pregnancy.

"He's gotten other girls pregnant too, but my baby is the only one he's keeping."

Mitch Kramer was the same coward and loser who didn't take responsibility for his sperm.

I didn't want to waste any more time. I hated deceiving a family member, but she'd gone too far. If I gave Yolanda another chance, she wouldn't hesitate to hurt Kiera. What if her delusion and jealousy pushed her to hurt Grandma too? I couldn't let that happen.

"I could go on vacation with you. I'll have to shift my schedule around though. Do you think you could set up a meeting with me and Red Venom and your boyfriend? I have a proposal for them. I want to get it over with before my schedule packs up again. Work has been stressful."

"Really? You mean it?" She squeezed my hand. "I don't want you stressed, baby."

I squeezed her hand back. "We could make a lot of money together." I glanced at my watch. "I have a commitment tonight, but I'd cancel it to meet them instead. Do you think that can happen?"

Her eyes brightened, and I knew she was hooked.

"They're reviewing a drug shipment tonight at the dock. I can take you there."

"What dock? What time?"

She gave me the time and name of the warehouse. It matched the location the PI had uncovered.

"I'll text Mitch right now." She got out her phone.

"Tell him that Black Mamba is excited to meet Red Venom. That I'm a wealthy man going by a nickname, and that I have a cunning vision that could make them a lot of money. Do your sales pitch. You know how wonderful I am. You'll get a nice percentage from this transaction."

Yolanda smiled. "Should've asked you to join sooner."

"What about the names of the elite members? I'd like to know who I'm dealing with, you know? You wouldn't want your lover to be taken advantage of by other men, would you? I'd like to research my competition. Where are they located?"

I should've held back on the questions when she gave me Red Venom's location.

She narrowed her eyes and smiled. "I'll tell you after we meet at the dock."

It was time to end this conversation. Rising from my seat, I said, "I'm done."

She got up as well and looked at me. "Done with what? What do you mean?"

Four FBI agents emerged from the café and surrounded her, spewing the Miranda rights.

"I've done nothing wrong." She looked at me. "Forrest! Tell them!"

I took out my phone and showed her. "You need to pay for your crimes, Yolanda. Everything you've said has been documented."

The phone had been recording since I sat down at Java Jitters. Remi had contacted his friends, who had dressed up as FBI agents. They had been watching our meeting and listening in from the building across the street. Remi had been monitoring the recording on his end, waiting for my signal as well. I couldn't risk one mistake. I needed to ensure I got enough information from Yolanda before letting them take her. They'd hand her over to the real FBI agents who would meet Remi in a few hours at his restaurant.

I didn't want the real FBI to hear everything and ruin my meeting with Red Venom. They'd want to take over the mission, and I wasn't ready for that yet. They'd receive the edited version of the recording later today.

Yolanda screamed, cursed, and begged me to help her.

As I watched the agents take her away, sadness cloaked my heart. Yolanda had been a sister to me, but I couldn't save her. At this moment, there were no winners. I lost a sister, and she lost her family. Sorrow and disappointment clung to me as I closed this chapter of my life.

CHAPTER SIXTY-NINE

I parked my car a block away from a warehouse facing the Providence River. Eight in the evening brought out a crowd of people wandering the streets, taking in the late September air. I could sense the last wave of heat and humidity before the weather turned to the chill of autumn.

A sense of inevitable ending stirred in the air. The seasons changed, and there was nothing anyone could do to stop it.

Unlike the seasons, heinous crimes could be stopped. Everything would end tonight so I could return to Kiera and start my life with her.

My body was tired, but my mind was wired.

"You ready?" I spoke into a small earpiece.

"Everything's all set." Arrow responded. "Be careful."

Wearing a black innovative suit, which cost more than my other suits, I walked up to a shoe repair shop called The Shoe-smith. It was a small shop on the first floor of an old two-story brick building. I wouldn't have noticed it if I hadn't been searching for it.

From what I knew about shoe repair, a cobbler only used

old leather, while a shoemaker worked with only new leather. I doubted Red Venom would repair his inhumane shoes. How much did he pay these men to make the revolting shoes?

I entered the shop, and the bell dangled on the glass panel.

An old man with glasses sat in the chair, repairing a boot. Another man, dressed in a striped shirt, sat in an armchair in the corner reading a sports magazine.

A strange odor inundated me. Having worked in the hospital and research labs, I was used to various chemicals, and this space reeked of them.

"Can I help you?" The man placed the magazine on the coffee table and strode over to me.

About time you acknowledge my presence, fucker. "I'm here to meet Mitch and Red Venom."

"And your name?" He pulled out his phone.

"Black Mamba."

With my gun tucked inside my jacket. I was prepared for the worst. I didn't want the FBI to know what I was doing here. It would complicate my business endeavors. I had a history with Red Venom, and it needed to be resolved today. Then I could hand him over. Before Kiera, I wanted him dead. That had been my only goal. But now I didn't want any more deaths on my hands. I'd be satisfied if he rotted in a jail cell.

Voices echoed down the hallway, and I walked toward it. I found Red Venom and Mitch Kramer looking at something on a long table.

They turned when they sensed me. Red Venom studied me and made one step forward. He wore a black button-down shirt with black pants and red shoes, looking like someone from hell. Mitch Kramer wore a white button-down shirt with khaki slacks, looking like a filthy politician about to be punished in hell.

"You must be Black Mamba—a venomous snake," Red Venom said.

"That's right. Its vicious venom is suitable for those who get in his way." I smiled.

Red Venom laughed, looking at Mitch. "I like this guy."

"That's what we do best. Those who wrong us shall pay for their sins." Mitch looked at me for a while and a smirk appeared. "I remember now. You were at the auction. I hope the two beautiful women are serving you well. I hear you have a proposal. We are men in the business of making money. Let's hear it."

I had dreamed of this day where I stood in the same room as my enemy, showing him how he would die for taking the life of an innocent man. The rage that had once consumed me didn't exist right now.

Why?

Though I hated Red Venom, vengeance was no longer the dominant emotion. Love had overcome everything.

As I stood face to face with my father's killer, I realized something profound. The main reason I wanted to destroy Red Venom was to stop The Trogyn from expanding their network—and not because of my personal vendetta. That admission freed my heart from the chains of the past.

I didn't know how heavy the burden of vengeance had been until now.

Mitch looked at me suspiciously. "Where's Yolanda?"

"She's not feeling well. The pregnancy is making her tired."

"She's pregnant?" Red Venom asked Mitch, who didn't reply.

Mitch cocked an eyebrow. "What's your actual business here?"

"I'm interested in the production of your red shoes." I walked up to the table behind them, and rage spiked.

There were moments in life that tested my faith in humanity. This was one of them. I reined in my anger so the recorder in my jacket could register the conversation with clarity.

"Who pissed you off to have their skin on your table?" I asked.

Human skin was sprawled on the table like pieces of fabric ready to be made into accessories. I wanted to puke. This abhorrent display shouldn't have shocked me, but it did.

How could they stand there unaffected by this appalling crime? They treated humans like animals.

"Enemies." Red Venom grinned. "You cross me, you die. I mixed their blood in with the red dye. It's a fabulous creation, isn't it?"

A door slammed from the back.

"Dad, the new shipment just arrived—" Bruno stopped in his steps and stared at me.

Son of my enemy.

Recognition surfaced on Bruno's face, and his lips thinned. "You don't belong here." He dropped the box he was carrying onto a nearby table.

From the corner of my eye, Red Venom pulled out a gun and shot at me. I dodged but wasn't fast enough, so the bullet hit my arm. It didn't penetrate because of the high-tech suit made with Kevlar embedded in it. It had cost a fortune, but was well worth it.

I fired back and dashed over toward Bruno. Red Venom fired another shot. The bullet hit Bruno in the chest, and he collapsed to the floor, bleeding.

"Get down!" Armed men burst through the door, and the real FBI agents poured in.

Arrow had alerted the FBI, and the timing couldn't have been more perfect.

"Drop it." An agent gestured to Red Venom.

Mitch Kramer had already fled somewhere.

The agents aimed their guns at Red Venom, and he surrendered, staring at his son. "Fuck! Bruno needs medical help."

The agent handcuffed him.

"I'm a doctor," I told the agent with the beard, and dropped my gun, which I had a license to carry.

Dressed in black and armed, Arrow rushed over to me. "You all right?"

I nodded and told him about the preserved human skin, the dye, and the attached warehouse. He could relay that to the agents. They'd need a separate team to gather that evidence.

Sirens blared as I crouched beside Bruno, checking his wound. Red Venom had shot his son in the heart. His pulse was slow, and the way blood poured out of him showed me it was too late.

Despite my hatred toward Red Venom, I didn't want Bruno to die for his father's sins. But fate had plans no one could foresee.

"I'm sorry, Bruno!" Red Venom shouted as fear tugged at his face, making him seem older than minutes ago.

Bruno fluttered his eyes, trying to turn toward his father, but failed. The EMTs entered and surrounded Bruno.

I walked over to Red Venom and whispered in his ears, "How does it feel to see your loved one die and there's nothing you can do about it?"

"Who the fuck are you?"

"Do you remember Emanuel Navarro?"

His furrowed eyebrows told me he didn't know.

"It's hard to remember when you've killed too many innocent people." I described the village where we'd lived, and the rival gangs he'd fought. "Do you remember a man you accused of stealing your drugs? You shot him even after he denied it. He was innocent. He had a family—a mother, a wife, and a son."

Red Venom's brows furrowed.

I assisted his memory. "You were with Afonso Moura and Bento Melo. They're both dead."

Recognition splashed on Red Venom's face, and he swallowed.

"That man was my father."

His jaw twitched, and he looked over at his dying son. "Save him. I'll pay for my sins."

"It's too late." That wasn't a lie, but he didn't believe me. In his eyes, I was avenging my father.

"Save him!" he shouted as Bruno succumbed to his injury.

Red Venom didn't know that even if I wanted to, I couldn't. God had already claimed his son. But I made him believe I *chose* not to save his son. He would forever remember that kind of pain.

As I walked out of the warehouse, Red Venom threw curses at me while calling for Bruno.

Arrow came up to me. "Red Venom's real name is Salvador Barbosa. Mitch Kramer is in the van if you want a word with him. They found him hiding in a storage room at the back of the building."

I walked up to the van, and Mitch sat in the seat with his cuffed hands on his lap. The agents were busy looking at the container, which I assumed were dead bodies.

"You're a piece of shit, you know that?" I asked.

"Fuck you! What did you do to Yolanda? She was loyal to me."

"Were you going to be there for her and the baby?"

"I don't have time for kids," he muttered.

"Ever heard of a condom, asshole?"

He rolled his eyes, and I lost it. I punched his face.

He jumped from his seat, charging at me even with cuffed hands.

"That hit was for Kiera. This one is for her mother." The second punch broke his nose. "And this one is for Yolanda. You and your fucking organization brainwashed her."

He dropped to the ground. "Who the hell is Kiera?"

"The daughter you don't deserve."

With that, I left him to the authorities and headed to the clinic to see my love.

CHAPTER SEVENTY

KIERA

While Forrest worked in the greenhouse, I sat at my desk in my spacious office—a room I recently decorated inside Forrest's home. I organized the greeting cards that were delivered by the printing company. I'd ordered a few copies of each to send to Grandma Morena. She'd asked that I address her that way before she returned to Texas last week.

It had been two weeks since the awful incident that almost killed me. But it was that near-death experience that showed me the abundance of love around me. I didn't know if I'd have survived if I hadn't heard Forrest calling me. I could have easily been lost in the darkness, never finding my way back to him.

When I'd regained consciousness and saw my mom and Grandma Morena, I cried with them. They'd taken wonderful care of me, especially when I tried Forrest's new medication.

Though the taste could be improved, the medication was a lifesaver. I recovered faster than when I had the flu. I was healthier now than I'd ever been. It boosted my body, instantly improving my energy.

That was proof that nature could heal any ailments. We just had to find the right blend.

The hammering stopped, and I grabbed a gift box I'd wrapped earlier and headed toward the back room. Forrest was expanding the indoor greenhouse that connected to the outdoor one. He'd bought more plants, and the area looked like a little forest. I loved it.

Last night, he showed me Goddess K, a character I had inspired in Level Four of his video game. She looked like me, dressed in beautifully sophisticated clothing. She grew these unbelievable Agoona fruits, which had magical blood that could heal people. He blew my mind with all the details that went into the game.

I stood in the doorway and acknowledged how lucky I was to be loved by him—to call this perfect man mine. He stood shirtless, with ripped jeans sitting low on his hips. He toweled the sweat from his face, neck, and chest while gulping down a jug of water. Every movement he made, his taut muscles flexed, arousing the hell out of me.

"Don't move," I said.

I set the gift box down on the table with the tools, pulled out my cell phone from the back pocket of my jeans, and snapped a photo of my BaMBu Beast. The image rendered him a sophisticated farmer, hunky doctor, and spectacular lover.

He tossed the towel aside, arched an eyebrow, and raked his eyes down my body, sending a sizzle through me. "Miss me?"

In three steps he stood in front of me, pulling me into him. He smelled of earth, masculinity, and security.

"Always. I love you." I looped my arms around his neck, running my fingers through his hair, which needed a trim. But that could wait another week. The long hair reminded me of our beginning—how I'd inspired him to grow it out.

He kissed me lightly. "I love you more."

"*Impossible.*"

He poked my ribs, and I squealed with laughter.

"According to that journal you love, there's no such thing as impossible."

I poked him back. "Glad you remembered."

"Are you done with the greeting cards?"

"Wanna see?" I grabbed the gift box.

"I've been waiting for you to show me." He took my hand, leading me to a bench in the greenhouse.

"Wow." I looked at the extension he'd built that was hidden behind the wall of giant plants. "What do you plan on doing with all this space?"

"Creating an indoor forest for you." The sage eyes sparkled.

"I already have the only Forrest I'll ever need." Smiling, I slid an arm round his waist, resting my head on his shoulders.

"Is that for me?" He pointed to the gift box.

"For my one and only." I straightened up, placing the box in his hand. "It's made with lots of love."

"I can tell." He tapped the box. "Before I open it, I want to ask you something. Be honest with me, okay?"

"I'm always honest."

"When you heard about your father's death, how did you feel?"

Two days ago, the news reported the sudden deaths of Red Venom and Mitch Kramer, which surprised me. Forrest mentioned they wouldn't have survived in prison because they knew too much about The Trogyn. The car collision during their transport to the prison was disguised as a "freak accident" so no one would investigate. The crime organization was getting nervous because their members and businesses were being eliminated one by one. Money spoke the loudest.

I met his concerned eyes. "Nothing. I don't know if that's good or bad. But I don't feel anything."

"That's good. I didn't want you to bottle up your emotion."

"We had no relationship. He was a stranger to me who did awful things. If I look at it objectively, then I'm glad he got what he deserved. But you were asking me from a daughter's perspective, and my answer is 'nothing.'"

He nodded, looking more relieved.

I touched his face. "What about Yolanda's death? You had a history with her."

"She was like a sister to me." Sadness and regret filled his eyes. "I wish I could've stopped her from taking the wrong path."

Yolanda had died at the hospital when she went in for a miscarriage.

"There are certain things we can't control, no matter how much we want to."

"Now that I know you're okay, let's focus on joyful things." He ripped the shiny wrapping paper away in one swipe, not considering how long it took me to wrap it. But it was fine because I was just as excited as he was.

Shifting on the bench, I watched Forrest open the box of greeting cards and postcards. Happiness shimmered in me as I watched him hold each card, studying it with fascination and delight. My heart palpitated, wanting to know his thoughts.

His opinion mattered more than anyone else's. The card collection was dedicated to him.

CHAPTER SEVENTY-ONE

FORREST

Sitting with her in this greenhouse meant the world to me. Just like our precious relationship, the greenhouse was in the beginning stages. This was the new beginning we both needed and deserved.

I'd spent so much time and energy searching for something to heal the wound in my heart, and I found that and more in Kiera. The nature lover who spent his childhood wandering the woods was now enchanted by a nature photographer. The innovative thinker who wanted to create a medicine derived from natural sources was blown away by her presence. The inquisitor who had been searching for something to fill the void in him was now full of love. The doctor who made an oath to heal others had been saved by her.

Nothing mattered in life more than love. Love was the blood that kept us alive, that made us feel and gave us hope.

As I held the greeting card with a matching postcard, I fell in love with her even more. I didn't think it was possible to love her more than I already did. She'd claimed my heart and soul, and inspired my heart to grow when I didn't think it could.

"I want to know something." Kiera looked at me with warmth in her eyes. "Around you and within you, there's so much to be loved, both in the darkness and the light." She placed a hand over my heart. "I love you the way all living things should be loved in nature—between the rivers, within the soil, amongst the leaves." She traced her finger along my jaw tenderly. "I love you the way mushrooms adore tree bark or a craggy rock. I love you like the moss decorates the forest floor, gracefully and silently."

My heart quivered at those powerful words. A force burst from deep within me, flowing with gratitude and so much love. This was the moment I knew the power of true love. It defied, refuted, and contradicted logic, and yet it was the only thing that was truly sacred and priceless. Love healed everything.

She swallowed, took a deep inhale, and emotions gleamed in her eyes. "I love you the way the Earth loves its Forrest."

That simple statement left me speechless. Where did this perfect woman come from? She owned me in every way.

"That's the most profound declaration I've ever heard." I embraced her, wanting to pour all my love and appreciation into her. "I love you so much."

Flipping to the back of the card, I read Greetings from the Forrest in large text. Below the title was a smaller line that read: Where the forest whispers its wisdom.

The words sank into me like a small pebble falling into the depth of my soul, slowly creating unseen ripples beneath the surface. She transformed me into a man full of mush today, but I didn't give a damn.

I ran a finger over the collection's name and the phrase, loving the words and what she'd done with her dream. "This is your dream come true. I'm honored that you dedicated the collection to me. Anyone who buys your card is receiving a burst of healing, whether they know it or not."

Her cheeks bloomed pink. "Thank you." She picked up a card with an adorable mushroom surrounded by moss and ferns. "When I think of nature, I think of you—strong, intelligent, free, creative, safe, mysterious, regenerative, and rejuvenating."

"Kiera, baby." I set the cards aside and wrapped my arms around her. "You're my heart and my soul. I love you more than I can explain."

"I know. Color me happy." She rubbed circles on my back. "You didn't see the rest of the gift."

I drew back, grabbed the photo book, opened it, and my cock hardened at the first image of us during the boudoir photoshoot. "The darkroom isn't finished. Where did you develop these pictures, and who made them into a book? *Who* helped you?" Jealousy clawed at me. "Where is he? I'm going to kill him."

"Stop it." She slapped my thigh playfully. "I rented a darkroom and bound the book myself when I took a class last week."

My lips stretched into a wide smile. "You're so resourceful."

"I learn from the very best." She kissed my cheek. "By the way, what are you growing in those four garden beds over there?"

I had filled two beds with soil, while the other two were waiting for the soil delivery. "Something pretty. You'll see soon enough."

The doorbell rang, and she jumped up and grinned. "It's here!"

"What's here?"

"Something for you, *sugah.*" Grinning, she pointed at me. "Y'all stay where you are. Don't move."

I smiled. What was she up to now?

A few minutes later, she returned wearing a cowboy hat.

"Howdy, handsome." She placed it on my head and squinted her eyes. "You make a handsome cowboy."

I yanked her into my lap. "You want a wild ride, sugah?"

She laughed. "I do, but we have to attend Remi's gathering soon. While you guys play your Level Four demo, the girls and I will have our own discussion."

"We have two hours." I grabbed her ass. "That's plenty of time to do cowboy stuff."

"Only if you wear the new overalls I got you." Her eyes gleamed with friskiness.

I supposed my Kitty K had wicked plans for me.

"My life's mission is to satisfy all your needs."

"Yeehaw!" She pumped a fist into the air.

Laughing, I stood up, carrying her in my arms. "I didn't know you had a thing for farmers and cowboys."

"I didn't until you," she said as I brought her to the living room. "Maybe next week we can pretend you're a prince being rescued by an irresistible assassin who captures your heart."

"Sounds like a plan. But for now, you're the untamed cowgirl who's going to show me the wicked wild west."

Her laughter filled my heart and home, healing every aspect of me. Life with Kiera promised to be filled with love, adventure, laughter, and everything a man could dream of. She was a special gift that changed me, and I couldn't wait to start my life with her.

EPILOGUE
SIX MONTHS LATER

Kiera

It had been a week since we got back from Texas, and creativity thrummed in me. I'd been busy meeting with local printers for my card collection and trying to find the right packaging to market it. I recently had a get-together with my friends, who gave me fabulous tips.

Audri offered to help with the marketing campaign. Michelle wanted to promote it on her blog. Natalie wanted to sell some at her store. People often came in to purchase her fashion collection as gifts and needed a card to go with the gift box. Vivian bought a bunch to give to her staff.

Forrest had been occupied the last week with meetings every day and him working in the greenhouse. He'd spent so much time in there, I wondered what enormous project he was working on. Maybe he was trying to find the right plants for another medication he was developing?

But he promised to spend the next few days with me. I wanted to lie low for a few days before rearranging my photo studio and darkroom.

Sitting in the living room, I smiled at the newspaper article I'd brought back from Texas. The media attended the special event at Full Circle Apothecary when I debuted Greetings from the Forrest to the public. The overall reception embraced my heart and validated this endeavor. I made the right decision by listening to my heart.

Several stores around the country had contacted me, wanting to know how they could carry my card collection. Some even asked if I could sell the photos as prints. I was open to everything, but that could start in a month. I needed to hire an assistant to help me.

So much had changed, and I was grateful to be with a man who loved me. My blood aversion had turned into fascination. When I accompanied Forrest to his research center, I couldn't stop looking at the images and videos about blood. Grandma Morena was coming up to visit next week. She and my mom were like besties now. They talked on the phone often. Mom took an online herbs class taught by Grandma Morena, and it was so informative. I wanted to learn more about this marvelous world of plant-based medicine.

From my last conversation with Olivia, I'd learned she was dating Levi, Forrest's friend, and had cut back on modeling to focus on her skincare career. I didn't blame her.

As I considered which images to send to the printer, a sigh drew my attention away from the images. Forrest leaned against the wall, staring at me with a smile that would sell a lot of GQ magazines. He wore a T-shirt and jeans, looking relaxed and sexy as hell.

"How long have you been standing there, weirdo?"

Chuckling, he pushed himself away from the wall and walked over. "How's that weird? I'm admiring *my* woman in *my* home. I have every right." He offered me his hand. "Ready to see the greenhouse?"

It was early April, and the trees in the city had just budded. Tiny leaves peeked out as though greeting a new life. I loved this time of year where colors and hope stirred in the air. The bamboos, trees, shrubberies in the greenhouse had already bloomed from the advanced solar light equipment and irrigation system he'd installed. I loved that he'd brought the outdoors inside, where I could enjoy it during winter.

I hadn't been inside the greenhouse to explore what he'd done. He didn't want me to see it until everything was completed.

"Yes." I grabbed his hand. The gleam in his eyes had me asking, "What did you do?"

"Everything I do is for you, baby."

We stepped inside, and the vibrant energy of nature embraced me. We stopped by an area with bamboos and pots of flowers.

A deep inhale invigorated my lungs. "This is like a sanctuary."

Forrest shifted to stand in front of me. "You're my sanctuary —my sky, my sea, my mountains. Everything in existence has more meaning because of you." His sage eyes held mine, and my heart galloped with anticipation. "If a picture says a thousand words, then you're my entire alphabet. Your words, your presence, and the sound of your voice vibrates in my body, my cells." He grabbed my hands, cupping them in his. "It's difficult to explain how I feel about you. You connect the dots for me where there are no dots. I only have to look at you, and everything makes sense. When I'm with you, even chaos has clarity."

My body thrummed with love and appreciation. I didn't know what to say, and I didn't have to because he continued.

"I love you not only for your heart, humor, intelligence, and thoughtfulness, but also for what I've become because of you. I love you not only for how much you've grown, but also for how much you've inspired me to grow. I love you for all the wonderful things you bring out in me—I'm a better man because of you."

Tears flooded my eyes, flowing down my cheeks. I didn't think I would ever experience profound love, but he gave me that and so much more. His love offered me the freedom to believe in myself and to go after my dreams. He made me acknowledge my self-worth, and that I was perfect.

"I'm a lucky woman." I kissed him.

"I'm a lucky man." He brushed my tears away with fingers. "I want to show you how you've inspired me."

Forrest

I led her down a pebbled path that I'd recently completed. "Like I said earlier, everything I do is for you. From this greenhouse to the holistic medicine that will be available worldwide in a few months."

She gasped with so much joy and pride on her face. "Really?"

I nodded.

"Oh my gosh! That's fabulous!" She jumped up, embracing me. "I'm so happy for you."

I swung her around and inhaled her scent. When her feet

landed on the ground, I held her tight. "You inspired the name."

She veered back, her brown eyes full of curiosity. "What do you mean?"

"Developing an alternative medicine that could heal people had always been my dream. My parents' deaths motivated me to continue their work with plants." I showed her the various pots taking over a corner of the greenhouse. "I'm a doctor, and I'm supposed to help and heal people. But when you fell unconscious, I felt powerless, not knowing how to heal you. All the years I'd spent studying the human body and medicine went down the drain. The fear of losing you ripped out pieces of my heart for every second that went by. Living without you would be meaningless." I brushed a thumb across her cheek. "You were the first person to use the medicine in its completed form—the first person to be healed by Kierit."

A slow smile slid onto her face. "Kierit? As in 'cure it?'"

"Right on the money." I tapped her forehead. "My smart woman. *You* are part of this profound movement that reminds everyone of the power of nature. That if we spent time to study it, we could find remedies for all the diseases in the world."

"Forrest . . ." she choked. "That's . . . beautiful. No one has said something like that to me ever." More tears filled her eyes.

"I love you. You are the remedy for all my needs. If nature loves and laughs through plants and flowers, this greenhouse will bloom with love and laughter. We could immerse ourselves in happiness all year round."

"When did you get so poetic?" she sniffled.

"Since I met you. Now stop crying." I kissed her forehead. "It'll blur your vision. I need to show you something." I positioned her in front of the first garden bed, which was tented with a tarp.

"Why are they covered?" she asked, glancing at the four beds.

"Because they weren't ready to be shared until today."

"Are you growing magical plants or something?" she teased.

"Something like that. Close your eyes."

Looking nervous, Kiera covered her eyes with both hands. If only she could see the nerves going wild in my stomach. I'd never done anything this life-changing before.

I yanked the tarps off of the beds, tossing them aside. "Open your eyes."

She did and gasped at the first garden bed where the herbs grew, forming the word WILL.

My heart pounded as I watched her walk to the next garden bed with a serious expression on her face.

Oh no. Was this too sudden for her? Was she not ready for this massive move?

Her hand shook as she placed it over her heart, staring at the word YOU.

She fell back a step, and I placed a hand on her lower back for support. "You okay, baby?"

Nodding, Kiera looked at me with adoration.

When her eyes darted to the third bed, she sucked in a breath at the word MARRY.

Tears streamed down her face as she stepped over to the last bed and cried even more at the final word ME?

Chococat sat beside the question mark, signifying a new beginning for Kiera and me. It had been there the first time we'd connected, and it would be with us for the rest of our lives.

"You built and planted all of this for me?" She wiped her eyes with the back of her hand.

"You deserve the best." I cupped her face in my hands. "I love you. A forest thrives because of the trees, plants, flowers, rivers, and animals that make it come alive. You're all of those things to me and more. I promise to do my best to prove how much I love and cherish you." I dropped on one knee. "Will you give me that chance?"

She gave me the biggest smile I'd never forget. "Yes! Yes! Yes!" Pulling me up, she gave me a big, sloppy kiss.

Drawing back, I searched her face, grinning. "You don't need a ring?"

"I don't need anything but you." She kissed me again. "But okay, I want to see. Where is it?"

Laughing, I walked her over to the stuffed animal. "Chococat has it." I reached for the shiny black box, turned to her, and opened it.

She gasped at the circular black opal with a gold band that I had customized for her. "Forrest, this is gorgeous."

I slid it on her finger, and it fit perfectly. Kiera was going to be my wife, and I was a blessed man.

"It's the most beautiful ring I've ever seen." She placed her hand up in the air, admiring it. It suited her splendidly.

"As far as I know, there's only one."

"How do you know?" she asked.

"Because not everyone can afford a black opal. They're worth more than diamonds. It all comes down to rarity and quality. And black opal is extremely rare." I tipped up her chin. "Just like you."

Moving her hand around, she admired the ring. The sunlight streaming down from the glass ceiling panel made the liquid fire in the gem appear brighter than usual. She made the ring more brilliant.

She smiled. "I really did get my Opals are Forever."

"What are you talking about?"

She told me about the challenge the SSG had given her.

"You should have just told me. I would have made all your

Super Spy Girl dreams come true. I would have said those three words sooner."

"It wouldn't have been as fun and would definitely be less meaningful. I only want to hear 'I love you' without provocation." She smiled. "I'm going to call my mom and then my friends."

I didn't tell her I'd already asked Ms. Ford for permission to marry her daughter. I wasn't a man used to asking for permission regarding anything, but I knew this was important to Kiera and her mom.

Kiera wrapped her arms around me. "But I want to celebrate with my fiancé first."

Her hands slid down and cupped my ass.

"What do you have in mind?" My hands slid down to claim her ass.

Her eyes sparkled. "Since you have a bunch of herbs, I want to make you a meal using them. I appreciate everything you've done for me—because of me. I want to be the best wife to you."

"You're already the best."

"I know." She winked, giving me a mischievous smile. "Want to help me gather some basil, mint, and cilantro? I plan on making a delicious meal to eat off of you."

I loved her heart, mind, and imagination.

"I'd be a fool to refuse such an enticing offer."

We rounded the garden, admiring its beauty, and prepared for our flourishing future.

THANK YOU so much for reading Kiera and Forrest's story!

. . .

For Vivian and Arrow's romance, order **The Strategist** (Book 5) now!

https://nadiahan.com/books/

If you enjoyed **The Inquisitor**, I would appreciate a review on your chosen platform(s). With your support, I can continue to write more stories.

BONUS SCENE
COWGIRL IN CAPE COD

Read Kiera and Forrest's **bonus scene here** or scan the code below.

KEEP IN TOUCH

For exclusive content, new releases, and giveaways, sign up to my newsletter.

https://nadiahan.com/newsletter/

Join my **Facebook reader group** for bonus features and exclusive giveaways!

https://www.facebook.com/groups/nadiahanselitebookworms/

WaterFyre Rising Series

The Mastermind (Book 1)

The Daredevil (Book 2)

The Innovator (Book 3)

Journals

Finding Your HeART

ACKNOWLEDGMENTS

The Inquisitor has taken me on a wild journey, which makes me even more grateful to those around me. My immense gratitude goes to the following:

Anna, thank you for being the magnificent editor that you are. Because of you, my story shines brighter.

Lindsay, thank you for the thorough copy edits that tighten up my story so well.

Melissa, you have a magical wand that wipes away all the errors. Thank you.

Jennesse and Karina, thank you for your insights on the Brazilian culture and the Portuguese language.

Sharon, you're the best cheerleader any author can ask for. I'm so grateful for you.

To my wonderful PA, Sara. Thank you for your support and helping me with everything so I can stay focused on my writing.

To all the readers on my ARC team. I am truly blessed to have you on my side. Your support means the world to me.

Thank you to my husband for creating a safe and loving cocoon so I can do what I need to do. And to my sweet and creative children, you are the reason I want to make this world a better place.

ABOUT THE AUTHOR

Nadia Han is a dreamer, a visionary, an artist, and a believer in karma and kindness. She lives in New England with her family and spends most of her time crafting stories. When she's not writing, she practices yoga, reads, creates art, explores nature, and eats all kinds of foods.

facebook.com/authornadiahan

instagram.com/authornadiahan

bookbub.com/authors/nadia-han

amazon.com/author/nadiahan